A Nate Temple Supernatural Thriller

Obsidian
Son

Shayne Silvers

COPYRIGHT NOTICE

NATE TEMPLE SUPERNATURAL THRILLERS

(Recommended Reading Order)

DEDICATION

Dedicated to a man among men, Scott Erwin

ACKNOWLEDGMENTS

Many were instrumental in bringing this story to life. Too many to name, but I will give it the ol' college try. First, I would like to thank my beta-readers, those individuals who spent hours of their life to read, and re-read, and re-re-read Nate's story, TEAM TEMPLE. Carol T, you are a gem.

Darja and Kim with Deranged Doctor Design for the gloriously epic artwork. To be completely honest with you, I was sold after seeing their company's name. Check them out at:

www.derangeddoctordesign.com

I would also like to thank you, the reader. I hope you enjoy reading OBSIDIAN SON as much as I enjoyed writing it. Stay tuned at *www.shaynesilvers.com* for updates on new releases, giveaways, book signings, merchandise, all things nerdy, and the fifth installment of *The Nate Temple Supernatural Thriller Series,* coming March 2017.

And most importantly, I thank my wife, Lexy. Without your love and support, none of this would have been possible.

So, without further ado… *let the magic commence.*

TRANSCRIPT THAT BIRTHED OBSIDIAN SON

Shayne:	I've thought about writing an urban fantasy novel, but I don't know where I should start. How would I make it unique?
Lexy:	How about Black-Ops Wizards?
Shayne:	Damn. Why don't you write it?
Lexy:	That's what I have you for… *Smooches*

GET YOUR FREE BOOK!

The family classic, Grimm's Fairy Tales, is not the collection of bedtime stories Nate Temple thought it was, but actually the keys to a veritable prison housing the most dangerous bloodthirsty hit men of the supernatural community. This reckless wizard must find a way to lock up the prison for good before his city becomes a buffet table for the Brothers Grimm...

SIDE NOTE: Be sure to read Obsidian Son first, as the Fairy Tale novella assumes you are already familiar with Nate's world and the characters in it.

Discover Nate's origin story, and get a sneak peek into the events that lead up to GRIMM, Book 3 in the Nate Temple Supernatural Thriller Series. To get your digital copy of FAIRY TALE as well as a digital copy of OBSIDIAN SON (*share it with someone who loves to read!*), and lots more exclusive content, all for FREE, you just need to tell me where to send them.

www.shaynesilvers.com/l/134

EPIGRAPH

Here be dragons.

— Hunt-Lenox Globe, 1503 A.D.

And Babylon shall become heaps, a dwelling place for dragons, an astonishment, and an hissing, without an inhabitant.

— Jeremiah 51:37

Come not between the dragon, and his wrath.

— William Shakespeare, King Lear

CHAPTER 1

THERE WAS NO ROOM FOR EMOTION IN A HATE CRIME. I had to be cold. Heartless. This was just another victim. Nothing more. No face, no name.

Frosted blades of grass crunched under my feet, sounding to my ears alone like the symbolic glass that one shattered under a napkin at a Jewish wedding. The noise would have threatened to give away my stealthy advance as I stalked through the moonlit field, but I was no novice and had planned accordingly. Being a wizard, I was able to muffle all sensory evidence with a fine cloud of magic – no sounds, and no smells. Nifty. But if I made the spell much stronger, the anomaly would be too obvious to my prey.

I knew the consequences for my dark deed tonight. If caught, jail time or possibly a gruesome, painful death. But if I succeeded, the look of fear and surprise in my victim's eyes before his world collapsed around him, was well worth the risk. I simply couldn't help myself; I had to take him down.

I knew the cops had been keeping tabs on my car, but I was confident that they hadn't followed me. I hadn't seen a tail on my way here, but seeing as how they frowned on this kind of thing I had taken a circuitous route just in case. I was safe. I hoped.

Then my phone chirped at me as I received a text. My body's fight-or-flight syndrome instantly kicked in, my heart threatening to explode in one final act of pulmonary paroxysm. "Motherf—" I hissed instinctively, practically jumping out of my skin. I had forgotten to silence it. Stupid, stupid, stupid! My body remained tense as I swept my gaze over the field, sure that I had been made. My breathing finally began to slow, my pulse returning to normal as I saw no change in my surroundings. Hopefully my magic had silenced the sound, and my resulting outburst. I finally glanced down at the phone and read the text. I typed back a quick and angry response before I switched the phone to vibrate.

I continued on, the lining of my coat constricting my breathing. Or maybe it was because I was leaning forward in anticipation. *Breathe*, I chided my-self. *He doesn't know you're here.* All this risk for a book. It better be worth it.

I'm taller than most, and not abnormally handsome, but I knew how to play the genetic cards I had been dealt. I had fashionably shaggy blonde hair, and my frame was thick with well-earned muscle, yet still lean. I had once been told that my eyes were like twin emeralds pitted against the golden tufts of my hair – a face like a jewelry box. Of course, that was after I had filled the woman with copious amounts of wine. Still, I liked to imagine that was how everyone saw me.

But tonight, all that was masked by magic.

I grinned broadly as the outline of the hairy hulk finally came into view. He was blessedly alone – no nearby sentries to give me away. That was al-ways a risk when performing this ancient right-of-passage. I tried to keep the grin on my face from dissolving into a maniacal cackle.

My skin danced with energy, both natural and unnatural, as I manipulated the threads of magic floating all around me. My victim stood just ahead, oblivious of the world of hurt that I was about to unleash. Even with his mil-lennia of experience, he didn't stand a chance. I had done this so many times that the routine of it was my only enemy. I lost count of how many times I had been told not to do it again; those who knew declared it *cruel, evil, and sadistic*. But what fun wasn't? Regardless, it wasn't enough to stop me from doing it again. And again. Call it an addiction if you will, but it was too much of a rush to ignore.

The pungent smell of manure filled the air, latching onto my nostril hairs. I took another step, trying to calm my racing pulse. A glint of gold reflected in the silver moonlight, but the victim remained motionless, hopefully un-aware or all was lost. I wouldn't make it out alive if he knew I was here. Timing was everything.

I carefully took the last two steps, a lifetime between each, watching the legendary monster's ears, anxious and terrified that I would catch even so much as a twitch in my direction. Seeing nothing, a fierce grin split my un-shaven cheeks. My spell had worked! I raised my palms an inch away from their target, firmly planted my feet, and squared my shoulders. I took one silent, calming breath, and then heaved forward with every ounce of physical strength I could muster. As well as a teensy-weensy boost of magic. Enough to goose him good.

"*MOOO!!!*" The sound tore through the cool October night like an unstoppable freight train. *Thud-splat*! The beast collapsed sideways into the frosty grass; straight into a steaming patty of cow shit, cow dung, or, if you really want to church it up, a Meadow Muffin. But to me, shit is, and always will be, shit.

Cow tipping. It doesn't get any better than that in Missouri.

Especially when you're tipping the *Minotaur*. Capital M.

Razorblade hooves tore at the frozen earth as the beast struggled to stand, grunts of rage vibrating the air. I raised my arms triumphantly. "Boo-yah! Temple 1, Minotaur 0!" I crowed. Then I very bravely prepared to protect myself. Some people just can't take a joke. *Cruel, evil,* and *sadistic* cow tipping may be, but by hell, it was a rush. The legendary beast turned his gaze on me after gaining his feet, eyes ablaze as he unfolded to his full height on two tree-trunk-thick legs, hooves magically transforming into heavily-booted feet. The heavy gold ring quivered in his snout as the Minotaur panted, corded muscle contracting over his human-like chest. As I stared up into those eyes, I actually felt sorry... for, well, myself.

"I have killed greater men than you for less offense," I swear to God his voice sounded like an angry James Earl Jones.

"You have shit on your shoulder, Asterion." I ignited a roiling ball of fire in my palm in order to see his eyes more clearly. By no means was it a defensive gesture on my part. It was just dark. But under the weight of his glare, even I couldn't buy my reassuring lie. I hoped using a form of his ancient name would give me brownie points. Or maybe just not-worthy-of-killing points.

The beast grunted, eyes tightening, and I sensed the barest hesitation. "Nate Temple... your name would look splendid on my already long list of slain idiots." Asterion took a threatening step forward, and I thrust out my palm in warning, my roiling flame blue now.

"You lost fair and square, Asterion. Yield or perish." The beast's shoulders sagged slightly. Then he finally nodded to himself, appraising me with the scrutiny of a worthy adversary. "Your time comes, Temple, but I will grant you this. You've got a pair of stones on you to rival Hercules."

I pointedly risked a glance down at the myth's own crown jewels. "Well,

I sure won't need a wheelbarrow any time soon, but I'm sure I'll manage." The Minotaur blinked once, and then bellowed out a deep, contagious, snorting laughter. Realizing I wasn't about to become a murder statistic, I couldn't help but join in. It felt good. It had been a while since I had experienced genuine laughter. In the harsh moonlight his bulk was quite intimidating as he towered head and shoulders above me. This was the beast that had fed upon human sacrifices for countless years while imprisoned in Daedalus' Labyrinth in Greece. And all of that protein had not gone to waste, forming a heavily woven musculature over the beast's body that made even Mr. Olympia look puny.

From the neck up he was entirely bull, but the rest of his body more resembled a thickly-furred man. But, as shown moments ago, he could adapt his form to his environment, never appearing fully human, but able to make his entire form appear as a bull when necessary. For instance, as he had looked just before I tipped him. Maybe he had been scouting the field for heifers before I had so efficiently killed the mood.

His bull face was also covered in thick, coarse hair – even sporting a long, wavy beard of sorts – and his eyes were the deepest brown I had ever seen. Cow shit brown. His snout jutted out, emphasizing the gold ring dangling from his glistening nostrils, catching a glint in the luminous glow of the moon. The metal was at least an inch thick, and etched with runes of a language long forgotten. Thick, aged ivory horns sprouted from each temple, long enough to skewer a wizard with little effort. He was nude except for a beaded necklace and a pair of distressed leather boots that were big enough to stomp a size twenty-five in my face if he felt so inclined.

I hoped our blossoming friendship wouldn't end that way. I really did.

CHAPTER 2

AFTER THE LAUGHTER DIED DOWN, THE MINOTAUR spoke, his shoulders relaxing as he assumed a less-intimidating posture. "I must thank you for testing me this night. I almost forgot *The Path*, and for this I must ask your forgiveness."

I blinked. "Uh, forgiveness?"

He nodded, relaxing even more, steepling his fingers before him as if in prayer. "I have been reading quite a bit lately on the Buddhist faith. Most intriguing. I can't fathom why I had never heard of it until recently. But I need not react to such an overt negative offense. Karma will come back to visit you... quite severely, I would imagine." He sneered.

It took a few moments for my brain to process his words. "Karma? You're a *Buddhist* now?" I practically yelled in disbelief. "Come on! It was just a practical joke. You make it sound as if Karma will be gunning for me."

Asterion began to lecture, his snout pulled back like Mr. Ed chewing a wad of peanut butter. "The severity of the Karmic retaliation is weighted against five conditions: frequent repetitive action; determined intentional action; action performed without regret; action against *extraordinary* persons..." He leveled a meaty thumb at his chest with a vain grin. "And finally, action toward those who have helped one in the past." He wasn't able to conceal his pleasure. "Having broken all five this night, I would say Karma's going to *destroy* you." I rolled my eyes and shrugged. The Minotaur switched gears. "My deepest condolences, but if this is about your parents' murder, I cannot aid you."

Before I could stop myself, the frozen ground around us vaporized to baking clay and cow shit in a fifty-foot radius, steam rising into a heavy fog. I could smell the soles of our boots burning like fresh tarmac. "What?" I hissed.

The Minotaur's eyes widened. "You are the heir to the notorious Temple wizards who recently passed. Why would you seek me out again if not to find their murderer?"

"The evidence revealed no foul-play. What do you know?" I whispered, voice like gravel, trying to blockade the torrent of emotions that had so suddenly swelled up inside me – the emotions I thought I had successfully walled away. Until now.

"Nothing! But come now, Temple, you know it to merely be a delusion. Are you claiming that you do not know a way to kill someone without a trace? You are a wizard. That is child's play for your kind. When a wizard dies, it is either violent or from extreme old age. For two to die within moments of one another is beyond calculation. Even Hermes wouldn't bet on that."

I had checked the evidence myself. Repeatedly. He was wrong. He *had* to be wrong. Calming myself, I came back to the reason for my visit, dispersing my abrupt magic out into the night with a flick of my wrist. The ground remained warm, but no longer smoldering. "Word around town says you deal in antiquities. Is this true?"

The Minotaur hesitated, glancing at the ground in relief. "Says whom?"

I glanced behind me as I heard the distant sound of sirens on a nearby road. Impossible. They couldn't be following me. Perhaps some kid had been caught speeding on the back roads. I was just being paranoid. "Says *Who*." I corrected, turning back.

"Irrelevant." He muttered.

That rankled me. "It is not *irrelevant*. It's paramount! The rules of grammar are just as important as the rules of engagement in war. Without them we are barbarians." I argued.

The Minotaur frowned pensively. "Then I must take that into consideration."

"So, are the rumors true or not?" I pressed.

"Possibly. What do you seek?"

"A book."

"I know *many* books. Perhaps you could elaborate?" He replied, sounding bored.

I weighed my options. My client wanted this badly. Very badly. And so far, I had turned up nothing. This was the end of the road. The sirens were closer now, and the flashing red and blue lights limned the fringes of the field. Fuck. It *couldn't* be for me. I rushed onward, anxious now. "I don't

6

know the title, but I can show you the symbol from the cover." I had to move fast in case the cops really *had* found me. Regardless, if they drove by, chances were they would either recognize my car, or at least wonder why such a beautiful vehicle was parked outside a field on a deserted country road.

The Minotaur knelt down to the ground, waiting. I noticed that his necklace was really a set of prayer beads, and shook my head in disbelief. The Minotaur, a reformed Buddhist. I traced my fingers just above the grass, releasing a tendril of fire like a pencil to burn an insignia into the now dry earth. It resembled a winged serpent over a flickering sun that appeared to be burning out, or fading. The Minotaur was still for several breaths, and then glanced warily toward the sky. After a long silence, he unfolded from his crouch, scuffed up the ground with his massive boot, and whispered one word. "Dragons." His horns gleamed wickedly in the moonlight as he towered over me. I blinked. *What the hell?*

"Dragons?" I glanced behind me as the sound of slamming car doors interrupted my train of thought, and realized that the flashing lights were just outside the field, right by my parked car. Shit. I *had* been made. Time to wrap things up. As I stood, I saw a flicker of silver in the air. I reflexively caught what Asterion had tossed to me, and found a dull, chipped silver coin in my palm. A worn image of a man holding the legendary Caduceus – the healing staff of doctors everywhere – was imprinted on one side, but the other bore only a pair of winged feet. "Flip once to save the life of another, and once to save your own." The Minotaur recited.

I frowned. "Why give me this?"

"I do as commanded. The book you seek is dangerous. I was told to pass this relic on to the first requestor." He fingered the prayer beads thoughtfully, glancing once over my shoulder at the flashing lights.

"How long have you held this?"

He answered a different question instead. "I have guarded the original version of the book you seek since I was put in that cursed Labyrinth, but I fear that copies might exist in the outside world. If they haven't been destroyed over the years. Humans are always destroying their culture." He snorted, eyes briefly flaring in outrage. "Both the coin and book were entrusted to me by Hermes." My mouth might or might not have dropped open in disbelief for a moment, but the Minotaur continued. "If your desire for this

7

book is strong enough, meet me here two days hence. We will duel at sunset."

"But you're a Buddhist now. Couldn't you, you know, just sell it to me?"

The Minotaur shook his head with a hungry grin. "Promises made, promises kept." I glanced at the ancient coin in my palm. "Oh, and Temple…" I looked up to see his boot flying at my midsection, so hastily threw up a last-second shield of air. It deflected only the fatal portion of the blow. "Karma says *hello*. Don't *ever* cow-tip me again." The force felt like, well, what I imagined a heel kick from the Minotaur *would* feel like. Then I was flying toward the pulsing lights. The Minotaur's guttural laughter stayed with me as I tumbled through the starry night, and then I landed chest-first in a moist pile of cow shit, sliding a few feet so that it smeared a perfect streak from chest to groin. I heard a surprised grunt, and then a knee ground me into the cold grass, mashing the molecular particles of shit firmly between each individual fiber of my six-hundred-dollar coat.

Cold steel clamped around my wrists. "I got him, Captain! He came outta' nowhere!" I couldn't help it. I began to laugh – hard – despite the lingering pain of Asterion's well-placed farewell boot.

"Fucking Karma!" I bellowed between giggles.

"I think he's hopped up on something, sir. Probably mushrooms, judging from all this cow shit."

"Whatever." A new voice – presumably the Captain's – said. "Let's just take him downtown. We have a few questions for him about his parents' murder."

I choked on my laughter.

CHAPTER 3

T HE HEAVY STEEL DOOR CLICKED OPEN AS A SECOND cop entered the room. I had time to notice a third young cop standing guard outside – nervously fingering his holster – before the door closed. The interrogation room smelled like cleaning solution and metal. I, on the other hand, sat with my hands cuffed behind my back, wrists slightly chafed, smelling like cow shit. Like a stain on the great cog that is the shining white bureaucracy of the United States government. I was rightly furious. And my car was parked out in the middle of nowhere. I'd have to get Gunnar or someone to drive me out there to pick it up later.

The cop already at the table watched me with an amused grin, as he had for the past twenty minutes. He was obese, his belly sagging over his weapons belt. His cheeks hung heavy on his face, reminding me of a melting candle, and his buzzed haircut made him look all the more ridiculous. He hadn't shaved, and looked like the kind of guy who needed to shave twice a day in order to look presentable. I wanted to slap the smile off his face. "Now that we're all here, Detective Kosage," I growled, "The cause of death, as your officers informed me, was inconclusive. Are you reneging on that statement?"

Silver streaks started at the man's temples to merge with his wavy black hair, and he was comically short – scrawny even – but he somehow still managed to compose an aura of authority. A modern Napoleon. He hesitated at my knowledge of his name, but then glanced down at his badge and simply nodded. Then he proceeded to sit down, setting a Styrofoam cup of burnt-tar coffee onto the table beside a manila folder.

It was a few hours until midnight, and my palate was not that of a refined Starbucks Barista. Coffee was coffee. I eyed it longingly.

"Mr. Temple," He began in a nasally voice.

"*Master* Temple," I corrected him with an icy tone of warning. The patriarch of our family had always been referred to as the *Master* Temple as far back as anyone could remember. In today's society, it sounded out of place, but it was a formality I was insistent upon pressing here. And the media ate it up since it sold headlines, so everyone knew of it.

He nodded. "Of course, *Master* Temple." There was no mockery in his whiny voice, just emphasis, as if he appreciated the concept of respect. "First things first." His badge glittered in the fluorescent lighting. "Trespassing is illegal. You managed to pass the sobriety test, ruling out mushrooms, so what were you *really* doing out there? Could our city's youngest billionaire really find nothing else to amuse him?" He looked genuinely puzzled, glancing pointedly at the putrid stain on my chest. "We could hold you for 24 hours, Master Temple. After all, I'm sure Mr...." he shuffled some papers from his file. "Kingston would not be pleased with your uninvited exploration of his property."

"Are these really necessary?" I jangled my hands behind my back.

Detective Kosage's eyes squinted thoughtfully before nodding. "For now, yes."

I scowled into his eyes, waiting a full ten seconds to see if he would change his mind. He didn't blink. I decided right then that I was going to have some fun with my situation. Regulars – as we named non-magical be-ings – were terrified of the concept of magic being real. Especially since the media had recently started fueling the fires with stories of magic happening all over America. The debate was on everyone's lips. Was it real? Was it a hoax? Regardless, most Regulars were unable to comprehend the possibili-ties of things they didn't personally understand, and it was *so* much fun to capitalize on that anxiety. It was who I was. My charm.

"Alright, boys. Have it your way." I lifted my hands above my head in a languorous stretch, my wrists already free of the cuffs, as they had been for the last nineteen minutes. I set the cuffs on the table, sliding them over to the other cop, Detective Allison. "Here you go, Ali." I tried to mimic the smile he had given me earlier, waggling a small bobby pin between my fingers. "It's amazing what one can learn on the web. Now, I'm not sure how you were raised, but it is considered the height of impropriety to have a conversa-tion without offering refreshment to your guest. Especially when the host has one. Unforgivably rude, actually." They blinked back at me in unison, shock apparent on their faces as the cuffs sat on the table like a pink elephant in the room.

As if on cue, the door opened, and the nervous cop entered with a steaming cup of coffee. He set it in front of me, and then nervously backed away from the room. I deduced that we were being recorded since my two jailers hadn't moved or spoken since my display. I had an audience. My smile stretched wider. Even better. Steam curled up from my cup. I invisibly casted a bit of magic into the coffee, dropping the temperature enough for me to down it in one gulp, which I promptly did. Again, both the cops' eyebrows raised in unison, amazed that the drink hadn't scalded my throat. I let them wonder at that. "Much better, gentlemen. Now, what do you two want to chat about next? Your future careers? Politicians and the media can be bought, and I have a few extra bucks to grease some palms. Elections are coming up." I waited.

The detectives stared from my hands to the cuffs again in disbelief. Detective Allison responded first, rising from his chair with a furious growl, but Kosage slapped a dainty palm on his forearm, the authority plain. "Let's continue this discussion... professionally." He glanced back to the folder as Allison glared hatred at me for a moment longer. He finally sat down, the chair protesting his bulk with a loud squeak. I arched an eyebrow at the noise, my thoughts plain. His eyes hardened, but he leaned back as Kosage read from a paper. "Let's talk about Temple Industries for a moment."

Temple Industries. The technology company my parents had started twenty years ago, headquartered in the thriving metropolis of St. Louis, Missouri. The company's fingers stretched wide, claiming over 3,000 patents (more than Microsoft) that ranged from software, to computer chips, and even to defense technology for the U.S. military. No one truly knew *everything* that the company concerned themselves with, just that they always seemed to produce the most cutting-edge technology. The company was vast, falling into the reputable *Fortune 500*. But I wanted nothing to do with it. "It might be a very, very brief moment, as I have nothing to do with my parents' company. Other than owning a hefty amount of shares." I added honestly.

Kosage stared back, eyes sharp. I kept my face blank. "Yes, well, the Interim President of the company, Ashley Belmont, is less than forthcoming about details of ownership. You're saying that you have no intentions of taking over the company?"

"Why would I?" I answered questions with questions when pissy.

Detective Ali leaned forward. "Money." He growled hungrily.

I glanced from face to face before leaning back in the steel torture device that doubled as a chair. "I assume that being clever and thorough policemen, you have already combed over my finances?" Kosage waited a moment, and then gave a brief nod. "Then you have no doubt noticed that I am already fairly wealthy from previous investments not limited to my shares in Temple Industries." Another nod. "Furthermore, that I run my own arcane little bookstore which brings me a *sufficient* amount of annual income."

"Plato's Cave," Kosage answered with a wry grin at my financial modesty.

I nodded proudly. "Have you also noticed that the stock in Temple Industries has dropped significantly since my parents' untimely… death?" The last word was hard for me to voice. Kosage blinked, reaching down for the coffee to cover his tell. "Ah, perhaps my previous assumption was too flattering. Not as thorough as you should have been. I have made no move to assume leadership of their company, and the value of that company has only dropped since the unfortunate death of the owners." I dramatically dimmed the lights with magic as I stood from my chair. Kosage's chair slid back as he hurriedly set the coffee back down to the table, glancing up at the lights with a frown. Regulars. They were still scared of the dark, refusing to believe that magic existed, even when it happened right in front of their faces. They didn't know whom they were toying with. No one knew I was a wizard. They probably just thought the lighting system was faulty, but it had the desired effect. "You *better* not be implying that I had *anything* to do with their deaths," I hissed.

As I allowed the lights to brighten back to normal, Kosage swiveled his nervous brown-eyed gaze back to me, no doubt wondering if he had imagined the lights dimming. "Of course not. Please sit, Master Temple." I didn't. He shrugged, regaining his composure, but Detective Allison remained on edge. Steel scraped the concrete floor as he scooted back to the table. "As I was saying, Miss Belmont says she will not speak to us until she has had a chance to speak with you. But you do not answer her calls. Then we get a pack of lawyers on our backs for questioning her. You can see our predicament. Things would be easier if we could simply talk to her. But why would she need to speak to you first unless you are indeed planning on taking over the company?" He was whining again.

I had no idea why she would want to talk to me, but I *had* been screening my calls lately. They were coming in from all over. *CNN, St. Louis Post Dis-*

patch, and every news channel within a hundred miles had somehow found my personal cell phone number. I shrugged in answer. "Are you arresting me?"

"There is no need for such words. We're merely trying to get to the bottom of this. We share the same goals, Master Temple. Finding the cause of their... death." He hesitated on the last word, but it was obvious that he had intended to say *murder*. "If you could please sit and answer a few more questions, we can get this over with in short order."

The Minotaur's words came back to mind. The St. Louis Police Department had been the ones to tell me that the evidence of their deaths was inconclusive. They had been found dead in one of their laboratories with no signs of struggle, drugs, poison, or any of the usual clues that whispered murder. They had simply died within moments of each other. My father had been found with a minor but precise, almost surgical, perimortem gash on his wrist, but not deep enough to be fatal, and no blade in sight. The detectives had even declared it as self-inflicted around the time of death.

Temple Industries had been their life, and ultimately, their death.

I felt the barriers of my will weakening, the brick wall of restraint crumbling against the tides of power and magic inside me. "I do not have the answers you seek, *gentlemen*." I dramatically flicked a finger as if to shake off a drop of water, and a blast of frigid air beckoned to my command. The sole door to the room flew inward as if hit by a battering ram from the hall, the lock skittering across the floor to rest at my feet, and the temperature in the room dropped significantly. Detective Kosage's cup of coffee tipped over, splashing the steaming liquid towards his face.

I snapped my finger as the door rebounded off the inside wall, revealing the startled guard outside now gripping the pistol at his belt in shaky fingers, the button latch safety rattling in the sudden wind. The steaming mass of coffee froze into a chunk of brown ice an inch away from Detective Kosage's bloodless nose. Several frozen coffee-cubed drops fell into his lap.

His chair slid back as his reflexes finally kicked in. Both of their eyes were wide now as they flinched from the door to me, panicked. I walked around him and Detective Allison on my way to the door. "I'll talk to Miss Belmont for you. Next time, don't bother with the cuffs. Just say *pretty-please*."

"What the fuck?" Detective Allison roared in shock. "How did he—" His face was pale with fear. "Was that..." he glanced from face to face, and then to the camera in the corner of the room, his eyes wide, "Magic?" He whispered low enough for only our ears.

I smiled, dimming the lights more dramatically this time as I leaned closer, whispering back conspiratorially. "Come now, officers. Don't tell me you still believe in *fairy* tales..." My grin stretched further, menacing, and they each leaned away. "Answers can be dangerous... *All men should strive to learn before they die what they are running from, and to, and why.*" I quoted. "Seems like you have faulty lighting here," I added.

Then I strode out of the room, leaving the words hanging like an axe over their throats. I had a client to meet. Then a well-deserved drink with some friends. I wasn't about to waste my time babysitting the city's men-in-blue.

CHAPTER 4

I LEANED AGAINST THE COLD BRICK WALL OF THE DINER, glancing at the sign hanging above my bookstore across the street through the light flurry of snow falling down to the ground in fat, heavy flakes. Plato's Cave was artfully painted onto the aged wood. I contemplated the events of the night as I waited for my client to arrive, trying to keep the wind at my back in order to avoid the sickly aroma of shit still painting my upper body.

The cops now thought my parents had been murdered. A week had passed me by since hearing the dire news. No prior health issues could have caused it. *Age* had been the predominant concrete answer.

But now I wasn't so sure.

First the Minotaur, and now the cops. I wondered what had made them change their minds. *Means, motive,* and *opportunity* were the three things cops looked for in murder cases, as my childhood friend – now an FBI Agent – Gunnar Randulf had told me.

The news of their death had wrecked me, but as an old Japanese friend from college had taught me long ago, *grieve fiercely for one day and then move on.* His ancestors had been Samurai, a hard-ass culture. So, that's what I did. The first day I had been a mess, sticking to my store, needlessly stocking shelves, and staying busy without thinking.

The next day I had sealed the coffin on those emotions, following the evidence clinically, detached after my allotted one day of grief. Then my present client had called on me, giving me something new to focus on. I had devoted myself to his request, ultimately leading to tonight's meeting with the Minotaur.

From time to time I obtained rare books for – as was most often the case – less than reputable clients with large bank accounts. I had a reputation for being able to find goods where others couldn't, and it had landed me a decent income. I had clung to my new client's request like a bloodhound – anything to ignore the pain inside me. But now the grief was threatening to come back as I discovered that the cops apparently hadn't closed the high-profile case. It wasn't their fault that their prime suspect was a rich heir. How many times had I seen a similar case go through the media?

And prove to be correct.

It made sense, but it was wrong. And infuriating. If I had learned of even one shred of evidence proving murder, I would have most likely gone vigilante, *Batman* style.

I hadn't been that close to my parents the last few years, but that was mainly out of stubbornness. As encouraged, I had double-majored in Physics and Philosophy at the age of twenty. But I had encountered an enchanting mistress while at college. *Books*. More accurately, the Classics: Milton, Sir Arthur Conan Doyle, Dostoevsky, Dante Alighieri, and a vast slew of philosophers. Not wanting to stand in my parents' shadow, I had started my own business, something more in line with both my talents and my interests.

Plato's Cave, my own Atlantis.

And I had been damn successful against the modern world of digital formatting, Kindles, iPads, and Nooks. It seemed that ancient books and classic volumes only increased in worth, and I had contacts that the rest of the world didn't.

Legends.

Many people think of Myth and Folklore as either the very first fictional writings, or the incessant ramblings of inebriated authors. Nothing more. But my family and I knew better. We were wizards, and being such, were deeply entwined with those mythical races. For better or worse, the myths were all very, *very* real: Hermes, the Minotaur, Hercules, wizards – and as I had just been informed – dragons. The trouble was finding them. They didn't want to be found. They had lived their glory days long ago, and for the most part, remained reclusive.

But sometimes they decided to socialize again, causing the occasional sighting or other unexplainable carnage, and that was usually where wizards came in. We were the unofficial police of the magical community, or at least the wizards I had met seemed to lean in that direction.

But I had ways of finding those recluses, and a significant amount of charm that helped me win them over to help me find those old, withered, and forgotten tomes. Like I had with the Minotaur. Thinking of that encounter, I couldn't help but wonder why the hint of dragons had set him so on edge. I was pretty sure I would know if dragons were in my city: big, scaly, hungry, flying lizards, stealing gold and virgins? Didn't ring any bells.

I briefly wondered why the Minotaur had been prepared for my request thousands of years prior, and what Hermes had to do with it all. I idly fingered the coin in my pocket. Old books were like that, most often entrusted to an individual for life, and then passed down to a loved one upon their death.

On the upside, the original might be able to fetch more money from my client. If I could prove it was authentic. It wasn't like I could tell him, *'Well, the Minotaur told me it was the real deal, and he just wouldn't lie about something like that. He's a Buddhist now. They frown on lying.'*

Impatient for my unpunctual client, I thumbed open my pack of cigarettes, placed one between my lips, glanced around to make sure I was alone, and lit the tip of the cigarette with only a thought. No fancy hand motions, words, or lengthy process used at all. It had taken a while to hone my focus enough not to light my face on fire. The first few times hadn't been as successful.

My magic was an ever-present companion of mine. I had been told that I was more powerful than most – things that were quite difficult for other wizards came easily to me. I saw the world through tinted glasses. A whole world of colors, vibrations, waves, and particles danced around me, and I knew how to tap into them; manipulate them to my desire with a thought. It was simply a part of me. I couldn't imagine it any other way. But I definitely knew I was a minority.

Content, I nestled my shoulders against the cold wall, bent my knee to rest my boot against the brick in an impromptu lean, and took a sweet, heavenly inhale.

Simply marvelous.

For those of you lesser beings that haven't partaken of this man-made Manna, you are missing out. I inhaled the menthol smoke, thinking of a favorite quote I had read long ago. *Man, controlling Prometheus' gift of fire between two fingers...* Relishing the cool smoke searing my lungs, I was startled by a sudden voice from the alley beside me.

"Those things are bad for you. Cancerous, even."

Recognizing the voice, my pulse slowly returned to normal as I turned to face my client. People were rarely able to sneak up on me. "My body is a temple, and every good temple needs some incense now and again. Something you should learn. Like punctuality, kid."

My client grunted as he stepped out into view, lighting his own clove cigarette by the smell of it. The fragrance surrounded us like a soothing blanket as he puffed it to life. "The brightest candle burns half as long, right?" He exhaled another cloud of the pleasant-smelling smoke from his nostrils. He somehow made it look dangerous, like a bouncer flexing his muscles, or a cop cocking his pistol.

"Hypocrite," I muttered.

He smiled. "You smell... bad," he finally concluded.

"I shit myself earlier. Deal with it."

He frowned. "Does this happen often?" I glared back, and he chuckled before shrugging it off. "Did you find it?"

I studied my client, trying to figure him out. Dark, lanky hair hugged his scalp down to his jaw, and his eyes were dark enough for me to have never placed a color to them. I peered closer, but seeming to sense my curiosity, he glanced away. His harsh angular jaw and cheekbones made stark shadows in the dim light. Tight leather pants clung to his legs, and calf-high boots that looked like they belonged on a *Pirates of the Caribbean* set covered his feet. The leather smelled clean and sharp. His white V-neck Tee contrasted the tight pants, and a thick silver chain hung against his chest, peeking out from underneath the fabric.

He looked like a modern James Dean. He wasn't even wearing a coat and it was snowing. Rebel without a cause, all right. I suppose many would have found him roguishly handsome, and I, being comfortable with my masculinity, realized this with a slight twinge of jealousy. "Possibly. I'll know for sure in two days." I noticed a new smell for the first time around my client – cold rocks, and... snakes. I know that neither of those things instill a familiar sense of smell to most people, but being a wizard, my senses were enhanced, and I could place associations to such things. I stored it away for later thought.

The *boy* – because he *was* younger than me – nodded. "Two days. That's perfect."

Unsure what *that* implied, I probed a bit. "Are you sure you want it? My contact seems to think it might be dangerous..." I paused the required amount of time. "Which raises the price."

He flashed me an amused smirk, took another inhale of his cigarette, and then dismissively flicked away the ash. "Price is not an issue." He leveled his dark, black diamond eyes on me. The irises *were* black. No color whatsoever. "It is vital that you get it. And no later than two days. Sooner is better, but *definitely* not any later." He glanced around warily, even up at the nearby buildings. Paranoid much? "Any other inquirers?"

That stumped me. "No. Why?" I asked.

"Just curious. I presume that this still remains a secret between us?" I nodded. "I have your word on that?" he pressed.

I knew that there was more to this than he was letting on, and that he was definitely not your Average Joe. He was wary, but unafraid – anticipatory. I repressed a shudder at exactly who my client might be. Everyone had his or her secrets.

"I've already told you that you have my word, but it's just a book. Why the secrecy?" The words sounded hollow even to me. Books were not *merely* books, at least not always. I've cracked a deadly spine once or twice in my day.

Like *Twilight*. Now *that* was deadly. The series had managed to turn normal adolescent girls into raving, hormone-filled psychopaths intent on dating vampires, and *no one* would *ever* knowingly do something *that* stupid.

He ignored my question. "Good... It's nice to know that some still honor their word." He rubbed his shoulders, signaling the end of business. "So, I'll meet you two nights from now? Where is our next cloak and dagger rendez-vous?" he grinned. "I recommend somewhere not so near to your place of business, wizard." He hadn't known that appellation last time, or at least hadn't revealed it.

I told him a place off the top of my head, and he began laughing. "Interesting venue. Ever been there?" I shook my head, and he laughed even harder. "Okay."

"I don't even know your name." I said, ignoring whatever he found so funny.

His nose crinkled as he scanned the street, muscles tensing slightly. "It's better that way. My name is on too many lips already. It seems I have many..." he glanced around again, muscles growing tighter, "Fans. See you in two days, Temple."

19

Then he stepped back into the alley, and... disappeared, even to my senses. He was simply *gone*. "Whatever." I muttered to the empty alley. I turned away, taking another puff from my cigarette, and my phone vibrated in my pocket. I glanced down, read the text, and then glanced across the street to my store. I saw my two friends, Gunnar and Peter, leaning against the door, staring at me. They were waiting for our monthly nightcap, as we had done for the last five years in order to maintain our friendship amidst diversifying careers, and, well, just life in general getting in the way. I stepped away from the wall and waved as I headed their way, eager for that drink.

CHAPTER 5

GUNNAR GLANCED BEHIND ME TOWARDS THE ALLEY as I approached. "Nate." I took another drag of the cigarette, and then stomped it out under a heel. Gunnar Randulf was built like a house, tall, strong, and skin as pale as fine alabaster. His face was hard, with a double-cleft chin, and a rough, but neat, blonde beard covered his lower face. Blonde hair brushed his jaws, looking expensively well-kept; he had been forced to use some bogus religious excuse so that the FBI wouldn't make him cut it short. Gunnar Randulf was descended from the Norse Vikings, his last name meaning 'Shield-wolf,' and he left a trail of broken hearts wherever he walked. But despite all the attention his looks gained him from the fairer sex, he seemed immune to the casual chase, instead searching for that one true love. It was like trying to find the perfect steak without ever eating meat before.

He was the worst wingman *ever*.

Peter on the other hand, was a study in contrasts – handsome, but unremarkable. Tall and wiry, with bright blue eyes, he looked like every other Yuppie in town. They each wore slacks and a shirt, not having changed from their respective jobs before heading over to my digs. I had known them both since childhood, and we had been friends ever since. Peter, being a Regular with no unique powers, was definitely the odd ball out, but it hadn't affected our friendship at all. "Who were you talking to?" Gunnar's face was curious, glancing into the alley.

"Whom. Fucking *whom*! Is everyone illiterate?" I grouched.

Peter chuckled. We were alone on the street. "I sensed him… *sensing* me. Then he was gone. And he smells like shit." Gunnar said.

"Sorry, but the smell is all me. I had an accident."

Gunnar's baby-blues weighed me, but ignored my hygiene. "*What* was he?"

If Gunnar couldn't even place what the kid was, then I had no idea. I shrugged. "A client. That's all I know. And they pay my bills. Sort of a *don't ask don't tell* policy. You two ready for our Round Table?" Peter and Gunnar both nodded, but not before both peering over my shoulder again. Peter looked curious, but Gunnar didn't seem satisfied with my response.

"Of course. It's our fifth anniversary, after all."

"Oh, *Darling*. You *remembered*!" I mocked. Gunnar rolled his eyes. I unlocked the heavy oak front door, closing my eyes for a moment as I turned off my secondary alarm system – a fine mist of magic was laced over the entire perimeter of the building. My friends, knowing the routine, waited patiently, although Peter studied me curiously, no doubt trying to see something of my magic. Peter had experienced its effects once, and wasn't anxious to see it happen again. The feeling of a thousand fire ants swarming your body left an impression, and very real bites. One reason for the secondary protection was the valuable and unique items stored inside, but the other was because I lived in the loft overlooking the front lobby – and what a lobby it was.

I had purchased the antique 1920's theater and performed a few minor renovations, redesigning the Grand Lobby into a bookstore with a more modern feel. Several steps led down into the store from the entryway. Six-foot-high, glass-walled dividers were randomly scattered about, effectively sectioning the room into a maze of couches, bookshelves, and even a European coffee bar tucked back against the wall. The convoluted maze was an extensive web of *Feng Shui* that a team of monks had helped me design. Modern, yet classic. Yin and Yang. Vintage movie posters, steam-punk paraphernalia, and vinyl records decorated the rough brick walls. It was the ultimate man cave.

Even though the place was empty at this time of night, it still felt homey and welcoming. The glass-walled dividers were covered with wax-penciled graffiti in a variety of different colors – quotes, ancient passages from classic works, names, and brief artwork – a rite of passage granted to my frequent customers.

I led the way to the back stairs that climbed the old brick wall to my loft.

Two of the three theaters nestled in the back had also been revamped. One was packed with almost every type of gaming system. I had even acquired a team of beta-testers to try out games in the developmental stages. Hence, installing the coffee shop in the lobby. Nerds needed caffeine to function.

And my business was the Atlantis for nerds across the land. Nerdlantis.

The second theater was now a vast library where I conducted my more profitable sales with those premier clients of mine.

The third theater was on a need-to-know basis, and not many needed to know.

My glass-windowed loft overlooked the entire store, both front and back, as I had gutted the old projector room to create a home within a home for myself – a *Sanctum Sanctorum*. The stairs creaked as we ascended my modern castle-tower, reminding me of the Captain's prow of a ship, overseeing the activity of the crew below. I shouldered the heavy oak door open and headed back to the bar against the far wall. Settling down into a pair of couches inside the large open loft, my friends took off their coats, relaxing as I began to work. I discarded my own ruined coat, tossing it into a nearby laundry basket with optimistic hope that it could be salvaged. I placed three cups before me.

Absinthe was the chosen poison for this auspicious evening.

The licorice-fired spirit had been the favorite drink of visionaries throughout history, including Oscar Wilde, Vincent Van Gogh, and Ernest Hemingway. But I wasn't about to attempt Hemingway's famous *Death in the Afternoon* cocktail of chilled champagne and Absinthe. I chose the French Method instead.

I bent to my task, the process of making the perfect drink now a familiar routine for me, as I listened to Gunnar and Peter's soft conversation. Salivating with anticipation as the thick aroma began to fill my nose, I placed several ice cubes into the drinks, set my creations atop a silver tray, and then carried them over to the table in the sitting area. I handed Gunnar and Peter each a glass, bowed my head, and then backed away onto my own aged Darlington Chesterfield couch. I snatched up the last glass, and reclined with a pleased sigh.

"What's new with you two?" I asked curiously.

Gunnar answered first, clearly excited, "I was given authority to put together my own field team. Special Agent in Charge, Roger Reinhardt, is letting me dance the gray area a bit with some of my recent cases since the traditional protocol hasn't been very successful. My... unique talents will be a benefit. Jurisdiction and red tape hold us back all too often, so he's turning a blind eye, as long as I produce results." He winked. "Off the record, of course."

I grinned. This was huge. "That's fantastic! You're implying that more of the recent crimes have been in our field of expertise? Involving magic?" Gunnar merely nodded, but his lips tightened a bit, apparently closed on any further elaboration of the subject. Perhaps Peter wasn't supposed to hear details.

He shrugged. "It will most likely fizzle to nothing, but it was good to hear that some people are wise to the fact that they are helpless to solving some of the newer crimes. It's only in the preliminary stages right now though. A temporary trial-and-error experiment."

Peter, sensing Gunnar clamming up, chimed in, "I've gained a bit of respect around the investment firm. They're letting me work directly with a new client, a new family in town with deep, deep pockets." To himself, he murmured something lower that I couldn't quite catch; thumbing a worn leather bracelet I had never seen before on his wrist. Odd. Peter had never worn any accessories. Was he in danger of becoming metro-sexual? Something *was* different about him, now that I thought about it. But I remained silent, not sensing anything specific. "It might even be my big break."

"Then I propose a toast," I raised my glass. "To women and careers, and the men who ride them!" They rolled their eyes, and we each took a deep drink. This was what our round table was for, setting aside a single night to speak of how we were attempting to impact the world. After years of hard work, it seemed my two friends were doing just that.

Gunnar opened his mouth to speak, but I interrupted him. "You almost got me killed tonight with your stupid text message."

He frowned before answering. "Speaking of that, was that some weird autocorrect mistake in your response? It said you were in a cow pasture."

"No. That was what I typed." I sipped my drink and sighed in appreciation as my taste buds were overloaded with fennel and anise.

"Okaaay... That's not mysterious at all," Peter's eyes twinkled as he leaned forward.

Gunnar was still frowning. "So, barring creepy clients and cow pastures, how have you been?" Gunnar asked carefully.

I grinned over the rim of my aromatic drink. "Both of those negations are actually related. I just got busted from the police station. Apparently trespassing is frowned upon. As is cow-tipping."

Peter choked on his drink. "Pardon?"

Gunnar wasn't so polite. "What? You know they are looking for any excuse to give you trouble! You even said that you noticed patrol cars hanging around the shop. And why on earth were you *cow-tipping*? Could you find nothing else to entertain you on a Thursday night?"

"I needed information," I began, settling deeper into the chair. I spotted my first edition of *Paradise Lost* on the table beside me, and recalled the last passage I had read before retiring the tome: *Do they only stand by ignorance, is that their happy state, the proof of their obedience and faith...* It reminded me of the detectives at the police station. It had been close to a week since I had read the passage, but I had an eidetic memory, so it was forever burned into my brain. A gift and a curse. I had never quite gotten used to how others couldn't do the same thing.

"How could you get information by cow-tipping?" Gunnar pressed, knowing there was more to the story. We had fallen into a strong friendship almost from the very beginning, and then upon discovering our unique similarities, the strands of friendship had only grown stronger. We each had one foot in a whole other world.

The world of magic.

Gunnar was a werewolf, able to change at a whim now, thanks to my parents' help long ago. As if sensing this, Gunnar idly thumbed the tattoo on his wrist – a gift from my parents. Werewolves normally couldn't control their change from one form to the other, but the tattoo served as a totem, allowing Gunnar to shift at will, no longer a victim to the cycles of the moon. Merely a thought or a finger on the tattoo would begin the transformation. White, snowy fur slowly began to curl up from Gunnar's forearm before he realized what he was doing. He removed his finger, closed his eyes, and the fur disappeared.

Peter watched with a distant, familiar envy. He was a Regular, just happening to fall into our lives back in school, and he had been there ever since. Despite having no powers, he was a good friend, and an even better man. He was one of the few people who knew our secrets. Even Gunnar's boss didn't know the truth, but he did know that Gunnar had an unusually high success rate for solving cases that other agents had deemed *unsolvable*.

The age of digital media had made the lives of our kind harder to conceal. *YouTube* had caught more magic on film than any number of cameras in the past. Even dismissed as hoaxes, a growing number of people throughout the world had begun to question this resurgence of magical evidence with some serious scrutiny. Luckily, they were mostly regarded as intoxicated conspiracy theorists. I could imagine what would happen once the lid finally blew on that subject. It would be the Salem Witch Trials all over again. Blood would flow in the streets, and the government would no doubt pass a litany of regulations and laws within weeks. I shivered at the thought, coming back to the question.

"I needed to speak with the Minotaur," I answered simply, taking another sip of the licorice fire.

Peter leaned even further forward. "*The* Minotaur? As in the one Theseus killed in Daedalus' Labyrinth? He's *real*?"

"Come now, Peter. You know better. Of *course*, he's real. Almost all the myths are real. But the Minotaur wasn't killed. True, he was *defeated* by Theseus, but he swore not to eat any more men – the first monster carnivore turned vegetarian – so was allowed to survive. He's still... *kicking* around, so to speak. And he's good at finding things. My kind of things." I still felt the impression of his boot on my stomach, despite my hastily thrown shield. I was sure it would bruise nicely.

Gunnar growled unhappily. "So, after cow tipping-him, why on earth did he agree to help you? He could have very easily killed you, you know."

I let the silence build until they were leaning forward. "He's Buddhist now." No reaction. "Or trying to become one. I'm guessing I survived because he struck a deal with Hermes long ago." I fingered the coin in my pocket, but remained silent on that gift. "It has to do with the client you saw earlier. He's looking for something, and my other sources turned up nothing. He was my last resource. He said I could duel him in two days for the item. Then the cops arrived. They must have been keeping tabs on my car."

"Well, it's not exactly discreet," Peter mocked.

I grinned back, showing my teeth. "Jealousy does not become you, Peter."

He grunted indelicately. "Did you find what you were looking for?" I nodded.

Gunnar looked relieved. "You risk too much, Nate. You have access to an almost limitless fortune, but you still risk everything for these pennies you get from clients."

"They aren't quite pennies," I murmured, again thumbing the coin in my pocket.

"You know what I mean, Nate. Don't bandy words with me. I know you."
He frowned. "I heard radio chatter on the way over here. I'm guessing it was
about you getting snatched up by the police. What did they want?"

"Just more questions," I waved a hand, not wanting to continue that line
of conversation. "About the company and everything," I lied.

Peter's interest peaked. "Have you finally decided to pick up the reins?"

"No. But apparently, everybody thinks I'm scheming to do just that."

Peter grinned. "You, scheming? They must not know you *at all*." I smiled
back, nodding. "Well if you won't do it, why don't you hire me to help? I
could use some creative financing to increase your profits."

Gunnar suppressed a grin behind his glass, but remained silent. "Your
track record is not so great, Peter. I can't risk that with my parents' company.
It's much too vast for anyone except well-experienced professionals. It's not
a toy to pass to my friends. No offense." Peter's eyes smoldered, his hand
idly brushing his new bracelet again. "Why do you think I haven't jumped in
myself, Peter? It's too big, even for me."

Gunnar leaned back, stretching his feet. "Say that again. Your parents
would roll over in their grav—" his face paled. "Oh, God. I'm sorry, Nate. It
slipped out. I didn't mean—"

I waved a hand to interrupt him, dampening my anger quickly. "No,
you're right. But choose your words more carefully next time." Gunnar
looked ashamed of himself. Good.

Peter finally broke the silence. "Still, Gunnar has a point. You don't want
to stay in this shit-hole for the rest of your life. What about Chateau Falco?
Are you going to sell it? You can't leave it empty. It's been in your family
for what, a hundred years? You can't just let it go."

"261." I murmured. Gunnar and Peter glanced at each other for a moment,
not comprehending. I rolled my eyes. "261 *years*. And I haven't decided yet.
It is not for sale at the moment, but who knows? I haven't been there for a
long time."

"But you are its new *Master*." Gunnar raised his arms to mimic a Hitler
salute. "*Master Temple, your wish is my command,*" he mocked.

I rolled my eyes before whispering softly. "The place ... scares me. It's
not just a home. It has secrets that even my parents kept close." I looked at
them, a serious expression on my face.

"You're not scared of *anything*. Hence, Minotaur tipping." Gunnar grinned.

"Well, I am afraid of *that* place." I answered honestly.

They blinked in disbelief, the silence stretching for a few moments. Changing topic, Peter continued on, wisely sensing that talk of the mansion was off the table. "At least you could hire me as a consultant. I couldn't hurt anything."

Gunnar laughed aloud this time. I shrugged as Peter scowled at Gunnar. "Wrong. I can't *hire* anyone because I don't *work* for the company. I'm just an investor."

"You mean they didn't leave it to you in the will?" Gunnar stammered in surprise.

"Years ago they asked me. I declined. Hence my fall from grace in their eyes. I guess they looked at me as God once looked at the young Lucifer."

Peter looked baffled, "I just don't understand you." He glanced at Gunnar's tattoo pointedly. "You either, Wolf. You each have the gifts of gods, and you do nothing with them. Well, *you* go cow-tipping." He waggled a frustrated hand in my direction.

"It's just something we were born with, Peter. It doesn't make us gods. And we *do* use it. When necessary." Gunnar idly caressed the crescent tattoo on his wrist again. He had been wetting panties before girls even knew what it meant back in Junior High – the only student with a full beard and a tattoo. Smug bastard. He was easy to hate.

"But you wallow in filth rather than taking the world by its balls!" Peter argued.

"Easy, Thrasymachus. Might is not right." I said softly.

Peter slumped in defeat. "Listen, if you two are going to talk philosophy again, I'm out. No more circle-jerking Plato for me, thank you very much. I've got work in a few hours." He stood to leave, downing his drink with a contented sigh. Setting it on a side table, he paused as if remembering something. "Hey, did you happen to find that book I requested a couple days ago?"

I frowned. For the first time my eidetic memory failed me. "What book?"

Peter turned to face me. "I left a note with Jessie. He's a new employee. Not one of your veterans."

"He never mentioned anything to me," I answered honestly. I had only

28

spoken to the kid once. My store manager, Indie, had hired him. "Why the sudden interest in a book? I didn't even know you could read," I teased.

Peter looked hurt. "What, I'm not allowed to read every now and then?" he grouched. "I left him a note with the title. He said he would leave it on your desk." I glanced back to see a crumpled piece of parchment on my ornate oak desk.

"I haven't been in the office for a few days. Just coming here to sleep. I've had... a lot on my plate."

Peter and Gunnar both nodded, faces grim. "It's no big deal. Just a book a client asked me to find. The rich one I was talking about earlier."

I nodded, suddenly distracted by an odd sensation on my arms. "I'll take a look around tomorrow." I mumbled, rubbing my forearm curiously as I stretched my mind out like a web, searching for the cause of the distracting warmth. It felt like a wave of steam.

Peter nodded, pocketing his cell. "Alright, gentlemen. I bid you—"

His mouth closed with an audible click of smacking teeth as I suddenly leapt to my feet without a word of warning. The sensation had cranked up a dozen notches, as if I was now standing before an open oven. I darted to the wall of windows that overlooked my shop, and then looked further out to the street. I had left two of the loft windows wide open for air circulation from the store below. The ice cubes clinked together in my glass as I stared hard, my skin pebbling with sudden anxiety. I felt my friend's eyes on me, but I couldn't peel my eyes away from the street. It had begun to storm outside, heavy snowflakes beginning to cover the cars outside.

I heard my voice before I consciously chose to speak. "*Once upon a midnight dreary, while I pondered, weak and weary... Suddenly there came a tapping, as of someone gently rapping, rapping at my chamber door...*" The world slowed as I abruptly sensed the presence that stood just outside the front door to my shop. Something powerful was waiting for me. The waves of heat intensified, contrasting my suddenly icy forearms.

Long ago, with my mother's help, I had created what some Tibetan monks coined a *memory palace*, a vast mental library where each item – whether a statue, painting, cabinet, plant or even a book – held a specific piece of knowledge or past memory. My mouth moved in pace with my racing thoughts as they wandered through the dusty library, the imaginary walls of bookshelves racing into existence all around me. I held a book in my

29

palms, but I didn't need to read it. Merely holding the construct transferred whatever memories or knowledge it contained into my subconscious.

Gunnar grumbled. "Eidetic showoff. What—" The bell from the front door chimed and a shadow slipped inside, interrupting Gunnar. I heard him draw his SIG Sauer 9mm pistol in a swift motion, but it was a distant, sensory feeling, my mind still focused entirely on Edgar Allen Poe. An appropriate black cloak was folded around a woman's shoulders like obsidian wings, the whites of her teeth seeming to glow as she stared up at me from the floor below. Her eyes were black coals, but a glint of yellow reflected off them from the light behind me. My voice was faint even to me as I continued the poem.

"Then this ebony bird beguiling my sad fancy into smiling, by the grave and stern decorum of the countenance it wore…"

Her voice hissed back the only acceptable answer. *"Quoth the raven, Nevermore."*

CHAPTER 6

MY FRIENDS STOOD BESIDE ME NOW, ALARMED. EACH syllable of her words was laced with magical seduction. Emphasis on *magical*. "You must read a fair bit, Temple."

Gunnar's eyes weighed me. "I thought you were the only one who read ancient crap like that. And how did she hear you?" he whispered.

The woman took several slow, seductive steps towards the main floor, hips swaying deliciously. She made it hard to focus. "I hear many things, *Wulfric*. But be a good doggy, and speak only when spoken to." Gunnar's jaw dropped further. She continued without missing a beat. "What kind of bookstore do you run, Temple?" She picked up a copy of *Atlas Shrugged* on a display case at the bottom of the stairs. "This isn't even a first edition." A slimy, oily fire suddenly spread from her fingertips, smothering the priceless tome. "Oh, my mistake. It was." The book crumbled to ash in seconds. What the *hell* kind of power was *that*?

I was sure that Gunnar comprehended the ancient appellation she had given him, as he was very adept at his Norse heritage. *Wulfric* translated to *Wolf King*. Treading carefully, I chose civility. Courtesy was a good bet when dealing with ancient magical beings – courtesy or raw power.

Having chosen the latter with the Minotaur, I gambled on the former this time.

"We're closed for the evening, Madame. Pray come back in the morning, and I'll allow you to pay for the damage to my book."

"Hmmm… But a girl can't be too patient. She wants *what* she wants… *when* she wants it." She dropped her cloak, revealing utterly nude ivory skin, unblemished, and perfectly contoured with pleasant curves. I tried to mask my surprise… and lustful admiration. I was confident that I had never seen a body look so good. "But I do know how to repay a favor, bookkeeper." Her hand crept between her legs, skimming her round breasts in the process, her nipples instantly tightening. A small moan escaped her lips, and her eyes became glassy. My pants tightened instinctively, and her moan grew lustier, as if she had somehow sensed my reaction.

Her eyes came back to mine, and I realized for the first time that her pupils were not circular. Not human. They were horizontal slits, and her irises were a vibrant yellow. The exact same shade as the oily fire she had used to incinerate my book. Remembering that touch helped me regain focus like a cold shower would a pubescent boy. "I am seeking a book. An ancient family tome, titled *Sons of the Dying Sun*. Find it for me, and your *payment* will be... *climactic*." She flashed me a sultry grin.

Her voice threatened to overwhelm me with more than mere words. She was using old magic. Powerful magic. I felt erotic fingers massaging the deeper areas of my brain, coaxing me to listen and obey her as she had so adroitly caressed the pleasure centers. A quick glance at my friends revealed they weren't faring well with the battle for self-control. Their feet began to carry them to the doorway leading downstairs. I laced my own voice with magic, hoping to break whatever spell she was casting. But her power grew thicker, stronger. I decided to stop speaking polite Old English. "I will keep my eye out, but I am not a big fan of creepy, naked women showing up at my place of business... despite any contrary rumors."

She grinned again, her magic growing ever thicker, as if flexing, but I continued, silently halting her with every ounce of power I had. I could feel my control slipping, wanting nothing other than to rip my clothes off and meet her downstairs for a quickie. Or a Longie. Whatever she would allow. I noticed sweat on my temples, and momentarily imagined her licking it away and I froze. Fuck that. I lashed out with my power, no longer playing defense, and cut through hers like a blade. It snapped back into her with force, causing her to stumble back and glare up at me. Gunnar and Peter shook their heads dumbly, eyes dilated. My hands were shaking with the effort. "This is quite unprofessional, and I am, in fact, in the middle of a business meeting. Come back tomorrow and I will see what I can do for you."

"A shy wizard. Very well. If you don't like an audience, I'm sure I could persuade them to leave for you," she whispered coyly. Her magic came back faster, and stronger, the very air quivering. Each of my friends sagged at the sudden onslaught. Jesus, she was *strong*! I had never practiced much mind magic, but hers terrified me. Without my help, my friends would become drooling sycophants to her every whim.

With a crack of power that made one of the windows panes shatter, I broke her spell a second time, and my friends visibly stumbled as they were released. I let out a breath. Gunnar tossed his gun onto the couch, thumbing his tattoo in anticipation as he risked a glance at me. What *was* she? I hadn't ever heard of mind magic like this before, but apparently, I was strong enough to simply outmuscle her. That or I was damn lucky.

"We can chat in the morning, but for now, leave. Twice asked." I said.

"We *demand* your service." The tone of her voice was damn intimidating. We?

"Why do you need my help? Have you checked amazon.com yet?" I snapped.

Her eyes tightened. "We want what is ours, and will tolerate neither thieves nor bystanders. I don't want to ruin the surprise, but I'm sure your friend already has an idea what we're willing to do to reclaim our property." She winked at Gunnar. His face slowly grew pale in recognition, as if he had suddenly made a grim connection in his mind.

I used the only name she had offered. "You see, Raven, I'm not that good with demands. And right now, you are trespassing."

"*Raven*... I like it." She sniffed the air and then froze. "Why does it smell like—" Then her entire nude form stiffened as if recognizing a scent. "Him," she hissed. "You gave it to him, didn't you? I will floss my teeth with your guts for this, Temple."

I stared back, lost. "Um, what?"

"Don't lie to me!" she shrieked, chest heaving. She must have mistaken my confusion for concealment. "So be it. I will just have to see for myself if your last scream resembles that of your father." The lights went out, and a menacing cackle erupted from the darkness.

My rage jumped at the unexpected mention of my father. *What did she know?*

Then all hell broke loose, and I quickly discovered that Karma is indeed a bitch.

CHAPTER 7

S EVERAL OF MY GLASS-WALLED DIVIDERS IMPLODED AS
she let out a feral cry that was entirely inhuman. As the carnage began, I distantly wondered about her creepy horizontal pupils, what
they might signify, and whom she thought I had given her book to. I also
thought of my father's last scream at her hands, and my magic responded,
filling me like a pool of frigid water.

Gunnar beat me to the stairs, leapt into the air, and *shifted*.

That was the only way I could describe it, and even having seen it happen
a hundred times or more, it was still a breathtakingly beautiful thing to be-
hold. His clothes exploded around him, and a huge, white-haired wolf with
long ivory fangs and ice-blue eyes landed gracefully at the base of the stairs a
story below; the remnants of *most* of his clothes raining down like confetti,
having been unable to accommodate him mutating into his full werewolf
form. But over his white haired rear-end was a pair of *Underdog* spandex
underwear. I blinked in surprise, momentarily frozen. *Underdog underwear*?

Peter hung back, clutching a liquor bottle in a shaky fist. But whether to
drink or throw, I didn't know. Regardless, he was wise to hang back.

I did the opposite. I was directly behind Gunnar, tearing down the stairs
three at a time, whipping up all sorts of nasty to dish out on this bitch. But all
my power was invisible. No pretty shape-shifting for the wizard. No one
could see all the beautiful raw energy surrounding me, dancing from my fingertips, awaiting my command like a one-man rave party. As I breathed in
more power, my senses magnified. Smells contained tastes, my vision was
sharper, able to pierce more of the darkness, and the tactile feedback of my
fingers sliding down the mahogany stair rail was as euphoric as a lover's lips
brushing an earlobe. But no one could see a damn thing for all my hard work.

The world was unfair. Gunnar had a fucking outfit, and he *still* looked
cool.

"Sic her, Gunnar!" I yelled as I threw pulsing blue lights into the air around her, hoping to confuse her or ruin her night vision. Then I let loose a hurtling streak of fire towards her beautiful rack, hoping to mar her perfect nudity.

Her face began to stretch, her tongue momentarily growing longer before a flicker of hesitation crossed her eyes and she became normal again. *What the fuck?* My fire struck the wall behind her, neatly slicing through a framed movie poster as she effortlessly sidestepped and unleashed a screaming yellow ball of her own fire at me. I ducked behind a divider, and the ball slammed straight through it, shards of wood and glass biting into my arms and neck. A particularly long sliver of glass sliced deep into my forearm, which instantly welled up with dark, thick blood. I grunted in pain as my whole forearm flushed with heat.

Oily fire rained down upon a table behind me, igniting a small stack of precariously balanced books. She was some flavor of shape-shifter, but with much more control than even Gunnar had. Freaky. And I still didn't know what she had been about to shape-shift into. A demon of some kind by the looks of it. That wasn't good. Demons were hardcore. But I didn't have time to call for backup, despite the rules. If it was a demon, I would deal with it and apologize later.

From the shadows, Gunnar abruptly appeared in his *Underdog* undies, shattering through yet another glass-walled divider to grab the woman by the throat. But his long ivory teeth snapped together with a loud empty *clack* as Raven dodged him and then used his momentum to throw him through yet another of my oh-so-expensive glass-walled dividers. She grinned, slinging balls of slimy fire from her fingers after Gunnar, but he was already gone, melting back into the shadows of my store like a wraith. The fire slapped into a window, the glass spider-webbing with cracks before finally shattering into the street.

I gathered my will and threw a battering ram of force straight at her smiling face. She leapt impossibly high into the air to dodge my attack, but the force caught her feet, sending her cartwheeling into the shadows with a groan of pain. I heard an immediate growl, the snapping of jaws, and then a sharp piercing whine as I saw Gunnar fly directly into the brick wall, the impact knocking a cloud of dust from the rafters high above. He struggled to his feet with another whine, shook his head, and then let out a piercing howl of rage that made my forearms pebble with gooseflesh.

Now he was pissed. Gunnar's icy werewolf eyes latched onto mine and I took a reflexive step back, wondering if his head had been knocked loose enough to now see me as a threat. But he simply stared. I held up a finger, and motioned him to circle around the edge of the store. He slipped back into the shadows without any acknowledgement of my plan. I hoped he understood, because it would take both of us to take down this monster.

Raven cackled again. "Is this all you've got? And I had heard so many tales of the legendary Temples. You're putting up even less of a fight than your parents did." My vision went red so suddenly that I almost froze, thinking she had cast a spell of some sort on me.

But it was just rage, an emotion that I was very, *very* comfortable with.

Again, I wondered what she had to do with my parents. Was she lying just to goad me? I shook my head. It didn't matter. Her blood was mine. She was close, just behind a bookshelf ahead. "It's time to end this farce." Her voice cut through the darkness.

I calmly strolled around the bookshelf, coming face to face with the demon shifter. Her eyes glowed yellow in the flickering light behind me, her horizontal pupils momentarily halting my advance. She washed her hands together dramatically, more of the oily fire growing in her palms, the exact color as her irises. Then she grinned, teeth suddenly needle sharp, and threw her hands out at me. I slammed my will into the approaching scream of fire and it splattered into the clear shield of air, exploding into droplets of fire like paint on a glass wall. The heat instantly bled through the shield, lightly burning my fingertips. I rolled away as I dropped the shield, and watched as the fire fell to the ground of my shop, burning weakly. She stared at me on the ground and shook her head, disgusted, like one would at a peripatetic cockroach on a kitchen floor.

Icy blue eyes trailed her every move from the shadows, but she didn't notice. I watched, clutching my arm in real pain, fingers wet with blood, and tried to look terrified, beaten, as I struggled to crawl backwards. Her grin stretched wider as she took a single step closer, hands dripping more fire, but her fingers were now scaly yellow claws.

Then my pet werewolf slammed into her with such force that her head snapped sideways, the breath flying out of her in a rush before he slammed her into a solid oak bookshelf.

It didn't even wobble, and her head struck the aged wood with a solid crack, her eyes briefly rolling back into her skull. I climbed to my feet as Gunnar clutched her throat between his finger-length canines, his eyes glancing at me. I brushed off my arms, and strolled closer, glancing around my store to assess the damage. Indie was going to be pissed in the morning when she came in for her shift. I sighed. At least we were alive. With a thought, I drew the cold moist air from outside and doused the remaining fires lest they destroy any more of my priceless books. I snapped a finger and lit the candles that were spread about the room, filling the space with a familiar glow.

I tied up my forearm with a shred of cloth from Gunnar's clothes lying nearby. At least I knew it wasn't his underwear. Glancing out the window, I noticed a few people standing near the diner, pointing anxiously toward my store. One of them was gripping a phone to his ear.

Great.

Peter had reached the bottom of the stairs, but stayed there. As I said, wise.

Then I leveled Raven with very angry librarian eyes. Her ample breasts heaved in fury. I felt her attempt mind magic again, but I shut it down violently. She glared back.

"You don't stand a chance, wizard. You think you can kill me without catastrophic repercussions?"

"I did ask you to leave. Nicely." I grumbled.

Peter piped up from the stairs, full of conviction. "Twice!"

An odd look crossed her face, and she eagerly tried to peer past my shoulder, but Peter remained a safe distance away, out of her view. Maybe she was surprised to find a Regular here with me. But there seemed something *more* to her look. Unsuccessful, she turned back to me. "You think you stand a chance against us when even your parents failed? My sisters will *destroy* you." The words actually frightened me with their simplicity. She wasn't trying to threaten. She honestly believed it. Gunnar's eyes flicked back to look up at me, questioning, but not releasing pressure. What did any of this have to do with my parents? Before I could ask, she began to move. "None shall escape the eclipse!" she screeched.

The woman's hand became a web of yellow reptilian talons again, darting towards Gunnar's furred throat. I prepared a blast of air to pin her arm down, but I heard a high keening wail like a mortar shell racing towards me from over my shoulder. I ducked, just missing the streaking projectile of ice that abruptly slammed into the woman's chest. Frosty smoke trailed up around the top of a liquor bottle that was now wedged firmly between her breasts, leaving a frosty crater of icy gore. Her eyes glazed over instantly. I studied the wound for a few silent moments, looking for the swell of a breath between her magnificent breasts, making sure she was dead. My gaze was thorough.

After a minute, I slowly turned. Peter was nervously wringing his hands together. I didn't say a word, stunned speechless by his display of magic. Peter began stammering. "I didn't know if you guys saw it or not. She was going to slice his throat." Gunnar had leapt back at the sound, barely missing the fatal swipe of Raven's talons.

Gunnar shifted back to his human form out of the corner of my eye, naked except for his Underdog undies. Imagine the actors in the movie *300*, and you'll understand my rage a bit better. I wasn't jealous.

I rounded on him. "Really?" I asked, gesturing energetically at his ensemble. "Have you no *dignity*?" His face turned crimson.

"I haven't done laundry this week! Spandex is the only thing I've found that works on the fly without being shredded. Do you have any idea how embarrassing it is to run around naked looking for clothes after I shift? Besides, I think I look kinda cool." He flexed proudly.

I groaned, waving a hand dismissively as I turned back to Peter. "And *you*! How long have you been able to use magic? Why didn't you tell me? All this time I thought you were just a *Regular*!" I roared, my legendary wizard temper rising to the surface.

He evaded my questions, backing up a step. "Look, there's a dead woman… thing on your floor, damage everywhere, and I just saved Gunnar's *life*. I can't be here when the cops—" he hesitated with a shudder, looking forlornly at Gunnar as he realized a cop was *already here*. If an FBI werewolf counted as a cop. "I have to leave. If anyone finds out I was involved in this, I'm a dead man." His words rang deeper than mere legal trouble. He sounded as if he meant his last statement literally. "I'll lose my job. Our company can't afford any involvement in," he waved a hand, "Whatever this is." His eyes widened for a moment. "I think I left my… phone upstairs."

"No—" I began, but too late. He was already padding up the stairs. I had seen him put his cell in his pocket before the attack. Gunnar and I shared a heavy look.

Peter raced down the stairs after a few seconds and then aimed for the door, intending to go straight past us. "Peter..." I began, reaching out an arm to halt him, but he brushed me off.

"I guess it was in my pocket the whole time." He looked panicked, eyes darting around the room before he continued, "and you didn't read my note about the book yet?"

"I already told you I hadn't," I answered with a frown.

"Oh, okay. Well, it's on your desk. Whenever you get a chance." He still looked nervous and confused. Shock, no doubt. "No time to chat, Nate. I'm gone."

"That whole 'might is right' conversation might be much more relevant now."

Gunnar chimed in. "Yes, and *Dead men tell no tales*. I *am* an FBI agent, Peter." He hesitated, glancing from me to Peter curiously. "And *whatever* you did, you didn't have to *kill* her. Murder is kind of a big deal."

He threw up his hands, exasperated. "But she wasn't even *human*!"

"Point for Peter," I said. "But still, magic is nothing to play around with. You need training. And, damn it, I am a *trainer*!" I added, hurt.

He fingered his bracelet as if seeking comfort from it. "It's pretty new to me too. I promise we'll talk. But not tonight." He forcedly shoved past us and out the door.

Gunnar and I stared at each other for a moment, and then down to the nude woman. Sirens wailed in the distance, coming closer. "This doesn't look good at all. What do you want to do about it?" He waved a hand at our feet.

"I'm not sure. You think Clorox will clean up the blood? Or will it ruin the lacquer finish on the wood?" I asked, clueless. I am a bachelor, after all. I paid people to clean. It was beneath me. Like it is for bachelors around the world.

Gunnar furrowed a brow. "No, idiot. The body."

I blinked. "Oh. That's nothing." I strode to the satchel that I had hung at the door earlier in the day, and withdrew two silver pennies from a Crown Royal bag tucked inside. I knelt down and placed them over her eyes, but not before thumbing back the eyelids to catch another glance at her oddly horizontal pupils. "Huh." Gunnar made a similar noise behind me. What I was about to do wasn't exactly necessary, but I tried to do it whenever I got the

39

chance. Last respects. I stepped back with a whispered, *"Requiescat in pace."* A low horn wailed, somehow far away yet also near. I felt it like bass in my chest. The body disintegrated into a yellow pile of ash before our eyes, and a ghostly hooded figure on a boat coalesced behind it, sweeping the pile out the door with a misty paddle as he glided past us. I looked up at Gunnar. His eyes were wide with shock.

"I thought he was just a myth!"

The boatman glanced back, nodding once before vanishing. I waved amicably. "The Boatman of the River Styx is as real as any other fable you've encountered. Charon helps guide the dead to their final resting place. You just don't see many people making his job any easier. I try to make friends wherever I can." Gunnar just shook his head. "You off the clock, or on?" I asked, staring him in the eyes.

He didn't answer for a long while, weighing his options. "Off." He said finally. "But if this becomes relevant, I'll have to put the badge back on." I nodded in answer, thankful. "Got any spare clothes for me?" I nodded, flipping my head towards the loft above. Gunnar darted away, looking like a freaking idiot in his stupid underwear. I grabbed a dustpan and broom, cleaning up the broken glass and burned books as questions raced through my head. My forearm ached, but it could wait.

I wondered what was so important about her book request, and why she had been so damn impatient to get it. The denizens of the magical world knew my reputation, knew I could find things for the right price, so why had she been so impolite about it? She had acted as if *I* was the thief; selling it to some unknown person she apparently held a grudge against. And she had mentioned my father.

Gunnar appeared as I was dumping the dustpan into the trash behind the coffee bar. I was muttering to myself as he slowly approached. Wizards were known for their tempers, and Gunnar had seen some of my most flamboyant. Not wanting a repeat, he waited. Again, I surround myself with wise friends. That thought brought me back to Peter, and a question I didn't want to think about on top of everything else. *How*?

I glared at him. "Four – fucking – thousand – dollars. Each!" I bellowed, brandishing my broom like a sword at the destroyed dividers. Gunnar expertly leapt back with an amused grin.

"You're good for it," he mumbled.

I scowled back. "Not the point. And you know it. What the hell just happened?"

Gunnar grew serious. "Honestly, I have no idea. Have you pissed anyone off lately?" My glare answered his question. "I mean, besides the Minotaur," he paused. "Or the police." He sighed. "Anyone more than usual?"

I thought, and thought hard, before answering. "No," I paused. "But she did say that you might know what was going on."

Gunnar's eyes instantly grew guarded. "Possibly. I'll look into it, and let you know in the morning when I pick you up for the... funeral." My shoulders sagged.

"My life sucks huge wang," I complained. Gunnar nodded sagely.

"Pick you up at noon?" he asked softly.

It was already three in the morning. "Whatever."

"Can you handle the cops? Just tell them it was a... burglar or something."

"Or something..." I replied testily.

I heard one last thing before I turned away. "Does your mind really store all that stuff you read, or did you just happen to read Poe lately?"

I didn't answer. My thoughts drifted away from my friend, lost in the unpracticed task of cleaning up the place. I barely noticed him leave, or the bogus answers I gave the cops, but soon all was silent, and I was back upstairs overlooking my wrecked shop, sipping a new glass of fiery absinthe. I spun the coin the Minotaur had given me earlier around a finger, thoughts questing for answers to the night's events. A gift from Hermes. I hadn't actually ever met any of the 'gods' before.

I grunted, pensive. But at least there were some positives. I now had three books to find – one for Raven & Associates, one for Peter, and one for my mysterious client – and one of those was already found, as long as I could beat the Minotaur in our duel. But I didn't want to think about the duel tonight.

I wondered what kind of shape-shifter Raven had been. I was almost positive she hadn't been a demon. As if sensing the risk, she had chosen not to reveal her true form. She had to have a reason. My thoughts grew darker as I watched the snowflakes continue to fall outside the shop's windows, as numerous as the questions drifting through my mind.

"*Quoth the raven, nevermore.*" I mumbled, downing the last of my drink as I began to scribble out a note for Indie to read in the morning – a list of laborers to call for the expensive repairs to my shop, and a vague explanation of how it had happened.

CHAPTER 8

"**A**T LEAST IT'S CONSISTENT," I OFFERED.

"Shut up, Nate." Gunnar slammed down the hood of his car. Licorice-smelling smoke clouded up from the engine block, filling the air with a sickly-sweet aromatic fog. "If you hadn't made me drive out to that god-forsaken field to pick up your car, we might have made it to the cemetery in one piece." His shoulders sagged. "Tow truck will be here in a few hours. We can call a cab."

"Let's just walk. It's not far. I could use the fresh air." I waved away a particularly heavy tendril of smoke creeping towards us. Gunnar nodded, following my lead. I immediately looked around a bit, acting conspicuously nervous.

"What?" Gunnar asked, tensing.

"Isn't there a leash law in St. Louis?" Murder shone in Gunnar's eyes. "Never mind." I smirked and continued on. He had been up all night, re-searching leads, seeing if it related to whatever Raven had been talking about. Apparently, several bookstore owners in town – and even across the river in Illinois – had been targeted over the last few days, some surviving, but most not. Gunnar hadn't elaborated on details yet. But I definitely wasn't the first bookstore owner to be visited by her.

"Why are you so annoying this afternoon?"

I grinned. "Have you ever had Cuban *colada*?"

"Cuban… Is that some kind of drug?" he threw up his arms in exaspera-tion. "Damn it, Nate. I'm an FBI Agent!"

"Down, boy. It's not a drug, but it probably should be. It's Cuban coffee. A form of espresso laced with sugar. Liquid Nirvana." I quoted my friend from Miami. "*Nunca comience un día duro sin una taza de colada*. Never start a tough day without a cup of colada."

Gunnar squinted, eyes bloodshot. "Where can I get some?" Whipping out a flask from my pressed suit coat, I passed it over. "You had some the whole time?"

"Of course."

"You're a real asshole sometimes, Nate. Capital A." I grinned in response. Gunnar's nerves steadied after a few sips. "This is really good." I held out a hand for him to pass it back. Instead, he slipped it into his own suit pocket. "You should probably get a flask like mine so you can carry it around when on the go," he patted the flask.

"You should probably get a new car, like mine," I answered dryly.

His smile instantly turned stony. "Capital A."

After several minutes of silence, we entered the infamous Bellefontaine Cemetery – the final resting place for both my parents, and also my every ancestor who had come stateside since the 1700's. The cemetery had been founded in 1849, and we had had all of our pre-1849 ancestors transferred here from their previous graves shortly after. William Clark – from the famous Lewis and Clarke expedition – and even Mark Twain were buried here. Only the best for the Temple clan.

Before I had a chance to admire the beauty of the Bellefontaine grounds, we were assaulted. Camera flashes nearly blinded us. A red carpet had even been rolled out over the blanket of fresh snow, looking like a bloody smear. We were momentarily descended upon, shoved bodily by a gaggle of reporters, all shouting to be heard over one another. "Master Temple, is it true that you're taking over Temple Industries?" One voice shouted. I wanted to burn the ground to ash, but instead, I chose civility.

Kind of.

I glared at a film crew standing nearby, staring down my audience of likely a few million viewers. "Greetings, carrion. Where there is a carcass, there will always be vultures. I hope you are all having a splendid feast on the decaying remains of two of the greatest minds St. Louis has ever known. Now, if you would be so kind… step. The fuck. Back." Cameras and microphones lowered. The ashen-faced cameraman looked pale as his boss ordered him to cut the feed. I took a few steps before turning back to them. "Oh, and have a nice day." Then I was off again, feeling marginally better.

Towering monoliths, marble angels, and skeletal, ancient trees surrounded me as I strode deeper into the cemetery, colder on the inside than I was on the outside. The wind was muted here, as if holding its breath in the presence of so many dead. Gunnar walked beside me, a wry grin on his face. "That was efficient, and polite."

"They're lucky I was only mildly perturbed. A cemetery is a convenient place to commit mass murder," I glanced at his badge, which was prominently displayed on his belt. "Hypothetically," I added.

Gunnar nodded, awed as we came into sight of the towering Temple Mausoleum. It was the largest private plot in the cemetery, safe in a wide swath of fresh grass that ringed the entire perimeter, secluded from all other nearby graves. Due to its sheer size, many at first mistook it for the caretaker's residence, but only until they came close enough to witness it in its entirety. It was nicer. And bigger. Much bigger. The marble colossus was astoundingly extravagant, having been built to house our first ancestors on this side of the Atlantic, and their descendants had pulled out all the stops, trying to recreate the more lavish mausoleums found in their former European homeland.

It was a study in contradictions, almost every culture fused together for its creation. Corinthian columns climbed two stories to hold the massive marble roof overlooking the cemetery. Marble sentinels of all sorts stood guard between each column: armed Roman soldiers, nude men and women entwined in Raphaelian ecstasy, or less profane romantic embraces, Spanish Kings, Queens, and even Arabic scholars. Several gods and goddesses could be seen in the mix if one looked closely enough: Anubis, Zeus, Odin, Athena, and a few others from a spattering of different faiths.

I spotted a small group of executives and lawyers from Temple Industries just outside the door, obviously waiting to speak with me. Didn't I already have enough to deal with? Then I spotted a discreet hand gesturing to get my attention behind the trunk of a large tree beside the path. Weird, but definitely preferable to more talk of my parents' company.

I flicked open my pack of smokes, stabbed one between my lips, and lit the tip with a thought. I pointed emphatically at the swarm of suits near the entrance, feet planted firmly, a maniacal scowl on my face. "Gunnar, *sic 'em!*" Gunnar stared back at me as if I had finally lost what little sanity he thought I had been clinging to. With the perfect moment lost, I lowered my wounded arm and sighed. "I just need a moment. Stall them." Gunnar glanced around warily, obviously reluctant to let me out of his sight after last night's events, but finally complied.

I ambled aimlessly, waiting until no one was looking my way, and then darted behind the tree where I had seen the hand. "Hello, wizard," A gruff voice greeted me.

I assessed the speaker, who was decked out in full-blown soldier gear, but it was a mixture of ancient leather armor and modern weapon belts. Very, very authentic. He looked as rough as his battle-hardened leather, creases marring his eyes in vicious crow's feet. A crude scar cut across his jaw, and another ugly slash zippered the side of his neck. His eyes were a milky green, reminding me of absinthe. "Ah, hello, Sir LARPER. You are correct that this is a field of death, but not the one full of battles you no doubt seek. I'm afraid the field where your brethren await is over at the Park of Carondelet."

He studied me, measuring me up and down for a moment without amusement. "I'm from Brooklyn, idiot. We don't participate in Live Action Role Playing games." He had said *we*, even though he seemed alone. "Name's Tomas. I'm here to tell you that you're in danger. We're looking for someone, and we believe he came to St. Louis."

"I did have an unexpected visitor last night." His interest perked. "She was naked, pale skin, dark hair, and naked. Oh, and she had yellow eyes." He frowned, but shook his head, not recognizing the description. "I guess I had to pay extra because of the eyes. Although she wasn't worth the money."

"Yellow eyes… That doesn't ring a bell, but be careful. Something big is going down here soon. Maybe real soon. Bookstore owners have been dying pretty nasty deaths. Watch your ass."

I nodded as he turned away, taking a pleasant pull from the cigarette as I watched him leave. "Oh, and she had horizontal pupils." He stiffened, turning back to me.

"What?" he asked quietly.

"Judging by the arsenal at your hip, I think you know what she was. She mentioned having sisters before I killed her," I let out a stream of smoke. "Tell me."

He blinked. "You killed her?"

"Wasn't all that hard, really. Kind of a breeze," I lied.

The man weighed me with his eyes. "She never shifted, did she?"

Damn. "Well, she started to," I answered defensively.

The man began laughing, wheezing even. "Spoken like the pup that thinks he killed a mama bear, only to discover that it was just a cub," he laughed even harder, before my scowl silenced him.

"She didn't seem to appreciate a glacial liquor bottle to the heart very much, shifting or not. Now, what was she, and what is your stake in this?"

He reeked of military, or perhaps mercenary training. "Dragons have been rumored in the city, but we came here only to find one in particular. A man. A very dangerous man. I guess he could possibly have a group of lady dragons at his beck and call. It would make things…interesting."

"Oh… like, real dragons?" I asked weakly.

The man blinked as if I were daft. "Of course. But I guess they're technically were-dragons. Able to switch between human and dragon form at will."

I inhaled my cigarette again, postulating. "I've never encountered one before last night." I answered honestly. "So, what do they want?" Assessing his gear again, a new thought hit me. "Are you supposed to be some kind of dragon hunter?"

The man grinned darkly as he slipped me a business card with a number on the front. "Why, yes. *We* are." His eyes fixated halfway up a particularly tall oak. I followed his gaze to see a human form tucked back against the trunk, almost invisible. The figure nodded down at us, tipping a fedora with a grin, balancing what looked like a grappling gun in the crook of his shoulder. I suddenly wondered how many more men this man had in his employ, and why they were so wary. And then the man was walking away again, leaving me alone by the tree trunk as he spoke over his shoulder. "We're not sure what they are doing yet, but we're keeping tabs on 'em. We've also got our eyes on you, Temple." I looked back up where the sentry had been, but he was gone. Not a rustle of movement. Damn good.

Dragons again. So, that's what Raven had been preparing to shift into. Not a demon, but a were-dragon. But why had she stopped? Surely, she could have protected herself against us if she had simply shifted into her dragon form. What irked me the most was that I hadn't known that dragons could shift at all. I had always assumed that a dragon was just another big, scary monster, lurking in caves and guarding treasures. Not something that could go unnoticed in a large city. But if they could appear human…

Gunnar called out my name, probably noting the other man's departure from the tree. I stepped back onto the path leading up to the Mausoleum. "Coming." I took another drag on the cigarette before snuffing it out on the path.

Gunnar tried to intercept me before the group of gnarled lawyers and ancient board members could swarm me, but failed. "Master Temple, my deepest condolences. I have been trying to reach you for the past week, but it appears your cell service must be unreliable." A stunning, tall redheaded woman spoke, stepping out from behind the group of geezers around her.

Despite the fact that she was significantly younger than her companions, I realized that not one of them had spoken a word to me. They watched the firecracker woman with respect and... fear? Her eyes were tight with stress, strain, and Corporate America-itis. But it did nothing to hide her beautiful cerulean eyes. I had heard of Miss Ashley Belmont before, but had never met her, and hadn't expected such a big aura from such a frail package – maybe 110 pounds despite her height. My parents had referred to her as their right hand. Maybe I should have started working for Temple Industries after all. I realized I was staring, so quickly fumbled for an answer.

"No, I just didn't answer your calls." The woman blinked in surprise, and I almost slapped my forehead with my palm. *Think first, Nate*, I chided myself.

Her response was whip-quick. "Understandable. I have been meaning to talk to you about—"

"I don't give a damn about the company," I growled at my misperception of her. The fairer sex had always been my kryptonite, able to instantaneously make me lose focus. She looked hurt at the interruption, but I barreled past her, closer to my linebacker, Gunnar.

"I was going to say *your parents*, Master Temple." She said softly behind me. I looked over my shoulder at her. Her long legs, wavy red hair, and secretary glasses seemed to shelter a cunning intelligence and rare compassion.

Gunnar stepped forward, "I'm honored to introduce Ashley Belmont, stand-in CEO of Temple Industries. It is very rude to keep a woman waiting, Nate. I think you owe her a minute of your *oh-so precious* time." He said, leveling a condescending glare at me.

The woman nodded appreciatively, tugging her open Burberry coat closed about her. Damn it. Gunnar was right. "My apologies, Miss Belmont. What can I do for you?" I asked politely.

"To be honest, I'm not quite sure myself. The information is confidential..." She glanced pointedly at Gunnar, and the silver badge glinting off his belt. He didn't even blink, unsnapping the badge and tossing it underhand to me. I turned to face her bright stare as it sailed at my face, using magic at the last second to stop the badge an inch from contact. I reached up, plucked it out of the air, and stuffed it into my suit's inner coat pocket. Luckily, none of the older gentlemen were looking at me.

"I don't see any cops." I said.

She dipped her head, not even blinking at the show of magic. Huh. Magic didn't impress her, which meant she must be privy to my world. My parents must have shared things with her. Or she was a Freak, like Gunnar and I. "That is all well and good, but I'm afraid I can only give cursory details here. The location isn't secure." She flicked her gaze over to a man silently climbing down from a nearby tree. He wore the same fedora I had seen earlier. "Perhaps you could permit me to join you at Chateau Falco following the eulogy?" she asked softly, eyes returning to mine.

I nodded after a moment. I definitely didn't want to go to my parents' home, but I did owe her at least a discussion, especially after a week of radio silence. And it was the perfect location for such a talk. She was acting like the perfect daughter to my parents' last wishes, regardless of her bloodline, and I was acting like their spoiled son. "Consider the invitation offered, Miss Belmont. I have a few things to wrap up first. Perhaps this evening over refreshments?" she nodded in response.

"See you then, Master Temple." She glided into the Mausoleum on stiletto heels. Gunnar's eyes followed her like a dog watching a steak.

"Pretty impressive gal." Gunnar spoke beside me. I nodded distantly as I saw Peter inside the Mausoleum, frantically engaging Ashley – no doubt attempting to secure a job. She was courteous to him, but I could see the denial in her posture. A tough woman. It seemed my parents' company was in good hands. "Any idea what she wants to talk to you about?" I shook my head as I strode forward.

"No, but we'll find out soon enough." I handed the badge back to him. "Let's get this over with." I stepped inside the Mausoleum, ready to see my parents sealed away forever. I only hoped that I could also bury my grief this day. The wings of the building hungrily embraced me as I stepped inside the citadel of death that had marked the end of so many of my ancestors. If a building had emotions, this one seemed hungry, anticipatory.

CHAPTER 9

I WAS IN A FOUL MOOD AFTER THE FUNERAL. I HAD stayed longer than anyone else, wanting to be alone with my parents one last time. Now, I was blessedly alone. A cab was going to pick me up in an hour. The service had been a blur, speeches from friends and associates causing many tears and tight throats, bringing back all the grief I had attempted to hide over the past week, but both my friends had been there for me.

Neither said a word, nor did they try to comfort me. They just remained by my side, twin guardians determined to keep me safe during my moment of weakness; rock solid men. Now alone, I wandered the main floor of the vast Temple Mausoleum, studying the private alcoves on either side of me which each held an elegant tomb and statue of a fallen ancestor. You would be surprised how many relatives could be found in a quarter of a millennium. Ornate benches sat before each tomb, the design dating back to the particular time period of the individual, or – as was most often the case – couple. A locked glass-encased leather-bound book rested on an elaborate pedestal before each tomb, sharing a not-so-short biography of each resident. A large fountain gurgled just inside the main dome-ceilinged nave, emitting a soothing, bubbling sound that was made all the more beautiful by the stained-glass windows shining down from high above.

Oh, and my parents had recently made the windows bulletproof.

They had upgraded the security of the family Mausoleum, installing security cameras, reinforcing walls, motion-sensors – which I assumed would be totally unnecessary in a building occupied by corpses – and what compared to a bank vault door on the main entrance. It was the Fort Knox of Mausoleums, but I had never understood, nor received an explanation as to why.

I glanced up at the back wall past the fountain. A large mosaic of tiles decorated the wall in a huge family tree, except the names of the relatives weren't on the branches; they were on the roots. Sapphires marked each woman, and rubies each man, their names etched deeply beside each gem. My name was the last and lowest part of the root system, having no other relatives to share the nutrient production for the massive tree.

I was the last Temple.

After perusing each of my distant ancestor's tombs, I finally came to the task at hand and turned around, retreating back towards the entrance to rest in front of the one tombstone I had avoided after everyone had left. The one now belonging to my parents.

My feet dragged as I reached the newest area of the crypt, and I sat down heavily on the firmly padded leather divan a few feet away from it. Ever so slowly, I looked up, and saw my parents staring down at me through lifeless marble eyes. Sadness threatened to overwhelm me now that I was alone, and I felt a heavy guilt that I hadn't spent more time with them in recent years. Now the chance was lost forever.

The funeral hadn't really been legit, merely an excuse for all the distant friends and celebrity crowd of St. Louis to come say their peace. The real funeral procession, and the first goodbye, had been only a day after their sudden demise, and I had been the only attendee. Not even my friends knew of it. That was the day that I had called Charon to give them their last ride home, as I had done with Raven at my store last night.

The door leading outside opened quietly, and I looked up to see an elderly bull of a man step inside, tugging in a janitorial cart. "You shouldn't be here." I growled. "It's private property."

The man looked back at me with an unperturbed smile. "I've been here more times than you, Laddie." His Scottish brogue was thick. "I kept the place clean for 'yer father going on forty years now. I guess I work for you now." He continued pushing the cart inside, the 8,000-pound door closing behind him with a dull thud. Soundproof walls – yet another addition from my parents. Maybe they hadn't wanted to disturb the rest of the cemetery with their after-life parties once they passed on. Courteous of them, really.

"Well, if you work for me now then get out."

"Not in my contract, Master Temple." He began mopping up the spotless floor.

"Cantankerous old bastard," I grumbled under my breath.

"Aye, Master Temple. That I am. Ye have a mouth like 'yer father." I blinked over at him, but he was engrossed in his work, so I let him be. He obviously had the code to get inside the mausoleum, so I trusted his story. I resumed my study of my parents. I thought of their deaths, and the lack of evidence the police had obtained from both the scene and the morgue. The facts flipped through my mind like a speed-reader on crack, but I came to no new conclusions. If Raven had been telling the truth, why had the dragons wanted them dead? Apparently, my parents had made some big-league enemies.

A hand brushed my shoulder, and I jumped, realizing that I had dozed off. "Better clean yourself up, Master Temple." He dropped a silk kerchief into my lap, crimson lines showing through some of the thin material. "Never let 'em see you sweat." I stared down at it, listening to the cart shuffle away behind me. I slowly unfolded the cloth.

A larger game is afoot. Beware of the coming Eclipse, my son.

I stood in a rush, thrusting a finger out at the old man to halt him in a tight cocoon of air as he neared the door. My magic wrapped around him like a straightjacket, one foot lifted off the ground as if I had stopped time. "What's the meaning of this, old man?"

The janitor stared back from his invisible prison. "The name's Mallory, Master Temple, not 'old man.' I found that next to your father before the police arrived. You haven't been answering your phone, so I decided to meet you the old-fashioned way. Didna' want the Bobbies' to find it. Awkward questions, and such, no doubt." *Bobbies* was an English term for Policemen. Without preamble, the janitor rolled his shoulders, and my spell simply evaporated as if it had never existed. He continued tugging the cart through the heavy doors, and then disappeared outside, the door thudding closed behind him. I remained frozen, unable to even wonder how the senior citizen had so easily disarmed my magic. My gaze shifted from the door to the kerchief, and then to my parents' tombstone.

The message had been written in crimson ink.

No, not ink. Blood.

Then I was moving. I bolted outside, ready to interrogate Mallory further, but when I got there he was simply gone. His cart sat just outside the door, but of him, there was no sign. I saw the cab I had called earlier idling just outside, waiting patiently. After a few seconds of bewilderment, I decided to lock up the mausoleum via the electronic keypad, and angrily climbed inside the vehicle. "Did you see an old man leave the building a minute ago?" I growled in response to his jovial greeting.

"Just you, sir." He answered with a frown. I looked back. The cart was gone. *What the hell?*

"Never mind. Plato's Cave in Soulard." I calculated in my head. 7.5 miles. "Get me there in eight minutes." He nodded eagerly as I flashed a fifty-dollar-bill at him. I leaned back into the worn leather seats, satisfied by the adrenaline-inducing formula-one driving abilities of the cabby. I closed my eyes with a sigh, thinking. I now knew the reason for the odd perimortem gash on his arm. What had been so important that my father had wanted to leave a message in his own blood? And what did that have to do with the upcoming solar eclipse in three days? Wait, two days now. I hadn't even remembered the big event until the message on the kerchief. It just hadn't seemed important. There was a big convention of astronomers in town awaiting that very spectacle, but I'd be damned if I knew how it was connected to my parents' deaths. Something nagged at me, but I was too exhausted to worry about it.

I began preparing a plan to acquire – or at least look into – the book that Raven had wanted me to find. Not knowing what it was about, or why it was so important, I figured that finding it might at least protect some of my fellow bookstore owners around town. Perhaps I could barter with one of the dragon sisters she mentioned. Either way, it was better to have it in my possession than it remaining an unknown. I spoke a quick reminder into my iPhone, commanding the feminine intelligence queen to transfer it to my calendar in case I forgot later. I was meeting up with Gunnar in an hour to discuss the information he had dug up on Raven and her vague hints. He also had all the information on the latest bookstore attacks. Maybe if we kicked up enough dust we would find a trail.

The taxi screeched to a halt in front of my bookstore. I glanced down at my phone. Seven minutes. I threw him the bill and climbed out. He tipped an imaginary hat at me, and – much more responsibly this time – pulled out into the street, adhering to the legal laws set aside by the grand city of St. Louis.

CHAPTER 10

M Y PHONE VIBRATED BEFORE I HAD TAKEN TWO
steps. "Temple," I answered.

"Hey," Gunnar replied, sounding grouchier than earlier. "My
car died today."

That brought a brief grin to my face. "I know. I was there."

"No, it *really* died. It's going to cost twice what it's worth to fix it, so I
will be a public transport kind of guy for a while."

"Well at least there's tons of babes on the public bus."

"Not in this town. New York, maybe, but not St. Louis."

I tried not to laugh. "Still want me to swing by?" I answered instead.

"Yes. I've got everything together now. You sure you want in on this?"
he sounded guarded.

"Um, someone tried to… hurt us last night." I changed what I had been
about to say. Police were kind of nit-picky about overhearing unreported
murders. Even if it was self-defense. "Pretty sure I don't have much of a
choice." I hadn't told him about the dragon hunters at the Bellefontaine
Cemetery. Nor the kerchief from Mallory. It would have to wait. With newfound resolve, I mumbled a confirmation. "As much as I would like to catch
a flight to Cabo, there's no getting out of it for me. I found out some information that might help us a bit."

"Maybe you *should* get out of town. The cops are already watching you."

I shook my head firmly. "I'm not running away from this."

"Alright." He sighed. "See you in an hour, then." I clicked the phone off,
and shoved it in my pocket. I placed a hand on the heavy door to my shop
and strode inside. Standing there for a moment, I let the building's heat wash
over me. Plato's Cave was doing a brisk business for a Friday, despite the
new renovations due to Raven's visit last night. A few workers milled around
the broken window leading to the street, the sound of hammers striking nails
filling the air.

A stunning, tall young blonde hung near the register, her *Got Jesus?* Tee stretched much too tightly over her breasts. A cartoon depiction of our savior was waving a thumbs-up in the most inappropriate of places, but the fabric was long enough to remain decent. Barely. Her name was Indiana Rippley. Her eyes reminded me of glacial chips of ice, almost a neon blue. She was my second-in-command at the shop, my store manager, and was privy to more classified information than the other employees.

"Hey, Indie. What's happening?" She had started as a simple part-timer, but had rapidly forsaken using her degree when confronted with some of the darker clients I sometimes entertained. Her skills at running a tight ship had proven necessary; she was smooth sailing where others would blanche.

"Not a whole lot, Cap'n. Other than the remodel." She added with a curious brow. I nodded back. "Game night tonight," she scanned a paper before her. "Gods of Chaos IV, if I'm not mistaken."

"You're never mistaken, Indie," I answered, rolling my eyes.

She beamed up at me, dancing up a bit on her toes, a pleasant jiggle making the cartoon Jesus dance a quick two-step on her shirt. "We got the store cleaned up after you left for..." Her face grew tight. "Need a drink? I'm on break in five." She offered, knowing I had been through a tough ordeal today.

"I'm fine, Indie, but thanks." But all I really wanted to do was succumb to her offer. I had crushed on her for years, but never made that final leap to show her my true feelings, fearing the nuclear fallout if things went south.

"Okay." Her eyes were full of doubt. "I just want you to know that you aren't alone. If you need a shoulder to lean on, don't forget about us little people." She said with a friendly grin. Eye candy for sure, but she was a trusted friend, and extremely intelligent. Her IQ had been clocked at 187 on three separate tests – well above genius level. Harmless flirting had been a part of our relationship since we had met so many years ago, and it had never crossed the line into anything more. I was protective of her, and she of me. But I still found myself wondering if there could be more.

"Thanks. But I'm fine. Maybe next week I'll be ready to talk about it."

"You know where to find me, Cap'n." She was also the only employee who didn't always refer to me as *Master Temple*.

I leaned over the counter, whispering conspiratorially. "Any particular guests I need to know about?"

She glanced about, making sure no customers were near. "Nope. We're all prepared for the worst though." She discreetly slid open a drawer by her long, pale thigh, revealing an empty LockSAF PBS-001 biometric fingerprint pistol case. Every employee had one, and the necessary paperwork for concealment, happily paid for by yours truly. Even with rubber bullets, the guns could impact a world of deterrence. Noticing that Indie wore a tight black pencil skirt, I tried not to imagine where she had hidden her weapon. She smiled sweetly up at me, as if sensing my thoughts.

I leaned back, and nodded. "I just need to step up to my office for a sec, then I'm off again. You mind holding down the fort tonight? I'm not sure where I will be, but my plate is kind of full right now."

She glanced at the schedule, feigning a frown. "Well, I'll have to cancel my dinner plans, but if my employer doesn't mind compensating me for it, I don't mind. My date is kind of a douche anyway."

"You debutante!" I laughed. "You know I'm good for it. Rain check for next week, and I'll take you out for lunch so you can hear all the boring details."

She nodded. "Only if it's somewhere good."

"Your pick."

She clapped her hands, and I had to force myself to walk away rather than study the reaction of her anatomy. I climbed the stairs to my loft, unlocked the door, and stepped inside, expecting a class five cluster-fuck of a mess, but I was wrong. I had woken up late this morning, and had momentarily turned into a tornado while looking for my suit. A smile split my cheeks, and I strode over to the window. Indie was glancing up at me. I mimed a worshipful pose, recognizing her deft hand at cleaning up for me. She deserved a raise. Her smile grew wider as she waved back up at me, and then she returned to her duties.

I changed quickly, and then scanned my desk for Peter's book request. Spotting the parchment, I shoved it into my jeans pocket, threw on a comfy tee and a jacket, snatched up my Fendi satchel full of magical goodies – including the SIG Sauer X-five pistol Gunnar had gifted me – and locked up behind me. Curious, I approached Indie again. "Any reason I never got the message from Peter earlier in the week?" I waved the note at her. She frowned, unknowing, "Peter said he left it with Jessie." Her eyes instantly became guilty.

"He seemed like a good guy when I hired him. He's an odd duck, but he's still trying to learn the particulars for working for you. Want me to talk to him?" Her face was set in a frown, no doubt anxious to rectify this situation with a Defcon 1 approach. *And you wonder why I was hesitant to risk our friendship for a chance at romance.*

"No worries. Just see that it doesn't happen again. I have full faith in you, Indie. If you thought he was worth hiring, then I trust you." My voice grew darker as I picked up a pirate accent. "No need to make him walk the plank... yet."

She grinned back, nodding once. "Aye, aye, Cap'n!" She bellowed loudly.

From around the store, all my employees dropped what they were doing to salute in my direction; a chorus of shouts that startled the customers. "Aye, aye, Cap'n!"

I saluted back. "See you later, Ind—" She held up a finger, commanding my obedience. I frowned, but waited. As slowly and deliciously as an exotic dancer, she raised an arm from behind the counter, dangling a white paper sack like the dancer would dangle a pair of panties. Her face glowed with pride. "You. Are. An. Angel," I said, snatching up the bag of freshly brewed colada. She nodded before turning to a nearby customer, engaging them with her full attention. *Raise for Indie. Check.*

I headed out to my car that was parked in front of the store. It had cost quite a bit to get the city to allow me to purchase the space as a permanent spot, but it was definitely worth it. After all, like my father always said, *money doesn't spend itself.* I gunned the engine with a throaty roar, and sped off towards Gunnar's office. *Time for answers,* I told myself.

CHAPTER 11

"**A**NY WAY YOU CAN TIGHTEN UP THE PIXELS?" I asked, squinting. "It looks like an Etch 'n Sketch. By a blind amputee." I studied the screen. "With cerebral palsy."

"If you would just give me a damn second," Gunnar snapped. "We aren't all billionaires who can afford a year's salary on a stupid Apple desktop. The neighbor's call only came in five minutes ago, and I tapped into the street cam three minutes ago."

I waited; sipping a shot of the still-steaming colada that Indie had given me. Dusk had begun to descend upon the city as I reached Gunnar's office. Being in one of the higher levels of the FBI building, I had a pleasant view of the city from my chair. Gunnar's fingers shot toward me – imploring – as I began to take a meditative sip. With a sigh, I poured him a shot of his latest addiction. He downed it, never moving his eyes from the screen.

I had created a monster.

As if fueled by the caffeine, his fingers flew across the keyboard of the desktop in a blur. Moments later, the picture on the digital screen cleared, revealing a recognizable image this time. He clicked play.

A female in a long trench coat entered a downtown bookstore. Nothing scary about that. Then Gunnar jumped ahead ten minutes. The same woman walked out, the street slightly darker now. She dipped into an uninhabited alley and dropped her trench coat. As the garment fluttered to the ground, there was a flash of pale nudity, and then a long, red tail knocked over a trashcan before disappearing into the shadows. Gunnar was watching me. "Damn. Dragons again. Must be one of Raven's sisters."

"What, like *real* dragons?" He asked.

"Of course, *real* dragons," I grumbled; mimicking the dragon hunter, Tomas, I had met at the cemetery. I explained his description of the shape-shifting dragons to Gunnar. "You were telling me that this isn't the FBI's first sighting?"

Gunnar shook his head, leveling me with angry eyes. "Third. One book-store owner died of hypothermia, but the thermostat in his store was set at 73 degrees. The other was found covered in infected blisters, oozing puss and bacteria. But he had been to the doctor a few days prior, and had walked away with an impeccable physical report. Neither of them makes any sense. Then this. But at least this one is still alive. It's my first case in charge of the new team I was telling you about last night, and I still wouldn't even know what we were dealing with if you hadn't just told me. Which is the whole *point* of the new team." He glanced around warily. "A team that is more ca-pable of dealing with *our* kind of stuff."

"We need to go check this out. Now." I stood, curious about the odd par-ticulars of the other deceased victims.

Gunnar nodded. "Alright, I'll call my squad to swing by after we check it out. I kind of want you off the books, for now," He added sheepishly. "But tell me what else you found out, and how."

"On the way," I answered. Gunnar snatched up a coat the size of a tarp, locking his computer and darting out the door behind me. "We'll take my car." Gunnar scowled. He opened his mouth to ask another question, but I held up a finger, motioning to all the agents swarming around us. He clamped shut, unhappy, but understanding. The elevator door whisked open before me, and Gunnar's boss, Special Agent in Charge, Roger Reinhardt, stepped out. He was also a large man, full of authority. He wore short-cropped dark hair, looking every inch the politician, but I knew he was good at his job. He knew how to play the bureaucratic games with the big boys. His eyes widened at the sight of me, quickly searching for my visitor's badge. I waved it at him so he wouldn't have a heart attack.

"Nathin Temple. My deepest condolences," he offered sincerely.

I nodded back, wordlessly stepping past him into the elevator. He turned to Gunnar. "Any progress on the attacks, Agent Randulf?"

"Working on a lead now." Reinhardt looked dubious, glancing at me. "He's under my protection." Gunnar continued. "His shop was broken into last night, just like the others, but the perp escaped. He might be able to iden-tify the assailant." Reinhardt still looked unconvinced, but finally nodded.

"Have you found any... *special* consultants yet?" Gunnar shook his head. Interesting. It meant that Reinhardt didn't know that *I* was a special consult-ant, which also meant that my secret alter ego as a wizard was still safe.

59

Goody. "I'm taking a big risk with your task force, Agent Randulf. Consulting with alleged... *gifted* individuals to help us catch *gifted* criminals still sounds like some bad Hollywood movie, but I have to admit that things are getting... weirder out there." He grimaced at that, as if it left a sour taste in his mouth. I tried to keep my face blankly innocent and aloof. "It still feels like making a deal with the devil. Don't make me look a fool." He studied me curiously for a few seconds, sizing me up, and then he strode away.

Gunnar joined me in the elevator as I hit the lobby button. Music played in the tiny steel box as we descended, not speaking. It was a huge deal for Gunnar to lie about the Raven escaping, even though the cause was worth it. It was also worthy of note to hear that Agent Reinhardt assumed that Gunnar was simply 'consulting' with other Freaks, and not that Gunnar was one of those Freaks himself.

"Consulting, eh?" I offered.

Gunnar glanced at me, eyes tight. "It's the only way... for now. We need a home run. Neither the local law enforcement, nor the FBI can handle this type of thing. That's why Reinhardt is allowing me to do this. He knows, even if he won't admit it, that the crimes in this city are growing beyond his scope of understanding. He saw one of the other videos. I thought he was going to faint when he saw the tail."

"Well, then. Time to roll the dice," Gunnar grunted as the doors chimed open. Exiting the secure building, we hopped into my car and rode downtown. I handed him the kerchief from my pocket on the way, explaining its origins.

He studied it critically, even sniffing it. I guess it's a wolf thing. "Mind if I run some tests on it?" I shook my head, paying attention to the road in order to bottle away the pain of parting with my father's kerchief. "The solar eclipse... Raven mentioned that too. Any idea what it means?" I shook my head again. "And you say you've never seen this old man before the funeral?"

"No. But he knew some pretty heavy magic. My power slid off of him like rain, and then he simply walked out. His appearance could have just been a cover, but he obviously has access to Temple Industries, and my parents hand-selected each and every employee. He also knew the code to the Mausoleum. As far as I know, only three people knew that code, and two of them are now dead."

"Could he be one of the... dragons?" the word was tough for him to say aloud.

"I don't think so. He gave me a lead. I'm pretty sure that's out of countenance with the Evil Bad Guy Bible." Another thought hit me. "And he didn't have horizontal pupils." Snow was still piled up on the street banks from the night before.

"I almost forgot about that. Creepy." I nodded, glancing over at my friend; he was practically hugging the dash of the small sports car with his massive bulk.

"Her magic matched the color of her irises, and even her hand when it started to change into that nasty manicure job that tried to slice your throat. At least that's what caught the Dragon Hunter's attention."

Gunnar sputtered. "What? Dragon Hunter?" he demanded.

"Oh, yeah." I did my best to look apologetic. "At the funeral I met a guy when I was having a smoke. He told me to watch out. Said I was in danger. Apparently, something big is going down soon, and him and his crew are hunting a particular dragon in town. A man. He said he was keeping tabs on the bookstores, so I'm sure we'll run into them again."

Gunnar opened his mouth to say more. "We're here." I interrupted, changing the topic as I pointed at the deserted shop doors. I pulled my car into a parking space, and we climbed out. Gunnar was staring at the store, so I studied his silhouette against a streetlamp. He looked like an ancient Valkyrie, his Norse heritage obvious. Raising my gaze, I scanned the nearby buildings, appreciating the beauty of the ancient little city. The courthouse loomed over us, powerful, resolute, and regal, her white climbing columns and vast marble façade intimidating and imposing. My gaze flicked over the top of the courthouse directly across the street from the bookstore, and I immediately tensed. "Gunnar..." I warned.

He followed my gaze in time to see a long red tail swinging gently in a gust of wind between two gargoyle statues. He slowly turned to me, eyes surprised. "Well, that was easy. Want to go have a chat with her?" An expensive car pulled up behind mine, squeezing into the last parking space on the street amidst a blare of angry honking as they cut someone off. The driver remained inside, studying a map.

I nodded to Gunnar. "Have you brushed up on any Dale Carnegie lately?"

Gunnar grunted, smiling as he brushed his tattoo subconsciously. *"How to*

61

Win Friends and Influence People... Yep."

I decided to leave my bag of tricks in the car, feeling confident in my power. Magic was fueled by emotion, and I had plenty of that. Tools helped wizards focus their powers, but I had enough power and control that I rarely needed a focus for doing things. Unless I was trying something completely new. But I wasn't planning on experimenting tonight. Plus, I had a werewolf to back me up. Besides, Peter had killed the first dragon with a frozen liquor bottle, and he was untrained. I would rely on sheer power, because I was fast and efficient at destroying things when I needed to. The only other thing I trusted to use was the handy-dandy pistol that I had stowed in the glove compartment, but heading into a federal courthouse with a gun seemed idiotic. There was nothing discreet about the weapon. Gunnar carried a small backpack with a change of clothes inside in case he needed to shift into his werewolf form.

We crossed the street and headed inside the beautiful stonework courthouse. The five-story pillars held up the roof, reminding me of the Greek Parthenon. The moving tail was no longer visible, but I knew it was up there amidst the stone gargoyles that guarded the roof's perimeter. Gunnar had to wave his badge several times as security questioned our entrance, but we were finally admitted. They waved us on, turning back to their duties.

We took the stairs two at a time – swift, but not fast enough to alarm anyone we might run into – feet slapping the cold marble as we continued up to the roof. We didn't encounter anyone else at this late hour, but kept our eyes to the shadows just in case. What if the dragon was back in human form? I decided to pay very close attention to the eyes of any person who came near me. Any horizontal pupils and I would have to neutralize them. And why had she remained so close to the scene of her break-in? The emergency call from the neighbor had informed Gunnar that the owner was alive, but scared shitless. Understandably so. Perhaps the dragon was waiting on the storekeeper, seeing if he went out in search of her request. That would mean that he had offered up some information to her that had somehow spared his life. Interesting. I'd have to talk to him about it, if we survived our own encounter with the dragon. We climbed to the top floor of the building, and looking both ways, chose a direction in search of a roof exit. Windows lined the wall, allowing a splendid view of the city below.

Seeing no one around, I spoke, my heels striking the marble with each step. *Tap, tap, tap.* "So, tell me more about this strike-force you're putting together. I can't imagine many Freaks are in the bureau, so how much good could it do?" *Freaks* were how the few unenlightened individuals – like the cops – referred to us. No one had yet confirmed, officially, that we existed, but plenty civilians already knew or at least had a very good suspicion. Crimes were simply becoming too 'unexplainable' with the new advanced technologies revealing truths that had historically been hidden under reams of paperwork. A Kentucky Senator was even demanding that all Freaks should furthermore be termed Wizards since it had to be our fault that they all existed in the first place.

Idiots.

Gunnar looked at me heavily, saying nothing.

"Wait, you said hush, hush. Do you even have any jurisdictional lines? Are they just going to put up fliers in every police station in the country, seeing if any Freaks are stupid enough to move to the buckle of the Bible-Belt?"

Gunnar scoffed. "Of course, there are lines. Like I told you, this is just a test run. Reinhardt knows weird stuff keeps happening, and that more often than not, we remain aloof to the criminals and their capture. This is merely a beta testing of an idea I whispered to him. He's a Regular, but a damn good agent. He has no idea what he was *really* allowing me to do. What I was really asking him. So for now, I basically just have a wider line than the other agents. Instead of a razorblade, I'm dancing on a steak knife." I pondered that. Crime was getting nastier each year, and while most of it was the normal, run-of-the-muck kind of crime, some of it *did* need a firmer hand. Guns were fine, but sometimes not enough, and all too often, red tape plugged up said guns.

"Can't hurt, I guess. Any recruits yet, or just *consultants*?" I mocked, scanning the glass walls around us for a roof exit. Gunnar said nothing, so I stopped and glanced back. *Tap, tap, tap.* The sound of heels striking the ground continued.

He pointed a finger at me, face ashen. "*Me*?" I stared back, dumbfounded. "Oh, no way. I'm not even a cop! I don't know diddly about all the minutiae that took you *years* to learn. I'm a terrible recruit." Another thought struck me. "And I don't even *want* to join! I've got enough on my plate, thank you very much." Gunnar continued staring, but I realized he wasn't pointing at me. He was pointing behind me. Then he abruptly shifted into his *Underdog* underwear-clad werewolf form, clothes exploding into shreds. I only had time to hope that it wasn't the same pair of underwear from the night before.

Tap, tap, tap. The noise continued, and this time I realized it sounded quite different from our heels striking marble. It sounded like something tapping on glass. I turned, and found myself facing a massive grinning red dragon, snorting fog onto the cool glass from her scaly visage outside. *Tap, tap, tap.* A giant talon let out a staccato drumbeat. I was momentarily reminded of a sadistic child tapping on a glass fish tank.

Then the glass exploded inwards, and a massive arm wrapped around my waist, tugging me out onto the windy rooftop. "Ack!" I yelled as the grip squeezed the air from my lungs. Muscles bunched around me as the world tossed and turned. I heard Gunnar howl – a piercing lament – but we were moving fast, and between being tossed about like the victim of a drunken operator controlling a Ferris wheel and not being able to breathe, I felt positively unpleasant. Which pissed me off. Which is when I get a tad reckless.

Everything halted, and I abruptly noticed a sad statue on the roof from inches away, his face pitying my dilemma. Then my body was hoisted out over the city streets five stories below, the grip loosening enough for me to breathe. Cars flashed by beneath me, oblivious of my predicament. "Now that we're alone, I propose we have a little chat," a woman's voice spoke. I lifted my head to stare straight into the dragon's fiery red horizontal pupils, ignoring the blood pounding in my skull. I gathered my will, ready to unleash hell.

"Ah, ah, ah." The blood-red dragon's voice cooed as she released one of the talons holding me up above St. Louis' beautifully paved streets. My body dropped an inch and I squawked in alarm. "I just wanted to have a few words with you about a family book," her voice was that of a phone sex operator, full of empty promises that one couldn't help but buy. "Oh, and also about my sister, since she never came home last night."

Another talon let loose, dropping my upper torso entirely, leaving me to hang upside down by my knees. I laughed, fighting my panic. "Your sister won't be coming home any time soon."

She cocked her head quizzically. "Start talking. Now, wizard." My pack of cigarettes fell out of my pocket, sailing down into the night.

And down, and down, and down.

I swiveled, quite composed, and pointed an angry finger at her. "That.

Was. A. New. Pack. Bitch."

More glass burst outward from atop the roof, out of my immediate sight. Her eyes swiveled towards the noise with a hiss and tongue of flame.

I am not above sucker-punches.

A rumble of power began to build at her throat as she prepared a counter-attack at the noise. I summed up my will, calling on the wind this high up, and bulldozed the sad-faced statue that had shown me a moment of compassion. A cloud of dust and rock exploded out, but a big portion of the statue sailed true, slamming straight into her wide-open mouth as she was ready to let loose her blast. Napalm fire, unable to go anywhere else, splashed all over her crenellated head, bathing her in a sick wash of flames from snout to chest. She shook her head with a roar of pain and surprise. "Eat that!" I crowed, still hanging upside down. Then the fire died out from her scales, causing no lasting harm. Blood dripped freely from her scaled lips thanks to my thrown statue, one tooth dangling by a thread of her gums before it too fell to the roof like the drops of blood.

The roof around her flared with the liquid fire. I heard a shout, but not Gunnar's voice, and then three sizzling blue and black spears sailed through the night towards my captor. She dodged two of them, sending them off down into the nearby park, and hopefully not into a wandering pedestrian, but the third slammed home, tearing a jagged hole in one of her wings and piercing her thigh. Blue sparks sizzled up from the wound and she roared in pain.

She took one shaky step, freeing her wing, and then glared at me. "It appears that your time is up." With a smile, she let go of my leg and I fell.

Fast.

I realized I was going to become a nuisance to the street-sweeper on the morning shift. The dragon launched off the roof with a snap of wings, sailing away into the night sky. Gunnar, in his giant white-haired werewolf form, stared down at me from the roof, jaws stretched wide as if howling. But the wind whistled in my ears as I dropped, so I couldn't distinguish his familiar roar, and then I spotted a freaking black boomerang racing towards my face from another building across the street.

My scream was in no way similar to that of a frightened little girl.

The black boomerang unfolded into a trio of interconnected rubber balls attached to a net of rope. Apparently, *Spiderman* was watching over my fair city. The web slammed into me, and then the weighted balls swung around and around my torso until finally hammering into different sections of my body like a boxer working a heavy bag. One was about a hair away from permanently ruining my chances at continuing my family tree, and luckily none hit me in the face or I would have officially been Mike Tyson-ed. The force of the impact was strong enough to alter my trajectory directly into a window on the side of the building.

And then *through* the god damned window.

The heavy glass didn't impede my entrance in the slightest, sending a tinkling shower of shards before me into what seemed like a plush office. I bounced off a very sturdy bookshelf, and then slid face first onto a long, wide wooden desk, my face efficiently clearing everything off the top of its surface: a stapler, a jar of pens, a book, a pile of papers, a keyboard, a monitor, and at the very end of the desk sat a steaming mug of coffee. I squinted my eyes shut in anticipation, trying to brake with my feet, but they were all tangled up in the damn web. Again, I inform you that the impending shriek sounded in no way similar to that of a frightened little girl. I slid to a halt, my nose brushing the scalding mug. But it didn't spill. I tried to steady my breathing, and cautiously peeled open the only eye not squeezed shut from the web, staring at the room's only occupant.

A man had wisely scooted back from the desk. He reminded me of Father Time. Older than old, but he was apparently still spry enough to dodge a sailing, web-encased, wizard who happened to burst through his fourth-floor office window. He glanced down at me, long, heavy caterpillar eyebrows frowning with disapproval. A heavy authority was contained within his stare. Then I noticed his getup. A thin black robe settled around his shoulders, and I noticed a wooden gavel on a bookshelf behind him.

I gulped. "Your Honor." I offered. The rope web pressed my nose flat against my face, and another lifted my mouth into what would pass for a world-record hair lip.

Without a word, he reached over my face, carefully plucked up his coffee, and stepped out of the room. He had a damn good poker face, I thought to myself as I heard pounding feet racing towards me from just outside the open door. Then a swarm of security guards burst into the room, guns leveled in my general direction as if anticipating a ninja to disappear into a cloud of smoke and throwing stars. The lead guard blinked, and then suppressed a grin as he tucked his gun away. "I don't think he's an immediate threat."

I squirmed angrily, hoping to unhook one of the balls on the web, but I merely succeeded in slipping off the desk to fall straight onto my back on the hard wood floor. Pain flashed in my side as the wind was knocked out of me.

"Thun of a vitch!" I wheezed through the web.

CHAPTER 12

I T DIDN'T TAKE LONG FOR GUNNAR TO SORT OUT THE
mess and get me out of handcuffs. That's two times in twenty-four
hours. Impressive, right? Gunnar had changed into his spare clothes,
and no one seemed to notice. At first, Justice Simpson hadn't been very
pleased with my interruption, but after checking my wallet for identification,
he had burst out laughing so hard that I actually started to blush. His last
comment still aggravated me as we stepped outside, past another set of
chuckling guards. I flipped them off. "Pricks." I muttered, rubbing at the rope
burns on my neck. They laughed harder.

Gunnar glanced over at me, amused. "He did say that you could *drop by
any time*. Quite courteous of him, given the situation."

"I take it you're walking back to the office?"

Gunnar grumbled back. "Thought you might like a souvenir." He offered
me one of the dragon's teeth that I had knocked out. It was almost as long as
my pinkie.

"Nifty." I smiled back, pocketing it. A beautiful blonde woman in a track-
suit was walking across the street from us, and I swiped back my shaggy hair
for a semblance of dignity. Gunnar followed my gaze, nodding his agreed
approval. Her hair was cut short along her jaw so that the bangs formed
wicked points near her chin, layered perfectly around her thin oval face. She
grinned at my obvious interest, and I winked back. She giggled and began to
change direction towards us, limping slightly as if she had sprained her ankle
while running. God, girls giggling! What a delicious sound. "That's a nice
Cherry Danish," I said for Gunnar's ears only.

Gunnar stared at me askance. "Do you always refer to women as dessert
dishes?"

I pondered that as we climbed into my vintage car. We waited for the jogger to approach us, her dazzling white teeth reeling me in as her long legs
brought her closer. She leaned into the window, studying us both. "Got a

pen?" She asked in a breathless voice. I silently slipped her one. Her eyes were like almonds, and the smell of clean sweat quickly kicked in my hormones, which had barely survived the *Spiderman*-like assault. She furiously jotted down a number on my hand. No name. Her fingers were feverish. "Whom do I ask for when I call?" I asked with a grin.

"You'll find that out *if* I *answer*. Or *if* you even call." She grinned, and then turned to walk off her twisted ankle.

"Gold-digger." Gunnar complained.

"But I've got gold, so it's a win-win." I answered, grinning.

"Money doesn't make you happy..." He recited the well-known adage.

I started the car, revving the gas into a throaty growl beneath my feet. "Well it sure as shit doesn't make you sad either, Gunnar." He rolled his eyes, but couldn't mask his grin as I pulled out into traffic. A few seconds later, the car parked behind us also pulled out. Was it the same car that had parked behind me before we went into the courthouse? Was this what a tail felt like? I was too intrigued to be scared. I mean, I had just survived a joint attack by a wannabe *Spiderman* and a red dragon. What danger was a mere Regular? I answered Gunnar's first question. "I guess I just haven't met a girl who classifies as a dinner dish. But that's okay. I adore dessert." Gunnar belted out a laugh.

"So, who saved your ass with that net launcher?"

"Spiderman?" I offered.

"Seriously, Nate. There are three possibilities. One, they were trying to catch the dragon, and missed horribly. Two, they were trying to catch you for some dark reason. Three, it really was our friendly neighborhood webslinger saving your pathetic life. In that case, I might have my first recruit, even if he does seem to have poor character judgment."

I grunted my displeasure at his quip. "I like number three best, but I guess you should look into the alternatives since *Spiderman's* just a comic book character. So, who was that other guy on the roof with you?" The car was still behind me, but further back.

Gunnar looked frustrated. "I'm not sure. He appeared out of nowhere, shot the dragon with that electric spear gun, and then he was gone. Maybe he was one of those dragon hunters..."

I nodded. "Mind looking into it for me? I have to swing by Chateau Falco."

Gunnar arched a brow. "Need backup?"

"Pretty sure that's one of the safest places in town right now. I'll call you after."

I pulled up in front of the FBI building and he opened the door. "My team should be finished with the bookstore in a short while, so I'll let you know what we found out later. See you soon, Temple. And watch your ass." The tail continued on past me. I was simply reading too much into things.

"That's what I have you for, sweetie." I winked. He shook his head and slammed the door with more force than was necessary. I continued on, still on schedule to meet Miss Belmont at Chateau Falco.

CHAPTER 13

I WAITED OUTSIDE THE GATED FORTRESS OF CHATEAU Falco. A tall, thick, brick and rebar-enforced wall surrounded the grounds, and an arcane Damascus steel forged gate impeded my path. A life-sized nude statue stood atop the wall to either side of the gate – a man and a woman armed for battle. It had been rumored that the cremated remains of our first ancestors to settle here had been used for the mortar. Before I could beep in on the intercom, a familiar voice emanated from the speaker. "Greetings, Master Temple. Your fortress awaits. Lowering the bridge now." The gate began to slowly swing inward.

"We live in the 21st century, Dean. People don't have bridges. They have gates."

He ignored me. "Bridge lowered, Master Temple. You can safely cross the moat now." Then he signed off. I sighed, shifting into gear and driving up the mile-long cobbled drive, passing lush gardens on either side of me. Well, lush for this time of year anyway.

After a few minutes of driving – Dean, the Temple family's Chief of Security and Butler, didn't appreciate speeding, and was known to let the air out of the tires if one disobeyed, even if said one was now the current Master Temple – I pulled into the wide circular drive leading up to the courtyard, parked, and left the keys inside. I didn't see any other cars, and wondered why for a moment, but then recognized Dean's skilled hand as I spotted tire tracks leading to a large remodeled stable. He had already parked the guests' – whomever they may be – cars in the stable in case of more snow or rain. Chances were that the cars were also being detailed by one of the family employees while inside. I shook my head wearily. I didn't belong in this type of atmosphere, which is why I had left several years ago.

The fountain in the center of the drive was off this time of year, but the stonework statues in the center were still spectacular. I leaned back, taking the looming four-story structure before me. Built over two hundred years ago, each generation had added onto it, but none dared stray from the original colonial design. The old pile now stretched close to 17,000 square feet, containing two wings, two large libraries, twenty bedrooms, three kitchens, a theater room, a glass greenhouse attached to the side, and even a mediocre observatory.

I sighed, fingering the quickly-made leather thong that now held the red dragon's tooth around my neck. It was so sharp that it scratched my chest a bit, but it was a badge of honor in my eyes. A warning. I walked up to the massive front door with the Temple Coat of Arms emblazoned in the wood. A pinprick light studied me from a corner in the sheltered Porte-Cochère, blinking red with a motion detector. Beside it, a screen came to life to reveal Dean studying me critically. "Ah, Master Temple, please come in. Follow the guiding lights to come entertain your guests in the Master Study. All are here, as the Master has requested." I sighed, having requested no such thing. It was as I had feared. Whether I wanted it or not, I was the new Master Temple, and not just in name. The family reputation was like royalty, inescapable. I began to take a step. "Ah, ah, ah. Please remove your shoes, Master Temple." Then he signed off. Dean remotely unlocked the door before me, and I stepped into the dim house, a nostalgic grin on my face. Even after years of hiding from this place, it seemed we picked up right where we had left off.

It was comforting.

And disturbing.

I kicked off my shoes, and finding no others nearby, I placed mine just inside the door, and followed the trail of dim LED lighting embedded into the marble floors, escorted by the technology of the house as it led me down one hallway, and then another, and on, and on, wondering all the while who else might be here waiting to speak with me. Trudging on, I decided that my parents should have bought an electric golf cart for inside the house. Since it was now mine, perhaps I would act on the idea. I passed rooms of cabinets filled with odd bits and ends from archaeological digs, or acquired through auctions or inheritance from past family members.

The rooms I passed held a timeless quality even amidst cutting edge technology. But I didn't let my guard down. The beauty of the house was one of its many defenses. A sleight of hand. If one looked close enough, one would notice that some of the paintings always managed to be staring at the people

72

in the room, no matter where they were positioned. And I'm not talking about the paranoia one gets when they *feel* like the pictures are watching them. I mean that they might literally be watching you. I shivered, moving on.

Despite the chill outside, the floors held thermal-controlled piping beneath the marble tile, heating the stone to a comfortable temperature underneath my socks. It's nice what money can buy.

Reaching a large stairway, I ascended, following the lights and continuing on for another few minutes until I reached my father's old study. I hadn't needed the lights to guide me, but it was a nice comfort, as well as an intimidating show of power for my guests. I took a deep breath before opening the door and stepping inside. The pleasant, aromatic whiff of frequent cigar smoke hit me first, and then the heart-wrenching memory of seeing my father behind the now-empty desk at the end of the room, smoking his precious Gurkha Black Dragon cigars.

One of his five hand-carved, camel-bone chests sat on a corner of his massive desk. Each chest of a hundred cigars set my father back $115,000. Half-a-million dollars to kill yourself, slowly. Hypocrite, I may be, but at least I wasn't as reckless about the cost. A thick glass window covered the entire back wall, but this night it was basked in the soothing glow of many antique lamps.

I immediately studied the people in the room, uncharacteristically wary after my recent adventures. Ashley Belmont stood to one side, speaking to an older gentleman who had his back to me. She smiled over his shoulder at me. I waved back. "Miss Belmont. A pleasure." Her smile grew warmer.

The man beside her turned, smiling knowingly at me. "Nasty bit o' news about the courthouse this evening. One should be careful when dealing with dangers that might be attracted to blood in the water. But of course, ye know this already, Laddie." Mallory grinned, striding over and pumping my hand enthusiastically.

"How did you..." I began, and then slapped my forehead. "You were the one tailing me. But why?" I was genuinely perplexed.

He discreetly pointed a thumb at a long-barreled spear gun leaning against the wall, but flicked his eyes over his shoulder, reminding me of Miss Belmont's presence. "Just making sure the Master Temple is safe. Did ye think I was only a janitor?" His grin was infectious. Reassessing the older man, I realized that he was rather stout, with thick, heavy forearms. Coarse, iron-grey hair covered his skin and knuckles, reminding me of an old-school sailor. An old man for a guardian, I grunted. But he had most likely saved my life tonight. Having seen my magic slide off of him at the mausoleum, I deduced that he was most definitely dangerous. Which is a good quality for a guardian.

"Well, thanks, I guess. You could have just told me, though."

"Not nearly so much fun." He answered. "But I do believe that be a discussion for another night, over a glass of scotch. You have business this night, Master Temple." He pointed a finger across the room, indicating a sharply dressed man standing beside Dean, Chateau Falco's Butler.

I walked over with a familiar grin, and bumped knuckles with Dean as he extended his hand for a professional handshake. He had served as our Chief of Security since I was a child, but vehemently denied all titles except Butler. He came from a very different time, when the term *Butler* was a highly-respected profession. Dedication, Loyalty, Honor, and Prestige were his life-blood. "Pleased to see you again, Master Temple." He was about chest height, and his eyes seemed to shine like Caribbean ocean water surrounding the black island of his pupils. "Bad hygiene is not indicative of a respected gentleman, especially the last heir of the renowned Temples. Do not disrespect yourself like this again." I grinned back, shrugging. If I wasn't wearing a suit, I was slumming it in his eyes.

"I showered last night, Dean." I argued.

"Then perhaps the finer points of how to properly groom oneself need to be relearned after years of bachelor-hood." He droned, respectfully, of course.

I grinned even further. "I know just the women to teach me. Thank you for the reminder, Dean. I will practice studiously with them. Several times, to make sure I learn it correctly." Ashley made an embarrassed sound behind me.

Dean blushed. "Incorrigible. Completely incorrigible."

I smiled, patting his arm affectionately. He was family. I studied the last sharply dressed man out the corner of my eye. Would we dance this night? He waited patiently, fighting the urge not to introduce himself and rudely interrupt my reunion with Dean. Years of training came back to me in the blink of an eye, the training of the European Courts; the cloak and dagger dance of smiles and knives, where winks could mean assassinations, and glares could mean life-long alliances; the dance that had been ingrained into each and every Temple child. I turned to him after a heavy silence, face utterly blank, letting him know that this was my home, and he was here by my choice, not the other way around. Seeing my obvious attention, he broke first, as was proper. "Greetings, Master Temple. My name is Turner Locke."

I nodded at him. "A pleasure to make your acquaintance, Mr. Locke. Be welcome in my home." Dean glided closer to the wall, blending in like a piece of furniture, trying not to disturb the Master and his guests, but ready to serve in any capacity I required at the drop of a hat. I studied Mr. Locke. "What firm do you represent?"

He blinked in surprise. "None, Master Temple. I worked exclusively for your father after our first interaction."

"Then you must be a very adequate lawyer, Mr. Locke. My father wasn't easily impressed."

He nodded humbly in answer. "May I ask how you knew my profession?"

"What other profession would deem to speak with me so urgently after my parents' deaths?" I smiled coldly. "Now, what is the purpose of this mysterious meeting I unknowingly called everyone to attend? I abhor unknowns, yet here I find myself wading in a plethora of them." My tone filled the room. Smiles lowered, and Mr. Locke gestured toward a semicircle of chairs before the desk. "If you could please take a seat, Master Temple, I have pledged to share your parents Last Will and Testament."

I inwardly groaned. On top of the funeral, this was the nail in the coffin, so to speak. It was so real now. They were dead. I was alone. I mustered my resolve so no one would see my weakness. They each began to take a seat, and I paused, realizing there were not enough chairs. I began walking to the side of the room to pull up another, but Dean hissed for my ears only. "Master Temple. Do not abase yourself so!" He flicked a discreet finger at my father's chair behind the desk. I opened my mouth to object, and Dean revealed a serrated blade in his deft fingers. "Tires," was all he said. No one else had noticed. I smiled and nodded, approaching the chair behind the desk with trepidation and an overwhelming sense of foolishness, like a nine-year-old child putting on his father's shoes. Slowly, I descended into the worn leather, waiting for someone to declare me an imposter. I fought to keep my face blank.

The three seated before me grew tense, watching me as if a rabid lion had been let loose in the room. Dean oozed approval as he glided up a few paces behind me, in full view of the three subjects before his Master Temple. Jesus, I didn't belong here, regardless of what Dean thought. I tried to sound like my father. "Would anyone care for refreshments?" Each of their eyes cautiously settled on the drinks already sitting on coasters before them, but they didn't speak. "Ah, of course. Thank you, Dean."

My butler nodded as he set a perfectly weighted glass of scotch in front of me. I leaned back, taking a pleasurable sip, having no fucking clue what I was supposed to be doing. I could dance with the best of them when I knew the game, but my father's game made me look a fool. I felt as if I should know a different language for this. I decided to stop pretending. I didn't want to live in my father's shadow. I would simply be myself.

"Well, since I am the only one in the dark here, why don't we just cut straight to the point? You obviously want my permission to do something, or you are expecting me to tell you that I will pick up right where my parents left off. Well, I can quickly dissuade you of any false assumptions. I will *not* be taking over the company, and you will *not* use me as a phony symbol of the company to increase shareholder value. I am *not* my father. I am sure that Miss Belmont is fully capable of running Temple Industries, or she wouldn't have been promoted to her position. By all means, please finish your drinks in peace, and Dean will escort you out as soon as you are ready." I took a sip of my drink, and leaned forward, baring my teeth in a smile.

A heavy silence blanketed the room. Dean sighed disapprovingly, but I ignored all of it. Mr. Locke spoke up first. "If I may be so bold..." I waved a hand, setting my glass down for fear of shattering it in my clenching fist. "You remind me very much of your father, more so than you might believe. Please understand that what I am about to say comes word-for-word from your parents' lips. I have it written and notarized if you would prefer?" I didn't blink, burning him with my eyes, and very seriously contemplating a dangerous display of magic to quickly evacuate my guests. But remembering that Mallory was here, I chose against the latter, unsure if he would simply make me look like a pouting child.

"Proceed," I said.

He withdrew a closed envelope from his briefcase, broke the rather impressive seal on the outside, and handed a small letter from inside to each person in the room, including Dean. As he handed me mine, I unleashed a thought and it burned to ashes in my hand. "Not interested," I said coldly. Ashley inhaled sharply, leaning away as if I might bite. Mallory watched me with disapproving eyes, discreetly shaking his head.

Mr. Locke didn't even hesitate, reaching back into his bag to withdraw another letter. "How many copies do you have?" I growled.

He looked embarrassed. "Your father warned me of your... disdain for authority. I have brought enough copies to be sure that you read one in its entirety." I sighed in defeat, nodding for him to read it aloud. He held it firmly, his hand quivering slightly as he began to read:

Nathin Laurent Temple,

Please do not do anything rash, my Son. I have asked my good friend, Turner Locke, to read this aloud, as I am unsure of its safety in your hands at this emotional juncture. Mr. Locke has several copies in case this one happens to be destroyed prior to complete evocation.

Typical of my father.

Two items of importance must be discussed. I wish you to assume control of Chateau Falco, as we both know it cannot and must not fall into Regular hands. It is a legacy of our family, and must be preserved. Everything on the grounds has already been transferred to your name, and whether you sign the deed or not, measures have been taken, bribes paid, to see that my wish comes to fruition regardless of your wishes.

Mr. Locke has three rather small gifts to bestow upon you at this time.

Mr. Locke reached inside the envelope, and produced three small, plastic credit cards, each a different color. He handed them over to me. On the back of each was a post-it-note with a number... followed by much too many zeroes. *Small gifts,* but oh so big at the same time. My eyes grew large, but Mr. Locke continued.

The numbers are approximations, as you fully comprehend compounding interest.

Second point. If you do not assume ownership of Temple Industries, it will be sold, along with all of its patents, to a dozen competitors in China. This will create a massive job vacuum in the city of St. Louis, our founding heritage town, and a rather unhappy reaction from the Mayor, Senators, and Representatives. A letter has also been sent to the President of the United States, warning of this possibility. You will most likely be shunned by the en-

tire city you live in, and Plato's Cave will no doubt drown in the bad publicity.

I regret informing you of my decision like this, but your mother and I wanted you to chase your own dreams while able. Temple Industries is much too vast to leave out of the family's control. It must pass on with you. We respect and applaud your decision not to join the company sooner, having time to pursue your own business with Plato's Cave. We couldn't be more proud of you, Nathin. You are the apple of our garden, and we hope you will always remember that. Try and bring your unique light to your new company.

Know that Chateau Falco was like a child to us all, witnessing many family secrets and stories never before uttered aloud. All one must do is listen to discover those secrets...

With all the love in the world,

Your Mother and Father.

Always the last word. Turner handed me the letter. A drop of blood stood below each name, and an elegant signature flourished beneath each name. My eyes watered and my shoulders sagged. My voice was dry. He was right. Damn it. "Very well. I humbly stand corrected. This is much bigger than myself. I accept." The tension in the room evaporated. Ashley's shoulders sagged with relief, but I couldn't fathom why. I feared that I was about to drive Temple Industries in a new direction all right, and faster than anyone thought possible. Straight into the ground. I didn't know a damn thing about such a large company. I was just a bookstore owner. I was way out of my league. I turned to Ashley. "I expect you to maintain your position, doing what you already know how to do. I will help in any way I can, but you must understand that I am really not equipped to wing this kind of thing."

She nodded, smiling sadly. "Of course, Master Temple. It will take time, but I am not going anywhere. Temple Industries is my life. I will run it as if it were my own."

"I will hold you to that. I don't wish for my lifestyle to change now that I am CEO. For all intents and purposes, things will remain the same as before."

She smiled sadly, a tear falling onto the personal letter in her own hands. "Your father said you would say that. You are very much alike," she tucked her letter away, and I didn't have the heart to ask her what it had said. I wondered how close she had been to my parents. They had worked together every day. This must be the ultimate tragedy for her as well.

I shook my head as Turner finished reading his own letter. "What did you get? A Rolls Royce?" I asked snidely.

"Among other things..." Turner answered in a whisper. His eyes were bloodshot. "As with your father, I will always be at your service, Master Temple. Retirement or not." He straightened his spine, attempting to clear the remorse from the room. I nodded with a genuine smile of gratitude. "One more point of concern." I nodded. "I must ask that you refrain from any actions that might be deemed notorious in your dealings with the police or FBI." I frowned. Word got around quick. Or he was just well informed. "The CEO can't be seen to be involved in official matters. It wouldn't be good for business. Could you manage this last favor?" I grumbled, but finally nodded to appease him. There was no way in hell I was backing off Gunnar's case, so I would just have to be discreet about it. "That includes private inquiries into your parents' deaths. The police can handle it. It is their job to do such, and we can't have you devoting all of your time to such matters. It would be seen as weakness to the shareholders. Especially any... unplanned meetings with judges." He added carefully. *Damn you, Mallory*, I thought to myself, but I finally nodded.

"In that case," I spoke, "I will need Miss Belmont's full cooperation with the police. I have been hassled lately by them in regards to the company and their... deaths. If you could please talk to them and have it all sorted out, it would make things much easier for me to leave alone. Make it clear to them that my taking over the company was not a sneaky move on my part, but that it was the last request of my father."

"Of course, Master Temple."

Dean piped up. "Well, if business is concluded, would anyone care for steak?"

Everyone politely declined, not interested in such a heavy meal on such heavy hearts. Mallory leaned closer. "Now that ye have a few nickels, Laddie, what ye gonna buy?"

A smile tugged at my cheeks as I thought of Gunnar. "I know just the thing."

CHAPTER 14

ITseemed we had many people in the St. Louis area on retainer for late hour transactions. It had taken one phone call, and only a twenty-minute wait for them to have everything prepared. It was good to be king. Now I was racing down the interstate well above the speed limit, dialing Gunnar on speakerphone. The car kept attempting to pair my phone with the built-in Bluetooth, but I kept declining until it devolved into a shouting match between the technology and me. Gunnar finally answered. "Hey."

"Gunnar! Where are you?" I bellowed, cool October wind roaring around me, the acoustics surprisingly adequate for a hardtop convertible. I cut someone off with a squeal of tires and furious honking.

"Should I turn on the news? Because it sounds like you're in a high-speed car chase," he answered.

"No cops. Yet. Listen, where are you?" I answered, a shit-eating grin on my face.

"Still at the office, why?" I checked the rearview mirror. Mallory was furiously trying to keep up with me, but American Muscle couldn't match the handling of my ride. Still, he was doing a fair job, cutting off the same guy I had a moment ago, producing another peal of blaring car horns.

"Good, good. Come outside. I'll be right there."

"Is everything oka—" I hung up, howling like a wolf into the wind.

I took the next exit, swerving across three lanes to take the turn downtown. I paid no attention to traffic lights, savoring every shade of red I blew through as only a thirsty vampire could appreciate, hoping to lose Mallory, but he doggedly pursued me. No doubt he was going to chastise me, but I couldn't help myself. Seeing the building, I downshifted, and slid into a 180-degree spin, pulling pretty damn close to the curb. Gunnar was standing outside the door, staring at me with wide eyes, a hand on his gun. Two agents also stood outside, a forgotten cigarette raised halfway to one's mouth as he stared from Gunnar to my car. The smell of burnt rubber filled the air as I reversed – much more cautiously – to the curb in a nice, orderly parking job... facing the wrong way. I climbed out, brushing a hand through my tousled hair.

Gunnar trotted over. "What the hell is going on? You showed up like the devil himself was chasing—" He froze as my '69 Firebird skidded to a halt in the middle of the street, her throaty grumble soothing in the cool night air. Mallory leaned out the window, grinning like a teenager. "Bloody smooth lady, Master Temple! *Bloody smooth*!"

Gunnar stared from me to the old man in my car. "It's him! He was the one on the roof with us!" He stared at me, eyes still wide.

"I know. He works for me. Mallory, this is Gunnar. Gunnar, this is Mallory, the man who gave me my father's kerchief at the mausoleum." My friend looked as if his brain had shorted out. I capitalized on his moment of confusion. "You're going to love it."

His eyes snapped back to me, not comprehending. "Love what?"

"Only the best for my BF."

One of the agents burst out laughing behind us. I turned to him, smiling broadly. The other agent grunted, handing him a twenty-dollar bill. I shook my head, not understanding their transaction, and saw that Gunnar's face was beet red. "I'm sure you meant BFF, as in *Best Friend Forever*, and not BF, which means *boyfriend*." He growled, angrily glancing back at the agents.

I was quiet for a second and then burst out laughing, unable to contain myself at my *faux pas*. After my laughter receded, I spoke louder than necessary, turning my mistake into a blade against Gunnar. "Whatever you say, sweetie. I just wanted to show you how much you mean to me." I tossed him the keys to the gleaming orange Aston Martin DBS, already walking towards the driver's seat of my own car as Mallory climbed into the passenger side.

Gunnar stared from the car to me, stunned. "For me?"

"Of course," I answered, climbing into my car. "My first act as the new president of Temple Industries."

The agents were shaking their heads in disbelief, their homophobia momentarily overcome by the sleek sports car. No doubt they would sell this information to the first reporter they could find, but I didn't care. They stepped up closer to the car, appraising her majestic curves. "You really queer?" One asked me.

"Read the tabloids and get back to me. I have somewhat of a reputation with the fairer sex." I winked, revving the engine.

The second agent chuckled. "That's putting it mildly. If I took your reputation literally I would lock my daughter away somewhere you could never find her."

I leaned out the window with a lecherous grin. "Maybe you should." His smile wavered a bit before the car regained his full attention again. "Pick me up at the Chateau in the morning, Gunnar, we have much to discuss." Then, before he could argue, Mallory and I sailed off into the night in a flurry of burning tires.

Mallory's cheeks were huffing. "You don't lead a boring life, Master Temple."

"Stick around for the next few days and you'll see just how right you are."

"My old bones don't be ready for sleep after such a thrill as this beauty." He declared, patting the dash affectionately.

I glanced at the time. "You mentioned a discussion over scotch." He gave an excited nod. "If we hurry, I know where we can find a different type of beauty to enjoy that scotch with us. She'll be more entertaining than the 50-year-old Macallan I have stashed away."

"Beauty, eh? Two ways to warm an old man's bones," He ticked off a finger for each. "A fine young lass, and Macallan. And I do feel a chill. Let's hurry." He buckled up, grinning.

CHAPTER 15

AN EARTHQUAKE RATTLED MY NIGHT STAND; THE sound shredding what was left of my cerebral cortex. I managed to peel open one bloodshot eye to see that it was just my cell phone vibrating, and realized that I was in one of the guest rooms at Chateau Falco. My head pounded from the night's activities. Mallory apparently had a cast-iron stomach, and had put me to shame as he, Indie, and I shared one of my father's $17,000 bottles of Macallan Scotch. We had caught up with Indie just as she was closing up shop, and Mallory had effortlessly snookered her in to join us on our haunt.

"I be an old man, but I amma' no dead yet. Would ye care to join us for a nightcap, my wee bonnie-lass?" She hadn't been able to decline. We had stayed up late, sharing stories about my parents, how Mallory had been first to find their bodies and take the note from my father, his history with the family, and definitely Indie. A whole lot about Indie. Mallory had been infatuated with the stunning manager of my store, and she had eaten it up like candy. I briefly remembered vocally agreeing with Mallory on all points, enthusiastically sharing my interest in Indie, and shuddered. Had I said something I wouldn't be able to take back? Had I told her how I truly felt about her and possibly ruined our friendship?

Damn it all.

There was only one way to find out.

I seriously considered blasting my phone into oblivion, but managed a semblance of humanity, and answered. "Ow."

"Nate! You all right?" It was Gunnar, and he was – dare I say – giggling. "This car is *incredible*! You had breakfast yet?"

"Shhh…" I fumbled at the nightstand and almost knocked over a glass of water. Three Advil sat beside it.

God bless Dean.

I considered crushing the pills and snorting them. Gunnar interrupted my thought.

"I can't hear you very well. Must be the fact that I'm driving a *convertible!*" He bellowed, shattering my eardrums like a swarm of pygmies reenacting a Stomp concert in the auditorium of my skull. "I'll see you in a minute. I'm at the gate now." The sound lessened and I heard him speaking to someone else. Then, "Thanks, Dean! See you in a minute, Nate!" My phone beeped in my ear as he hung up, piercing my eardrum anew.

I fell out of bed, kneeling on the floor as I snatched up the pills and water. I guzzled them down and managed to stumble to my feet before I noticed that I was naked. The room swayed slightly, and I chuckled, realizing that I was still slightly drunk. I shambled over to a wardrobe, threw on one of the heavy robes from the closet, and carefully zigzagged my way to the bathroom. After four tries, I managed to tear open one of the packages of toothbrushes that were stored in each bathroom, and brushed my teeth from a fresh tube of Aquafresh, my favorite. I opened the door, and stretched my toes into the shag rug over the marble floor just outside the room, letting out a groan of contentment. Shuffling down the hall, I almost ran straight into Dean, who had no doubt been coming to warn me of the inbound intruder. He studied me with an amused grin. "Did Gunnar receive the gift well?" Dean asked.

"He giggled," I answered.

"Hmmm… a grown man, giggling. Inappropriate." He turned his back on me, clapping his hands together like Zeus casting twin thunderbolts. "Breakfast is served in the main kitchen!" He bellowed for all to hear. I heard a feminine grunt from the room next to me, and then a thud as said someone fell out of her bed. I smiled, glad that I wasn't the only one still intoxicated. Then Indie began laughing.

The door burst open beside me and Indie flew out of the room in a drunken stumble, eyes glowing brightly as she bumped into me. She wore only a silk robe, and it was apparently very, very cold in her room, according to the little protrusions threatening to tear the silk robe over the centers of the pleasant swell of her breasts. Her bare feet arched as she stretched out, wrapping her arms over my shoulders and collapsing into me for a totally indecent hug. She leaned back, still holding on, and beamed up at me. Her breath smelled of fresh mint, and she had washed her face. Her soft, wavy hair tickled my neck. I needed a cold shower, stat. "That was so much fun! You've been holding out on me, Nate. We should do it again some time." I spied

84

Dean squinting at me in disapproval from the staircase, as if I was contemplating corrupting Indie's virtue in the hallway.

I cleared my throat, and patted her back neutrally. "Too true." I glanced back at the stairs, but Dean had left. "Are you still... a little drunk?" She nodded, grinning wider. I brushed a hand through my hair. "Good. I had hoped it wasn't just me. They should put a warning label on that bottle."

"I'd do it again. In a heartbeat." Still pressed against me, she patted my chest with her hand, mimicking my heartbeat. "Thump-thump." She said, giggling. She curiously fingered my dragon tooth necklace with a frown, but didn't say anything. "Let's go eat!" She dragged me down the stairs bodily, never letting go of my hand. Her eyes roamed her surroundings as we walked. "This place is so beautiful! Why do you live at the loft when you have *this*?"

I shrugged, catching her as we both stumbled and almost knocked over a priceless vase. She laughed, and then danced forward a few steps, spinning in a cute pirouette with her hands above her head. I jumped forward to catch her again as she almost fell. She stared up at me for several moments, complete trust filling her eyes. Neither of us turned away; we just stared. "Always there to catch me..." She raised a hand to brush my cheek affectionately, her fingers as smooth as silk. "But who do you have to catch you, Nate?" Her eyes grew sad, almost wet.

"Me strong. Need no help." I growled in a caveman voice as I tugged her back up.

She shook her head with a smile. "Maybe, but it doesn't always have to be that way. You deserve the world, boss." With a wink, she tugged me ahead again, leading me into the kitchen to find Dean serving three plates of eggs and bacon onto the large table. A fire was roaring in the fireplace, making the air toasty and warm. Indie's frozen form slowly thawed, much to my disappointment.

I wondered if I was reading too much into our drunken dance through the halls, or if I was really too obtuse to see it any sooner than now. Did Indie care for me too? She tugged my hand to a nearby chair, plopping down with a grin. Her hair was a mess, but she somehow managed to look alluring, a natural beauty, nothing like the magazine covers. Her beauty was pure. I found myself glancing at her often. I noticed that the top of her robe hung loose, revealing an impressive expanse of rounded bosom. I felt her eyes turn to me and I quickly looked away. She stretched her arms above her head with an amused grin as she stared me in the eyes, knowingly. My face grew heated.

"How is Mallory?" Indie asked Dean, still smiling.

Dean glanced over a shoulder, slapping a kitchen towel over his neck. "He was up an hour ago, going to the gym, if I recall correctly."

Our jaws dropped. He was working out? We were still tipsy, and he was working out. He was like eighty-years-old. Indie turned to me with raised eyebrows. I shrugged. "Bon appetite." I shoveled a fork in my mouth, groaning at the pleasant taste. I heard a chime, and Dean glanced down at his phone.

He punched a number on the screen, and then spoke. "Come in, Agent Randulf. Just follow the lighted path, and you'll find us in the kitchen. I set out a plate for you." He typed a rapid staccato on his phone, no doubt illuminating the correct lights to guide Gunnar to the food.

I could vaguely see the video chat on the phone. "Thanks, Dean. I'll be right there." Dean clicked off the phone, and tucked it back into his pocket.

Gunnar appeared a few minutes later. "Hey, Nat—" He halted, seeing Indie. "And the plot thickens..." he said with a face-splitting grin. "Good morning, Indie. I didn't realize you were occupied, Nate. I don't want to intrude on your breakfast." He was barely hiding his smile as he noticed Indie's silk robe, and my own heavier robe. She grinned wide, turning to face me expectantly.

"We had a few drinks last night. I mean, not just *us*. Mallory was there, too."

Gunnar grinned. "Oh? Where is Mallory now?"

Indie continued smiling, remaining silent as she glanced back and forth, egging Gunnar's false assumption on. "He's at the gym." I realized how lame it sounded after I spoke. "Shut up and sit down, Gunnar. Or leave. Whichever is fastest." He chuckled and sat down, sweeping up the third plate without shame.

Indie kept the guilty smile on her face, leaving me to the wolves. Or wolf, in this case. "How have you been, Gunnar?" Indie asked, immediately followed by a full body hiccup that didn't go unnoticed by any of the present males.

"I've been good, Indie. And you?"

"Great! We had such a fun time last night. We sampled some delicious scotch... well, more than sampled, I guess." She giggled at him, and Gunnar smiled back.

"Nate knows how to have a good time. Too much so sometimes, but he's a good man. He's lucky to have a friend like you around to keep him out of trouble."

She nodded, serious. "I know." They shared a smile.

"Thanks for that, Dr. Phil. You almost finished?" I growled.

Gunnar apparently wasn't. "So, moving on up, huh?" He waved a fork at the house in general.

"Package and parcel deal from the surprise last will and testament read to me last night. The same package and parcel that got you your new car." Gunnar nodded, a mixture of sadness at the reason and happiness at the result. "I'll explain later," I said as he opened his mouth to ask another question. He nodded, tearing into his plate hungrily.

We ate in silence, the two of them grinning wide, but remaining silent. I stood, set Indie's empty plate atop mine, and attempted to carry them to the sink. Dean swept past me like a shadow, snatching up the plates with a frown, and continued on to the sink, offended. He took his job very seriously.

Gunnar stood, but Dean was faster, snatching up the plate with a derisive sniff. Gunnar merely shook his head, grinning. "Thanks. Ready when you are, Nate."

"Good. Let's saddle up. I'm just going to grab my things from upstairs." I wobbled, quickly regaining my balance. The food was helping, but I still felt the lingering effects of the nightcap. Wait, plural nightcaps.

"I need to change too. I'll walk with you upstairs." Indie said.

Gunnar rolled his eyes; amused at implications only another man could derive from the statement. "Meet me out front when you're...finished."

Before I could hit him, he left through a different hallway, leaving Indie and I to walk upstairs in peace. Indie tucked an arm through mine, supporting herself, or me, I wasn't sure. After a few minutes, she spoke. "Nate... I had a wonderful time last night." I murmured acknowledgement and she smiled. "Thank you for letting me spend some private time with you. It meant the world to me. Ever since I started working for you, it's been harder and harder for me to make friends outside of the crew at Plato's Cave, and to them I am merely an authority figure. I work, and then go home. It was nice to get out

87

and have fun with… you."

"But you had a hot date planned," I argued.

"A lie." She answered softly. "I've seen too many weird things since meeting you." And that was true. She had seen me do magic, and had spent time around some of the more dangerous private clients I dealt with. The curtain had been pulled back for Indie, revealing some truths about the world that would definitely make it difficult to cope in mundane normalcy, and I was only pondering those consequences now. "To be honest, I haven't been able to find anyone who really interests me enough to spend time with. I really enjoy working for you. But it's more than the secrets you keep. I think it's just you." She slowed to a stop in front of her room, not letting go. "I guess that I'm trying to say that you are probably the best friend I have. I don't want to push you or anything, but just know that I'm here for you. Always. In whatever capacity that you need. Whether as a friend, a confidant, or…" Her deep eyes studied me intently, her silence speaking volumes.

This was a line I had never thought we would cross. Indie was a knock-out, and one of the most brilliant women I had ever met. Aside from appreciating both her beauty, and cunning skills as my store manager, I had forced myself to maintain a professional distance. "Is that why you let Gunnar think what he thought?" I asked softly.

She thought for a moment. "Maybe. Maybe not. He approved of his assumption, approved of *me* with *you*. That was a very special thing for me to realize. But on the other hand, my denial would have merely served to confirm his assumption anyway. So, I remained silent. It felt…nice." Her eyes crinkled in thought. "Like Gunnar said, you really are a great man, Nate. One of the last. I just want you to know that I have never felt about another man the way I feel about you. I… adore you, and couldn't imagine not having you in my life. In whatever capacity that I am allowed. It's hard to talk at work without sending the wrong impression. You have everything, but just know that you could have nothing, and my feelings would remain the same. I'm lucky to have you as a friend."

"And I, you," I answered honestly.

She smiled. Then she leaned close on tiptoes, and kissed my cheek, holding her warm, soft lips against my skin for longer than necessary. "Thank you, Nate." My body reacted on its own, and I pulled her in close. She didn't resist. We stared at each other from inches away, tasting each other's breath.

My heart raced wildly, my brain trying to logically sort my emotions. I found myself leaning closer, her silk-encased torso pliant against my desire. I knew, beyond a shadow of a doubt, that she craved my touch in a not so professional manner, and I craved to be touched by someone who actually knew me and cared for me. She was genuine – a rare find. Maybe even a meal to be savored rather than the desserts I had known my whole life. Others saw the Temple heir, but Indie saw Nate. Just Nate. Her skin was hot beneath my fingertips, and her breathing grew deeper as she studied my face.

"Oh, Indie..." I whispered, my fingers shaking as they pulled her closer. "This is a line that cannot be uncrossed..." I began.

"Cross it if you wish it." Her pupils dilated with honest lust. "But know that you can have me however you desire. I know your heart better than anyone, Nate. You live a lonely life. I only want to see you smile. I only want to *make* you smile..."

I leaned in, resting my forehead against hers as I closed my eyes. I felt her lips softly brush mine as she whimpered delicately, her skin on fire now.

Then my fucking phone vibrated in the other room.

We both stepped back instinctively, my heart thudding with adrenaline as if a bucket of ice water had suddenly been dumped over my head. Then, in a twirl of silk, Indie skipped into her room, pausing at the threshold. "Think about it, Nate. I've made myself clear, I believe, and I am not ashamed to say it. Not to you. Never to you." She smiled coyly, untying her silk robe, and letting the two halves separate slightly, revealing an unbelievably toned torso. Her grin stretched as my genitals threatened to mutiny against my still-ringing phone.

"We'll talk. Soon," I promised. I took a step to her door, trying not to look away from her eyes. I pressed my car keys into her soft hands, squeezing them closed. "Take my car. I can pick it up later. Can I do anything else for you before I leave?" Her eyebrows lifted as her gaze swept over my body from head to foot, and then to her own scantily clad frame, before returning with a hungry twinkle.

"Do you really want me to answer that, Cap'n?"

"Right. Time for me to leave before I fall victim to your feminine wiles."

"One must use the weapons available to her." She smiled.

I turned, instincts screaming against me, and I heard her sigh softly behind me. I glanced over my shoulder in time to see her robe billow to the floor of the hall, and her naked silhouette slowly strut out of sight as she went deeper into her room to change. I almost walked clear past my room. I glanced at the phone, and saw that it was Plato's Cave. I listened to the voicemail on speakerphone as I began to change, and a roiling ball of ice slowly built up in my stomach as the words crashed home.

"Nate, it's Jessie." The new employee Indie had hired. "I don't know how to say this, but…" He took a deep, nervous breath on the other end of the line before blurting out in a rush of forced air. "The shop was broken into last night. They did a number on your loft, but the rest of the store seems okay. Books were tossed from shelves, but I don't think anything is missing from the store. The third theater room wasn't broken into either. The cops are here. You should be, too. Call me when you're on your way, I guess." Then he hung up.

The dragons were playing hardball now. I sat down on the edge of the bed, wondering if they had broken into the store in pursuit of their precious book. If they thought I already had it they were grossly mistaken, but at least they thought highly of me. It was something to remember, a card to exploit later. Another thought hit me a second later. What if I hadn't picked up Indie last night? A chill ran down my spine at the possibility of her being kidnapped and used as leverage against me. If the dragons wanted an angry wizard, I would give them the angel of the Apocalypse. I finished changing, rounded up all my things, and flew down the stairs to meet Gunnar, trying to focus on anything other than Indie and my fucking shop.

Indie's scent remained close, replacing the last fog of the drink from last night with an altogether new high. A whole body high. The high of future possibilities.

CHAPTER 16

"SO," GUNNAR BEGAN. "INDIE LOOKED PRETTY GOOD. She also looked tired. You keep her up all night?" He was grinning, his beefy hands massaging his new leather steering wheel.

"You like the car?"

He shot me a stupid smile.

"Interesting, because they haven't sent out the title yet. One phone call, and I put the car in my name instead of yours. One teeny-weenie phone call, and your dream car becomes my demolition derby car. I will drive it off a goddamn cliff, and send you the *YouTube* video."

Gunnar grumbled back, but kept the smile on his face. "Fine. Just asking."

I watched the shop windows fly by past the car, still feeling on cloud nine from Indie's touch. "I think she likes me."

Gunnar scoffed. "And I thought you were a genius. You really are an idiot sometimes, Nate. Of course, she likes you. She's worked for you for, what, five years now? She's not staying around for the health benefits. More like possible fringe benefits."

"The health benefits are completely free to my employees."

"Oh, well maybe she is staying for the benefits then."

"Just forget it. Let's get back to business. We need to swing by my shop."

He frowned. "Why?"

"It was broken into and tossed last night."

His grip on the steering wheel creaked. "What?" he demanded in a low growl.

"I got a message from Jessie while I was changing. The cops are there."

Gunnar swerved across incoming traffic to take us to the shop. We drove in a brittle silence, both furious and nervous at the implications of dragons breaking into my shop. He didn't even need to ask who it was. We both knew it was the stinking reptiles. Then a thought crossed his face. "Do all your employees have their paperwork in order? They're all packing, right?"

I waved a hand, looking out the window as we turned onto my street and I saw my shop swarming with flashing red and blue lights. "They're set. Don't worry."

He parked a safe distance away and we climbed out into unusually warm autumn air. My heels pounded into the now dry sidewalk as I prowled up to the caution tape surrounding my shop and home. I glanced at the surrounding rooftops, hoping to see a dragon that I could blow to smithereens. Nothing.

We halted as a cop held up an instinctive hand at our approach, not even looking at us. "Sorry, this is a crime scene. No shopping today." I didn't move; staring at his badge, imagining all sorts of frightening magic I could use to get his attention. Then I recognized him as the young cop who had been standing outside the interrogation room two nights ago, and grinned. Perfect. Before I could scare the bejeezus out of him a second time, Gunnar whipped out his badge. The rookie turned to us then, and his jaw dropped as he all but leapt back a step upon seeing my smiling face. "M-master Temple! My God. Where have you been? Never mind. Get in there. The Captain wants to speak with you."

"I take that to mean Kosage?" The rookie nodded nervously. I stared into his eyes until he began to squirm, and then whispered in a dramatic voice as we ducked under the caution tape. "Thanks for the coffee." His legs all but quivered as I glanced back at him, wiping his forehead with his sleeve. I briefly wondered what he thought about the display of magic in the interrogation room the other night, but the thought evaporated as I stepped inside Plato's Cave.

Cops milled around everywhere, taking pictures and sipping coffee from my coffee bar, probably not even paying for it. Damn the pigs. The shop was a mess, but not nearly so bad as it had been after Raven's visit. I chided myself for not setting the wards last night when we had picked up Indie. Then I saw him. Our eyes locked together at the same time, but mine tightened in anger.

"Kosage. What happened?" I hissed, as if blaming him for the invasion.

"Ah, Master Temple. Nice to see you again. As you can see, your shop was broken into. It seems they just broke through the tempered glass window, which was quite a feat given their makeup. They practically would have had to shoot it in, but no one reported gunshots. I take it you live in the loft upstairs?" He asked, flicking his eyes up above. I nodded. He flipped open a small notepad. "Where were you last night between the hours of two and three in the morning?"

"At Chateau Falco."

"Can anyone vouch for that?"

I leveled my hooded wizard eyes down on him, making his short, delicate stature an obvious distaste. "You've already tried that tack, Kosage. Be very careful. Don't dare accuse me without solid evidence." My threat rolled off his back like water on a duck.

"Speaking of *that tack*, it seems my notes were mistaken from our previous discussion." He flipped a page. Then another. "I quote. *I have nothing to do with my parents' company*. Seems that's changed now, hasn't it?" my eyes were coals, but he continued on. "Any known enemies who might have wanted to steal from you?"

I hesitated, sensing Gunnar's apprehension. "No. But I do have some very pricy merchandise. Was anything stolen?"

"Your employees are checking the inventory as we speak. But so far it seems like nothing was taken, although they put up a hell of a search."

I nodded, thankful they hadn't tried breaking into the third theater. My secrets would be over if they had succeeded in opening that door.

Kosage closed his pad, lifting his eyes. "We should be done shortly. We haven't found any smoking gun, so to speak. And all your employees' paperwork for their firearms are up to date, so there isn't really anything else we can do. Do you have anything to add that might aid us?"

I glanced around the store, sensing all eyes on us. After a few seconds, I shook my head. "Nothing."

Kosage assessed me for a few seconds, but then shrugged. "Thank you, Master Temple." He began to turn away, but stopped. "I see you are spending time with the FBI. Might I ask in what regards?"

Gunnar's hackles raised territorially, but I spoke instead. "You may not."

"Interesting. I think we'll be keeping our eyes on you over the next few days. For your own safety, of course." His smile was slimy. "Parents murdered, making you the new CEO of Temple Industries, which you seemed to lie to me about. Bookstore broken into while you are conspicuously absent, but nothing stolen. Escaping handcuffs without permission. Arguable assault when you departed the interrogation room. And playing with the FBI, but…"

he looked me up and down. "No credentials to that effect. Those things could give you some trouble down the road, Master Temple. There's already blood in the water. No point in thrashing about."

"I think your work here is done. Pack up. Now." He turned to look at me then, a hint of anger in his eyes at the loss of face in front of his men. I smiled.

"You heard him, men. Pack up." He slowly turned to face me, clasping his hands behind his back. "I've got my eyes on you, Temple. If I hear even one whisper of your name at another crime scene, things will get ugly. And I know just the judge to call. I believe you met him last night." His smile stretched wide at my reaction, then he left.

My employees slowly materialized from around the store, watching me carefully as if they felt that they had somehow failed me. "You were all hired for your unique qualities, your ability to roll with the punches. Show that to me now, and get this place up and running within the hour. Business as usual."

"Aye, aye, Cap'n!" They crowed, soothed by my subtle compliment.

"Anyone seen Jessie?" I asked aloud after a few seconds.

"He left after he called you. Had to get to class or something." I heard someone answer. I grunted.

"Alright. I need to head out with Gunnar. You guys got it from here?" The only answer was the bustle of work as they began cleaning up the store like a team of pixies. "Oh, and can someone call that window guy again?" Someone laughed before answering an affirmative. Then I whisked out the door with Gunnar on my heels.

"Nothing fazes you, does it?" he asked as we climbed into his car.

"It wouldn't change anything. I've heard that you can either choose to smile or cry about problems, but either way, it doesn't change the fact that they still happened."

He was silent for a spell as he pulled out into the street. "Wise words. Who told you that?"

I smiled as I stared out the window. "Some Amway guy." The buildings whizzed past me, threatening my unsettled stomach. The cops would now be breathing down my neck at every turn. And the dragons had crossed a very dangerous line. It was time to take off the gloves. "Smiles and cries... either way, it doesn't change what I'm going to do to them when I see them next," I

94

almost whispered.

"Within the limits of the law, of course." When I didn't answer, he continued. "Right, Nate?"

I traced my fingers along the magic around me, spinning it around my fingertips like a silk ribbon in the wind, imagining what horrors I could cause with my power. It felt more vibrant than usual, stronger. I shrugged noncommittally. "Sure, Gunnar. Sure..."

CHAPTER 17

W E WERE SILENT FOR A WHILE AS GUNNAR DROVE,
pondering the day's events. "What have you got?" I finally
asked him.

Gunnar's face became stony. "I had a technician run the kerchief. It was
human blood, and it was a match to your father. He had his blood on file
from the... murder."

I nodded, letting out a heavy breath. I hadn't doubted it, but it was still a
lot to take in. Gunnar handed me the kerchief sympathetically before continuing. "Well, a lot of people are coming into town for the eclipse event. All
the hotels are practically full, so no luck on your dragon hunter friend."

"Plural. He said *we*. He's got friends."

"Irrelevant. Did you hear me say that every hotel is full? I need more information if you want me to find him."

I fished out the card the dragon hunter had given me. "Does this help?"

Gunnar scowled back, snatching the card from my fingers. "Tomas Mullingsworth." He blinked. "Have you tried simply calling him?"

I nodded. "Late last night. No answer. Think you can find him?"

"Yes, but you could have given me this last night, Nate."

"I was too busy buying you this Aston Martin. Want to guess how much it
costs?"

"I'd rather not. Then I might feel like I'm indebted to you."

"Oh, you *are* indebted to me for this." I showed him my teeth. "Besides, I
have so much going on right now that it kind of slipped my mind. I have to
keep my participation in this out of the media. A request from my lawyer.
And now the cops will be sniffing around my every move after the break-in."
Gunnar nodded, looking pissed.

"And there's all this other stuff to focus on. I mean, Peter, a closet wizard,
asks me to get him some bullshit book for a client, a dragon attacks me at my
shop, then I go to my parents' funeral and receive a message from beyond the

grave by a creepy old man, wizard, bodyguard, and then I was attacked *again*. And apparently, some Spiderman-wannabe has gone rogue, teaming up with these dragons, or dragon hunters." Another thought came to mind and I groaned. "And *tonight*, I'm supposed to duel with the Minotaur in some shit-infested field over a dumb book about—" My mouth went dry as I recognized the connection. Everything had happened so fast that I hadn't even thought about it. "Dragons…" I finished.

Gunnar gazed at me askance, making sure I was all right. "Huh. That's the kind of thing that we in the Bureau call a *clue*." He turned left at the light and continued on, the Aston Martin purring as he downshifted. "Still no idea who this client is? Or *what* he is?" I shook my head. "Seems pretty sketchy that he wants a book about dragons that is dangerous enough to warrant risking your life for, right around the time that a group of dragons is also seeking a *book*. One that they say belongs to them. One that they're willing to kill for. Then a group of dragon hunters arrive, saying they are hunting a rogue dragon." He was quiet for a moment. "How much is this book worth?"

"Fifty-thousand-dollars."

Gunnar swerved the car a bit, stripping a gear in the process. "I need a new job."

"You can fight the Minotaur if you want." I smirked.

He considered that for a moment. "I think I could take him."

My eyes widened, and then I began to laugh, deep belly laughs. It felt so good after all the drama. "You? Take the Minotaur? An immortal monster? Do you have any idea how many innocents have died by his hand? Theseus was the only one to ever defeat him, and he was lucky, having help from the goddess Ariadne with her ball of thread to help him navigate the Labyrinth."

Gunnar was quiet for a time. "I'm guessing a ball of thread won't help us, right?"

I smiled. "No. No it won't. But then again, he's Buddhist now, so maybe we'll just have a nice political debate or something."

"Probably not, Nate."

"Yeah. Probably not." I had no idea how I was going to fight the Minotaur. I had magic out the Wahoo, but Asterion knew that, and was probably ready for it. I was just going to have to wing it. This book could give me answers about my parents, or the kid might know something. Either way, I had to win. That settled, I took several deep meditative breaths, trying to banish

97

my anxiety. The sound of Gunnar's scanner going off with a squawk almost made me jump out of my skin. "I think I just peed a little." I said, glancing down at the seat.

Gunnar shook his head. "Gross." He fiddled with the radio, hit a button, and then spoke into the mike. "Agent Randulf, here." Gunnar's boss answered, voice garbled.

"Looks like you got another one just over the river. Owner found dead this morning after the neighbors heard a loud ruckus last night." Gunnar sighed wearily, and asked for the address. Reinhardt gave the store name, and forwarded the address to Gunnar's GPS unit. It blinked at us a few seconds later, instantly blaring directions at us in a feminine English accent. Neat.

"Alright. I can get there..." he smiled at me. "Pretty fast." He down shifted the car with a metal click, and the engine tried to tear free from the frame as we launched around an old blue-hair driving in front of us. Agent Reinhardt signed off with some jumbled response that couldn't be heard over the engine.

"It's just over the river," I noted, watching the GPS. "In Illinois."

Gunnar's teeth showed through the smile. "Which is what the FBI calls *jurisdiction*. This is the second attack across state lines, confirming our authority. We can kick the local police out easily this time." He looked over at me. "Which is a good thing, considering Kosage's hard-on for busting you. I wonder what you did to piss him off so much..." He trailed off, curiously.

I chuckled. "I spilled his coffee in the interrogation room."

Gunnar rolled his eyes. "I'm sure that was it." I leaned back in the seat, enjoying the G-force pull of the car as Gunnar broke every speed limit sign we passed. Street signs blurred past, then Interstate signs, and then I was staring out at the Mississippi river as the rails of the bridge whizzed past me.

My phone rang in my pocket. I plucked it out, glancing at the screen. Peter. "Just the man I wanted to talk to," I answered, reproachfully. Gunnar scowled silently.

"Yeah, listen. We should probably talk. You free now? I wanted to talk to you about that book." The line was quiet for a moment. "I think I wrote down the wrong title."

"No time now, I'm running errands with my new chauffeur." Gunnar's knuckles cracked on the steering wheel in disapproval.

"Oh. Well, where are you? Maybe I could meet you?"

I glanced out the window. "Not likely. Heading into Illinois to talk to someone near the warehouses just over the Eads Bridge."

There was a silence on the phone. "Okay. How about tonight? At the Cave?"

"Sure," I glanced at my watch, thinking of my schedule with Asterion, and then if I survived, the book exchange with my client. I also wanted to swing by the Expo Center to see if anything seemed off at the eclipse convention that was starting tonight, like maybe a group of dragons murdering the attendees. Maybe I could squeeze Peter between everything. If I wasn't dead. "How about around nine? I might be a few minutes late."

Peter answered quickly. "Sure, sure. Just leave the security down so I can wait inside. It will be cold outside tonight."

"You know, seeing as how I know magic, I seem to recall a way for the cold not to bother you. Just a simple spell for a *wizard* to teach another *wizard*. Might be something that, if I were just learning how to use magic, I would have sought out another wizard to teach me," I growled.

"I know, I know. We have a lot to discuss. My client is really pestering me about this stupid book. He'll pay whatever you wish," he added the last quickly. He didn't realize that money was no longer a motivator for me. Looking at the sticky notes attached to the cards I had been given had surprised even me. That many zeroes made things confusing.

I hesitated before speaking the truth. "What's the new title? I have to know that if you want me to help you. And how much is it worth?" I asked curiously. Having studied his note yesterday, I had soon found that I already owned a copy of the unremarkable book at Plato's Cave. It was even in my personal collection in the loft, not downstairs in the shop. But now he had fudged the title. Nothing is ever easy.

He paused, speaking into the background. "High five-figures." I repeated his answer aloud. In the span of a week, I could make six-figures by selling two books. Gunnar grunted in disbelief, shaking his head. "I'll tell you the title tonight."

"Okay. You realize I can't find something if I don't know what it's called, right?" Peter sighed on the other end. "And I am doing no more favors until we have a nice long chat about your new ice cube making ability." I added.

I could feel Peter tense on the other end. "Okay, okay. See you then."

I hung up. We drove on in silence, Gunnar glancing at me now and then, but saying nothing. So far, I had accounted for two of the three books that had been requested of me. Now, just one, thanks to Peter's inability to write down the correct title of the book his client wanted. It should be simple enough to find though. If it was in any way similar to the original request. The important one was the odd book the Raven lady had asked me about, *Sons of the Dying Son*. I pondered several possible sources, my mind distant from the sounds of traffic fleeing the British sports car. But it would have to wait until after my duel.

"Is that the first time you have talked to Peter since...?" He waved a hand at the air, implying the attack two nights ago. I nodded. "What do you think it means?" he asked carefully. "Wouldn't you have known a long time ago if he had..." he searched for a word, "the ability?"

I looked over at him, thinking. "Perhaps." I turned back to the window, feeling his eyes on me. "But perhaps not. It's not exactly a science. Some come into it early, with training and foreknowledge, like me. With others, it might take a traumatic experience for it to manifest." I was silent for a minute, thinking hard for an explanation. "Have you heard those stories about mothers who were suddenly able to lift a car from their child's trapped body? Or those who survive an un-survivable accident, and have no idea why? Most often, those are people like Peter apparently is. It hits them all of a sudden, and they don't quite understand it. Then they normally hide from it, unable to explain what they remember lest they sound like an insane person."

Gunnar stared hard through the windshield, cutting off a motorcycle with a sharp swerve. "But Peter didn't seem too surprised by his reaction."

"No." I said softly, growing angry. "No, he didn't. Which either means that he already knew or that he's much more cool-headed than we thought. Since being around us his whole life, maybe it was an awakening for him. He had wanted it for so long, and then, suddenly, there it was. He was no longer the outcast. He was just like us. Maybe his joy overrode his shock."

Gunnar spoke as we exited the highway into a seedy warehouse district just off the bridge. "It seemed more like the former to me. Cool-headed doesn't sound like Peter." I nodded, fury barely contained. "But then why didn't he come to you? I mean, you are one scary, talented wizard, and he never told you." His words trailed off as he waited for me to speak. I remained silent, anticipating our *talk* tonight. I would get my answers then.

Gunnar drove through a warren of dilapidated warehouses, glancing at the

GPS every few seconds for our turnoff. A large truck pulled out in front of us, laden with construction debris, and a smeared sign that read 'Not responsible for falling debris.' Gunnar was glancing down when the back of the truck suddenly flew open. I yelled and Gunnar slammed on the brakes by reflex, then he saw the contents, and we both hesitated.

Stone gargoyles filled the back of the truck, but it continued moving down the street, blocking us from passing him. The driver must not have realized that the door came loose. Gunnar swerved to the side, trying to get the driver's attention in his side mirror. The driver apparently remained aloof to our honking, because Gunnar cursed and pulled back behind the truck, resigned to follow behind him until our turn.

We were still going the speed limit when I thought I saw one of the gargoyle statues move.

CHAPTER 18

I LEANED FORWARD, HOLDING MY BREATH AS I STUDIED the huddle of lifeless gargoyles staring at us from the back of the truck. They were all demonic gargoyles of some kind, but were each subtly different. Some had wings, and some bore weapons, or massive claws. But none moved.

As I began to relax, one of them blinked, turning its hideous head to stare straight into my eyes amidst a puff of dust and crumbling gravel that cascaded down its torso. "No fucking way," I whispered, my forearms pebbling.

Gunnar looked over at me. "We'll pass this schmuck in a minute or so, and then we can get on to the crime scene." He said, attempting to sooth my impatience.

I shook my head and pointed. "The gargoyles. They're alive."

One of the gargoyle statues snapped out its wings, and Gunnar jolted as if he had been Tasered. "What the hell?" he exclaimed, slowing down. The gargoyle shook out its wings. Then it turned to look directly at us, curious. Gunnar went still. "Nate…?"

"I know, I know! I'm thinking!" I argued, keeping my eyes on the waking statues. It looked like someone had raided the wrong house, getting more than they bargained for. These statues weren't planning on staying in the garden for the owner's pleasure. I tried to recall everything I knew about gargoyles. I remembered that they could wake, but only for short bursts, turning back and forth from life to stone for mere seconds at a time, but only if they were strong. Really strong. Which explained the stories about people waking up the next morning and swearing that their statues were in a different spot than the night before. And it usually had to be night for them to have the kind of power needed to do so. Or if something traumatic had happened to them. Like suddenly being moved from their home. Shit. My hopes were that these statues would look around a bit, and then turn back to stone. Content. Not angry and vengeful. Yeah right.

"Just stay calm. Don't do anything to startle them. Don't slow down, and don't speed up. Since we're staying the same distance away from them, they might just fall back asleep."

Gunnar nodded slowly, shifting only his eyes to me. "Okay. You're taking this pretty calmly. Has this kind of thing happened to you a time or two?"

I nodded. "At Notre Dame. But that was at night when they are known to have enough power to wake. I've never seen one come to life in daylight. It's kind of against the rules. Things can be believed at night, explained away as just a trick of the dark. Day time makes it all too obvious, and we Freaks need our secrecy."

"You're preaching to the choir. But how are they awake now, then?"

I explained my theory about a traumatic shift in their home, but even I wasn't so sure. These gargoyles hadn't fallen back asleep yet, and a couple more woke up while we were talking, flexing long-unused muscles. "What are the odds of this many bad things coincidentally happening to you in such a short span of time?" he asked.

"Not high." Another statue woke in a crack of stone and dust. They began looking at each other curiously, silent conversations traveling between their eyes as if asking *so, now what?* Several of them began to smile as if they had an idea. "Technically, a wizard could raise them, but he would either have to be close, very powerful, or have some kind of tie to these specific statues. I haven't heard of any wizards on this side of the river, but I guess I can't discount the possibility..."

As one, all of the statues turned to stare at us, cocking their heads like a cat spotting a laser light on the floor. Another gargoyle's wings snapped out, knocking the head clean off of one of the others. Okay, friendly fire was a good thing. "If nothing startles them, then they should just fall back asleep. I think. Just keep pace with the truck." Gunnar nodded, focused on a goal.

Then the truck swerved abruptly, and the driver honked his horn furiously as a car cut across the intersection just ahead of him. The gargoyles crouched, reacting defensively. We hadn't seen any other cars on this street, so the statues focused on the only sign of life near them.

Us.

I could see the hatred as they stared at us, and then they leapt out of the moving truck, landing like a group of paratroopers in a war zone – eyes wary, and claws out. Gunnar swerved as one of the gargoyles drew a club

103

strapped to his back and swung it at us. The tip of the stone club screeched down the passenger side of the car. "I am *definitely* going to sue that driver!" Gunnar bellowed.

"You can't. His truck said that he wasn't responsible for falling debris." Gunnar turned murderous eyes on me. I almost yelled for Gunnar to floor it so that we could get away, but then I thought about these monsters loose in the city, left to do as they pleased. "Gunnar, stop the car! We have to stop them!"

He pulled the emergency brake, spinning the car in a 180-degree turn so that we were facing the huddle of gargoyles. "Damn it, Nate! How the hell are we supposed to fight them?" He wasn't scared, just genuinely asking what we were supposed to do. "I will not ruin my car by running over them." He folded his arms defiantly. Drama Queen.

"The heads. I think if we can take the heads, they'll become inanimate again."

Gunnar cocked his SIG Sauer and climbed out of the car. Before they could move, his gun roared, blowing the head off the man with the club. I arched an eyebrow at him. "He scratched my car," Gunnar growled.

"My mother always said that a pistol is the Devil's right hand." I grinned. Gunnar smiled back, showing teeth.

Then they began to break up, moving on us like well-trained predators. But they weren't expecting a wizard and a werewolf to crash their party. They were just looking for a little entertainment. If I had my way, the entertainment would be completely one-sided, leaving only a whole truckload of gravel behind.

I suddenly had an idea. Something my parents had briefly taught me, but that I had never truly practiced. I guess this would have to count. I yelled to Gunnar. "Cover me, but no matter what you see, make sure you don't shoot me!"

Knowing my weirdness, Gunnar just nodded, popping off a few more shots at one of the more demonic-looking gargoyles. I took a deep breath, and instantly found the calm reservoir of power deep inside me. It actually helped clear my head a bit from the hangover. I waded into that power like it was a hot spring, allowing the tension to ease out of my muscles. I knew it took only seconds, but in my mind it felt like an hour. Once relaxed, I began drawing that reservoir into me, through me, and then projected it over my skin like stone armor, doubling up over the most vulnerable areas. It was easier than I remembered. My skin felt like ice as the stone encased every section of my body, efficiently turning me into a stone version of myself – statue Nate.

Once satisfied, I opened my eyes back to the real world. The gargoyles had taken no more than a few steps. Gunnar was efficiently picking off legs and heads where he could, but I knew it wouldn't be enough. There were close to a dozen of them. I glanced down at my stone hands in wonderment, twisting them this way and that.

To any passerby, I most likely looked like a human statue. Except that I wore clothes, and I could move. Neat huh? I felt like a stone manikin, and I knew that if I looked into a mirror, my face would still be there, but cast in stone. I could move without impediment, but with this armor I could take just about as much damage as one could dish out, but each hit tore off some of that shielding, so it was only temporary.

I turned to look at Gunnar. His eyes were wide as he looked from me to the statues, and then he began to laugh. "That is so cool! Why do you bitch about my power when you can do *that?*" he asked, cracking off another shot to send one of the gargoyles down permanently.

I shrugged and turned back to the horde of gargoyles with a grin of my own. "Play with me?" I asked one who was warily approaching me, unsure whether I was ally or foe. It cocked its head in confusion. I reached out, grabbed its throat, and crushed the stone in my fist. The head toppled to the ground with a heavy thud. I pointed at one of the winged gargoyles. "You're next." The gargoyle let out a dusty roar, wings snapping out as if preparing to fly. Not today. I rushed the gargoyle, batting down one of its wings as it crouched to take to the air. The wing shattered under my fist, knocking the beast off balance, then I punched it straight in the nose, knocking it clean off. The gargoyle stumbled, preparing to defend itself, but I kicked it in the chest so hard that its head flew off from the abrupt whiplash. The body skidded into the last few gargoyles, knocking them down like bowling pins. "Strike!" I roared.

Gunnar's gun blasted until two straggler gargoyles died at his feet. He was panting as he jogged towards me. I didn't wait. I dove into the pile of gargoyles like a wrestler, trapping a leg here, an arm there, until I found a hold. An arm bar tore off its appendage completely, and then I punched its throat until I felt pavement on the other side. A blow to the side of my head made me see stars for a few seconds, and then Gunnar's gun blasted off the sucker-punching gargoyle's head from inches away. My ears rang, and I could feel some of the stone sliding off my face where I had been hit, leaving naked, vulnerable skin underneath. Gunnar noticed immediately.

"We need to finish this fast, before your armor fades completely." I nodded back, but was picked up in a bear hug from behind. I kicked out with my heel and connected with the gargoyles knee, shattering it so that he fell down. As my feet touched ground again, I angled my head to protect the soft skin, and head-butted his nose with the back of my skull. He fell back immediately, tottering on his one good leg. I turned, crouched, and superman tackled him down to the ground. Gunshots continued as I pummeled the statue until only dust remained of his neck.

All was silent. I looked up to see Gunnar scanning the area. "I think that's all of them," he said. "But we need to get out of here before someone shows up and starts asking questions. I'll tell the cops that we drove by here when we heard the shots, but saw only broken statues in the road. Can you do something about your… appearance?" he asked with a wry grin.

I nodded, climbing to my feet as more pieces of the armor slid off of their own accord. With little effort, the rest of the armor began cascading down my body like roof tiles, crashing to the road in piles of slate. After a few seconds, I could feel the wind on my skin again, and rubbed it for warmth. The stone armor had been cold. I was now covered in dust like some vagrant homeless person. "I might get your car a little dirty."

Gunnar shrugged. "Nothing to be done about that." He checked the car for scratches, but other than the first scratch, it was surprisingly unharmed. As we pulled out, Gunnar spoke. "That wasn't too bad. But it's too much to be a coincidence." He paused, face thoughtful. "Someone is gunning for us, but the question is who? The dragons?"

I nodded. It was either the dragons or there was a third player in the game. Gunnar was right. It was just too unlikely to be a coincidence, but I couldn't imagine who else it could be, or why they would use such an obscure way to take us out. I mean, they were dragons. Why wouldn't they just eat us? Or burn us? Gunnar interrupted my thoughts.

"This might be a bad scene, Nate. You up for it?" I grunted affirmation, watching the warehouses pass by us as Gunnar finally found our destination.

We pulled into a parking spot just outside a trio of flashing police cars.

"Put on your party dress. It seems all the boys showed up for this one. Let's crash the ball, shall we?" I asked. Gunnar grinned, opening his door, and strutting like a peacock as no less than a dozen Illinois police stared open-jawed at the brilliant Aston Martin parked just outside the tape. The severe contrast of such a specimen in such a seedy district was perfectly satisfying.

"It's nice having a billionaire as a friend, you know that?" he laughed. With a nod, we strode towards the barricade like gods among men. At least, that's what Gunnar looked like. I hoped to establish the same sense of self-confidence as I followed behind him, covered in dust and gravel. A billionaire vagrant for a friend, more like it.

CHAPTER 19

W E WERE QUICKLY PAST THE HORDE OF POLICE officers and into the shop, thanks in no small part to the heap of silent questions behind their eyes as they glanced from the towering Norwegian FBI werewolf in their midst, to the gleaming sports car parked a dozen yards ahead of them, to the dusty and dirty celebrity billionaire civilian in tow. They lifted the tape for us to enter. "Need backup, Agent Randulf? It's pretty… disturbing."

"Not necessary. Give us a few moments in private." The store was in shambles. Paperback and buckram books decorated the floor, torn open to leave loose pages lying about like the useless guts of an eviscerated animal. Fury smoldered deep down inside my stomach, as if I were looking at heaps of dead children lying about the room instead. Books *were* my children. It was sacrilegious.

Hundreds of spiny, silver needles covered the scene, as if a dozen chrome porcupines had exploded in a last act of martyrdom against the written word. Glancing about, I noticed that the needles were embedded into the walls, bookshelves, tables, and even through one of the side windowpanes, shattering glass out onto the street. Kneeling, I spotted faint droplets of blood on some of their tips.

Gunnar was still, scanning the small shop from the center of the carnage: the calm eye of a hurricane. Then he stiffened. I turned to follow his gaze, and I couldn't help but take an involuntary step back. On the far wall, the owner of the establishment hung six feet off the ground, crucified by much larger silver stakes at each appendage. Some of the wounds had shed more blood than the others, staining the wall in a viscous smear as it made its way down to the floor.

For instance, the one spearing the man's genitals into the brick wall had bled the most, belying that it was one of the first inflicted.

I shuddered at the thought, remembering my close encounter with the net-launched web the night before that had almost made me permanently sterile. Gunnar arched a brow. "Pretty sick. Who carries around a bunch of stakes to hammer a person into a wall?"

I pushed back the emotions that were screaming for me to run away, and stepped closer to the body. It was riddled with tiny silver needles as well, like a bad advertisement for acupuncture. He had not died easily. I climbed onto a nearby table and studied the large stakes. After a moment, I glanced back at Gunnar. "They weren't hammered into him," Gunnar scoffed, stepping closer.

"Then how in the hell were they—" He blinked, noticing the polished, rounded edges of the stakes. No hammer marks marred their surface. I reached out and tentatively touched the cold metal. My mind immediately crumpled, folding in on itself in utter defeat. I was falling, falling down into a black abyss with no one to catch me, and I was screaming with no one to hear me. Indie's words came back. *Who's there to catch you, Nate?* My sub-conscious immediately answered. *No one. No one cares enough to catch you. You're all alone. Who are you to fight something this strong? You don't stand a chance. You should just leave it all alone and go back to your shop.* I was terrified, completely terrified, and I was still falling into the blackness, a blackness like a thousand dying suns...

Something struck me across the face like a bitch slap from Jesus. I grunted in shock, my head instantly clearing up as everything came back into focus. I wasn't falling. I wasn't alone. That hadn't been my thoughts. I realized that I had fallen down from the table, and that Gunnar was holding me protectively on the ground. "Nate! You okay? What happened?"

I grunted, fumbling my shaky arms to hold myself up. He let go and slid back a few feet, watching me nervously. My eyes watered from the blow, and my head rang, but I wasn't angry with him. He might have just saved my sorry ass. I looked back up at the body and felt breakfast ready to come back up, so I quickly turned away, breathing deeply. Hangover *plus* dead body *equals* projectile vomit. "They were," I shivered convulsively for a second, the fear trying to overtake me again. I managed to take a breath and try again. "They were cast at him. Thrown."

Gunnar looked from me to the man spread-eagled on the wall. "Cast? Thrown? Do you have any idea what kind of precision that would take?"

I nodded. "Positive. And to hold his," I studied the man. "190-pound weight into a brick wall required unbelievable force." I turned to face him. "This was a dragon, for sure. The same mind-magic as the Raven tried to use is present here. Except much stronger. Instead of lust, this one used fear. Unparalleled fear. She mind-fucked me just by touching the metal, and that was, what, twelve hours later?" Gunnar nodded, remembering the details from the cops outside. "I can't imagine what this man experienced before he died. He didn't even deal in the type of circles that would come close to what Raven asked me for." Studying some of the book covers on the floor, I growled angrily. "History. He was a fucking history book dealer. Nothing even remotely spooky. They must be getting desperate."

Gunnar nodded, eyes darting to the body again. "Another dragon. With silver stakes..." He sighed hesitantly. "Your ball."

I stared, momentarily clueless. Then it hit me. Silver stakes were anathema to a werewolf. To hear that one of these beasts harnessed such weapons was beyond scary, even for me, but to Gunnar it was deathly so. "I didn't think of that. I guess this one's on me." Gunnar nodded slowly. "You know, our partnership feels one-sided, Gunnar. I'm handling all the nasties while you read reports. Very bureaucratic of you."

He grinned, but seemed unhappy about it. "But I'll be there for motivation. From a distance. With a wall between us." He glanced at the brick wall holding up the body. "A couple walls between us, but I'll be there, cheering you on with a megaphone, you little dragon-slayer, you," he said unashamedly. As a werewolf, Gunnar could handle a world of pain, but he wasn't immortal. One stake to the chest and his world would end in a blazing eternity of pain. Or so I had read. Not a simple death for a werewolf, more like a Dante's Inferno, seventh circle of hell, type of death.

"Gee, thanks." I muttered. I looked at the corpse one last time and then spoke to Gunnar. "Mind if I send him off?" Gunnar shook his head. I didn't bother with the coins, but spoke the words, filling them with my power. "*Requiescat in Pace.*" The familiar wail of a horn rumbled deep inside my chest, and Charon drifted out of nowhere to pluck the victim's soul away from the body, laying it down in his boat as he continued on, nodding once at me in gratitude before he slipped out the front door. Of course, the cops outside saw nothing. They were blind to beings such as Charon. And Charon only took the *souls* of Regulars, as opposed to taking the entire *body* like he had with Raven.

Gunnar shook his head, and began taking pictures of the corpse in situ, various angles, and close-ups. Cop stuff. Me, being utterly deficient at police procedure, decided to go peruse the items in the store, verifying and cataloguing the victim's selection. Had the owner's loving fingers brushed off that particular buckram cover recently? I used my toe to flip over several books, glancing here and there at loose pages. The wind howled through the broken window, hungry to be the first to explore the virgin building's insides, and then abscond with the equivalent of a pair of panties for its conquest – in this case, a collection of pages from the destroyed books.

I sat down in a clear area of the floor amidst the chaos, quieting my mind, and drew a mental circle about me, lacing it with power. I needed to think. One by one, I blocked out my senses. First, sound; the fluttering pages, the incessant clicking of Gunnar's camera, the general creaking of the building, the muffled voices of the police outside, and then the wind. I closed my eyes to kill visual feedback. Then smell, and then touch. Next came sensations of a rather difficult-to-explain nature: the sense of life lingering in the room from Gunnar and I, the sense of death from the corpse on the wall, and then the overwhelming sensation of love that stained every article in the room. It covered everything: the books, the tables, the windows, and even the walls.

The owner had dearly loved his establishment, not looking at it as merely a potential source of income, but as a living being, demanding all the requirements for life. Nourishment from books, care from the owner, praise from sales and contented customers, and vitality from the elements that were the store itself: the wood, windows, floors, insulation, stairs, furniture, and even the pot of coffee on the back table. The place was alive, and to think clearly, I needed to first empathize that life and then discard it.

Finally content, I floated in blackness; complete peace. I had to fight my mind in order to remind it that this was nothing like the blackness I had just experienced from touching the silver stake. This was a peaceful tranquility with no sense of falling or fear. I managed it, barely.

In my mind, I folded myself comfortably into a wingback chair that was suddenly floating in the emptiness. Then, as if it were the most normal thing in the world, I flipped on a Tiffany lamp sitting on a stand beside me. It was dark in my imagination, both literally and emotionally. I whipped out an aging leather journal, and began jotting down notes. All the information I had acquired over the last week that might be relevant to the dragons or my parents was splashed onto the journal, all in question form, and then I took a calming sip of a Mint Julep sitting on the table beside me, contemplating anything else I might have missed. Satisfied, I set the journal down in my lap, and finished my drink, enjoying the cooling freshness of the beverage. I glanced down at my writing, thinking calmly.

Dragons. Dragons were searching my city for a family book, *Sons of the Dying Sun*, killing anyone who got in their way, allegedly even my parents. My father and Raven had both mentioned tomorrow's solar eclipse, which had attracted thousands of tourists to the convention center where speakers had arrived from all over the world to discuss the science, physics, and even mystical extrapolations of such an event. Some kid client wanted me to find a book that also had something to do with dragons. Dragon hunters had a mark on a particularly dangerous dragon they believed to be in town. My shop had been broken into, and I had just survived a random hate-crime by a truckload of gargoyles while driving to the scene of another dragon attack. Maybe that last one was just my luck…

I couldn't think of any particular dangers surrounding the eclipses in history, so what was so important about this one? Perhaps when this scene was finished I could go do some research on dragons and eclipses. To be honest, I knew nothing more than your average idiot about them. Arcane master of knowledge and wisdom, a wizard should be, but there were simply too many myths and fables to study to know them all before one might encounter them in the real world. I wasn't one of those librarian warrior Grimm brothers. I needed ammunition.

That settled, I spent the rest of my solitude pondering possibilities of tonight's encounter with Asterion. How would a reformed Buddhist want to duel? What would it consist of? Good old-fashioned arm-wrestle? Political debate? Chess? Surprisingly, none of these seemed appropriate.

I came back to myself to find Gunnar finished with the scene.

He was flipping through a particularly old book without interest, restless. His heightened sense of smell had to make this place exceptionally unpleasant. He saw me move and placed the book down, waiting for me to speak. I stretched out my legs, careful of any silver needles, waiting for the feeling to come back from my meditation. After a minute, I stood, and he spoke, "We have to find this book soon if we want to stop the killing."

I stretched my calves languorously. "I think I know a way. A way that might actually get us ahead of them. But it might skirt some grey areas with the law," I added the last bit carefully.

Gunnar studied me for a long while in silence. "How about I have my men do their job, and pretend I didn't hear whatever you just said. You can be on your merry way, and do whatever it is you feel like doing while they work this scene. In a couple hours, we will have a chat, and perhaps we'll have information to share with each other."

My eyes widened. Gunnar was a stickler for protocol, and here he was, urging me to do whatever would get us results. I simply nodded at him. "Good idea. Why don't you drop me off at Plato's Cave, and I'll call an old friend?" He nodded, turning his back on the scene, and heading out of the building. I followed behind him like a good little sidekick. In some cases, it could be helpful to have a cavalry behind you like the FBI, but in many other ways it slowed them down, making them impotent to perform as agilely as was often necessary when dealing with sociopathic Freaks.

CHAPTER 20

THE ILLINOIS COPS WATCHED US AS WE LEFT, ALREADY being bombarded by FBI agents parked nearby. They didn't seem in the least bit upset about passing off the responsibility of this particularly grim crime scene. They seemed elated in fact. "Agent Jeffries," Gunnar called to one of his men. A slim, rough, Midwestern looking man came up to us obediently. He reminded me of Chuck Norris. An American good ol' boy.

"Yes, sir?" His voice was light but gravelly, with a faint Texas twang.

"Take over for me. I'm going back to HQ to look into some other leads on this sick bitch."

"Yes, sir. You found out it was a woman?" Jeffries asked.

"Yep." I answered for Gunnar.

Jeffries shot me an appraising glance. "You must be Nate-," He corrected himself. "*Master* Temple." It wasn't mocking, merely obliging a deluded person their wishes. I nodded, maintaining eye contact with my face still grim from the crime scene. He studied me harder. "How are *you* possibly going to help us catch this… bitch? Pay her off?"

I smiled back darkly. "Kill her, maybe. But definitely not catch."

He looked surprised, turning from me to Gunnar. "Pardon?"

Gunnar maintained his poker face, but I knew he was just as surprised, so I elaborated. "I assume that your men have an idea what we are dealing with? The *real* story, not the politically correct report? And also about my… specialty?"

Gunnar nodded. "They saw the video with the tail, and were briefed last night. They don't know about your specialty though." Gunnar grinned. "But word circulated pretty fast about how my *boyfriend* bought me a new car." Jeffries smiled.

I chuckled. "Okay. Catching her will be impossible. She breeds fear into all of those near her. This crime scene is more than twelve hours old, and when I touched the body I simply collapsed, overwhelmed with panic. I'm sure I don't have to tell you this, but make sure you have gloves in there, or else things could be difficult."

"Why in the hell did you touch the body? You could have ruined crucial evidence!" Jeffries said, furious.

I waved a hand dismissively. "The dragon that attacked here was silver. Not grey as in color, but silver, as in the precious metal."

"Okay. How does a civilian possibly expect to help us catch a..." he paused, as if not believing he was about to say it out loud. "Silver dragon?" I couldn't blame him. I mean, dragons, come on!

I waggled my fingers dramatically. "Remember, kill not catch. It's my forte." Doubt was still apparent on his face, so I glanced around me, judging the proximity of the other policemen. "You trust him for a little show and tell, Gunnar?"

Gunnar smiled with amusement. "Light petting only."

I could have called a ball of fire. I could have summoned a miniature whirlwind. I could have made him freezing cold. I could have done so many things, but not many knew my secret, and with the cops, that was a cover I hoped to maintain as long as possible. I merely trapped him in icy wires that none around us could see. I extended my hand, offering for him to shake it. Jeffries couldn't move, his eyes wide. "My, my, such a lack of courtesy among men these days. Really, Agent Jeffries, it's considered the height of impropriety not to shake an offered hand."

The tough man's eyes widened further. To me, it looked like when you went out and bought a Christmas tree, and they wrap it up nice and tight in that plastic net so that you can fit the monstrosity on top of your car, but I was the only one who could see the fine threads of barbwire-like cords. His mouth opened and closed wordlessly as he struggled for a few more seconds before giving up. "You... you're a—" he glanced about cautiously to make sure we were alone. Point for him. "Wizard," he whispered finally.

I let him go, nodding as if he had commented on the weather.

He shivered again, but his composure wasn't broken. "So, the stories are all true. If you can do that without even trying, then I am not ashamed to say that the idea of this... dragon's magic overpowering you scares me shitless."

"I play for keeps, Agent Jeffries. Which means I am not going to risk a capture. I will just make sure this bitch dies quick, if I have any say about it."

Jeffries nodded, but glanced to his superior. "He's obviously got... secrets, but he's still a civilian. How are we going to describe the outcome if we end up... killing her? I don't think there are even rules about this kind of thing..."

"Statistically speaking, you can get away with murder," I said quietly. They both stared at me, slightly horrified. I shrugged.

Gunnar finally spoke, pointing a thumb at me. "He's one scary fuck, that's for sure. But you leave me to handle Agent Reinhardt. This is the whole point of our new team. We must step out of the lines... but only when we have to. I'd like to keep my conscience as clear as possible." He turned a decisive eye to me. "We are not assassins."

Agent Jeffries glanced from Gunnar back to me, studying me curiously. "How have you kept it a secret for so long? You are famous. Does anyone else know?"

"Several people, but if anyone finds out prematurely, let me just say that I will know exactly who leaked the information. And what I just did was only... *foreplay*."

He blinked. "Are you threatening a federal agent?"

I touched my chest innocently. "Who, me?" I made my glare heat his face. Literally. To him, it must have felt like an oven door opening from inches away. He staggered back with a surprised grunt. My smile never wavered.

"Okay, okay. I'll play nice. As long as you do too." I nodded. I didn't know what steps I could or could not take without ruining things, so I merely trusted Gunnar to keep me out of the frying pan when it came to the red tape.

"Just make sure I toe the line according to your procedures. I wouldn't want to mess anything up. You trust me to be scary, and I'll trust you to make sure I'm as... *bureaucratic* as possible." The word tasted foul on my tongue.

"Bureaucratic is not a word you are familiar with. Not at all."

I motioned for them to follow me over to Gunnar's car. Jeffries spoke up once we were out of earshot of the other cops. "Why don't you tell me what your attacker looked like so we can put out a description to the local law enforcement?" Wise advice, but totally impossible for me to reveal since we had killed her. We had to keep that secret or face jail time, or at least a trial, and I didn't want to air out my dirty laundry to these pristine officers. I also didn't want to go to jail, or see Peter go to jail for simply protecting Gunnar.

With magic.

Fuck. This was getting complicated. Withholding information while trying to pass out crumbs to help them. I wanted to help, but I was just out of my depth. I was not a team player. At least not as big of a team player as you had to be to be a part of the varying police branches. But I had to say something.

"We won't be seeing her any time soon. She jumped a boat out of town after our encounter and said that her sisters would finish off what she had started." There, all true statements, sandwiched between a fuck-load of emptiness.

Agent Jeffries watched me with cop eyes. I fought not to look guilty, opening up my power to calm me, slow my pulse, and ease my breathing. "Just tell him, Agent Jeffries. He won't shut up if you don't, and it would just be more embarrassing for him."

"Gee, thanks, Gunnar." I had no idea what was going on, so I waited.

Agent Jeffries' eyes were harder than before. Like brittle diamonds. "Sugar-coated lies. My favorite." He said. I blinked.

"Pardon?" I asked. "You would fucking *dare* to—"

Gunnar laid a hand on my arm, smiling. "Wait, Nate. Just hear him out."

I folded my arms across my chest, checking my power so that I wouldn't blow Agent Jeffries across the parking lot. "Okay, what's so funny, Gunnar?" I finally asked.

"Tell him the color of the car is black." I frowned, but complied.

"Lie." Agent Jeffries said softly.

"So his IQ is around a 24." I spat.

Gunnar sighed. "Say anything then, true or false, and hear what Jeffries has to say. Tell me if he's right or wrong."

Okay, I'd bite. I had a killer poker face. "I just inherited seven billion dollars."

Agent Jeffries didn't even hesitate. "Lie."

Gunnar looked startled at my statement, but arched an eyebrow in question.

"He's right. It was eight." They both stared back, dumbfounded. "Let me try again," I said, determined.

"Wait a minute. You inherited eight *billion* dollars last night?" Gunnar whispered violently. I just nodded, trying harder to trip up Agent Jeffries. He leaned back on the hood, concentrating.

"I've been in an orgy."

Agent Jeffries immediately grinned, impressed. "True." Gunnar choked on something, starting a violent coughing fit.

Damn. "I voted for Obama."

"Definitely a lie."

I dug deeper. "My parents were murdered."

Agent Jeffries stared back. "You aren't sure."

Was this a power or was he just damn good at reading people? I opened my mouth for one more, but Gunnar had regained his composure, and interrupted me. "He can sense lies." I started to protest, but Gunnar held up one big Viking hand. "I'll prove it." I grumbled, leaning back on the car too. Gunnar was silent for a time, but when he spoke, it was a doozy. "I am a werewolf," he said, smiling as if it were a game.

I jumped up. "Whoa, whoa, whoa. Sounds like Gunnar lost his *fucking* mind there for a second. Excuse us, Agent Jeffries, but I think we'll be leaving now."

Agent Jeffries slowly turned to Gunnar, face serious, not hearing me. Was Gunnar trying to lose his job? I didn't know anyone who had blatantly outed themselves like this before. I know some had been caught shifting on video, but this was a first for damn sure. "True." Agent Jeffries finally whispered.

I looked from one to the other, wondering if I had just become Gunnar's new source of income. He was fucked. No one would keep a known werewolf on the books. The *first* admitted werewolf in the government, at that. Gunnar took a step towards Agent Jeffries. "Trade for trade. You told me your secret, so I told you mine. Only fair." Gunnar said calmly. "And there is a group of crazy bitches hurting innocent people in our town. But now, more importantly, do you still trust me?" He set his shoulders, and used a hand to lift Agent Jeffries' jaw so they locked eyes. What would Gunnar do if things went wrong? I didn't even know what the FBI would do when they found out. Would they just fire him, or hunt him down like a criminal... like an animal?

"You don't even have to ask the question, Randulf. Of course, I won't tell. You've saved my ass more than a few times, and I would never forget that."

"That might be enough for Gunnar, but not enough for me," I said protectively.

Jeffries abruptly drew a knife and sliced his finger before I could even react. Then he did the impossible. I felt the hum of power instantly surround him in a small circle. He knelt with one knee up, touched his forehead with the bloody finger, and then licked it clean. "I swear that I will never betray you, Gunnar Randulf, or Nate Temple."

Shit. He knew more than just how to sense lies. He knew a bit of arcane ritualistic magic. The circle snapped shut like a rubber band, and I knew that he would never be able to break his oath.

Over time, people had begun to assume that the ritual Jeffries had just performed was merely a formality, and had decided to simply trust another man's word, his honor. But it had begun here, with this ritual, when one literally swore an oath that could not be broken. Gunnar arched a brow at me, surprised himself. I nodded back. "He's telling the truth. He literally cannot betray either of us now. No matter what." My voice sounded surprised, and I didn't even care to hide it.

Gunnar smiled down at him. "Thank you, Jeffries, but it really wasn't necessary."

Jeffries nodded. "It was for him." He pointed a thumb back at me as he stood, tucking the blade away into a pocket.

"Well, he does know how to make a fucking point. I can do nothing but trust him on this now, because there's no way for him to renege on his oath. Where did you learn that, Jeffries?"

"My parents," was all he said. Looking to Gunnar, he continued. "All this time I thought I was the only Freak around... It's good to know that I'm not alone. I can't wait to work with you two, even though he's a civ," Jeffries said with a grin at me.

"A civ who can kick some serious ass when necessary," I argued.

He nodded back. An agent was walking our way now, obviously intent on interrupting us. Jeffries spoke. "I need to get back to the scene."

Gunnar nodded back. "You do that. I'll be on my cell. Get back to me as soon as you hear something. We'll chat later." Jeffries turned to intercept the agent.

Gunnar looked at me and shrugged at the look on my face. I silently climbed into the car, saying nothing. He started the car and began to pull out

119

from the curb, heading deeper into the seedy warehouse district. We drove in silence for a time.

Then the skin between my shoulders began to itch as if I were being watched. I glanced out the window, but blew it off as simple weirdness from the conversation I had just experienced, and the brief attack by the gargoyles. Gunnar finally broke the silence. "Did you really inherit that much money?"

I turned to him, thinking. "What time is it?" I asked.

He glanced at the dash and told me. "It's increased by about half a million by now, then." Gunnar stared at me, eyes lifted in confusion. "Interest," I added as I looked back out the window. Gunnar was silent for a time.

"Nate?" I heard him ask.

"Yeah?"

He was silent for a few seconds. "You said there were nicer cars than this..."

I rounded on him, blinking in disbelief. "Are you really about to *bitch* about not getting a *nicer* car?" I bellowed. We were about a mile away from the scene in a deserted stretch of vacated warehouses, probably converted to crack houses now.

He shook his head and opened his mouth to answer, but the back of the car suddenly shuddered, and the whole back windshield blew into the car, raining pebbles of glass over both of us as the car began to skid, the sound of screeching tires mingling with the tinkling of broken glass. When Gunnar and I had stopped screaming and he had regained control of the car, I turned back to see what had hit us. Gunnar merely gunned it, screaming, "No fucking *way!*"

A silver dragon was chasing us down the street, long neck stretching her beautiful chrome head no further than a yard away as she kept up with us going sixty miles an hour. Her silver scales slid and writhed against each other like a computer technicians wet dream. "Hello, boys... I think you might know where to find a book I was hoping to peruse." She purred, not even out of breath.

"Deceptacon!" I yelled, frantically saying the first thing that came to mind.

She let out an erotically sensual peal of laughter that tightened my pants with the thrill of dark sex. Fantasy dark sex. The kind that only belongs in the back of the mind where one knows they will never actually act upon it. The thrill and danger of pleasurable pain.

I was too startled to break her wave of fear and power. She had caught me off guard, and now I felt like I was drowning in that dark pleasure-pain. Nothing I could do but ride it. Gunnar and I had already lost. She was just too powerful. Then Gunnar snapped me out of it with another strong Viking slap to the face. His eyes were wide as I came back to myself. "Do something, Nate!" Gunnar bellowed, panicked afresh at my choice of words combined with the mountain of werewolf kryptonite on our bumper.

I was our only hope, as long as Gunnar could keep us away from her claws and jaws, I was free to battle this legend in the seedy warehouse district in which we were racing.

CHAPTER 21

TWO TIMES IN TWO HOURS WAS SIMPLY NOT acceptable. I had had enough near-death experiences in my life to know that I didn't particularly enjoy them. Now, having *overcome* all those past scenarios was definitely preferable, but it was getting ridiculous how many times I found myself in them. And the baddies always got bigger, stronger, and meaner while I seemed to remain the same.

Totally unfair.

Her power swamped me like a lead blanket, making me shake and break out into a cold sweat as I struggled to grasp hold of my own power that was screaming defiantly deep inside my core. She was simply too strong to battle solely within the mind. I idly wondered how old she was, and how many decades or centuries she had to perfect her talents. *How many centuries I have been alone*, her thoughts invaded my own, meshing together seamlessly. *It's helpless. Just give in. I can take away all the pain in the world, so that you only have to live with me. No more responsibilities, no more fear of death, no more stress. I will protect you. Why would you want to fight someone who only wanted to help you?* Another slap from Gunnar snapped me out of it, almost unhinging my jaw.

I reacted instantly, using my fear and the pain to do something, anything that would help get us out of here. I whipped up a wall of razor-thin air, hoping to slice her ankles off, or at least trip her up so that maybe she ran into a building. I cast it out the rear windshield like a trip wire, about a foot off the ground. It caught her immediately, and she let out a very human shriek of pain and rage, momentarily shattering her onslaught of mind magic.

My magic cut into her huge reptilian feet, tripping her up expertly, but after her first roll over a random parked car – squashing it beyond oblivion – her wings caught air and she gracefully regained control. She landed back on her feet easily and resumed her pursuit; yards further back from us, but still too close for comfort. At least she had a slight limp. She let out a roar that shattered windows in the blur of warehouses. Car alarms began squawking within a full block. We had to be going eighty miles an hour, but she was still keeping pace. I had to think of something. I extended my shield of power over both Gunnar and I, hoping to protect us from her magic before it caught hold.

Using magic to protect myself like I had with the stone griffins wouldn't keep Gunnar safe, and I was reasonably sure it wouldn't do much to impede her anyway, so I had to think outside the box.

I spotted a street sign racing towards us and instantly knew what to do. Our only choice if I could pull it off. "Gunnar! Get onto the Eads Bridge!"

He turned to me, eyes wide. "No. There are too many innocent drivers up there! Whatever you're going to do, do it here. It can't be worth the risk to go up there!"

I wanted to scream as she let out another roar behind us, making Gunnar swerve a little, startled. I grabbed the wheel and turned us onto the on ramp with a screech of tires, before Gunnar could argue. "It's our only chance! Stay near the rail and I'll take her out!"

Gunnar was forced to regain control of the car, but he spit out a curse in my direction. "How many will die with your plan, Nate?"

"I hope none, I really do, but it's our only chance. She's too strong."

My phone rang, making me jump in surprise. Not recognizing the number, I hit the speakerphone.

"Really? A fucking *phone* call? *Now*?" Gunnar yelled between offensive driving.

I ignored him, speaking urgently. "Temple. Kinda busy. Who is this?" I glanced back behind us, hoping the dragon took the bait. She let out a roar of pleasure at us directing the chase to a place with so much potential for collateral damage – so much more fear to feed on from innocent drivers – but I was sure I caught the faintest hesitation in her features, just like Raven in the bookstore. Then it was gone and she was chasing us anew.

The voice of the car chose that moment to go haywire from the impact of her first attack against the rear end of the vehicle – frightening us all over again. "*Door ajar, door aja-ajaarr.*" Then the voice garbled, and a fizzle erupted somewhere behind the dash. Car horns blared around us as Gunnar swerved back and forth, zipping nimbly between them.

The voice on the phone was bubbly. "Wow. Okay, you *do* sound busy.

123

Are you in a parade or something? I didn't know anything was happening today."

"Facts! Speak faster or I'll hang up!" I screamed against the wind tearing through the open windows.

As we careened through traffic, I was glad to see that we were out of the dragon's reach. Then she swiped a car into the median with a powerful backhand and I cringed. The driver stared at the dragon, frozen in utter disbelief. I noticed he was alone in the car, and was grateful. No kids in the backseat to worry about.

I take solace wherever I can.

The car thankfully skidded without flipping airborne, but that seemed to only infuriate the dragon more. "Right, right. Sorry." The voice on the phone apologized.

Our car's voice momentarily interrupted her. "*Low fyool. Locate the nearest fyooling station at your earliest conveenience.*" The sexy British female voice had begun to transform into a demonically possessed version of the childhood *Speak and Spell* toy. "*Now entereeng Soulard. Your destination on riiiight—*" It grew worse by the second.

The phone spoke again, sensing the press of limited time. "Oh, I didn't realize you had *company*. I work for you. I'm Abby. Miss Belmont informed me to tell you that when we were inputting your personal information into the system, a private video feed popped up into a queue for you to watch. One of the security cameras, as far as we can tell. The system will not allow us to access it. If you could swing by here and check it out, that would be fantastic. I think it's from the room of..." her voice grew soft. "The attack."

I blinked, momentarily forgetting the chasing dragon behind us. "The attack on my parents?" I asked, punctuated by another dragon roar in the distance.

"Yes, Master Temple. When shall I tell her you will be here?"

"Um. In an hour or two, hopefully."

Gunnar interrupted, snatching my phone. "Right. Thanks. Bye." He tossed it back to me, glaring. "First, dragon. Then company. People are going to die if we don't stop her. Do something. Soonest." I nodded, shaking my head free of the sudden emotions as I numbly pocketed the phone. A security feed from the room of my parents' deaths. That might hold one of those elusive clue-thingies. Another roar startled me back to the present.

Glancing back, I saw the dragon inhale sharply, so I quickly prepared another volley of power, using my sudden emotion for energy. I had seen the red dragon do a similar thing when she had been about to let loose her napalm fire on the roof. I used the same tactic, hoping they hadn't shared war stories. I let fire roil inside me, drawing heat from anywhere and everywhere, willing it into existence until I could see it clearly in my mind. I saw cars on the opposite side of the highway slowing down as I drew the heat from their engines, even seizing some of them to an abrupt halt, much to their sudden panic.

Or maybe they had just stopped to stare at the freaking dragon tearing after us.

I shook my head, building the fire hotter and hotter, our own car slowing down. "Nate! What are you doing? We're slowing down!"

"Shut up, Gunnar!" I screamed as the power threatened to burn my blood to ashes. I had never called this much fire before, and I knew it was at my limit, or possibly even beyond it. When the pain began to make stars in my eyes, I let it loose like a rocket launcher. It slammed into her snout just as she began to spit silver spears into another car. The fire halted most of the silver, slamming it back down her throat, causing her to slam down to the ground on all fours, sliding across the concrete highway, her talons clawing into the asphalt like a hot knife through butter. Our car abruptly tore forward, compensating for the floored gas pedal as I stopped pulling the heat from the engine. Gunnar swerved around another car, honking and screaming at them to get out of the way.

They obliged in sheer panic.

I turned back to see the dragon retching a car-sized lump of steaming silver onto the road like a cat with one of those vile hair balls they seem to be able to produce at the worst possible moments. She shook her head once and then launched into the sky. A state patrol car slammed into the pile of silver before the cop could dodge it, no doubt racing after us for help, and the car instantly flipped up into the air, somersaulting wildly. I imagined the screams from inside.

Was he a family man? Was he close to retiring, or was he maybe a new rookie on the force, hoping to change the world? I sensed the dragon's pulse of power, and realized she was toying with me again. I steeled my resolve, blocking out the cries in my own head as the cop died. There was no question. If he hadn't died from the first impact, the height and speed of the second impact with the road would surely finish him off. He was already dead. I swallowed the lump of guilt, blocking the dragon's power of fear from my mind.

But before the cop car could strike the ground, the dragon swooped down and caught the wreckage in a snatch of talons, sharply banking away to continue her pursuit beside us over the churning river on the other side of the bridge's rails. I stared into the driver's side, hoping to see the cop alive, knowing the odds were against him. If I did what I was about to do, he was going to die anyway. One life to protect so many others. It was a sacrifice that made a small part of me die inside, but I had no other choice. Gunnar roared in fury next to me, partially shifting form so that huge, beefy, wolf arms gripped the steering wheel as he spotted the cop car dangling over the Mississippi River Levee.

"Nate! Do something!" I nodded, still searching, hoping the cop was still alive. Then an elbow punched through the window, and... it was a fucking girl! Not a mature, battle-hardened woman of the force, but a young, and small, beautiful female cop. She was suddenly leaning out the shattered glass, firing at the dragon's underbelly without the slightest fear. First Spiderman, and now Wonder Woman.

The dragon let out a shriek of furious pain, and then looked into my eyes as we sped alongside her. She smiled broadly at me, and then dropped the car into the icy river, smiling as she ate up the surprise and fear for the cop's life tearing through my eyes. The cop would die in the frigid water of the Mississippi River because I hadn't acted sooner.

Not today.

I yelled incoherently as I half leaned out of the open passenger window, ignoring the broken bits of glass. I heard the cop scream as she fell several stories down into the dark water. Pedestrians on the walkway were running in panic, screaming in disbelief. The city was about to discover that their beloved Temple Heir was a wizard.

And I didn't give one.

Flying.

Fuck.

I called the weather to my command like a cloak, drawing every molecule of water from every cloud within a mile, and then I reached even further. I

126

had never been that great with weather, but it was all I could think to do. She was made of metal, and I was hoping that she wouldn't have passed swimming lessons as a young dragonling.

The weather responded instantly, water slamming into the vacuum I had created in the dragon's chest. Every crack in her body, every millimeter of space between scales, was suddenly filled with water, weighing her down dramatically. Then I did the opposite of what I had done a few minutes ago. I simultaneously withdrew all heat from her body, and cast the frigid temperature from the river below into those same water molecules, freezing them instantly. She faltered as ice abruptly creaked in her every joint, preventing her wings from working properly, and then she fell.

Fast.

"Temple!" Her bellow of rage was impressive, but the splash of her massive body hitting the river was even better. Sweet vengeance, thy name is Temple. Water splashed up so high that we could even see it from above the bridge. Gunnar slammed on the brakes, and we bolted out of the car – now sitting sideways on the highway – kicking down one of the maintenance fence doors that separated the pedestrians from the roadway. We leaned over the river and watched the bubbles until they stopped, and all that was left was the cool waves of the Mississippi welcoming the dragon to her new permanent residence at the bottom of the river.

Gunnar pointed urgently off behind us, and I saw the cop floundering weakly in the water a hundred yards back. I thought she would have been further away, and deader. Relief flooded over me as I saw a nearby boat pull up to her and toss her a preserver. She was alive, and the dragon was dead. I collapsed to my knees, crying out in relief, unable to hold myself up. I heard the screech of tires, and then metal slamming into metal where our car was parked. A beautiful ball of fire blossomed up over the Aston Martin. Then the world went black as I passed out from exhaustion.

CHAPTER 22

I WOKE IN THE BACK OF AN AMBULANCE, WRAPPED IN cheap blankets, near the riverfront. I was freezing cold. Draining oneself with as much magic as I had thrown about today had killed wizards before, but somehow, I had survived. My thoughts were sluggish, but I saw Gunnar talking to another police officer who was also wrapped in blankets, skin visibly steaming underneath, and it all came back in a blink.

I stumbled out of my ride and attempted to walk over to the two of them. Cop cars were everywhere, red and blue lights strobing around us. I had been out for a while, judging by the height of the sun. Then another thought hit me and I tripped, barely catching myself. Temple Industries was awaiting me, and so was the Minotaur. A cop instinctively reached out to assist me but then halted, uncertainty and fear obvious on his face. I scowled at him and he frowned sheepishly.

Gunnar and the other officer had noticed my approach and were striding towards me. Gunnar hissed at the officer who had shied from touching me. "How dare you? He almost died saving Officer Marlin and countless others from a murdering sociopath, and you can't even reach out a hand to keep him from falling down on his face? Is that the kind of thanks St. Louis has to offer?" His chest was heaving, and I almost fell down again as his rage suddenly coursed through me like electricity. My skin was buzzing, and my equilibrium wavered as my skin suddenly felt on fire.

"No, sir. It's just that Captain Kosage said... and the stories about what he did... I was scared to touch him. They say he called down the power of a god to battle a silver demon. I'm not a religious man, but others ran to the nearest church as soon as they could. They're calling him Archangel, or one of the Four Horsemen. He battled a devil in the middle of a high-speed car chase... and won." He looked at me. "I'm sorry, Master Temple, it's just that... whatever you did scares me. I don't want to risk my family by being too close to you. Or my job, when Kosage hears about all this."

The other officer, Officer Marlin, I presumed, stepped up next to me and wrapped a delicate arm under my shoulder in thanks, supporting my sudden dizziness. She was short, maybe 5'5, and stunning. Her straight, dark, almost black hair would have ended just below her breasts if it hadn't been tied back. Her thin face was perfect for it, and her bright green eyes were fiery with a hidden power that I could only guess at, and were big enough to drown in. "Now that I'm here, what are your other two wishes?" I mumbled, feeling slightly giddy from the sudden warmth and power that had filled me upon seeing Gunnar.

She laughed delightedly and my heart melted. Girl's laughter just flat did it for me. Her teeth glowed white as she grinned, "I like him." Her fingers squeezed my shoulder affectionately, and it was as if the pressure broke something inside me, and then my body coursed with even more energy and power, refreshing me like a long night of sleep followed by a healthy breakfast. Her faith wrapped around me like a giant oak tree trunk for support. I felt stronger, more awake. What the fuck? How was I sensing others emotions, and how was it fueling me? The petite officer spoke again, the blanket making her look frail and delicate, but I sensed there was more to her. "Well, I, for one, am grateful for his help. Never hurts to be friends with an archangel. You should be ashamed of yourself, officer."

The man's shoulders shrugged in defeat, but he turned and began walking closer to a small crowd of police officers. Then I felt my perception of the world abruptly jolt, like I had experienced only a few times before, and I grew instantly nervous. *Not again...* A man suddenly darted out of nowhere with a purse tucked under his arm, and slammed straight into the departing officer. He fell, dropped the purse, and a slew of jewelry spilled out across the grass. The stunned cop reacted quickly, cuffing him, and then a man and woman burst onto the scene. "He stole my purse! Thank god you caught him!" She latched onto her boyfriend in relief. Gunnar and I stared at each other in disbelief as the cop carted the man off to a nearby squad car, the couple in tow behind them.

"Odds are never that good. He's either the stupidest criminal in the world, or god is looking down on us." Gunnar said softly. I nodded, but suddenly felt very aware of the power high I was experiencing. The last time I had felt a shift like this some very strange things had happened around me. Odds had run wild. Things that would have never happened naturally suddenly did.

Things like this. Was it happening again? Had I reached a new power plateau, distorting chance all around me? I shrugged, not speaking my fear.

Instead, I glanced down at Officer Marlin beside me, changing the topic. "I'm glad I could help, but I seem to remember that boat saving you, not some archangel. I am no hero. I did what anyone else would have done, and a better man would have done it sooner without risking your life."

She was tiny – and dare I say cute – as she shot me a reproachful grin. When Gunnar stepped closer, the odd energy sensation tripled – filling me up like an overflowing teacup. I shook my head, studying my body for clues to this new power. I knew my body better than most people know their own, having studied the relationship between it and my magic over the years, but I came up with no alternative theories. It was happening again. I had reached a new plateau, and it was feeding off those magical beings around me – namely Gunnar and Officer Marlin – as it matured. But that meant she was...

"Whether I think you are an archangel or not is my own business, not yours. I know what I saw. You were glowing with... power?" She fumbled at a choice for words. "And you saved all of us. There's no telling what that..." she glanced at Gunnar for the correct word. Gunnar gave it, face serious. "*Dragon* would have done if you hadn't slain her." She let out a light laugh, like only cute little girls could manage, and shook her head. "If you aren't a dragon-slaying hero, then you're a Savior Archangel. Pick your poison, but you're one of the two. I would be honored to join you and Agent Randulf here in your next dragon slaying. But please, call me Tory."

I shook my head immediately. "You almost died today. We can't risk anyone else. Especially Regul—" I cut myself off, feeling like I had almost dropped a racial slur.

"It's okay, say it. Regular. But I think you'd be surprised..." She stepped back from me for a moment and reached out to Gunnar. My werewolf friend sighed and withdrew a bent piece of metal from behind his back, handing it to Tory. The petite bombshell took it, frowned for a moment, and then placed one of her dainty fists on either end of a long, straight segment of the bar. She lifted her eyes to mine, watching me with a grin, and began to bend the metal perfectly in half, not an ounce of strain crossing her face. It bent like a twisty tie at the grocery store. My eyes widened in surprise and her smile stretched wider. "I am no *Regular*, Master Temple."

I remembered her shattering her patrol car window with one blow of her

130

elbow, and realized that in most cases it wouldn't have been possible for even another man. Maybe adrenaline would help, but most would need a cushion to protect their elbow joint from permanent damage, or would have to take several attempts to shatter it so efficiently. She had made it look simple, easy. And she also showed no signs of an injured elbow.

She tossed the bent metal bar into the nearby grass. No one but us had seen it, as they all seemed preoccupied with the random thief they had just caught. "Agent Randulf offered me a job with his new team, although he didn't tell me what the team was called..." She glanced curiously at Gunnar, but the werewolf's face remained stoic. "He just told me what the goals of his team are, and what kind of criminals we'd be going up against. He said that he needed your approval before he allowed me to join the pack."

She waited for me to speak. Even energized, I was still a little slow. "Pack?" I asked with a frown.

"That's what he called it. A Band of Brothers kinda' thing. Or sisters, in my case. Is it like the He-Man Woman Hater's Club? Because I don't want to crash your groove or anything." She grinned, making my testosterone respond. It was definitely a bedroom grin: dark, dirty, and full of improper yet enlightening insinuations. Or maybe I was still thinking of Indie from this morning. "Is there a reason that he needs your permission for my help? Are you in charge?" she asked politely, face neutral of any disrespect.

I shook my head, and began to speak, but Gunnar answered. "I trust Nate... Master Temple with my life, and now you've seen why. We all have secrets, as I showed you mine a few seconds ago, but he is one of the scariest men I have ever met, and if he says you aren't up for recruitment, then I'm sorry to say that I would have to agree. This is a hobby of his, and he's survived encounters that are even less believable than what you experienced today. *Many* encounters like this, in fact. And the dangers will only escalate, with probably even scarier bad guys. He has veto power on my recruits."

I watched Gunnar, surprised that he had told her his secret. Was it National *Come out of the Closet Day* for werewolves? "I didn't even want to be in your... pack, and now I have veto power? That is... so cool," I added sarcastically. Gunnar and Tory laughed. "I have to be honest, Tory. This harem of dragons is nothing to scoff at. Today was a close call, but she has sisters, and I have no idea how powerful they are. We can hope that the silver one was the strongest, but I doubt it. It's kind of like the Billy Goats Gruff. The next one is always bigger than the one before. I had thought dragons were extinct until a few days ago, when we were attacked at my bookstore." Tory waited respectfully for my answer. Damn. I was hoping I could scare her off. "Do you have kids, a family?" She shook her head. "Boyfriend?" Again, she shook her head. "Manfriend?"

She laughed at that, the sound tickling the sensitive parts of my neck like a kiss. "I know my way around a bedroom," she spoke lasciviously, "but have yet to find a lover who could accommodate my... lifestyle." Before today it had just been me helping Gunnar, but now we had two new pups to take care of, and I didn't know if either were strong enough to benefit our cause or if I was simply setting them up to die a horrible death like pawns in a game of chess.

"One thing that I think is essential is absolute honesty on the team. Everyone needs to know the other's strengths and weaknesses in order to play to those strengths in a life or death situation. You've seen what I can do, well, some of it. I'm a wizard. I can harness, control, and manipulate energy to my will, but I'm no archangel. I use magic like others use guns. It's just a part of me. I was born into it. But it can be dangerous to be around me." I waited for her to run screaming, but if anything, she looked more content than before, relieved, as if finding a new home. Damn it, damn it, damn it.

"What else can you do, Tory? Is bending metal the extent of your power? Try and explain whatever you can. We need to know in order to see if it will help us."

Gunnar nodded approval, waiting for Tory to speak. "My whole life I've been strong. I never realized how much stronger until I was involved in a fatal car accident on a date." Her voice grew distant. "My date was trapped under the car on an old country road, dying of severe blood loss due to several deadly wounds. I was scratched up, but fine. Kind of like now. I climbed out of the car, looked down at him, and knew that he was going to die. It shouldn't have been possible, but I knew if I didn't help, he would die. I grabbed the car, and lifted it off his legs. It wasn't adrenaline. I know that now, because adrenaline can make me... scary strong. I managed to drag him out from underneath the car, and then the cops and medics arrived. A Good Samaritan must have called them. My date was too delirious from blood loss to remember what happened accurately, so no one ever knew about it. I decided to become a cop the next week."

132

She stared inward at her own memories, and I struggled not to drop my jaw. One handed car curl? Jesus. That might help out in a pinch. Tory's eyes refocused. "I wanted to use that strength to help people, and I've been careful about stepping too much out of bounds for others to notice, but anything to do with my muscles is simply superior to others. Running, lifting weights, punching bags. You name it. It's almost as if I have extra fuel inside me waiting to ignite my muscles... like Nitrous in a car. It's just there."

Gunnar was quiet for a spell, as if deciding if this petite cop was worthy of the club. I nodded at him to proceed. "I vote for her, Gunnar." I said, confidently. "We can't have a gang without the token cool girl. We need some estrogen on the team." I added with a smile. "Even if she can arm wrestle better than us."

"Everything is better with a girl around." She added with a mysterious smirk.

I frowned at that. "This isn't like your usual beat as a police officer. This will be..." I struggled for a word, finally saying the first thing that came to mind. "Black Ops."

Tory and Gunnar both stared at me as if I had spouted a prophecy. "Well, damn. That's exactly what it is, isn't it?" Gunnar said in surprise, nodding. "I'm not saying that it can be our official title or anything. We aren't spooks, but it does have to be hush-hush from the traditional police force, so that's a pretty appropriate name."

Tory spoke conspiratorially. "Let's go hunt some dragons then, shall we?"

I smiled back. "Soon. I have to go beat up the Minotaur first, and then we can go hunt dragons. Well, after I swing by Temple Industries."

Her eyes widened in disbelief for a moment, but Gunnar spoke up. "He's being literal. We'll get in touch with you after the fight, and the meeting at his company, and then we'll figure out a plan." Tory simply shook her head, mouthing *Minotaur* to herself.

Thanks to the odd addition of their energy to mine, I was somehow refreshed, and I didn't even care how at the moment. Wizards needed nutrition to use their power: water, food, sleep, and vitamins. If I ever forgot to eat, or drink enough liquids, I found myself lethargic, and utterly useless in the magical department. Which meant I probably needed to grab some food and water stat, but for some reason none of that had hindered me today. In fact, I felt stronger than ever. As long as this odd recharge gave me strength against the Minotaur, all was just dandy. Without it, I wouldn't have been up to battle him, or even light a cigarette with my magic. At that thought, I beamed. I placed a cancer stick between my lips and lit the tip with a thought. "Well, driver, where's the car?"

Gunnar's eyes flicked away instinctively. "Expensive car go *Boom*." He mimed an explosion with his hands. I groaned in frustration as I suddenly remembered the bloom of fire where our car had been before I had passed out. Gunnar spoke fast. "But everyone survived," he added. "Oh, and I managed to get your man purse before it was destroyed." He held it up, smiling.

"Satchel, asshole. Indiana Jones carried one, and he called it a satchel."

Tory laughed, tossing him a set of keys. "Officially, you can commandeer a car when necessary. I think the police owe it to you. Just try not to scratch it up. I already destroyed one, and that will come back to bite me in the ass, no matter what the story. The bottom line is always money, ya' know." She added with a grin.

"I bet you dress up nicely, Tory." I offered flirtatiously, hiding my anger at the totaled car.

She smiled carefully, studying me. "As a matter of fact, I do. Why?"

Gunnar rolled his eyes. "Come on! *Really*, Nate?"

I ignored him. "We might have need of a stunning piece of eye-candy to accompany us to a gala tonight. You have something to wear?"

Gunnar looked unhappy, but resigned to the fact that she was now part of the group. "I don't know if I have anything nice enough for a VIP event." I peeled off a thick stack of hundreds from my wallet and handed them to her. "Get something. I don't know if you will be going, but I would like you to be prepared just in case." She backed away from the proffered cash with manicured hands up. "Stop. Just take it. It's for a good cause. I'm not trying to bribe you or anything. We will need you to look convincing if you are to accompany us. We need to reek of money or they will think we don't belong. *Master* Nate Temple can go anywhere," I said mocking my own title. "But not with shabbily-dressed peasants." Gunnar grumbled at that.

She finally agreed, making sure I knew just how uncomfortable she was about it all. But I recognized the smile she was hiding. Girls loved to shop, and they loved even more to show off the results of all that hard work. We exchanged numbers so that we could get a hold of her on short notice, and then we set off. Less than one day, and the beautiful Aston Martin had been destroyed. I wanted to beat Gunnar to a pulp, but that was risky in front of all the other frightened police officers. Oh, well. Nothing to be done for it.

Maybe I would get Gunnar a Hummer next. Or a tank.

CHAPTER 23

GUNNAR DROPPED ME OFF AT PLATO'S CAVE, WITH ME telling him I would call him when I was ready. I spotted Indie behind the counter, but no customers present. She was wiping off the counter with a focused gleam in her eyes. Spotting me, she straightened with a smile. "Evening, Cap'n."

"Indie," I breathed the word like a man dying of thirst. Her smile turned inappropriate, and her cheeks reddened.

"Well, you sure know how to pronounce a name. I don't think anyone has *ever* said my name like *that* before." She eyed me up and down, eyes tightening at the dust and debris all over my clothes. She plucked out a few pieces of windshield glass from my hair, her thumb brushing my temple in the process. "You're a mess, Nate..." she whispered softly, her eyes concerned.

"Yeah, and I have to head back out. The *company* requests my presence." I made the word *company* sound like a curse.

"Not like this, you can't. Come on." She grabbed my hand, and began weaving through the glass dividers, guiding me upstairs to my loft. One of my other employees watched us curiously. Indie noticed also. "Nate's run into a bit of trouble. I'm going to doctor him up a bit before he leaves again. Can you watch over things for a bit, Alex?"

Alex, a blonde-haired Greek med student nodded with a grin. "Doctor him up, eh? Sounds... *nice*. Can I watch?" His grin grew wider.

Indie glared. "Careful, Alex. Look at him, and tell me he doesn't need it." Alex looked me up and down for the first time.

"Shit, Cap'n. You all right? I'm the med student, maybe I should help you."

He took a step towards us. I held up a hand, grateful for his help, but knowing that I needed to say some things to Indie that no other ears were privy to. "Thanks, Alex, but it looks worse than it is. She'll be fine. Her *doctoring* probably means something more like 'Chew Nate up and down for his poor safety choices this afternoon.' My pride would appreciate it if no other males were present to witness my downfall. I've got a reputation to uphold."

He grinned again, nodding knowingly. "Ah, in that case, good luck. She's got a tongue like a razor. I'll watch over the ship for you. We managed to get it all cleaned up after the break-in. Whaddya' think?" He spread his arms at the shop proudly.

"It looks great. Thanks for taking care of everything today. And also, the premiere for Gods of Chaos IV last night. I'm glad you all made it out of here before the burglars peeked their noses in." He nodded agreement. "Good turn out?"

He laughed, shrugging. "Didn't take much convincing, I mean, Gods of Chaos IV? Seriously? Divorces have resulted from keeping a guy away from that franchise. It was fantastic. They really upped the visuals, and—" He realized he was babbling, and stopped. "It was great. I'll update you at the meeting next week. Go get doctored up. We can't have our fearless leader looking like a stray now, can we?" With that he turned away.

Indie mouthed *Thank you,* before leading me up the stairs. I spoke my thoughts before thinking. "I don't think you have a tongue like a razor, but I have wondered lately..." My implication was instinctual, still slightly dizzy from my new power high.

She stumbled up a step, turning a red face at me. "I've made my intentions clear, Nate. If we were at Chateau Falco right now, I might just have resorted to the kind of *doctoring* every man wants from a woman. I can be such a *good* nurse."

It was my turn to stumble. She laughed lightly, her hand squeezing mine as she led me into my loft. She closed the door behind us, and began to reach for the blinds to the windows overlooking the store. Instead, I snapped a finger, and they instantly closed. She turned to me, eyes moving slowly, dreamlike. "Makes a girl wonder what else a wizard can do."

I grinned back. "You have no idea..."

"Oh, but you are wrong. I have many *ideas*, just no *facts*. Yet..." She winked, gliding towards the bathroom in that seductive sway that only girls can do – the grace of movement that could somehow make men physically hungry. She strode into my bathroom, and I heard the water turn on. My employees had even cleaned up my loft so that it was almost unnoticeable that anyone had broken into it last night. A few minutes later, she leaned out the door, smiling. "Here, boy." She patted her thigh as if calling a dog. I grinned, shaking my head, but complied. I did need a shower.

I entered the room, the mirror already fogged over. Candles were lit, and they filled the room with a warm glow, made more appealing by the steam from the shower. I didn't see her because it was a big bathroom, and the change in lighting slowed me down. The door closed behind me, and I felt Indie's fingers touch my coat. "Clothes off." She said softly from behind me.

"Indie…" I began, feeling worse for what I needed to say next.

Her fingers touched my lips, tasting sweet like strawberries. Must be her lotion. "Trust me, Nate. You need help to get all the shards out of your hair." Her breath was like a breeze of fresh mint, not gum or candy, but the herb. Spicy. I complied, tugging off my coat and shirt, and tossing them on the floor. She hissed when she saw the wound on my forearm from Raven's attack. I waved off her concern with a smile.

"It's okay. It's already healing." She frowned, and moved behind me. Her arms encircled my bare waist, and I immediately flinched in pain. "What's wrong? That shy?" She asked softly, curiously fingering the leather thong with the dragon tooth.

"I think you brushed a bruise." I said, surprised that I hadn't noticed it earlier. She leaned to my side and inhaled sharply. I looked down to see three large black bruises around my sides where the red dragon had dangled me over the courthouse. Then I saw more from the net launcher. "It's okay. I just didn't notice it until now," I mumbled.

She was breathing heavy against my back, her cheek pressed against my shoulder blades, and I realized that I was sore there too from one of the several fights I had been in. I peeled off the rest of my clothes until I was standing in only my *Superman* boxers. She circled me, hungrily looking me up and down. "Off," She said, motioning at my boxers before turning away with an amused grin. She sat down on the edge of the tub, and I realized that it wasn't a shower, but a eucalyptus-scented bubble bath that she had drawn for me.

She held out a hand, still looking away as I undressed. "I won't peek," she whispered. Dropping my boxers, I grasped her fingers, sensing the warmth under her skin, and just stood there for a minute. Her hand finally tugged at mine, so I obeyed, climbing into the steaming tub. I groaned. It was perfect. Not too hot, not too cold, and I had made sure to buy a tub that was big, wide, and comfortable enough to hold two… or more people. I plan ahead, folks…

Once safely settled underneath the foam, Indie turned back to me, snatching up a nearby pitcher. Her shirt stretched tight across her breasts. She leaned over me and scooped up some of the warm water, her hand dipping below the bubbles. The motion drew the shirt up a bit above the waist of her jeans, revealing a tanned expanse of hips and flat stomach, as well as a tiny ribbon of red panties.

She raised her hand, now coated in bubbles, and began pouring it through my hair, slowly, sensually, with her lips slightly open. She lathered some tea-tree shampoo in her palms, and then stretched her fingers through my hair like a cat pawing a soft blanket. Her manicured nails gently raked my scalp, making me shiver despite the heat as she plucked out several glass shards and tossed them into a trashcan. Huh. I had never experienced anything quite like this before.

"Keep your eyes closed, Nate." My mind went all sorts of adolescent on me, but I listened. The pitcher brushed my inner thigh, but she continued pouring the water over my head, washing out the shampoo without comment.

"Talk to me, Nate. I know you have a lot going on right now, but I'm here for you." She tugged on my shoulder, making me open my eyes, and sit upright. She had a washcloth in one hand, and began tenderly scrubbing my back as she waited. Macho man that I am, I managed to suppress grunts of pain when her cloth brushed any bruises.

I said the first thing that came to mind. "I got a call from the company. They discovered some video surveillance from the room where… my parents were found. It is password protected for me, so they haven't seen it yet."

"If it's password protected, do you even know the password?" she asked softly, her washcloth creeping lower down my spine.

"My parents gave me a list of potential passwords that I could use – depending on the severity of the need – in the event of a problem. I'll go through them, starting with the worst scenario first, I guess."

She murmured to herself as she leaned closer, one hand squeezing my shoulder for support as she reached even lower, cleaning the lowest of my back, and the top of another area entirely. I almost lost it when her breasts brushed my arm. "So strong," she whispered, massaging my shoulder unconsciously. Or consciously. Either way was fine with me. "You have scrapes on your back. Is that from this afternoon?" I shrugged.

"Or possibly yesterday. Before I picked you up I got in a bit of a tussle, but Mallory and Gunnar helped me out of it."

Her lips tightened, but she nodded. "What really happened today? I don't think your condition has to do with a business meeting at Temple Industries. Or the break in."

She climbed down from her perch on the edge of the tub, and knelt beside it to better reach my sides. I chose honesty. Somewhat. "I have to duel someone tonight. Someone strong, and I don't know if I can win. Then I have to confront another group of…" I hesitated, not wanting to scare her. "Bad guys who want something very badly. Enough that they might have even had something to do with my parents' deaths." Her hands paused at that, but quickly resumed their work, pressing me back against the tub so that she could move to my chest. Like an expert, she started high, saving the lower area for last.

I realized that as much as I cared about Indie, I didn't know if I could ever fully bring her into my life. It was just too dangerous. Even for me. But she was a Regular. She was defenseless. Well, she had martial arts and firearm training, and was damn good at both, but not enough training to jump into my weight class of bad guys. Dragons were out of her league. Hell, they were out of mine too. I had to decide if I was going to keep allowing her to assume we were an item, or if I was going to shatter that potential outcome. Her washcloth came to my abs and I tensed instinctively.

She smiled at my reaction. "Well, if you were asking my advice, I would say that it's pretty damn important that you win your… duel?" She made the word a question. I nodded. "I didn't know people still used that word anymore. But I guess your life is not of our time, is it?" I shook my head, glad she had steered the conversation in this direction, but also hesitant to squash my feelings for her. Maybe once this fight was over I would be able to calm down. Slow down my life. Work for the company, and stop taking on such dangerous clients. Her advice was right though. I *had* to win tonight. Everyone depended on me surviving, so I could deal with the dragons after.

"You're right, Indie. I *do* have to win tonight. I just don't know how. Some… strange things happened today. I fought some things that I had never dealt with before, and luckily, I came out on the right side. But I wasn't ready, and it could have cost others their lives. I can't be reckless when it comes to others. When it was just me, I didn't mind, but now..." I looked her in the eyes, placing my fingers atop hers. She stared back, eyes defiant. "My life is too dangerous, even for me. I couldn't bear having someone I care about hurt by something they could never defend themselves against. Like you. It's why I've always kept you at arm's-length. As good as you are, my enemies would make a game of hurting you, just so that they could see me hurt more, before they finished me off.

"I can't allow that. You've been my rock through some pretty rough parts, but I run two lives. I just can't seem to help it. I know it's dangerous, but it's a part of me that I can't give up. Those are the only moments where I truly feel alive. The other life is just a balance – safety and security for the dangerous half. Sometimes they overlap," She smirked at that, "But I must attempt to keep those I care about safe."

She waited, and then, as if I had said nothing, continued washing my abs, her delicate fingers massaging deep into my muscles through the soapy cloth. My blood was hot, seeming to melt the weariness from the muscles underneath her expert fingers.

She finished cleaning all the appropriate places. Her hand paused for a moment, and then she spoke softly. "I think you should handle the rest, Master Temple," she whispered with emphasis. She opened her eyes to stare at me, a feral, hungry gleam twinkling in the blue ice chips of her irises. "Alex might begin to wonder what kind of *doctoring* I am doing." I nodded dumbly.

She climbed to her feet, bending at the waist as she plucked up a stray piece of glass on the floor. Her face was close to mine, and her warm, soapy fingers caressed my temple. "I seem to remember you saying something about danger, but the steam must have made me forget. It must not have been that important. Teach me how to protect myself better, because I am not going anywhere unless you make me. Words are not enough to impede me from taking what I want, and what I know you *also* want. Danger is something I love just as much as I care for you, and it's why I am still around. Man up, Nate. I am."

She smiled to ease the sting of her words, then turned on the balls of her feet, and left me. I would hurt later. Any more cleaning, and I would have had to tip her. As it stood, I would remember this bath for a very long time. First pleasantly, and then with an ache that isn't entirely unpleasant in its own right. Guys are different from girls. Teasing can cause pain later if the teasing was good enough.

And yes, her teasing was glorious.

CHAPTER 24

I STEPPED OUT OF THE BATHROOM IN MY ROBE, NOT wanting to leave the safety of my home. It wasn't just that I was scared, because I was terrified. Battling the Minotaur was not on my bucket list. This could be a very short day for the last Temple heir. And it wasn't just because I didn't want to go to Temple Industries and see whatever digital feed they had told me about, even though I didn't want to see that either. I couldn't imagine what kind of clip I would see, but if it was password protected from even their most trusted employee, Ashley Belmont, then it was not going to be pleasant.

No, it was more than that.

I could still feel Indie's touch on my skin. The whole process of her bathing me clung to my soul. I felt stronger, more sure of myself, and I didn't want to leave that behind. I had experienced frequent dalliances with the fairer sex, but never before had I experienced such a strengthening as she had just shown me with a simple bath. I wanted to relish that feeling, and knew that the moment I stepped out the door, all hell would break loose, and the feeling would evaporate like the intensity of that first spray of cologne that leaves the skin somewhere during the middle of the night, when you want it on the most.

I sauntered over to my desk, the robe brushing my knees as I moved. I sat down before my desk, steepled my fingers, and glanced at my phone. I needed to make a call, a legally questionable call to an old college friend. To do that, I needed to use the scrambled sequence *she* had given me so that neither call could be traced to us. Paranoid?

Yes.

She was one of the most wanted cyber-criminals in the country. Possibly even the world. Her true identity was still a secret to the governmental agencies, but as I didn't know how close anyone was to catching her, or even if she was still being hunted, I couldn't use a social call to talk business with her. She would also be less than pleased if I did such a thing. I flipped open my iMac, and clicked the hidden icon on the desktop that she had sent me: an Encryption software that was years ahead of even most governmental branches. I typed in my cell number as prompted, and clicked *enter*.

The software began bouncing my cell phone number from one country to the next in five-second intervals, making triangulation impossible. I watched this all happen on a Google Maps image of the earth. Then it began switching my number at each location shift, until it revealed a temporary number for me to use, good for only the next seven-seconds. I hesitated. Did I want to do this? No.

But I had to.

Othello would probably relish the call. It had been a while since we spoke. I quickly typed in a number from memory. The system chimed, and then began tracing the number, the sequence of digits actually a code she had given me, and not necessarily a true phone number. But the system knew what to do with it. After a few seconds, her voice came to me through the speakers in Russian. I smiled at that, anxious to use the language after so long. That was, after all, where we had met in college. Taking Russian together. It was my fourth language, but I think it was her ninth. Ninth fluent language. Not counting any of the others she merely dabbled in.

"Привет, Фарос. Как дела?" I grinned. *Hello, Pharos. How are you*? Pharos was the nickname she had immediately given me upon discovering that I was a wizard. The Alexandrian Lighthouse, because she said that I shed light on shadows for a living, while she created shadows in the light so that she could work in concealment for a living.

"Очень хорошо, а ты?" I answered, already missing her, but knowing we wouldn't be able to talk personal matters over such a secure line. No breadcrumbs could be left behind for others to follow.

"Not bad. Very, very busy. As much as it pains me to shorten our conversation, keep it fewer than three minutes, if you please. What can I help such a dear flame with this morning?" I could practically see the smile on her face as she said it. I realized that wherever she was, it must be morning. Or she was simply throwing false trails in the event someone had hacked into our conversation. One never knew with Othello. We were still speaking Russian, and it took me a few seconds to phrase my questions correctly.

I heard her chuckle once I was finished. "Your Russian is growing stale,

Pharos. Perhaps you need to find a new Russian bedmate to fine tune that precious tongue of yours. You are beginning to sound rudimentary at best." That was one place we had frequented together, studying our... inflections between marathon bouts of, well, you know. She continued, conscious of our limited time frame. "Now, may I ask what Pharos finds so interesting in such an old book, and what it might have to do with the coming eclipse, or the... Minotaur?" She said the last word in English, but with a heavy accent. I felt proud, realizing that I wasn't the only one who had trouble translating that particular word.

"You may not." I answered, smiling.

"No fun. You will receive an encrypted email shortly with all the pertinent information. May I ask why the interest in this Tomas?" I watched the screen still bouncing our calls throughout the Google Maps image of the earth.

"Just a new face in the game I find myself playing. And I don't like new faces when my life is on the line."

Her voice grew clipped. "No one is allowed to hurt my Pharos. Do you want me to arrange an accident? I have new friends who specialize in such things." She spoke very softly. Was she asking if I wanted to place a hit on the dragon hunter?

I shook my head. "Not necessary. Yet. But thank you." I said quickly, very aware of the time ticking down. I asked her a few more questions, and she said she would include it all in the email within the hour. "You might need to expand your search to include myths. Anything might be helpful, even though it may not seem so to you. My... specialty finds useful tidbits where others would not."

"Oh, I don't doubt that. I know your... specialty very, very well." She purred with a thick Russian accent. My already testosterone-laden body responded, memories of tangled sheets filling my mind. She laughed at my silence. "No need to be prude, Pharos. We shall chat soon. I may have need of your help in the future, but next time our conversation should be closer. I very much wish to witness your *specialty* firsthand once again. Check your email soon." Then the line went dead, and the software shut down immediately. My computer rebooted of its own accord, running diagnostics that changed my IP address, and a slew of other safety precautions, basically erasing that my computer had even been running for the last twenty minutes.

Pretty neat.

I leaned back in my chair, sighing. I hadn't thought about our bedroom tussles in years, but she had been one of my best. That brought my thoughts back to Indie. Judging from my bath, I assumed she might even be able to top Othello's skills. Sensing something was out of place on my desk, I scanned its surface, and was shocked to see a satin red thong hanging off my lamp. I flinched, quickly snatching them away as if trying to hide them from any witnesses. I felt a piece of parchment folded around the tiny triangular crotch, and grinned. I unfolded it, reading the hastily scrawled lipstick note. The color matched the thong perfectly.

"I have read that Warriors were usually dressed by their lovers before battle, but I hope that what I did will suffice. I have also read that Heroes carry a trophy into duels for good luck. So, I left you a trinket... Touch for touch, Nate. Your turn next..."

A grin split my face as I stuffed the thong into my robe pocket. Good luck indeed, and also motivation to get my ass home as quickly and as intact as possible. Maybe I had found a dinner after all. No more dessert-dish women for me. If I survived the next few days.

I dialed a phone number and waited.

"Mallory," he answered.

"Heya', Mallory," I said. "I was hoping you could pass on a message for Dean." Mallory grunted affirmatively. I made my request, listening to him scribble the note down on a pad of paper. "Repeat the address, if you don't mind," I asked at the end.

"I don't need to repeat the address, Laddie. We both went there the other night. Ye should have it within the hour. I believe yer father already paid for this specific beauty, and I hear it's just come out of surgery, so it's sitting there now. The trick is how to list it..." he paused. "Dean has Power of Attorney will be able to complete the last request though, since he has Power of Attorney, and he wonna be none too pleased to leave Chateau Falco."

"It's important. I'll make it up to him."

Mallory grunted. "It will be done, Master Temple." Then he simply clicked off.

I nodded, wandering around the room for an appropriate change of clothes for the order of unusual events I would be facing tonight. I knew I would be back to meet with Peter this evening, so I could grab the last change of clothes then. If I was still in one piece after the Minotaur.

I realized I was thumbing the thong in my pocket and grinned to myself. They were still warm. Very warm.

CHAPTER 25

D RESSED, AND PREPARED FOR BATTLE IN MY *HUGO Boss* suit, I picked up my phone and dialed the number Officer Marlin had left me. She answered on the second ring. "Officer Marlin."

"Master Temple," I quipped, following her terse response. She chuckled.

"You mean, Archangel, I'm sure. One should hear the scuttlebutt around the water cooler after the event at the bridge."

"I think I'll stick with Master Temple. It's catchier."

"Still, Archangel has a nice ring to it."

I made a disgusted sound. "You ready to entertain a less than deserving gentleman caller at an expo this evening?"

"Your… gift made my choices much easier than I was accustomed to. I found something rather flashy. I hope it won't be too much."

"No one would dare complain that a flower blooms."

I heard a surprised, but definitely pleased, intake of breath. "Well, *that* wasn't what I was fishing for, but thank you. How many times have you used that line?"

"Alas, just this once, but if you vouch for its effect, I might keep it up my sleeve."

"It's definitely a keeper."

"Noted. I shall pick you up in an hour or so. Is that enough time?"

"More than enough. I've already been preparing, just in case."

"I'm sure you didn't have much difficulty. You were already more than halfway there when we met."

She sighed on the other end of the line. "From a near death experience to a ball. Young girls imagine stories about this sort of thing."

"But they imagine those stories with a gentleman or a prince. I am neither."

"Debatable," she answered with a demure chuckle.

"Gunnar has your address, so we'll see you then." I hung up.

My phone chirped back at me almost as soon as I set it down on my desk, Richard Wagner's *Ride of the Valkyries* blaring loudly. I let it play for a few seconds, enjoying the jingle, then answered. It was Gunnar. "Nate. There is a man outside my office adamantly waving car keys at me, declaring that I left them at a restaurant that I have never visited before. Do you have any idea why he's here?" I suppressed a grin.

"Not the foggiest." I paused. "Why don't you do one of your FBI things, like running the plates to see who the keys really belong to?"

"We're not supposed to use government resources for personal reasons," he answered, very textbook.

"Someone out there is looking for their keys, and someone happens to bring them to your attention, and you are not going to try to discover who they belong to?" I argued derisively. "And you wonder why bureaucracy doesn't work, why citizens are so concerned."

"Fine." I heard him fiddle with his keyboard, rapidly typing in commands. His voice was distant, speaking to someone else in the room. "License plate number." A shuffling of paper and then utter silence. "You're kidding me," he said in disbelief, voice full of disapproval to the agent in his office. I managed to tap the *mute* button on my phone before I burst out laughing into Gunnar's earpiece. A muffled argument took place as the agent vehemently defended his information. "Fine. *Fenrir* it is then." Gunnar snapped. I heard more keys tapping and then another deathly silence. It stretched on for a full minute. Then longer.

"Did you mean to hang up on me, Gunnar? You haven't spoken for a while," I said neutrally.

"Fuck you and the horse you rode in on," he growled.

"I take it you found the owner?" I asked.

I heard him dismiss the agent before speaking to me. "The report declares that a certain Gunnar Randulf and Nathin Temple have owned this 2012 Land Rover Defender Hard Top for the last three months. Funny, because I don't remember ever using my home as collateral for a..." I heard a few more clicks. "$80,000 SUV."

"I remember you having it, but you sent it off to Vilnar for customization, which added on close to $100,000, if I remember correctly."

"Hmmm… It's not as expensive as the Aston Martin," he said disappointedly.

"You destroyed the Aston Martin in less than 12 hours. This thing has bulletproof glass, and all sorts of other additions that would make it practically impossible to total. Unless you wanted to play chicken with an armored truck heading out of Fort Knox. That might be a different story. Then again, with as much as was spent on this guy, the armored truck might just die in shame."

"Nate, this is definitely crossing the line."

I argued back, ready. "It's registered to me with you as a co-owner. Should be fine. Just take the keys. Public transportation would cramp our style tonight."

"I will be fired for this. You ready for your chauffeur?" he asked, resigned.

"If you please."

"I don't."

"Then I'm afraid I must insist."

"Twenty minutes then, asshole."

"I love it when you talk dirty to me."

He hissed. "You do realize that this call is probably being recorded, right?"

"Of course. My company provided the tech, pro bono. See you soon."

He sighed on the other line. "Nate?"

"Yes." I answered carefully.

"Thanks." It sounded like he had been tortured into saying that single word.

"Men don't say 'thanks.' That's gushy girl talk. Just drive the shit out of it when necessary. It's really just an insurance policy for our survival. The way you drive anyway." I knew I was supposed to be staying out of the investigation into my parents' murder, as Turner Locke had informed me, but I couldn't just leave this on Gunnar's shoulders. It was my responsibility too, and I knew shit would hit the fan soon, and he would need my help.

"Asshole." He muttered. "By the way, I've tried calling your dragon hunter a few times, but he hasn't answered. I also can't find a speck of dirt on him, let alone any hard facts. Think it's an alias? Have you heard anything?"

I began to speak when my phone beeped. I looked down. "Huh. Speak of the devil. I think that's him on the other line. Be here in twenty and I'll tell you what I find out." He grunted and I clicked over.

"The very magnificent Master Temple at your service. How can I assist you, you wicked dragon hunter, you?"

He growled back. "We haven't had much luck hunting any dragons, where it seems you've been doing nothing but that." He didn't sound pleased.

"Need me to train you on my extensive skills? So far, I count two, possibly three dead at my hand." I fudged the number a bit, because technically, Peter had killed Raven, but Tomas didn't need to know that. "And I haven't even been *trying*."

"Your survival skills are rather impressive, but I seem to remember a net launcher saving the city of St. Louis from having a wizard-shaped smear on her sidewalk yesterday." He said suggestively.

"So it wasn't Spiderman. Damn."

"What?"

"Nothing. Listen, I'm kind of busy. Need the lesson or not?"

He grunted. "We're fine. But it seems they really have a hard-on for you. If we had simply been following you around, our job could have been over by now."

"You mean your contract would be finished."

He was silent for a minute. "Perhaps."

"Who hired you? Because I'm sure that would give us one of those clue things that seem to help one understand complicated situations."

"Not important," he answered immediately.

"Okay, fine. Does the eclipse have any significance to you?"

A longer silence. "Perhaps. Why do you ask?"

"I don't know if it is related, but shortly after we had our pleasant introduction, I found a note my father had left me, warning me of the eclipse."

"How cute. Your father left you a napkin note, and you think it's relevant. Typical—"

"It was written in his own blood…"

I felt him stiffen through the phone. "I apologize. I know what it's like to have a family like yours, and to suddenly lose the patriarch. My family is very old, tracing our lineage back to the crusades."

"Uh-huh." I answered, not hiding my boredom. My laptop chimed behind me.

"You don't sound surprised…"

"Hold on a minute, if you would be so kind." I answered, clicking the email open on my laptop. After a long password, I opened the encrypted file from Othello, and read quickly, catching the highlights. "Tomas Mullingsworth … Ex RN. I thought you said you were from Brooklyn?" I added curiously. Silence answered me. "Served in Afghanistan. Much redacting, but wait…" I made the false sounds of heavy typing and then came back. "Questionable operations: Three. Drunken bouts with superior officers: seven." I paused. "Really? That's quite impress—"

His voice was full of rage. "How dare you? That is personal information."

I let the silence build, his furious huffing the only sound between us. "My *life* is quite personal to *me*. And when it has been close to taken a handful of times in a span of days shortly after meeting with your targets, I decided it wise to learn more about all the players involved. Was I wrong? Would you have done any different?"

The silence built, and then he let out a breath. "You are a very dangerous man, Master Temple. I see why some have declared this city 'Poach-free.' Your research seems quite extensive. No one has ever been able to redact that information, let alone find it. I made sure it was buried. Deep."

"Never deep enough for me, Tomas, and you should remember that. This is my being polite."

"Good to know. Now, what do you want?"

"The eclipse. Ring any bells?"

"Not directly, but I have heard stories. Legends, really. Some dark ritual the dragons have been searching for. But they have never found what they need to perform it. I don't know exactly what they need, what they seem to be missing."

"I think it's safe to say that they have discovered it somewhere near my city."

He grunted. "But I don't know what this has to do with my mark. I have heard neither hide nor hair of him since we arrived. Just a trail leading here, and then nothing."

"Tell me about him." I said carefully. "If you trust me. Perhaps we can help each other. I just want this all to stop, I don't care who gets credit for it."

"I was hired to take out a rogue black dragon. Sometimes he goes by the name Raego. Ever heard of him? Seen him?"

I shook my head, and realized he couldn't see me. "No." I searched Othello's documents for the name, but came up with nothing. "Why would your client want him dead? Or whatever it is you do."

"Questions aren't part of the job. Just the money for a head. I have never met a good dragon, so it is pretty cut and dried. But this one is dangerous. Comes from an old family. Have you ever heard of a black dragon?" He asked me very slowly.

I could sense the seriousness, so I kept my answer formal. "No, but I've recently seen a rainbow of others. Even silver."

"Yes, I heard about that one on the news. Also very dangerous. But nothing compared to the black."

"I was on the news?" I asked, surprised.

"Yep." He let the silence build, but I knew Gunnar was on the way.

"I've seen a red one spit fire." I added.

He growled, a familiar sound from Tomas, I was beginning to realize. "We almost had that one on the courthouse until that crazy old man harpooned her with a lightning stick. He one of yours?"

"Yes." I answered carefully.

"Damn. Maybe we *should* have you teach us a thing or two. You're mighty resourceful for a Noob dragon slayer."

"I'm *mighty resourceful* with anyone who tries to kill me. Whether I know dick about them or not." He laughed deeply. "I saw the yellow one create oily fire. And the silver one could spit bullets in all sorts of shapes and sizes." I thought back. "And they all had some kind of mind control power. Is that common?"

He was quiet for a few seconds, and I realized he was taking a drink, obviously something stiff because his voice came back raspy. "Not common at all."

"So you're saying that the first dragons I have ever encountered are uber-dangerous? Cream of the crop murderers?"

"Seems that way."

Of course they were. "Okay, so what's so special about the black one?"

He took another drink, and then he spilled his words in a rush. "It is said, because I have never met someone who has survived one, that they can bend shadows, appearing and disappearing at whim. Their mind magic is so subtle and powerful that their victims won't realize until days later that they have acted any differently than normal. They can melt fire, petrify with a look, shape-shift into different people entirely, mind-fuck other dragons, et cetera, et cetera. Point being, the most dangerous of the bastards. Do you have any idea what kind of reputation a kill like that could make?"

"If he is guilty, of course."

"Right, I show up in town hunting rumors of the most badass dragon in centuries, and all of a sudden you have a reptile dysfunction in your city."

I began laughing. "Nice. I will have to remember that."

Tomas grunted in pride before continuing. "A flock of lady dragons murdering and pillaging for no reason. Probably just a coincidence."

"Harem." I corrected.

"What?"

"I like to think of them as a harem. A bunch of females at your beck and call? Harem, definitely a harem."

"Fine, a harem." He chided, sounding upset he hadn't come up with it himself.

"But why would a book be so important to them?" I pondered aloud.

Tomas was quiet. "A book? Is that what this is all about? Why they've been killing all you nerds?"

"See? Information trading is beneficial. And I am one rich, motherfucking nerd, thank you very much."

"Spill it, Temple."

"Each one I have encountered, or scene the aftermath of, was searching for a book. *The Sons of the Dying Sun*. Does that mean anything to your extensive knowledge on dragons?" I mocked.

"Can't say that it does. Do you think it's what they have been searching for all this time? For their ritual?"

"I haven't the foggiest." I admitted. "But it seems awfully important to them. Enough to risk losing a few of his flock to the local wizard billionaire."

"Billionaire?" He gasped. "Why in the hell aren't you in Bora Bora, fucking, drinking, and fucking your problems away?"

"Already done as much of both as I could before becoming a local nuisance."

"Damn. You do this for fun then?"

"To be honest, I didn't know what I was getting myself into. The first dragon just kinda stumbled into my lap." I remembered that first encounter and grew angrier. "She pissed me off by destroying a treasured tome. One of a kind type of book."

"Did you just say the word *tome*?" he asked, barely containing his laughter.

"It is what an educated man calls those flippy, heavy things with pieces of paper and strange symbols inside. They also have some with pictures, but those are usually not called tomes."

"Alright, Merlin." He chuckled.

I scanned the email from Othello, catching Hermes' name a few times. Interesting. "I haven't been able to find much on this book. Barely that it even exists. Just mentions and vague references, but no hard facts. I didn't think I would be even that successful, or they would have undoubtedly found it by now."

"True."

I heard Indie shout my name from downstairs. "I gotta run, Tomas. I'll be visiting *Artemis' Garter* tonight, a club in the Central West End. Judging from my track record, no doubt I'll run into some interesting people there. You should have men there just in case, that way you aren't bitching at me tomorrow about stealing your glory and all that."

He laughed for a long time. "No way. You're picking *there* to hang out in the middle of all *this*? You really are a reckless bastard."

I frowned. "Never been there, but it has an open roof, which is good for quick escapes. And Artemis is the moon goddess, so it fits." I offered.

"Whatever. See you there." He laughed again as he hung up.

Why did everyone laugh at my choice of locale? Guess I would find out later. I gathered up my things, pocketed my phone, and raced down the stairs. Indie was watching me curiously. I fingered her thong in my pocket and shot her a smile, revealing a bit of the thin satin so that only she could see. "I will return them to you as soon as I am able, my lady."

"Such a gentleman," she cooed. "Like the note?"

I simply stared back, undressing her with my eyes. My look must have worked because her cheeks tinted the slightest red. I used a bit of magic to pinch her behind, and she squeaked. "I shall see you soon." I laughed.

"Quite literally." She winked back seductively so that only I could see.

155

Alex looked back and forth between us, apparently not understanding. "You two are acting kind of weird." He said, but appeared aloof to our true conversation. Indie intended for me to *see* quite a bit more of her soon. It sounded like a good idea to me.

"There's a monstrosity of a vehicle parked diagonally in front of our store. Just because he has a badge doesn't mean that he gets to block your customers from the entrance." Indie grumped, very manager-like.

"Agreed. I'll file a complaint with the FBI." I bolted out the door and saw Gunnar pressing buttons on the dash, a look of pure joy on his face. He was early. The silver SUV gleamed in the sun, shiny rims, and military-grade tires lifting the body up high. I slid inside with aid of the 'oh-shit' bar just above the inside of the passenger door and smiled back at him.

"This is so cool!" He grinned.

"Glad you like it. The manager of Plato's Cave would like to file a complaint against the FBI for a terrible parking job that is blocking my front door from customers."

He smiled back. "Call Captain Kosage, I'll just run his little ass over with my shiny new tank." I laughed, nodding. "Temple Industries?" he asked loudly, pressing a button.

I began to answer when the Navigation unit spoke back. "Estimated trip duration, twenty minutes. Please buckle your seatbelts." Gunnar pounded the wheel like a child with his new favorite Christmas toy and took off.

CHAPTER 26

MY DRESS SHOES CLACKED AGAINST THE FLOORS AS I strode down the marble hallway of my new palace, Temple Industries. Receptionists, scientists, engineers, mail clerks, and lower peasants all, gawked openly as their new CEO meandered through the halls, hopelessly lost. I had been too stubborn to ask for help, and my minions had been too terrified to hurt my pride. So we walked, Gunnar behind me, glancing here and there at different labs and offices.

I had no fucking idea where we were.

"So, is this the tour?" Gunnar mocked.

I sighed, finally pointing a commanding finger at one of my new minions carrying a bundle of papers. "I need to speak with Ashley Belmont. Would you be so kind as to guide me to her office?"

He bumped into a copier, almost dropping his stack of papers. "Me?"

"No, the woman behind you." Bless his heart; he actually turned around to look. When he turned back he was blushing furiously.

"Um, follow me?" he said nervously, voice rising higher on the last word.

"Sure thing. But let me offer a word of advice. Don't incline your voice at the end of your sentences. Apologizing is a sign of weakness."

"Sorr—" He hesitated. "Right. This way then, Master Temple?" His face turned even darker as he did it again.

"Just think on it." I sighed reluctantly, motioning him onward.

He led us through the labyrinth of offices and labs, zigzagging this way and that until he finally came to a set of thick black doors and a desk. An aged receptionist glared at him, and then us. "Appointment?"

"No." I answered, feigning frustration.

"Miss Belmont is rather busy, what with that rapscallion Temple son doing nothing around here. I swear. If he walked in right now, I would give him a piece of my mind. It just isn't right to run a company like this." I nodded back. The tour-guide looked about ready to swallow his tongue, but remained silent out of corporate fear. "Be that as it may, you need an appointment. Honestly, I don't know how you got in here without beeping somebody." She arched her neck to study Gunnar. "He looks like a cop. Is that why you're here? A couple of upstart detectives looking for a case-breaker? Well, you can just leave like all the others. Appointments are like the Ten Commandments around here. Followed to a T." She leaned back, face smug with satisfaction.

I smiled, unable to help myself. "I hear all sorts of things about this Temple son. Is he as bad as all that? Have you never seen him before?" Gunnar and the tour guide stiffened as one, not wanting to be a part of the conversation.

"Off the record?" She asked, squinting her eyes. I nodded. "I hear he's into all sorts of depraved acts. Why, I hear he even..." she glanced around to be sure we were alone. She lowered her voice, leaning forward. "Has premarital sex. Frequently. With all types of women. It isn't right. It just isn't. He needs a strong role model. He needs to be here running his company. I hear he even smokes and drinks. Bah. If he were my son, I'd grab him by the ear and teach him a thing or two. That's what I'd do. But who listens to old Greta? Nobody, that's who." She composed herself, patting her coffered hair. "Now, names and identification, please. I will schedule an appointment at Miss Belmont's earliest convenience."

I strode forward, grinning like an idiot. The tour guide looked apoplectic, searching for an immediate escape. I handed over my driver's license with Gunnar's on top. She scanned his and opened her planner, flipping pages a few weeks ahead knowingly, speaking aloud. "There is an opening in three weeks on Wednesday. Shall that work, Agent Randulf, and..." Her eyes widened, looking up at me, horrified. "Master Temple!"

"The one and only." I grinned.

"Oh, bother! An old lady does have a loose tongue!"

"It's quite alrig—" I began.

"Oh, it certainly is *not*! Foolish, foolish, *foolish*! I'm terribly sorry. I'll just page Miss Belmont, and be packing up my box then." She was flustered, rearranging papers back and forth, utterly lost. I spotted a tear at the corner of one eye.

I opened my mouth to speak, and she leveled a gnarled finger at me. "Oh, no you don't. If I'm to be fired, I'll do it with all the dignity an old lady can muster."

"But—" She slapped her hand down onto her desk like a clap of thunder.

"*No!* You should be ashamed of yourself, letting me rattle on like that, digging my own grave. You are everything I heard about if you would do such a thing to an old woman. You don't need a *role* model. You need *Jesus!*" The last was a shriek.

The door to Ashley's office flew open then. Gunnar was pathetically trying to suppress a laugh, doubled over with his hands clasped around his knees. "What in the *hell* is going on out here?" She saw me, and blinked. "Master Temple. Is everything quite alright?"

I shrugged. "I was trying to tell Greta that all is well, and that I appreciate a little honesty now and then. Even a *lot* of honesty." I added with an appeasing grin. She scowled back. "Anyway, no harm done. Mind if we talk to Miss Belmont, Greta?"

Her eyes were twin coals, her cheeks reddening with embarrassment now. She waved a hand, shooing us on, but her gnarled finger locked onto our tour guide and her voice was low, dripping with venom as she proceeded to strip away his hide. Ashley looked bewildered, but stepped aside so that we could enter. The doors closed with a soft click behind us. "What happened?" Ashley asked carefully. "She's an old woman. I don't know how you managed to get her so worked up. I was outside just five minutes ago. How could you have possibly gotten such a reaction in so short a time?"

Gunnar spoke up between bouts of laughter. "He has a gift. Oh, god. My stomach." He wheezed. "It hurts. Laughing so hard. Sometimes I wish I had his charm, and then other times..." He waved a hand towards Greta in the other room, and began laughing all over again. Once he got a breath he continued. "I'm glad I don't."

Ashley looked at me and I shrugged. "She saw us, and began talking about *that rapscallion, Nate Temple.*" I mimicked her aged voice. "I should have stopped her sooner, but it was hard to get a word in. She's a tough old bag. I like her."

Ashley studied me, fighting a grin. "Me too. I'd like to keep her around for a while... without her having a heart attack on me."

That sobered me up. "Sorry."

She nodded, motioning towards her desk. We followed, declining her offer of drinks. "So, you have come about the video feed?" she asked carefully, eyeing Gunnar a few times when he wasn't looking.

I nodded. She typed a series of commands on her iMac desktop.

"Well, I can't say I quite understand it. It seems to be a feed from a security camera that runs separate from the rest of the system. Nobody even knew of it until we had input your information into the system as an employee. As soon as your social security number hit the system we got a critical ping. Any time something important or dangerous happens at the company, the upper echelon of management gets a 911 email. This one came only to me and you." I leaned forward, interested. "I haven't been able to open the feed. It's encrypted, and I have no idea what the password could be. Your... parents gave me a list of potentials, but I regret to inform you that none of mine worked. I have been efficiently locked out. Our only hope is to see if you have access to it."

"May I?" I asked, pointing at her desktop. She nodded, getting out of her chair and holding it out for me.

"I already logged off." Gunnar leaned back in his chair, curiously watching the scene unfold, or possibly just watching Ashley. Puppy love. Did they even realize they were each checking the other out? She guided me through the logon process, and then helped me open my email, which in turn asked me a series of questions that only my parents could have arranged years before. Successfully answering the questions, my email finally opened. There at the top of the page – marked with a blinking exclamation mark – was the 911 email. I double clicked it, and a password warning popped up. I looked back at her and she grinned sheepishly, stepping back and turning her head.

I typed in the verse from Dante's Inferno that my father and I had frequently discussed through a tough semester in college. I flourished my finger dramatically, and asked her a question. "How many attempts did you have before it locked you out?"

"Three." She answered nervously.

"Here, we, go." I said, then pressed enter. The password box wiggled a wrong answer. "Hmmm." I mentally glanced at the list in my mind, wondering if any of the other passwords might work, depending on the severity level of my father's warning. I hadn't tried the last password yet, as I had been hoping that it might not be as serious as we all thought. I mean, how would the video feed know how important it was? It had to be something my father frequently monitored as a security precaution if it was automatically logged as such an important breach. Something others wouldn't have access to. Not even Ashley, judging by the fact that it had only appeared to her after my information was logged into the system.

I leaned back, thumbing my lip at the puzzle.

The room was as tense as a china cabinet in front of a live orchestra. Not thinking of a better idea, I typed the last password on my parents' list, realizing that the irony must be a coincidence. The title of a journal written by Isaac Newton about Nicolas Flamel, the Alchemist who supposedly discovered the philosopher's stone: *The Caduceus, the Dragons of Flammel.*

I typed *Caduceus*, remembering that the coin the Minotaur had given me depicted that very staff on one side. It was in my pocket now. Another discreet reference to Hermes. That bore looking into.

The password box shook again in angry denial. Ashley unbuttoned the top button of her blouse, breathing heavily. "One more shot. I don't think it was one of the passwords on their list." She added respectfully.

I leaned back again, closing my eyes. She was right. It would have been too simple if it were the last password. I was letting my infatuation with dragons overwhelm my logic, but it had been the direst password on their list, so it had been worth a shot. I mentally zipped through memories of my father, trying to catch something, anything, that might give me a clue. An everyday password he would undoubtedly use. If it was to a secret video feed, then it was something he wanted kept separate. Something he could privately monitor at his own leisure. Which might mean a secret project. But why keep a project secret from his company? It must have been dangerous if he didn't deem it worthy of his employee's knowledge. I began to get a terrible feeling in my stomach. Was something here, in my new company, that he didn't trust any of his employees with, even his protégé, Ashley Belmont? My memory snagged on a brief conversation we had had while on a yacht in the middle of the ocean on my 21st birthday. Something I had only heard once. Something that *only* I had heard.

I slowly leaned forward one last time. Surely it couldn't be. That had been a night of hard drinking, a sharing of talk like we had never had before. An introduction into manhood, he had called it. We had talked until the sun came up, on everything from ancient alchemy to modern day particle theory at CERN; from Aristotle to Ayn Rand; from Greek myths to the Bible's Revelations; from one topic to another in almost every field of study. Then we had briefly discussed extremes. Extreme *measures* in particular.

My forearms pebbled as I remembered the two words that he had uttered as we had drifted off to sleep on the deck. He had repeated them three times, and then fallen asleep. I had merely assumed it was a disturbing thought from some vague mention of one of our topics, as we were both heavily intoxicated, but my eidetic memory was profound, and I had remembered these words despite the fact. Only now did I consciously dreg them up from the bottom of my memory, and the feeling of that wonderful night threatened to break me.

I hunched over the keyboard, shivering both in fear at the tone of voice he had used to utter the words, and also in profound loss, realizing all over again that I would never have the chance to speak with him again.

My fingers punched in each key, slowly, robotically. *Pandora Protocol*. I hoped my capitalization was correct, or that the password was even correct. It was a far-fetched idea, and to be honest, it didn't feel right. One drunken night, years ago? My father was much too methodical for that, right?

I looked up at Gunnar. His eyes revealed how much it hurt him to see me so grief-stricken. I turned to Ashley. Her eagerness was gone as her eyes filled with empathy. She slowly reached over to place a hand on my shoulder. "If this isn't it, then it doesn't matter. He can't expect us to type in a password that we were never given. It's no one's fault but his own if he created an unbreakable encryption that was important enough for us to see, but not important enough to receive a hint. He couldn't expect that," she repeated.

"Oh, yes. Yes, he could. He would *demand* it," I whispered.

Without further preamble, I pressed my finger to the *enter* key the same way I would have pressed the lethal injection button at a sanctioned execution of an innocent man. The computer chimed above me, as my eyes were still locked on the *enter* key. Realizing the password had worked, my shoulders slumped further. *No, please not this. He couldn't have...*

My father had kept his promise then. His secret project had indeed been real. Was that why my parents had been killed? Had someone discovered his secret work? I slowly lifted my gaze to the screen. Ashley was shifting nervously from foot to foot behind me. I clicked *play*.

It flickered to life instantly. I read the timestamp on the recording as I waited for something to happen. It must have been a motion-activated camera, because it jumped ahead at random intervals, and only when someone was walking past a particular door. With each person, a name would materialize at the bottom of the feed. *Jenna Davis. Accountant. Regular.* I began to frown after seeing the first few people caught on film. Each time one passed, their name, title, and the word *Regular* would appear at the bottom of the screen.

I felt a chill at the back of my neck. Each person would walk by the door as if it didn't exist. One woman dropped a paper and it landed directly in front of the door. She glanced down at the ground, searching back and forth as if trying to see the paper that was barely two inches away from her toes. But she didn't seem to see anything. She checked a few papers in her hand, frowned, and then glanced at the floor again. With a sigh, she turned back the way she had come. Five minutes later, she reappeared on camera, walking briskly past the discarded piece of paper on the ground without a care in the world.

We looked at each other curiously. Gunnar had stepped behind the computer to watch. "Is she blind? It was right in front of her."

Ashley spoke up. "She has perfect vision. She also isn't a Regular." Sure enough, the word *Regular* hadn't appeared at the bottom of the screen, but no elaboration had been listed either.

We turned back to the camera to watch a few more people enter and leave the frame. Then, my parents came onto the screen. Their forms sparkled like radio disturbance on the feed, but all else was clear. They conversed casually, leaning against the wall beside the odd door, glancing out of the camera's view frequently. Then, in the middle of speaking, they both darted inside the door and then closed it behind them. A minute later, someone walked near the door, looked back and forth, searching, then turned away, as if he had been searching for my parents.

"Creepy," I said warily.

"Can you pause it?" Ashley asked.

I did, and turned to her. "That door doesn't exist," she said simply. I arched a brow at her. "Look at the symbol above the door. It's the Omega symbol. I recognize the hallway, and know I've walked past that stretch of camera at least two dozen times in the last week. But I have *never seen that door.*"

"It's cloaked then." I told them. It was as if I spoke a foreign language.

"Hidden. Secret. Hocus pocus." I waggled my fingers.

"Then how can we see it on this feed? And how does the camera know all the information about each passerby?" Gunnar asked.

I pondered that. "It must be why this camera is off the main system. It's unique. It can see anything, even through magic. I bet it could even sense—" I began, looking at Gunnar, and then stopped. I had been about to say that it would probably reveal his wolf form, but Ashley didn't know about that.

"You were going to say that it would probably show Gunnar's werewolf form," she said simply, as if reading my mind. "You're right. It would. I designed the software, but never thought of merging it with live cameras."

We each turned to her, eyes wide. "I know almost every Freak in town. Your parents kept tabs on everyone. You would be surprised at some of them, but your secret is safe with me, Agent Randulf. No one else here knows." She smiled, unabashed.

"Well, isn't that something." I added.

"You will be granted access to the Arcanum that your parents compiled whenever you wish," she told me as if it were nothing out of the ordinary. My thoughts were racing. My parents had indeed pursued their secret then. It couldn't be anything else.

"I'm going to keep playing the feed." I said. Everyone nodded, leaning closer.

The feed jumped forward seventeen minutes. Then my parents bolted out the door, each leaving in a different direction. Odd. Ten minutes later, a shadow blinked across the hallway, and a new figure stepped into view. A string of question marks appeared at the bottom of the screen. The figure didn't sparkle like my parents. He seemed to be cloaked in shadows, as if outlined by them. He looked each direction, and then slipped up to the door he shouldn't have been able to see. He fiddled with the handle a moment, and was then inside the room, the door closing behind him. The feed blinked red for a few seconds, the word *unidentified intruder* blinking instead of the string of question marks from before.

The feed jumped ahead seventeen minutes again, and then he slipped out of the room, darting down the hallway in the same direction my mother had left. Less than a minute later, my dad entered the feed, sparkling with his name at the bottom of the screen. He studied the door, seeming nervous. Then he lifted his eyes to the security camera and spoke silently. His face was haggard. I studied it carefully, reading his lips, and my blood ran to ice. Then he set off in the same direction as the intruder. A steel door slammed down over the invisible door, securing it from any future tampering, and then the feed stopped. The video feed jumped ahead half an hour and then froze, blinking the date and time in large red letters. The only other letters on the screen were *Titan!*

Then it shut off, the whole computer shutting down, and rebooting.

I stood urgently, pacing back and forth. No one spoke. My mind scattered, rebelling against my futile attempts to control my fury. I felt my power rising up inside me like a tidal wave. I finally spoke, panting uncontrollably. "The feed stopped within one minute of the Time of Death announced by the coroner. That feed was somehow tied to my parents' heartbeat, stopping as soon as they died. That can't be possible," I said, exasperated.

Still, no one spoke. I rounded on Ashley. "Do you know anything, *anything*, about this?" I demanded.

She shook her head urgently. "Nothing. I swear."

Gunnar spoke softly. "You understood what he said to you." It wasn't a question.

I turned to him, slowly. "Oh, yes. I understood it perfectly." I continued pacing, trying to keep up with my fleeting thoughts.

"Care to share?" he asked sympathetically. I ignored him as the computer chimed back to life. I flew to the desk, logged back in, and signed into my email, but the video feed was gone. I logged off, and strode out of the room, Ashley and Gunnar barely keeping up.

Greta stood, looking horrified as she saw my face. A box was neatly packed on her desk. "You," I leveled an angry finger at her, my power leaking out enough to launch a flurry of papers from her desk into the air. She squeaked like a child, terror filling her eyes as the tempest of papers floated down around her like snow. "Are not leaving my company. Sit. Down." My voice was rough with emotion. She obeyed, collapsing into her chair with a faint squeak of hinges. Then I was off again. I called over my shoulder. "We'll be in touch, Miss Belmont. We will *definitely* be in touch." I turned my head to look her in the eyes over my shoulder. "Soon."

Gunnar followed in my wake like a good dog as the Master Temple stormed out of his castle to pick a fight with a dragon, or the Minotaur, or some helpless bystander who happened to tick him off on the way.

Someone was going to die. Soon. By my hand. And I was going to relish every second of it. But first, we were headed to the expo center to try to learn something about the dragons' sudden interest in the eclipse tomorrow afternoon. Maybe I would get the chance to kill someone there.

One could dream.

CHAPTER 27

W E HAD PICKED UP TORY AND WERE HEADED INTO
the parking lot at the *Eclipse Expo!* Or so the signs said. The
hotel was vast, full of auditoriums designed for conferences
and proms, loaded with luxurious restaurants, several spas, and a smattering
of gift shops. I had been in a daze since leaving Temple Industries, pondering
the implications of my father's last message to me. He had known it was the
end, or at least seriously assumed it to be the case. He had relied so heavily
on my eidetic memory, and skill of lip reading, and even the knowledge of a
password that had mostly been a lucky guess. Now I had one answer, but it
only led deeper into the rabbit hole, giving me countless more questions.
When this was all over I would bury myself in solving their secret before it
was too late. If it wasn't too late already… It was too volatile of a project to
be left unattended. And it had been over a week.

Being so distracted, I had barely noticed Tory joining us. She and Gunnar
had made small talk while we drove, complimenting each other's clothing,
but I had been mostly ignoring them. Not purposely, just so enveloped in my
own thoughts that nothing else had mattered. My phone vibrated in my
pocket. I plucked it out, glanced at the screen, and then answered.

"Master Temple—" I recognized the nasally voice instantly.

"Go fuck yourself, Kosage." Then I hung up, calmly placing the phone
back into my pocket. I didn't give one flying hell about the cops right now.
The silence that ensued in the car was as delicate as brittle glass. Gunnar
turned the car off and waited for me to compose myself. I blinked, looking
around as if surprised. "You two ready?" I asked.

Gunnar nodded, and I heard Tory agree. I opened my door and rappelled
the twelve feet down to the pavement. I quickly unlatched Tory's door and
opened it for her. Her hand was reached out to do it for herself. I held out a
hand to help her since she was wearing bright blue heels. She stared at me,
slightly surprised. "How did you move so fast?" she whispered very seri-

ously.

I blinked back. "Pardon?"

Gunnar was watching me warily. "All I saw was a blur, and I'm a were-wolf. You have never moved like that before…"

I looked from one to the other for a few moments and then shrugged uneasily. "My guard is down. You might see me do a few things tonight that shouldn't be possible. A wizard's life is all about control, and presently I seem to have none. I'll need you to be my compass between right and wrong, normal and irregular. Do you think you can do that for me?" I asked, unsure of myself for the first time in a very long time.

I never asked others to help me, but I honestly felt like my head was stuffed with wool, and yet somehow that I was thinking clearer than I ever had before.

"Perhaps it would be wise for you to wait in the car while Tory and I search the Expo Center." Gunnar offered. "And hanging up on Kosage probably wasn't your best idea."

I shook my head urgently. "A werewolf and the she-hulk might not be enough if we run into company. They could mind-fuck you without me there to protect you. Remember the Raven at my shop? She almost had you until I stomped all over her mind web." His face turned red, remembering all too well. "Just keep an eye out for me. I seem to have less restraint than usual, and I feel stronger. Which doesn't make sense. It almost feels the same as when I was first coming into my powers as a teenager. Perhaps I am reaching another plateau of strength." I didn't mention the oddity of the thief stumbling directly into the cops by the river. The less they knew the better. Plus, my distortion of chance might work to our advantage inside the Expo Center.

Gunnar's eyes widened at that. "Aren't you already stronger than most other wizards?" I nodded. "Is this spike normal?"

I chewed my lip for a moment. "I don't think so. At least not to this degree."

I reached further with my hand, offering it to Tory. She finally accepted, and allowed me to help her out of the SUV. I stepped back, eyeing her up and down speculatively. "Stunning. Simply stunning." Her cheeks warmed at the obvious interest. "And you call me Archangel. You look like Aphrodite." Her sleek white dress hugged her hips, leaving little to the imagination. It was slit at the side to revel a thigh somehow still tanned from the summer.

Either that or she carefully maintained a natural-looking fake tan. She looked classy, yet dangerously seductive. Like a James Bond girl.

I reached out a hand, but hesitated. "May I?"

After a glance to Gunnar, she nodded, obviously wary of my previous warning. "You two have nothing to fear from me. I don't think..." I delicately brushed her curled hair back to reveal her bare shoulder. I appraised her as if contemplating a purchase. Without asking, I unclasped the delicate chain necklace around her throat, and replaced it with a heavy diamond choker from my suit pocket. Not my intended purpose for the jewelry, but I had backups. Her eyes widened at the obvious quality of the necklace. I handed hers back and she tucked it into her purse. "This is better. It's flashier, and less likely to get in your way if you need to move," I said. I studied her face, admiring her skill with a brush. The makeup was definitely eye-catching, but it was missing something. "Do you have any bright red lipstick?"

She nodded, digging in her purse. I motioned for her to continue. She applied it expertly. Gunnar watched with apparent interest as she finished. It was as if she had suddenly found a spotlight, lips gleaming like fresh blood. She looked perfect. I glanced at Gunnar, looking him up and down, calculating. "I don't have any lipstick, Nate, so don't bother." I smiled back. He looked every inch the modern Viking. Nordic features flashed harshly in the afternoon light. I simply nodded approval and he rolled his eyes. "Who gets to judge you?" Gunnar grumped.

"How about our delicate Tory?"

"I can think of nothing that would make your outfit better." She appraised my tailored silver suit with more than approval. As if I was a dinner plate and she was starving. "I even like the James Dean look of the loose tie. You look very rat-pack. Rugged, yet refined. Is dress really that important to you?"

"Sartorial skill is a powerful weapon. Sometimes that is a huge advantage. Ever read Sherlock Holmes?" I asked.

She shook her head. "I saw the new movie."

"An adequate portrayal, but one should read Sir Arthur Conan Doyle in order to glimpse the full scope of how vital the right set of garments can aid one in a time of need. Disguises are a perfect sleight of hand. Think of a strip club. I assume you have visited one?" I asked without thinking. Her face turned a shade darker.

169

"Once or twice," she answered, guardedly.

"I just know that someone in law enforcement must see the darker shades of life in order to be competent at his or her career. Imagine a dancer wearing nothing at all." Her face flushed darker.

"Nate..." Gunnar warned. "Compass says *no*."

"Point heard, but allow me to elaborate..." He finally nodded, protective of Tory. "Her natural curves..." I carefully brushed Tory's side, making her arms pebble, and her moist red lips opened instinctively as she took a breath. "Will no doubt catch the eye, but the surprise has already been given. There is not much more to see. Boring.

"Now imagine an extreme outfit on a dancer. A nurse, for example. Catches one's attention, but without the right circumstances, it's too flashy to keep your interest. She's flaunting herself too obviously. You know she's there to take it off. Again, boring.

"Now, lastly, imagine a stunning woman step out onto the stage, fingers adoringly caressing the pole, eyes intent. She is wearing a flattering dress like Tory here." Tory's lips were still parted, her breathing deeper as she stared into my eyes. "Her hair is tied up with chop sticks. Then she stares straight into your eyes, and pulls the chopsticks out, her hair cascading down her shoulders like a waterfall." My fingers flipped Tory's hair before I trailed the back of my nails down from her shoulder to her elbow. She shivered again.

"You don't know what's about to happen next, or how long it will go on, but you can't turn away from her gaze. Then her hand carefully unzips the dress down the side, revealing an artfully tattooed ribcage, and then she begins to swing around the pole, masterfully, owning everything in the room. No one moves. Then she looks over her shoulder at you, and *clack*! She slams her stiletto down onto the stage, making you spill your drink slightly. You can't decide whether to meet her eyes or stare at the tease of flesh where the zipper dangles loose. She bends down at the hips, coming to hands and knees, and slowly crawls towards you with the grace of a predatory feline, eyes pinning you to your seat."

Tory was panting, and Gunnar looked stunned. Tory stepped back, resting a hand against the SUV for support. I didn't realize I had stepped closer to Tory. "Now, tell me which has a bigger impact?"

Neither spoke, so I continued. "That is the power of one's attitude and choice of dress. It ruled the European courts for centuries, power flashing from one to another with every change in fashion. There is a reason for every thread, every smile, and every flick of the hair. Everything matters. You live by this, or you can die by a smile that you didn't mean to give. The people we will be running into in the future live by this. You better learn it, but until you do, I will be the group's *fashionista*. If that is okay with you two?"

They nodded, regaining their breath. Tory looked at me as if she had never seen me before. "Was that magic?" she whispered.

I smiled back. "Yes." Her shoulders sagged in relief. "But not directly. Artfully choosing your attire and the attitude to match it is a very, very powerful magic. But it isn't magic like you saw on the bridge. I simply tapped into your imagination, feeding the flames of my point against your own personal experiences. What you felt was entirely genuine, and came from your own mind. I just helped reveal it to you." I leveled her with my eyes, smiled confidently, and then turned away. "Shall we?"

They followed me towards the entrance. I hoped I was right. I didn't *think* I had used magic in my example, but with as much power as was coursing through me, I honestly wasn't sure. As soon as I had met up with Gunnar, I had felt my strength bubble back up, my skin tingling. Then after seeing the video feed my power had threatened to burst out of me. It had taken a long meditative car ride to Tory's house before I was confident that I was in control. But once she climbed inside the car, it had gotten worse.

Something was happening to me, and I hadn't the slightest idea what it was. I had never heard of such a large jump in power around my age. Not without aid, but I hadn't done anything that would increase my power base. There were ways to measure it quantitatively, but I hadn't had any time to sit down and do so with my usual spells. It was like weight lifting. I knew I *felt* stronger, but without pushing myself to max out on the bench press, I had no way to know exactly *how much* stronger I truly was. I would have to keep it under tight control for the time being.

Power could be good, but it could also be bad. It was up to the user, and as power increased, it sometimes had a tendency to change an individual.

Here's to me not becoming an all-powerful sociopathic wizard over the next few hours. Huzzah!

CHAPTER 28

ORIGINALLY, I HAD BEEN SURPRISED THAT THE EXPO was taking place during the day, but after further contemplation, it made perfect sense. A solar eclipse couldn't be experienced at night, hence the word *solar*. Sometimes I can be thick, but I blamed it on the rough few days before me. There was a surprising number of people at the expo, wandering from table to table in the main atrium, accepting fliers, drink samples, and various other marketing ploys hoping to cash in on the tourists. And there were tourists aplenty.

I heard a speaker from behind the closed doors of an auditorium, but ignored it. We each had accepted stickers for our names upon arrival, and Gunnar and Tory chuckled at my choice of names. "Discreet, very discreet." Gunnar laughed.

I spied a police officer near the entrance, and his face visibly paled upon seeing me. I grinned back, showing teeth. Gunnar shook his head. The police officer began urgently speaking into the radio attached to his shoulder – no doubt informing my good friend, Captain Kosage, of my whereabouts. Gunnar and Tory were stunned at the cost of tickets at the front door, but then relieved to find that I had already paid for them in advance. Tory tried to pay for hers, but Gunnar knew better after years of friendship. "Please, your money is no good here," I answered softly, hiding her offer of cash from any casual passerby.

I was buzzing with power, and I had to find an outlet. Flirting helped. There was magic in flirting. That rush of endorphins when it's win or lose, and you're trying to impress the fairer sex. I just wanted to make it out of here intact, and I needed Gunnar and Tory to be on their game to accomplish that. Before Kosage found a reason to drag me downtown.

I whispered, leaning close to Tory as if for a kiss. Gunnar took his cue, and snatched us each a flute of champagne as if he had been waiting too long for the waiter to make his rounds. "I need you to play the part. *Expect* me to pay for you. You are a treasured gem on my arm, nothing more. A casual dalliance for the evening. A flower on my lapel." I traced the backs of my fingers down her neck in a very, very intimate way as I sensed her shoulders tightening at my words. "*Doucement*, my precious orchid..." I said a pitch louder as the Mayor and his wife walked past us.

The Mayor winked knowingly at me, nodding approval before his wife elbowed him sharply in the ribs. I continued on with a knowing grin to the Mayor as he frowned at my nametag. "Remember, this is a charade, a play, and we are the leads. I need you to watch my back, because *here there be monsters*." I breathed, pulling away with a dark smile. Her eyes dilated as she studied me, and then gave a brief nod.

I placed my other hand on her waist, looking to the entire world like a man staking a claim on his prize. "The less others think of you here, the better. It makes any change of character all the scarier." I gently pressed my lips against the carotid artery on her neck and then leaned back. I held out a blind hand expectantly, and Gunnar placed a flute of champagne in my fingertips. I raised it to Tory's lips. "Drink, my sweet."

She nodded weakly, accepting the drink with shaky fingers. I noticed her knees were quivering, so kept my hand on her waist. Gunnar offered me my drink and I took a long pull, savoring the pricey bouquet. Cakebread, if I had to guess. Palatable. Tory leaned in close to me. "Are you a vampire?" She asked, face smiling in a good mask.

I shook my head, curious. "Why would you ask such a thing?"

She trembled. "Because I can't help but listen to you. You're just so *adorable*. It's like *Twilight* is happening to me!" I blinked at her sudden change of character. She didn't seem like the *Twilight* kind of gal. "Do you have this effect on all your girls? If *that* isn't magic, I don't know what is?" She giggled oddly, a sound that seemed out of countenance for her. Then her eyes widened in sudden delight. "Oh, I'm going to go freshen up!" She took off like a rocket to the restroom. I turned to Gunnar, but he just smiled, amused. I took a swallow of my drink, barely keeping the shock from my face.

I had always been good with women. In fact, I was very good, but never *this* good. I groaned. She was right. It was as if my power was oozing out of everything I did. Without an outlet, it was making its own release. That meant that I had gained even more power than I realized after the attack on the bridge. But why?

I frowned thoughtfully. "It seems we might be in a bit of a pickle, Gunnar."

I noticed that one of his cuffs were loose, allowing him easy access to his tattoo. His eyes roamed the room like a lion, lazy, but hungry. "Why?"

"I'm leaking power on you two."

He arched a brow. "So?"

I blinked. "Have you noticed anything out of the norm? You are unusually copacetic towards me. You usually disagree and make everything more difficult. You are good at acting, but without question you wandered off to grab us each drinks. That is something Dean would do, but never you. Something is wrong. I think my power is pulling whatever attitude I want out of you two."

He sipped his drink. "I just feel peaceful. But now that you mention it, I don't think I've ever felt this mellow before. Calm. I mean, we are here to hunt murderers, or find why your father left you that note, but I am not stressed out at all." He thought about that for a minute. "I'm not even worried that I am not stressed."

"See. I was worried about myself needing a compass, but it seems that I have gained control of myself at the expense of you two."

"So, what's different about Tory? You barely know her, so why do you think she's acting different?"

"I think she took my eye-candy advice literally, and has lost all common sense. She called me *adorable*. And apparently, she has a thing for *Twilight*."

"Despicable movie. Werewolves get shafted the whole time. Jacob totally kicks more ass than Edward." I wanted to slap the shit out of him, but he continued. "Adorable, eh? Man, I hate being the third wheel." He grumbled. "But it's cool, I guess." He said, already falling back into his easygoing manner. I groaned inwardly.

Tory was walking out of the bathroom, eyes dancing with joy as she smiled at both of us. "Right. We need to hurry this up. I'll try to guard you two, but I don't know how well I can manage it." I said for our ears only.

"Whatever, Nate. I'm fine," Gunnar said casually.

"He's cute when he pouts." Tory giggled, snatching up a second flute from a waiter. She guzzled the majority of it. "I love this necklace. Does it look pretty on me?"

I nodded, studying her acutely. Gunnar frowned, snatching up his own re-fill of champagne. "I am not cute." He took a pull from his drink. "And I'm not pouting." I wanted to scream, but we had to maintain our profile for the guests. Any one of them could be my parents' murderer, or they might know something that could help me with the dragons. I placed my palm on Tory's wrist, and concentrated. My mind finally quiet, I suddenly noticed the creep-ing tendrils of power oozing from me to my two companions.

I quickly withdrew them, but a dozen more tendrils shot out into the peo-ple around us. The attendees had been studying us a moment ago, but now they each looked around, confused for a moment before turning away from us as if we didn't exist. I groaned. Tory shook her head with a frown, and then blushed furiously. Gunnar was instantly alert. Tension knotting his brow.

"I am so embarrassed," Tory began, trying to tug her arm away.

I held her hand tight, feeling slightly off balance. "No, it was flattering. Please don't be embarrassed. Remember how I told you I needed you to be my compass and keep me in line?" She nodded. "Well, I seem to have tem-porarily passed off my lack of control onto you two. It's my fault."

"I *despise* bimbos. I never act like that! And I *hate Twilight!*" She ada-mantly whispered. Then her pupils began dilating wider. "Do you think this dress looks good on me? Because I think *hers* looks like trash." She pointed at the mayor's wife, and the woman blanched, hearing her. Shit.

"Can we check out some of the souvenir tables?" Gunnar asked calmly.

The power was hitting everyone now. I hastily drew it all in to myself, and my eyes grew dazed, flecks of sparkling white flickering here and there as I steadied myself. The power tendrils were diminished, but several still latched onto my companions. Tory and Gunnar were more alert again, study-ing me. "I'm confused." Tory mumbled, rubbing at her temples. This was crazy. I had no idea what was happening to me. Was it dragons? I mentally examined myself, but realized that it was all me.

"Let's just get this over with. Follow me." I commanded sharply. They each shrugged, Tory quickly snatching my hand. I was unable to fully block them from my draining power, but it was a bit better than before. I used a brisk pace to help distract us. Just keep everyone moving. Maybe that would help.

As we slipped through the crowd, I allowed several tendrils to leak out of me whenever a group of people I didn't want to talk to would attempt to move towards us. I was, after all, a celebrity in town. Everyone wanted to be seen conversing with the Master Temple. Photographers mingled here and there. I pointedly used my power to guide them away from me. I didn't want a swarm of paparazzi following us. I wanted to find out anything that might help us, and then get the hell out of here. I had, perhaps, two hours until sunset when I would have to fight Asterion. We needed to hurry.

Without warning, a thick tendril shot out of my control, darting through the crowd to latch onto a curvy, tall woman in a red dress. As if in slow motion, she turned to stare at me over her shoulder. I saw a grin split her cheeks. It was the jogger I had seen outside the courthouse with Gunnar. The one who had given me a number, but no name. My cherry Danish. Gunnar grumbled about the world being unfair, then *gold digger*.

Tory's hand tightened in mine, her nails pressing into my palms. My control slipped a bit as the jogger approached. "Well, well, well. I've been waiting for you to call me, but it seems like you found a different piece of candy for the evening. Perhaps later?" She purred. She studied Tory from head to toe, nodding her approval. "Nice choice." Her eyes focused on my chest, exactly where the dragon tooth lay. I shivered, imagining that she could see it.

Gunnar laughed loudly. "I need a stiffer drink."

Tory's hand squeezed tighter, and I knew my control was slipping even further. "She's really pretty, but am I prettier?" she asked softly.

The jogger stepped in closer, and her body heat hit me like a wave of power. Her hips brushed mine as her warm palm touched my chest, her pupils dilating. Something slid across her iris, revealing a glimpse of a horizontal black bar, and I blinked. Contacts?

Shit.

I jumped back, slamming my lack of restraint solely into the jogger. She stumbled, and then shook her head as if dazed. "Dragon," I whispered.

She nodded, happy that she could please me with an affirmative answer.

Gunnar and Tory both started at that, momentarily refocusing.

Without a thought, I simply commanded her, and she obeyed.

"Who are you?"

"Misha."

"What color are you?" I asked, terrified that other dragons were possibly surrounding us. She tapped her finger against the fabric of her dress in answer. "Red?" A nod. "You tried to kill me on the roof of the courthouse. Then gave me your number after. Were you wearing contacts then too?" I asked, disgusted at my own stupidity.

She nodded; her edgy blonde bangs brushing her thin jaw. "It wasn't very nice of me to do what I did, but I can make it up to you..." Her eyes promised a very dark, and appealing, payment. Sex.

"Um, perhaps another time." I muttered.

"I'll go check out those tables, I guess." Gunnar offered, not seeming to care one way or another.

"Can you grab me one of those cute telescopes?" Tory clapped her hands delightedly.

"No, none of us are going anywhere." The girls sagged, frowning. Gunnar shrugged. "Misha, I want you to take me to your leader."

"But you are my leader," she answered simply.

Huh. That was... helpful. "No, before me, you were following the orders of someone else. Is he here?" She looked genuinely puzzled for a few seconds, and then understanding dawned on her. She nodded. "Can you introduce me to him?"

She squeaked in excitement and snatched up my hand, drawing Tory and me off bodily into a secluded hallway. "The Dragon Father is this way." Gunnar followed behind us, glancing unconcernedly at paintings decorating the wall. I was leading a pack of fumbling idiots, so what did that make me?

Tory whispered into my ear. "She works out, but her butt needs attention." She pointed at Misha's rear end. My face flushed, but luckily, Misha didn't appear to notice. "That one looks like you, Gunnie!" Tory giggled, pointing at a painting of Vikings.

Gunnar's chest swelled with pride as he nodded, not even hearing the pet name. What had I just gotten myself into? Meeting the Dragon Father? The one who had been trying to kill me for the last few days? *Hey, Dragon Father. I noticed that you had been trying to kill me lately, so just wanted to swing by and say, 'Hello.'*

Right, and I wondered why I always found myself in dangerous situations.

Gunnar began whistling lazily behind us, totally useless as a guardian. I struggled to withdraw a heavy tendril latched onto him, and his eyes immediately began to clear. He looked from me to the two stunning women pulling me down the hallway. "Is this a good idea?" He asked with a frown.

"Probably not. Try something for me. Touch your tattoo and keep your finger there." He frowned, but did so. "Alright, I'm going to release my restraint for a second." He nodded, and I let go of my precarious grip. Gunnar flinched for a second, and then growled at the air in front of him as if he could see the tendrils trying to latch onto him. His awareness was simply too strong for my careless tendrils to overcome him while he touched his tattoo. I almost clapped my hands, but of course, each was firmly trapped in a different girl's hand. "Keep touching it. It's the only way for you to stay focused." He nodded, now studying the hallway like a caged tiger as he followed us.

I let go of Misha's hand, smiling at her curious glance back, and motioned her on. Her dress was open to the top of her tailbone, revealing a flat, muscled back, and the gentle curve as it crept lower to her rear. I didn't at all agree with Tory's claim.

"Tory," I whispered. She beamed up at me. "I need you to focus on your strength, your unique ability. Can you do that?" She looked puzzled. "I think it's cute." I added.

"Really? You think it's cute?" I nodded, forcing a smile. "Okay then." Her eyes strained for a minute, struggling against my power seepage. I didn't want to risk pulling it away from her in case it affected Misha too. She took a quick breath, and then stared up at me, eyes clear but wide. "Wow. The stupidity is gone." She stated bluntly.

"I'm so sorry that I put you through that. Can you control yourself now?"

She nodded, face set in determination. "I want to make something very clear though, Nate. You scare me. Do you normally have more control than this?" I nodded. "Good. You just made me look like an idiot. I had no filter for my thoughts, and that is flat out embarrassing."

I felt guilty as hell. "How about we just pretend this didn't happen." I offered.

"Please." She answered, cheeks rosy. We continued on in silence before she spoke again. "Do you think she's cute?"

I blinked back. "Um. Am I still leaking power on you?"

Tory shook her head. "No, I just think she's cute."

I looked at her. "Sure, but she's a dragon, and she tried to kill me."

"There is that…" There was a longer silence. "Do you think when this is all finished – if she switches sides, of course – she'll go out for a drink with

178

me?"

I didn't have the slightest clue how to answer Tory. "Sure. You're beautiful." She smiled at that, so I chose subtlety next. "I take it you like girls?"

"I'm bisexual, but my tendencies lean more towards women most of the time."

I was quiet for a few moments before answering. "I'm pretty sure that if I was born a girl I would be a lesbian too. You girls are just so damn *adorable*." She turned to look at me, and then began laughing loud enough for Gunnar to grumble unpleasant things behind me.

My life.

CHAPTER 29

MISHA STOPPED IN FRONT OF A LARGE SINGLE DOOR. The number 901 stood above it, marking it as one of the priciest suites in the hotel. Two women – dragons, I assumed – stood outside the door, guarding their Dragon Father. They also wore contacts, hiding the horizontal slits of their eyes. I couldn't believe I hadn't thought of that sooner.

"Misha, what have you brought us, and why can I not feel you?" An African American dragon hissed. Her eyes were a bright green, but I didn't know if that was the contacts or her real eyes. "Snacks? A…" She sniffed the air in our general direction. "Wizard, a werewolf, and an appetizer…" She smiled at Tory.

Tory simply smiled. I spoke. "I wish to declare the Accords in effect. We chose to come in peace, and you will abide by that or the Dragon Nation will be destroyed by the Academy." I had absolutely no authority to command such a thing on behalf of the ruling body of wizards, but they didn't know that. The dragons tensed, grimacing as if tasting something displeasing.

"Then where is your gold? Your diamonds? A gift befitting the Dragon Lord must be offered, lest he feel slighted." The second dragon argued, her orange eyes smoldering. "Or is this appetizer our diamond? She does have a fine collar on. Perhaps she's an obedient little kitty cat."

Having already given Tory the diamond necklace, I produced a gold bar from my pocket instead. Gunnar and Tory's eyes widened. My suit had been reinforced and tailored to hold heavy objects without dragging the entire suit down in a noticeable way. I liked to carry odd things on my person every now and then. "I bring gifts. Even for the guard dogs." I tossed the bar to the first dragon, and she practically quivered at the slight. "Open the door, Misha. I won't be kept waiting."

Misha complied, still pleasantly grinning at the apparent promise I had made of sex later. We walked inside, and there he was. I idly wondered whether I should address him as Dragon Lord, or Dragon Father since I had heard both titles, but didn't really care if I ended up using the wrong one. I already had enough friends.

He was older, but looked to be in the prime of his life. Silver streaks jetted back from his temples, fading into his golden blonde hair. He was built like a football player, and wearing a tan custom-made suit. He reeked of money. He stood before us, curiously watching us enter, and then he smiled. "Greetings, Master Temple." He grimaced at my nametag. "Or should I call you by your politically incorrect nametag, *Archangel*? I had hoped to meet you soon." He looked at Misha. "I assumed she had been killed when I could no longer sense her, but I see that she has simply found a new master. Good luck. She is quite unruly. And obviously incompetent since she couldn't even kill you at the courthouse."

Then he turned his back on us, and walked into a vast sitting room with a fireplace roaring near one wall. I gambled. "So, what are you doing here, Raego?" I demanded.

He frowned, looking momentarily confused at my knowledge of his name. "First things first," he answered instead. "I believe you announced the Academy Accords." I nodded. "Then we must exchange gifts." He clapped his hands and three more women entered the room, completely nude. I couldn't make out their eye color, but they probably wore contacts as well. They carried a chest between them, setting it on the ground before their master. He flicked a finger, and the dragons moved about the room to what seemed like pre-informed positions.

Two of them stood near my party. One of them stared at Tory a bit longer than the other, and then sized me up and down hungrily. Hungry for eating me or sexing me, I wasn't sure. It looked like it could have been either. "Since you have requested my hospitality, it's only fair that you present your gift first. But I can't imagine what else you could possibly be hiding on your perfectly tailored frame. One gold bar was impressive, but I do not sense another on you. Perhaps the girl really is the gift?" He smiled politely.

I smiled back icily. "No, she is not. She is my snack to nibble as I please." I sensed absolutely nothing from Tory.

I noticed my power was still draining out of me, drifting around the room for a target. The Dragon Lord scowled. "You are leaking, wizard. That is not wise. I have already taken precautions lest you take any more of my harem."

181

"I *knew* it was called a harem!" I exclaimed, grinning. Gunnar shrugged as if losing a bet. "Speaking of your little harem, what's up with all the different colored dragons? It's like a bag of skittles in here." I motioned at the array of dragons around us.

The Dragon Lord nodded. "There is a uniqueness to our genetics that doesn't guarantee a child will end up the same color as his or her parents. Just because I am a golden dragon does not mean that I will have a golden heir. I collect as many colors as I can in hopes of increasing my chances of getting the color I desire. But that really isn't why we're here, is it?"

I nodded, contemplating his words, and idly wondered what color dragon he was hoping for as his heir. He had said he was a golden dragon, but the dragon hunters had said Raego was a black dragon. Maybe he was lying about being gold. I knew I was missing something. I reached into my pocket to withdraw a heavy piece of paper. "Title to a small diamond mine in Africa, ready to be signed over to you at your leisure. I dare say that this is better than whipping out a bag of uncut diamonds, or another bar of gold." I added sarcastically.

The Dragon Lord seemed surprised. "How very thoughtful of you. How long has it been in your family?" He asked, growing interested.

"Since 1631, but we have never mined it. Some of my ancestors searched for their engagement stones in the mines, but it has never seen a machine or work force since our ownership. It was estimated to be quite a promising mine, and my ancestors never had problems finding precious stones there when they chose to. I myself have five stones from the mine, ranging from two carats, to an impressive five carats. Of course, that is after it was cut. It was bigger when I found it." I added nonchalantly.

The Dragon Lord practically salivated. "I hope my gift can compare." I handed the deed to the closest dragon and she delivered it to her master without a word, and then came back to stand before me. Without preamble, she grabbed my wrist. Before I could even react, Tory slammed her hand down in a chopping motion against the dragon's forearm. The sound of bone snapping was louder than expected, and I felt my stomach shift as blood sprayed across both Tory and I from the dragon's bone tearing through the thin flesh and muscle of her arm. She shrieked, leaping back in surprise and pain. Then she took a step towards Tory, face contorted in rage as her arm dangled loosely at her side. "Stop!" The Dragon Lord commanded.

Tory wiped a bit of blood from her face, glanced down at her glistening fingertips and then the fine crimson arc across her white dress. She smiled. "My favorite color." Misha beamed approval as if it were a direct compliment to her.

"Oh, I *do* like her. You are quite right, Master Temple. She is no light snack. Nibbling would be the only way to taste such a bounty." The Dragon Lord chuckled. "But Aria was merely going to guide you to the chest. She really should have asked permission to touch you first. I believe her punishment will suffice?" He asked. I nodded. "She should be healed by tomorrow or the day after, at any rate." He said casually.

"What?" I asked.

"We heal rather fast, Master Temple. Take Misha for example. Took a lightning stick through the thigh last night, yet here she is." Misha nodded as she lifted her dress rather high to show me a bare expanse of thigh, as well as a quick glimpse of a red satin garter belt. Tory's eyes went hungry for a moment before she regained her control.

I strode over to the chest, wary of the prearranged gift. I undid the clasp and heaved the lid back. Inside sat a delicately worked music box. Tiny, really. Especially for such a large chest. I looked up at him, frowning. "This is a gift fit for a young girl, not a grown wizard. Perhaps I should give you a vending machine ring in exchange." I snapped.

He raised a finger. "The story is what is important." I waited, tapping my foot impatiently. "This was supposedly lifted from Temple Industries the day your parents died. In a mysterious room warded with magic. I reclaimed it from the perpetrator when he tried to flip it for cash. I paid heavily for it, assuming it to be quite valuable, but I have been unable to discover its purpose. No music. No magic. Nothing. Just a shiny box."

"Why shouldn't I believe that you just took it yourself?" I growled, power coursing through my veins as I remembered the video I had just seen in Ashley's office. I hadn't seen anything in the shadow-man's hands, but apparently, he had been a thief as well as a murderer. Gunnar and Tory took a step forward, unsure what to do. I held up a hand. "The Accords." I warned.

The Dragon Lord nodded. "I swear it on my power." He answered solemnly, drawing a sudden golden dragon talon down his forearm and touching the blood to his forehead. So he really *was* a golden dragon. The circle of power immediately thrummed around him, and his golden claw was back to human form before I could even study it. Well, shit. He had to be telling the truth or he would have simply fallen over dead. The magic was legit; any wizard would know that.

"Then who?" I asked, furious. "Give him to me. He is mine by right."

The Dragon Lord studied me. "Two gifts for one? That's not fair."

"I gave your guards a 1 lb. gold bar worth at least $17,000."

"True." He rubbed his lips, contemplating. "Come to hear my speech tomorrow afternoon, and I will give you the thief."

I pondered that. "Your speech is during the eclipse?"

"Of course. That is why we are all here." He smiled.

"That's what I don't understand. The eclipse is why your dragons are running amok, killing citizens in search of some old book. As a native, I take offense to that. You never asked to enter my territory, and you have murdered several people rather than simply asking someone for what you seek. As an arcane book dealer, I could have helped you, but you never asked. You chose threats instead. Breaking into my bookstore not once, but twice is a death wish." His eyes tightened, obviously surprised to hear about the second break-in. But if it hadn't been him, then who? I pressed on. "Foolish for a leader of any kind. It's no wonder you couldn't keep Misha from my control. You are weak."

His face grew tight. "Be careful. I can be a generous friend, or a terrible enemy."

"I'll take my chances." I answered with a disdainful shrug.

He prickled. "The book is a family heirloom, and does not belong in the hands of thieves."

"The people who are dead were not thieves, obviously, or you would have your precious bedtime story by now. Fucking idiot." I looked back at Gunnar. "Can you believe this guy? Dragon *Lord*? What a crock! Can't even get an old family book back."

He growled then. "You would dare mock me?" His face was scarlet.

"There is a difference between fact and mockery. Stating the truth is not punishable. If it offends, it is because it is true, and you have no grounds for argument."

"I will strip the flesh from your bones…" He began.

I brought my arms down with a snap, and whips of power suddenly exploded from each wrist: one made of liquid fire, the other of liquid ice, each crystal as sharp as a razor. The whips extended six feet to either side of me, shattering a table and a clay vase. The rug caught fire at the edges where the fiery whip rested, and a quick flick of my other wrist shattered a huge fish tank, instantly turning the water and everything inside it into a solid block of ice. My body reacted to the sudden release of power, pleased beyond measure.

"Try me, *Raego*. I fucking *dare* you." I hissed back, smiling through my teeth. Gunnar was in half wolf form, perched on his toes, and Tory had one of the dragons pinned against the wall with her hand squeezing the delicate throat, the dragon's legs kicking feebly as she tried to escape. Tory squeezed tighter and the dragon slumped with a final exhale, unconscious, I hoped. Misha clapped her hands, giggling. My rage was passing through them like extensions cords of my power, overriding their own conscious thought process. Creepy, but probably life-saving in this case.

The Dragon Lord blinked back, eyebrows furrowing. "I am not Raego, but I am very interested to hear how you discovered his name. My name is Alaric Slate. Why are you so fixated on Raego? Is he in St. Louis?" The man's eyes were anxious. "You can put away your weapons. I mean you no harm… this night. I stand by my word. As much as it displeases me not to kill you."

Sensing the truth, I drew back my power, motioning my friends to do the same. My whips of power snapped out of existence. My thoughts raced. If he wasn't Raego, then that meant there *was* a third player out there somewhere. Not good. Perhaps the third player had broken into my shop. "The feeling is mutual, but know that I will see the murderers dead before you leave town."

"Well, we won't be leaving any time soon, Master Temple, so I propose a truce."

"I give you until this formal conversation is over."

He pondered that for a minute, and then nodded. "Agreed. Bring me the book tomorrow, and I will let you see the thief." I began to argue, but he held up a finger. "I carry bargaining power. The thief is not all that I have that might tempt you. I have obtained one of your friends, and their limited existence depends on your cooperation."

I instantly thought of Indie. "Who?" I whispered, the whips of power immediately flaring out again. I was even surprised at my creation, because the more I thought about it, the surer I was that I had never created such a weapon as them before.

"You shall see when you accompany me at my short speech tomorrow afternoon."

"What is so important about this book? Or the eclipse for that matter?"

His smile grew distant, nostalgic. "The book is similar to the Old Testament of the Christian Bible. It explains much of our direct lineage from that first dragon. It is said that somewhere in that story is hidden a ritual to awaken a true Dragon Lord – the Obsidian Son – granting him the powers of our very distant, first ancestor. He will receive incalculable powers, and lead us into an era where we are respected, and feared. We have pieced much together from that ritual, but I would like to verify as much as possible before I attempt it. The eclipse is like the Solstices for the Faerie: A day of balance and power, where one reclaims control over the other. Alas, we will not be taking power from anyone, but rather reclaiming the power and control that was lost to us over the years."

He turned back to me, smiling. "It is very dear to me."

"So, you think that you are powerful enough to be this leader?" A nod. "A leader is more than power. A leader has a sharp mind, where you have the mind of a brute if you can think of no other way to obtain this book than by shedding innocent blood."

His eyes laughed at my childlike naivety. "We are *monsters*, Master Temple. We don't play by the traditional rules of your precious humans. They are all food for us, not worthy of existing but for our appetites. Check the guest list for tomorrow. You will see numerous aliases from all walks of life, but I guarantee that I will have *hundreds* of dragons to answer my call, from all over the world. If that isn't good leadership, then I don't know what is. Now, it is time for you and your friends to leave. Perhaps tomorrow I will discover how you gained your mind control powers. I must admit that I hadn't anticipated this ability of yours. It makes things… more complicated, but I could still have use for you when I take the city. Until tomorrow…" Then he bowed, and turned his back on us. He pointed at two particularly dazzling women, snapped his fingers, and pointed at a distant bedroom. He began undressing as he walked. "I trust you can let yourself out like good dogs?" He mocked over his shoulder.

We did. Fuming, I snatched up the music box, and we left.

Next batter up, Asterion, the Minotaur.

CHAPTER 30

I STEPPED OUT OF THE CAR, FEET CRUNCHING ON THE frosted grass. "You sure you don't want different backup? I would feel terrible if I helped kill the Minotaur." Gunnar added. I rolled my eyes. Some help he was. Misha and Tory sat in the backseat, looking anxious to join me. I didn't believe that I had permanently mind-fucked Misha, but she had switched sides at some point, and was proud of it.

"You two mind waiting here for us?" I asked the two women with a grin through the open rear window. They nodded, smiling coyly at each other. Maybe Tory would get her chance at that drink after all.

I began walking away from the car, speaking to Gunnar. "I doubt I will need your help, but you must obey my commands if you come. This is between him and I. No participation unless I say so." Gunnar looked relieved that he wouldn't have to get his paws dirty. Since when did minions become so useless? In all the stories I had read, they looked after their master's best interest, despite contrary orders. Maybe I was a crock leader also. I sighed, pushing the thought away.

We left the car running. The falling sun sat heavy and cold in the sky. We walked for a few minutes, past the point where I had conversed with Asterion two days ago. I began to grow nervous, wondering if I was too late, or at the wrong place. We finally stepped out of the proximity of the Land Rover's Xenon headlights and into darker pasture, the metaphor not lost on me.

I felt a tingle of power and we were suddenly in a different place entirely. Torches surrounded us in a wide circle, wicks crepitating loudly in the silence. Trees climbed high beyond the torches, allowing only a bit of the sunset to hit us. It felt old, ritualistic. In the center of the ring, limned by the firelight, sat a table, and before the table sat the Minotaur. Shadows wavered around the ring of firelight, swaying back and forth like dancers. I heard a snickering neigh from outside the light, but saw nothing except more shadows. There had been no visible sign that we were sharing the pasture with anyone while we had been walking through the empty field, yet here we were.

I looked up, and noticed that the sun had dropped significantly, resting just above the horizon, blazing with fire and warmth like it was the height of summer. Then I realized that I was warm, no, hot. As if it really was summer. I blinked at that. The grass wasn't frosted, but budding with life. Asterion was watching us, amused. "No wonder you convince all the heifers to do you. You have the coolest digs in the pasture."

He smiled back, shaking his head. "None of my partners have seen this place. It wouldn't be appropriate. It is always warm and sunset at the Dueling Grounds." He said.

The Dueling Grounds.

"You mean that this place is set aside just for dueling? Where are we?"

He studied us for a moment, face pensive. "You are between worlds, wizard. Not part of your world, completely, and not part of mine, completely. It is a rift between the two, just like sunset, stuck between two stark realities: day and night; myth and your world." As if that were answer enough, he continued. "I see you have brought a friend. That is, I suppose, in agreement with the Accords, but still…"

"He's a huge fan of yours. In fact, I doubt he'll help me kill one of his mythological heroes if he has any say." Gunnar nodded simply, glad that I had made his stance clear. He still thought that a simple discussion could solve things – how terribly naïve. I, on the other hand, was more certain of a different outcome for the night. One of us must die, or be severely injured, maimed, or incapacitated to win the duel.

"Kill? I have informed you that I am now enlightened, or attempting to achieve such a state. Why talk of killing, Master Temple?" Asterion snorted.

"That is the definition of a duel. And you did say that this was according to the old traditions, not your New Age protocol. *Promises made, promises kept* were the words you used, if I am not mistaken. And I am never mistaken when it comes to my memory."

"There are numerous ways to win a duel, Master Temple. Come, sit, we must converse like gentlemen." I heard another neigh beyond the flames, and then the scream of a dying animal.

"Um, do we have company that I should know about?" I asked. Gunnar looked uneasy as well.

"Grimm must have grown hungry…" Asterion said thoughtfully. He appraised me as I walked closer. "Your power has increased since last we met." I shrugged. He touched the air around me, feeling the tendrils that I thought only I could see. "Yet you leak all around you. Why do you waste your power?" He asked with a frown.

"It's kind of new, and when I don't leak, I become kind of reckless." I answered honestly. This was not the kind of duel I had expected, but the night was still young, so I remained guarded.

Asterion stroked his thin beard. "Your new power is seeking to fill you up, yet your cup – at the moment – is too small to hold it all in, so you spill over to those near you. You must deepen your cup." He said as if it made all the sense in the world.

"Thanks, Confucius, but I don't know what that means or how to do it."

Asterion tilted his bull-like head. "You must learn soon. It is not finished growing." I blinked. "In fact, I think it is only just beginning. But come, we shall discuss other things this night."

Armed with that assurance, I sat down across the table from him. Most of my newfound power centered in my chest, eager to jump out into whatever form I would allow, but the rest flowed loosely about me. "So, how does this work if we aren't going to bash each other's brains in?"

Asterion turned to Gunnar. "Does he always speak so boorishly, *Wulfric?*"

Gunnar nodded with a proud smile at the title. "He either talks like this, or like a man stepping out of a Dickens novel. No one really knows why he switches back and forth so much. Sometimes he acts like the perfect gentleman, but then others…" He waved a hand at me as if in explanation. Asterion pondered me with another stroke of his beard. I ignored it, but was surprised at Gunnar's perception.

A game board sat in front of us, black and white stones patiently waiting for our fingers to command. "Do you know the game? There are many different versions, but this one is quite unique, of that I can assure you…" Asterion smiled darkly, rattling a leather dice cup in one meaty fist.

"We're going to play a board game?" I asked in disbelief.

He nodded. "The game of the Gods."

"*Oi chusoi Dios aei enpiptousi…*" I muttered to myself, remembering a phrase from my father.

189

Asterion arched a brow. "The dice of god are indeed always loaded. I'm surprised at your languages, Master Temple. You are truly your father's son." He sounded sad.

"You were close with my father?" I asked softly, not even mad at the mention of them. It was almost pleasing to be able to talk to someone who knew my parents for who they really were.

"Occasionally. He would come to play now and again. Did he teach you the game?" I nodded. "Ah, then hopefully I will have a skilled opponent to battle this evening." His face lit up at the prospect.

I hadn't played it much, but my father had taught it to me, enjoying the complexity of the simple looking board game. Even with only two colors of stones, the possibilities were endless. I had seen many remakes of the game: *Reversi*, and *Go*, among others, but I had never seen one meet the difficulty of the original. They were like the children of this game – each merely a shade of the former glory of the original. I couldn't help but feel the same about myself. Would I ever step out of my father's shadow?

Asterion spread his sausage-sized fingers imploringly. "We shall roll for first turn. Abandon your power for the duration of the game."

"No." I immediately answered. "We are dueling, and for that I need whatever magic I have to be at my beck and call."

Asterion eyed me for a moment. "Then at least do not cheat. The game does not appreciate… manipulations." I furrowed my eyebrows at that so Asterion explained. "The game is powerful, and will punish any direct manipulation with force."

I withdrew my own dice cup, packed especially for this unlikely possibility, and plucked out the correct five dice. They were ivory, real ivory. Asterion scrutinized them, eyes widening. "Those are quite… spectacular. Which animal lost his life for you to play such a game with them?"

"Mammoth." I answered honestly, or at least as honestly as I knew. They could of course have belonged to some other creature, but that was what I had been told when my father had given them to me.

"Hmmm… They are not imbued with any devious magic, correct?"

I shook my head, offering them to him for inspection. "No, but yours are."

His fingers hesitated as they reached out for my dice. "Pardon?"

"Your dice are loaded. Weighted opposite the five's if I judge correctly,

190

but not enough to always roll a five." Honestly, I didn't know where the words came from, but I could feel the extra weight that would throw them off balance.

"I would never do such a thing." He said, glaring at me.

"You cannot fault something for acting in accordance to its nature. The nature of those particular dice is to cheat. Nothing in your new philosophy could possibly blame you for using them. Unless *you* made them to cheat, or are using them because you wish to cheat in order to win." I added, face devoid of accusation.

He watched me for a moment, and then snorted, slamming a head-sized fist on the stone table, and I jumped up to my feet. "I do not feel the mood for a game anymore."

"As you wish. Shall we have a dance-off then?" I threw down a quick dance move I had once seen a competitive break-dancer do to challenge his opponent. I thought it looked rather impressive, as I had practiced it quite a bit, but Gunnar burst out laughing.

"What was that? You looked as if you were having a fit." Asterion frowned.

"It's a perfectly good challenge move." I argued. Gunnar laughed harder.

"Do not mock me, wizard. I am not pleased to discover that these dice are loaded. Your father gave them to me. I always wondered why we played such an even game, attributing it to our sharp minds. But now I realize it was because we used the same loaded dice."

Interesting.

My father was a dirty cheat when necessary. Huh. Who knew?

"We could play with my dice." I offered.

"Like father like son. Yours are probably also loaded." He grumbled.

I squeezed my power tight, withdrawing all the tendrils to myself. Then I threw the dice on the table. *Five, three, six.* I scooped them up and did it again. *One, four, six.* I did it several more times, proving no consistent tosses. "Satisfied?"

After a moment, he nodded.

Then we began to play. It was a game of both luck and skill. Luck with the numbers rolled, and skill with how the player chose to use those numbers to move his stones. It symbolized life. One must make the best out of the cards they are dealt. I played rakishly in the beginning, but noticed a quick difference in this version of the game. Whenever I lost a piece to Asterion, I felt a sharp prick in my finger. After a few poor plays, the pricks grew more intense, one even drawing blood. Asterion had thicker skin than me, but he had also known about the consequences to the game beforehand. Gunnar inched forward as he noticed one of my flinches, watching us with both concern and interest mingling together.

After successfully goading Asterion into trusting me, I began to relax. He was leaning forward with excitement now as he watched the board, choosing where to place his stones. The board was heavily in his favor, as he had been playing more carefully, cautious of his new opponent.

Little by little, I released the restraint I held on my power, so that with each throw I was less and less in control of my power leakage. Asterion could sense magic, but I wasn't directly *doing* anything with my magic, merely releasing my hold on it. That's when the tables began to turn. I was hopelessly behind and it was his turn. He could have rolled almost anything and won.

But he didn't.

He sat staring at the dice on the table. Three one's, also known as the *Sisters of Fate* to the Greeks. It wasn't even enough of a roll for him to actually take the turn.

I scooped up the dice and tossed them disinterestedly, not thinking, not worrying. As they hit the table, I felt reality shift. It wasn't purposeful, and it was so discreet and natural that even Asterion didn't notice it. It was identical to when the thief had blundered into the cops by the river earlier. Odds running wild.

As a child, when I had hit my first new power plateau, strange things had happened. My parents had been baffled by it, saying they had never heard of such a thing happening, but over the next week or so the things that happened around me became too random to ignore: a phone call from a girl who had never before shown interest in me; a cop suddenly deciding not to give me a ticket when I had been doubling the speed limit; a fellow student deciding to apologize to me for being so cruel when we had been children; and even a fire starting in a chemistry lab where I was supposed to give a report that I hadn't yet written. Then they had ceased, and life had returned to normal.

And they had all happened after such a sensation as happened now.

I rolled three sixes. Asterion grunted, and I moved my pieces, slashing a third of his pieces from the board. He actually grimaced at the physical pain of losing so many at once, probably drawing blood on one of his beefy fingers. My luck had taken over. He had already lost. He just didn't know it yet.

He rolled again, and although it was a better roll, it wasn't anything that helped him. Within three moves, I sat staring at the board full of my pieces, only one of his stones left. He scowled up at me, and then flipped the board over in frustration at his loss. Gunnar hid his smile well. I didn't.

"The first part of our duel is in your favor. We shall have a discussion next." I nodded, rolling my shoulders for circulation, glad that he hadn't noticed the change in odds as anything unnatural. What bothered me most was that I knew he wanted to hand over the book, but he had to fulfill the necessary obligations that Hermes had bestowed upon him.

Now, I knew that compared to all the other problems I was facing, finding a book for a client was not that important. But I had given my word that it would be done. And that is something I do not give lightly. But Asterion had also mentioned that the book had *something* to do with dragons, which I was neck-deep in at the moment. So, here I was, playing a board game and risking my life in order to figure out what the fuck, exactly, was going on in my city.

Asterion's voice was harsh as he spoke next. "Explain these three weaknesses to me. Life, death, and love." I blinked, waiting for more.

"I don't understand." I finally answered.

"How so?" He asked, heavy eyebrows lifting slightly.

"I don't know how love could be a weakness." I gave as an example.

Asterion leaned forward, folding his arms before him across the table to support his bulk. His gold nose ring glinted in the firelight. I heard the stamp of hooves outside the circle, and shivered as I remembered the scream from earlier. "Answering one answers them all. You *love* to kill, yet *love* to promote life. You would *end* the lives of a few wicked to *promote* the lives of others. Yet you relish in the act. You kill too easily, and no executioner can be allowed to roam the streets without a check to that power. And finally, like the hummingbird, you *love* to flit from one pretty flower – a woman – to the next, tasting each, but never filling yourself. With humans, this hurts the woman, even if they presently do not understand it. Eventually they will. But by then it will be too late for them."

I thought hard about his words, because they were true, but I still felt I was right. On some of it. "The last is true. Something I was beginning to realize just recently."

"Oh?" He motioned for me to continue.

"Love is precious, and shouldn't be wasted on every passing whim, or it will mean nothing by the time you truly wish to share it with someone who matters." I said softly.

Gunnar grunted in surprise. Asterion smiled. "And the rest?"

"I seem to link them all to justice. I do not relish the *act* of killing, but what it signifies."

"But who are you to judge right from wrong? Is it because you have power?"

"Yes." I answered without thinking.

"Socrates would roll over in his grave…" Asterion began.

I understood where he was going. "Okay, hold on. Not because I have the *power*, but because I have the *ability*. I do not judge who is naughty or nice. If someone harms an innocent, then they are wrong. Especially if they do so to gain power. I *am* an executioner, but only on behalf of those who cannot protect themselves. I relish the act of delivering *justice*, but not in the act of delivering *harm*. There is a significant difference."

Asterion weighed me contemplatively and then smiled. "Then it seems I owe you a token of my gratitude." My shoulders relaxed. It was over.

"Does this mean I won? Can I tell people I defeated the Minotaur in a duel?"

"You *beat* me at a childish board game. But you *passed* a test." He smiled eagerly. "Now, we duel."

CHAPTER 31

ASTERION STOOD. "STEP AWAY FROM THE TABLE, IF you please. You may embrace your gift now." I did, and he led me away from the table, but still within the circle of firelight. I whipped up a hasty bit of magic behind his back, but he was too excited about the duel to notice. He turned to face me, bowed with hands formally folded together like a martial arts bout, and then he was rushing at me, head down. His horns gleamed in the flickering firelight. They pierced me below the stomach, and I screamed out in agony as I fell down to the ground. But as soon as my form touched the grass, it disappeared.

Asterion blinked, suddenly wary as his eyes darted about, searching for my wounded body. From the comfort of the table, I spun my spell a second time, creating a second visual replication of myself to stand off to Asterion's right. He turned, nostrils flaring as he saw the image of me flicker, bloody hands clutching the wound. The Minotaur darted forward again, flicking his head at the last moment to send me up into the air, but then I disappeared again.

I smiled from my front row seat atop the table, invisible to him and Gunnar. I crossed my ankles as I wove three more visual replications of myself, placing them evenly apart before him. He leaned back, face angry, attempting to judge which version of me was real. One had no injury, one had only the stomach wound, and the other had both wounds. I made them flicker in and out of existence, but not the uninjured form, luring him. He charged, tearing up the grass in his rage. As his horns struck the resemblance, gossamer ropes as strong as Kevlar snapped around him, limiting his mobility. He roared in fury, lunging at the second replication of me.

I smiled, pleased at my work, and also the raw fear on Gunnar's face as he watched the Minotaur maim me. Asterion pierced the second form as it turned to run away in mock fear. This time, the gossamer ropes of power latched around his arms even tighter, pulling them back to his sides, while several others restricted his thighs. Asterion bellowed triumphantly as he struck the last form hard enough to kill me for real. I let the spectral image vanish on contact, and the last of my gossamer ropes wrapped firmly around his boots, snapping tight as he fell to the ground, completely immobilizing him.

I withdrew the cocoon of magic around me, clapping my hands as I stepped down from the table, now visible to all. Gunnar and Asterion both stared back in disbelief, realizing that I had never left the table. My voice was soft. "You question me on life and death, and you were so ready to kill me just now. I saw you mortally wound me five times. Bad Buddhist. Bad, bad Buddhist." I waggled a finger at him. "I have not harmed you in the slightest, yet I have incapacitated you. How do you suppose this is, if I am so intent on killing everyone who crosses me?"

He smiled as he spoke three words. "Your turn, Grimm." The torches around us evaporated with a puff and I heard the strange horse-like neigh again. Then the sound of galloping hooves raced towards me from the sunset shadows. I heard Gunnar grunt as something slammed into him, knocking him completely across the clearing. But in the sudden lack of firelight, it was difficult for me to see clearly, even with the fading sunset, because the surrounding trees cast an army of shadows around us, and they still moved back and forth as if alive.

A place between worlds, the Minotaur had said. What was out there, and what were the shadows? A dark blur moved before me, and I leapt back onto the table, just missing a single gnarled horn from stabbing my thigh. Silky black feathers brushed my arm, and I leapt backwards off the table. I heard a heavy flap of wings as a huge silhouette rose up before me, and then it disappeared again. It was toying with me. I called Stoneskin around me before I consciously thought about it, just like I had against the gargoyles.

Panicked – but better protected – I swept the clearing with my eyes, trying to use my power to light up the clearing with fire so that I could see what the hell was attacking us. But my fire quickly flickered out, as if the darkness had simply swallowed it up. Before the light disappeared, I spotted Gunnar lying on his back, staring up at the sky, but he was breathing. I hissed at the Minotaur, not looking at him as the world plunged back into darkness. "This wasn't part of the duel."

"We each brought a pet. Don't you like him? He's rather territorial though, I must admit." I heard something behind me only a second before I felt the impact knock me forward enough to blow the air out of me in a rush, the sound of crunching stone armor filling the clearing. I landed on my chest and rolled. I remained kneeling, hoping to use the sunset to outline my assailant while hiding my own silhouette from view. I hoped it had been using my silhouette to find me, and not that it had some seriously kickass night vision.

Then it suddenly appeared in front of me.

A horse the size of a Clydesdale pawed at the earth with a silver front hoof, fire tracing away from the ground in a smoky burn, helping me see it clearly for the first time. Its eyes were like blazing orange embers, and it was mostly covered in feathers like a peacock, but black with fiery red circles on the tips instead of the usual pretty turquoise. Similarly-feathered, monstrous, black and red-tipped wings flared out behind it, tripling its size, and more feathers flared out around its entire neck in a lion-like mane, quivering as it snorted at me.

One massively thick barbed-horn spiraled up from its forehead, looking more like a trio of horns braided together with tiny spikes curling off the sides like thorns on a rosebush. Then it surged forward. To say it was graceful was an understatement. It was so beautiful that I was frozen still in admiration as I watched the red-rimmed mane of feathers tug back against the force of its sudden movement. Its horn struck my chest, and my Stoneskin crunched before the aged bone. The pressure was immense, but just as suddenly, it stopped.

I opened my very brave eyes, which had somehow closed as it hit me, and stared into a silky smooth-haired face. The beast neighed at me, stomping an angry hoof, but didn't bolt. Stupidly, I reached out a hand to pet the magnificent creature. Asterion and Gunnar both began to shout a warning, but stopped as my fingers brushed the snout. The feathers were just as smooth as they looked, but there was also regular velvety hair on its face. The eyes calmed as they watched me, and then it pulled its head away from my chest – as if apologizing – and snapped closed the red-tipped mane surrounding its head. I blinked, letting the stone slide away from my skin in sheets.

Asterion spoke. "It is finished. The book is yours." He was somehow standing up, my restraining cords of power gone.

I blinked at him, lost in the feel of the creature's fur beneath my fingers.

"That wasn't so bad."

"Granted, I should have taken into account the myths involving unicorns." Asterion muttered. "I should have remembered that they couldn't harm virgins."

I adamantly began to protest as Gunnar burst out laughing. "I am in *no* way a virgin! Of that I can assure you. Tell him, Gunnar"

The Minotaur smiled, reaching out a hand to help the werewolf stand. Instead of backing up my claim, Gunnar accepted Asterion's assistance with an awed gaze as he stared upon the myth towering over him.

For future reference, I mentally noted that Gunnar was useless in a duel.

Asterion clasped a meaty arm around Gunnar's shoulders. "That is where myth deviates from truth. You see, it's not just a virgin that is immune to a unicorn's wrath. It is also the last of a bloodline. It is just a coincidence that all of the documented survivors happened to be either a virgin, or both the last of their line *and* a virgin. It seems Grimm likes you."

Grimm knelt before me like a servant to a king. I stepped back, unsure. "This isn't really what I imagined a unicorn would look like." I said.

Asterion chuckled. "No, but you are imagining the adapted stories of Pegasus. This is his brother, Grimm. Perseus never met him... lucky for him, I should say." Until that moment, I had thought the unicorn and Pegasus were two different beasts, but didn't want to flaunt my lack of knowledge. I had a reputation to uphold after all.

Asterion judged Grimm as he knelt with head bowed before me. "Grimm is obedient, and takes care of himself. All one must do is call him when in need, and he will appear out of any nearby shadow to help." Just as quickly, Grimm suddenly disappeared. A single feather drifted down to the ground in his place. I picked it up, admiring the blazing red orb at the tip before carefully placing it in my pocket.

"What am I supposed to do with a horse?"

Asterion frowned. "You would be well advised not to demean his help. He is far more than a *horse*, as you just saw." I nodded back, swallowing reflexively. "You beat me fairly, Master Temple. But why didn't you simply battle me directly?"

"Sheer confidence in your superior ability to maim and murder, I assure you," I replied grinning. "I have friends that need my help, and I couldn't do that if I spent all my energy battling you directly. It was the path of the least consequences." The Minotaur smiled at the compliment.

"One can't die at the Dueling Grounds. You would have recovered from any injury in a day or so. *Any* injury..." He added with a grin.

I stared back in surprise. "Truly?" I asked, astounded.

"Truly." Asterion smiled.

With knowledge like that, I wouldn't have been so fucking stressed out about tonight, but I let it go with a heavy breath. *Woo-sah*, I rubbed my earlobe meditatively. "I would also like to add that your Karmic conversation with me hit a point that I couldn't refute. So, I tried the path that would be the least offensive. I incapacitated you, but didn't hurt you directly. Hopefully Karma will remember that when it comes my way again."

Asterion appraised me studiously. "How appropriate. You are, of course, correct. You would make an excellent student."

I shook my head. "I would look terrible bald. Or fat. With both I would look positively ridiculous."

Gunnar rolled his eyes. "Here." Asterion handed me a book that I hadn't seen him grab. "This is what you seek." I accepted the aged leather tome from his hand without asking where he had grabbed it from, and tucked it away in my coat, noticing the picture I had drawn for him on the cover, and the faint smell of cold stone and snakes. Oddly familiar, but I couldn't place why.

"Thank you."

"Perhaps I should thank you, Master Temple. It has been in my care for so long now, and one can only hope that a better guardian was needed, and that is why I lost today." Gunnar was still staring from one of us to the other, a stupid grin on his face.

"We must be leaving now, Asterion. I have dragons to face."

"Of that I am certain." He answered cryptically. Again, I wondered what the book was about, and what it had to do with dragons. He had said it was an original, but an original what? He turned to Gunnar. "It is nice to make your acquaintance, *Wulfric*. Perhaps the next time will be under a less stressful occasion."

Gunnar smiled back. "It would be my pleasure."

Then everything was suddenly gone, and we were left standing in the middle of a field, staring at each other. "You do lead the most interesting life, Nate." Gunnar said, glancing around in surprise.

"Tell me about it. Come on. We have a nightclub to visit, but I need to chat with Peter first. You can take Tory home to change, and pick me up after. We'll figure out something to do with Misha on the way." We walked towards the car, the headlights blinding as I realized it was suddenly night. How long had we been gone?

CHAPTER 32

I STUMBLED INSIDE MY SHOP, SHOULDERING THE DOOR open wearily. Some of the lights were on. Peter must already be here. I headed back into one of the projection rooms, following both the light and the sound of epic music and dying screams. Ah, what a peaceful sound.

I nudged the door open to find Peter sitting before one of the screens, playing Gods of Chaos IV, leaning forward eagerly as if it would help against the dozen enemies he was battling. "Hey," I said, falling down onto the couch beside him.

He started, but didn't take his eyes off the game. "Sorry, didn't hear you come in." He gestured at the table to a full drink he had made. Another sat empty beside it. "Poured you one of your elixirs of life. Absinthe."

"You will make a good wife someday, Peter."

"Yeah, give me a minute. Almost killed him." He continued playing, and I set down my satchel by the end of the couch, Asterion's book resounding with a heavy *thunk*. "Yes! Eat it, Minotaur!" Peter crowed.

I pondered the screen as I sipped my drink, warmth blossoming in my stomach and throat. "He doesn't really look like that, you know."

Peter finally turned to face me. His eyes were red-rimmed, and he looked tired, or extremely hung over. "I didn't even think about that. Here I was playing a video game against the Minotaur, and you fought him in real life tonight. I feel like an idiot. How did it go?"

I grunted, taking a deep gulp of my drink. "I survived, as you can see. I got what I wanted, and we parted on good terms. He was just fulfilling a promise he had made long ago." I leaned back, sighing. "Works for me, I suppose."

"Was it tough? I mean, he's tough in the game, and in real life you said that Theseus was the only one to ever defeat him."

"I didn't fight him directly. I played his philosophy against him. Gunnar saw it all."

"You took *Gunnar*? Why not me? I would have loved to see him! A real Minotaur!"

"*The* real Minotaur. And yes, I took Gunnar because I wanted backup." I let the silence build between us until I saw Peter squirm a bit. "Backup I could trust."

He looked at me then, cautious. "You don't trust me?"

I laughed. I couldn't help it. "*Trust? You?*" I spat. "I *used* to trust you. About two days ago. Then you just happened to whip out some magic like you had been doing it your whole life. And you never told me about it before-hand. How or why would I possibly trust you after that?"

He leaned back, resigned. "I was going to tell you. I swear. It just never came up. I wanted to be like you two for so long, and then I suddenly was, and I didn't want to be your weak-ass apprentice. I wanted to appear formi-dable, strong, dependable."

"Well, instead you just appeared untrustworthy. Satisfied?" I grouched. He shook his head, angry. "How did it happen? *When* did it happen? I would have known if you had an innate spark in you all these years. I sensed *noth-ing* of the sort though. What changed?"

He stood. "I need another drink first." He tried to step over my bag, but his foot got caught up in the strap and he stumbled before catching himself, spewing the book from the Minotaur onto the floor. Peter stared at it for a second, and then stooped down to pick it up.

"Don't, Peter."

He looked over at me, chastising eyes demeaning my warning. "It's just a book." Then it was in his fingers. I scratched my fingers through my hair. No harm in glancing at it, I guess. Besides, I hadn't had a chance to peruse it yet either. And I had risked my life for it. I watched Peter's face grow pale. He tried to speak twice, but no sound came out. When he cleared his throat, it was barely a whisper. "How did you find it?"

I squinted, taking another sip of my drink. "I already told you. I got it from the Minotaur. It's for a client."

He was shaking his head. "Is this some kind of a joke? This is the book I wanted you to get for *me*. The one my client *really* wanted. How did you know?" He looked hungry, and lost at the same time.

My forearms pebbled with sudden anxiety. "Alright, Peter. I don't know what you are talking about, but that book belongs to someone else. You look as if you have had enough to drink." I slowly stood, not wanting to spook him. He was ignoring me, reading the cover page. I leaned over enough to see, and read it myself. I somehow managed to keep my face neutral. *Sons of the Dying Sun* was written across an entire page. My skin pebbled even further. The book Raven had asked for. The one Alaric wanted.

"I thought that once that dragon lady asked for it, you wouldn't get it for me, thinking I was in league with her." He laughed nervously. "I ran upstairs to take away the note, but I guess that Jessie had written down the wrong title anyway, so I left it. Idiot kid."

"Who did you say your client was?" I asked, my mind suddenly racing.

"A rich old man who let me take over his portfolio. He said this was invaluable to him, and that I would be rewarded handsomely." He began idly fingering his bracelet with his thumb as he snapped the book closed. "I don't know how to thank you, Nate. I need to tell him right away! He will be thrilled! How much is it worth to you." He paused for a second. "Wait, did you say you got this from the Minotaur? Why would *he* have it?"

If my kid client had also asked Peter for the book, I'm sure he would have told me, but the brief description didn't sound like the creepy, secretive kid who had come to me a week ago. And the kid hadn't told me what the title was. He hadn't, for instance, told me that it was the same book a harem of dragons had been searching for, killing for. Alaric had said that there were many other dragons in town. Was there some kind of power play going on? If so, which side was I on? The kid didn't seem like he was working for anyone, if anything, he seemed to want everything on the hush.

I used the moment of confusion to strike, sensing the wildness in his eyes, and knowing something big was going on, even if I didn't have all the pieces. I snatched the book from his hands, and darted back a step. "I already told you, Peter. This book is bought and paid for by a client of mine. I work for myself first, others second, if at all. Your client has no right to this book."

"My client will triple what yours paid," he added, smiling.

"I don't change my mind after I promise something. My client asked me for the book, I obtained it, and he paid for it." The last was a lie, but I'd be damned if I was going to pass over such a high-demand book to a stranger when I had almost been killed several times to find it.

"Just hand it over, Nate. You will have your money tomorrow. Enough to drown in Absinthe for the rest of your life." Peter added with a slimy smile.

I studied him for a moment, and realized something for the first time. "Perhaps you hadn't heard... I took over my parents' company yesterday. The money you offer for this book is a mere pittance to me. Quite literally. Money is no longer a motivator. Just my word." I clinked the ice cubes in my glass, swirling the jade liquid as I watched Peter's eyes widen in surprise. "I take on clients that I trust, and I haven't met yours. I do know that a harem of dragons want this book mighty fiercely, enough to kill me for it. Perhaps I will keep it for myself. After all, I did risk my life for it no less than an hour ago. The Minotaur was no easy meat."

Peter watched me. "Why would the Minotaur have it?"

I held up a finger. "He didn't have it, he obtained it for me." I lied, not wanting to drag the Minotaur into it. There was a loyalty factor between my clients and I. I wouldn't sell him out just to get myself out of some hot water. Well, scalding water.

"Come on, Nate. Just give it to me. We are friends."

I laughed. "Funny. Because I thought friends were honest with each other, and I distinctly remember telling you that you would get nothing from me until you explained your newfound powers. I promise you nothing in exchange, but you do owe me an explanation. So, start explaining."

He fiddled with his bracelet. Then I understood. "Your bracelet gives you the power?"

He nodded. "It's a gift on loan, for now. If I can obtain the book for him, the power is mine. If I can't get it, then I get a whole lot of pain. I thought, with you as a friend, I could find any book in the world, so I agreed. How hard could it be if my client was willing to pay anything for the book? And then I could be a wizard like you."

"Deals with the devil are usually like that."

His eyes darted to the book. "I don't want to be hurt by this guy, Nate. He's really strong..."

He looked lost. "Then let me help you."

He shook his head vehemently. "No. I can't. He'll kill me."

"Who is he? I can make him back off. I have a reputation for this kind of thing."

Peter's eyes squinted. "I don't need your protection. Just give me the book. Now."

My anger was an immediate response to his tone. "Not happening, Peter. I think it's time for you to go beg forgiveness from your client. You should never make a promise that you have no way of keeping. It's time for you to accept the consequences like a man." My voice was low, furious that he would dare threaten me so that he could keep a power that wasn't his.

Something deep inside his eyes snapped. Madness danced there, where nothing of the sort had ever belonged before. The power had taken control of him. "Oh, I won't be begging anyone for forgiveness, Nate. You really should have heeded my advice and taken the offer."

He slammed his will against mine, sheer force against my hastily thrown shield. He was so *strong*. It was like a high school lineman trying to stop an NFL line, but I somehow managed to hold him back, and trip him up with a slash of fire at his ankles. As he lost his balance, his power lessened enough for me to regain my thoughts. Jesus, what the fuck *was* that bracelet, and where could I get one without the strings of servitude attached? I won't lie that it was an enticing offer from Peter's client. This was appealing even to me, and I had a considerable amount of power on my own. If he only had the finesse to match the power, he would be nearly invincible.

He regained his feet, lashing out with a rope of air to snatch the book. I tossed it behind me, cloaking it in shadows so that he couldn't see it anymore. He roared in anger. "I will have the book, Nate. Get out of my way."

"Peter, listen to yourself! You are willing to attack your best friend for a taste of power! What the fuck is *wrong* with you?" He didn't listen, but instead began tossing balls of fire at me in rapid succession. I swallowed them all with airtight pockets cast just before each, hoping to diminish the damage to my store as much as possible. Then my own power began calling out to me, that additional reservoir, and I used it. I cut directly through his attack, and slammed him into the wall, his head rebounding sharply.

He lashed out one last time, slicing a six-inch gash up my ribs with razor sharp air until I managed to shield him away from his power completely. I tied the knot around his core, allowing him to feel the power of the bracelet, but not tap into it. He slumped, arms hanging uselessly, and eyes rolling slightly. I was panting heavily. I didn't want him to keep the bracelet, but I was too scared to touch it, so I chose a different tact.

"The book is not yours. When you wake up, you will be home, and will have some time to think about all this. I doubt I will ever trust you again, but I expect an apology, if you survive your encounter with your client. I no longer care what becomes of you, Peter. I don't tolerate betrayal." Then I slammed my power deep into his brain, shutting it down into a deep unconsciousness that would last until morning, a hibernated sleep of sorts.

I prodded him with a finger to see if it had worked, and smiled grimly at my success. Wizards weren't supposed to use dark magic like this, altering the brain directly, but who would ever find out? Then I used flows of air to carry him outside my shop, and hailed a nearby taxi. "My friend has had too much to drink. If it wouldn't inconvenience you, I would ask that you take him home." The driver nodded. I waved a hundred-dollar bill at him. "I have an eidetic memory," I glanced at his name placard on the dash, "Ivan Petranov. You will carry him to his room, lay him down on the couch, and lock up behind you. Leave his keys with the doorman and you will have nothing to fear." I paused dramatically, and then hissed out the next words with a sound like a knife leaving a sheath. "If anything of his somehow disappears from his apartment, or if I hear that in any way you have deviated from my instructions, I will hunt you down, take away your license, and make sure that the only thing you can eat from this day forward is Borscht, because you will have no teeth. Agreed?" The man's face went from angry to pale, but he nodded. I handed him two more hundreds. "Pleasure doing business with you."

It was only as I stepped back inside that I realized I had been speaking in Russian. It was a perfect language for threats – full of harsh, angry syllables. Othello was rubbing off on me. I went back inside to ponder the book that had caused such a ruckus, waiting for Gunnar to pick me up so I could get the damn thing off my hands. Even though it was obviously dangerous, something about my client made me trust he wouldn't use it for harm. He was more concerned with keeping the book safe than anything else. He had even been making sure that no one else was asking after it, but of course, without the title, that had been impossible to relay to him. I hoped my instincts were right, and that I wasn't passing the book off to a psychopath. Oh well, we would see tonight.

At *Artemis' Garter*.

CHAPTER 33

I HAD TOLD MISHA TO SPY ON ALARIC WHILE I DEALT WITH my client. Hopefully she found something useful on her haunt. We pulled up to *Artemis' Garter* around ten, and I cursed when I saw the line snaking around the front of the building, and then on, and on, into eternity. Heads turned as we cruised by, girls primping themselves, or proudly revealing their cleavage to our pimped-out SUV.

As we cruised by I made eye contact with one of the valet's and he froze for a second. Then he jumped into the street, urgently flagging us down. Gunnar stopped, looking confused. The valet ran up to our window and waited. Gunnar frowned at me when I shrugged, but rolled down his window. The valet was heavily muscled, wearing a fishnet Tee despite the cold, but he somehow pulled it off. His nametag said Clyde. His short, spiky hair looked like a weapon, and I wondered if he doubled as such. If security tossed him into the crowd, his hair would no doubt maim several people. He smiled. "Good to see you, Master Temple. If you would please park over there, I will escort you and your party inside."

I looked where he had pointed. "That says reserved parking."

Clyde smiled again, amused. "Yes, reserved for distinguished guests and VIP. Join me at the front when you are ready." He stepped away, satisfied, and I felt Tory and Gunnar's eyes on me.

"Have you been here a few times or something?"

I shook my head. "Never." I answered honestly.

Gunnar looked doubtful, but parked the beast of a vehicle into the designated spot, and we all got out. Gunnar wore a crisp white dress shirt, a heavy silver medallion hanging in a nest of blonde chest hair, and dark expensive jeans. His boots were mid-calf under the hem of his jeans, but they also looked expensive. I should know. I had bought it all. Tory was wearing a single-piece white cashmere sweater that dipped low, wide-open almost to mid-stomach, allowing her breasts to hang free without a bra, and revealing quite a nice expanse of cleavage. Her long brown hair flipped down over her shoulders, the tips curling up just underneath her breasts.

A wide leather belt helped her appear taller, and the fabric continued down into a mid-thigh skirt, which when she was facing the other way, hugged her rear like a glove. She wore black knee high boots, laced up in the back with red ribbon lacing like a Christmas present. Oh, how anyone would love to unwrap that gift. Several of the women in line snorted in jealousy as they spotted her with us.

I wore a starched black dress shirt with white cuffs, and white jeans. My black boots were even more expensive than Gunnar's. All in all, we did look like VIP's. We skirted the line and found Clyde waiting for us, an eager smile on his face as he handed each of us a small paper bag with silver ribbon around the top. "Won't the rest of your guests be upset that we cut in line?" I asked.

Clyde shook his head. "VIP can do whatever they wish. They'll just want to get inside even sooner now that Master Temple is in the same club. It will be the talk of the town." He said with a grin.

"Right. How did you know we were going to be here tonight?" I asked, fiddling with the bag to see what was inside.

"I didn't. I just recognized you in the car. Almost every club in town awaits your arrival, Master Temple. Most of us have codes to follow that if you arrive, you are to be instantly treated as a VIP. Free marketing." He motioned us inside the first door to a bouncer. The beefy man's eyes widened upon seeing me, and then quickly shuffled us through. Clyde continued. "Our patron sponsor for this evening requests that everyone don contacts for the night's festivities. And, since drinks are covered at his expense tonight, we expect all guests to follow such a simple request. Even VIP." He smiled. "Now, if you will please put on your contacts."

Gunnar piped up. "I do not wear contacts. I have perfect vision." He was frowning as he held up a disposable contact case from inside the pretty paper bag.

"Already accounted for, Agent Randulf. None of the contacts are prescription strength. They're merely part of the event."

We must have looked startled at his knowledge of Gunnar's name because he smiled wider. "As I said, we follow news of you, and any of your known acquaintances." He frowned at Tory. "But she is not familiar to me."

He smiled very politely as he reached out a hand. "Miss..."

"Officer Tory Marlin," She answered after a look my direction. "And yes, that works perfectly fine, but I do not understand why we should waste time putting on non-prescription contacts." She argued.

Her last comment rolled off his shoulders. "Pleasure to meet you, Miss Marlin. Now, if you will please follow me I will show you the reason for the contacts." His eyes sparkled with anticipation. He led us up a flight of stairs, and I could feel the bass thumping from deep inside the building like the erratic heartbeat of some monstrous beast.

He led us up to the second floor, past two sets of security, and then stopped at a bar. He beckoned the bartender. The man jumped to comply. As he neared, I abruptly halted, instinctively grasping at my core of power to restrain him with cords of magic so he couldn't move. My eyes darted around, making sure no one had noticed. The bartender looked terrified. I leaned over the counter. "Who are you?" I growled, staring into his horizontal pupils. The pupils of a dragon.

The man looked about to soil himself. "I can't move! Why can't I move?"

"I'm a wizard, and am holding you still." I smiled back, pleased at the fear that I had caused the sneaky dragon. I wouldn't give him the chance to even attempt mind-games on me tonight.

His face paled, and Clyde looked mollified, as if suddenly realizing that he had done something to risk his job, but not knowing exactly what I had done to immobilize his bartender. "It's the contacts, Master Temple. That's what I was trying to show you. Everyone is wearing them. It's required by the wishes of the patron sponsor for tonight's dance competition." I blinked, and then looked around. One by one, I realized that Clyde was right. Everyone had the same horizontal dragon-eyed pupils. I shivered, understanding now how dangerous this situation had become – that we could very easily be outnumbered if everyone looked like a dragon. We wouldn't be able to tell Regulars from Freaks. And that was probably the fucking point. I was suddenly interested in who this patron was, fearing that the Dragon Lord had been working one step ahead of me.

I let the bartender go, waving him away. Instead of resuming work, he darted towards the restroom, holding the rear of his pants without embarrassment. I shook my head. I guess I had literally scared him shitless. That was a first.

A lingerie-clad hostess glided up beside Tory and Gunnar, her dragon-eyed contacts shining an icy blue, leaning in close to help them put in their contacts. A minute later, Tory and Gunnar had each donned their disguise, and were studying the crowd, ready for anything. Gunnar shrugged at my look, fiery-red dragon-eyes turning to me. "If we're the only ones without the contacts, it will be pretty easy to pick us out in the crowd." I nodded, but was still angry. I hated being one step behind.

"Who is this patron, and where are your contacts?" I asked Clyde as I slid on my own pair. They looked bright green in the case. I had worn contacts before in several Halloween costume contests, so knew how to do it fairly easily.

"Since I am normally outside, I wasn't wearing them. Same with the bouncer downstairs. Didn't want to ruin the surprise for the guests." He answered. "The patron, although I'm sure it is just a nickname, is called Raego. Perhaps he's a DJ, or a rising Rap star hoping to gain favor from the city. He is running a bit late, but said he would be here soon. He requested that if the Master Temple should arrive, he might be granted a few moments of your time. If it wasn't too much trouble, of course. It seems you caused quite the stir at the Eads Bridge this afternoon. It's all over the news. Archangel, they're calling you." Clyde said neutrally, no doubt itching to ask more. I said nothing, letting him think what he wished. The fucking news again. My secret was no more. Oh well, nothing to be done for it now.

Raego? That was the name of the black dragon that the dragon hunters warned me about. They would owe me big time if they were somehow able to bag him tonight after I tipped them off to this location. But how had he known I would be here? Had the Dragon Lord been lying to me? Was the Dragon Lord really Raego, and had someone followed us here? Or were the two working together?

"I was on the news?" I asked. Clyde nodded slowly, as if I were daft.

"Did you really slay a... dragon? They say you're a wizard." He asked as if embarrassed at the question. Then his eyes trailed back to the bartender who had run to the bathroom, and his shoulders tightened, as if suddenly believing the man's fear.

"More than one, but the news only heard about the one on the bridge." I basked in the shock on his face. "Perhaps I could spare a moment or so. I am meeting a client here myself, but if Raego arrives before I leave, then I might

210

say hello."

"Well, I will direct him your way when he arrives. It's been a real pleasure meeting you, but I need to get back to the front. If you need anything, anything at all, just tell the waitress 'Archangel.' And she will supply... *whatever* you or your party desires." The implication was heavy, and for the first time, I wondered what kind of club this was. Or was I reading too deep into things? Maybe I should have researched the place before telling my client I would meet him here. I had heard the name of the club through passing conversation and advertisements around town, and it had simply been the first place I thought of. Plus, I knew it had a rooftop bar. Always have a secondary escape option.

Maybe a little more research would have been smart.

Tory and Gunnar had moved over towards a balcony that overlooked the main floor below, and I saw their dragon contacts wide and clear as they watched the show below them in amazement. As I saw what had caught their attention, my eyes widened too. It was like Cirque De Soleil meets Hustler magazine. Three separate stages stood below us, with shiny steel poles climbing up to the ceiling above my head. As I followed the pole up, I realized that a nude woman was hanging by her thighs, arms outstretched, breasts hanging freely, and kissing the neck of a guest on the same level as me. She was thirty feet above the first-floor stage, barely holding on to the pole, and still seducing people on the floor above. The guest folded a twenty-dollar bill and tucked it inside a feather collar around the stripper's neck.

I shook my head, and noticed that Tory looked downright ravenous as she watched. I pinched her arm and she gasped, flushing red as she met my eyes. "Sorry, just incredibly... impressed." She said, but didn't sound convincing. I shook my head with an amused smile. Glancing back down, I saw a dance floor full of bodies writhing and thrashing to the music. Dragon eyes everywhere. I noticed a few strippers here and there, enticing couples into better positions, fueling their libido, but remaining just out of grasp of too-eager hands. Bouncers stood positioned through the room, ready to be anywhere at a moment's notice. I saw one stripper leading a young couple off to a back room, and shook my head in disbelief. A dance club, *and* a strip club. Who knew?

I pulled Tory and Gunnar's sleeve away from the railing. "So, I guess I didn't research the locale very well. I had no idea it was a strip club, I swear." Gunnar frowned at me, not believing a word. "Seriously. But let's go up onto the roof. Perhaps it's more G-rated up there. That's where I'm meeting my client anyway." They nodded, following me as I searched for the roof access to the top floor of the club, where hopefully nudity would be frowned upon by neighbors across the street, if not discouraged outright by the cold weather.

I found the door, and climbed up a narrow set of wooden stairs, my posse in tow behind me. We exited onto a wooden dance floor sheltered by a glass-ceilinged area with couches and divans around the perimeter where couples cuddled up beside each other or strippers performed lap dances in public view. Jesus. I felt like a prude. Don't get me wrong, I *love* the female body, and I have even visited a strip club or dozen, but I was focused on business tonight, and I had a female guest with me, making everything slightly more uncomfortable, even though Tory seemed to be enjoying herself just fine as she studied several of the dancers acutely.

Heat lamps dotted the roof, keeping the air tolerable, and hidden speakers thumped loudly with different music than downstairs. I scanned the tangle of bodies, even peering around the shoulder of a dancer writhing upon a black-clothed man in one of the plush chairs. Her breasts almost hit me in the face as she turned into me, startled at my cold-fingered touch. Her dragon eyes instinctively startled me, as she looked me up and down. "Care for a dance, love?" She purred.

I shook my head. "No, I was just looking for someone."

"I could be *someone*," she whispered sensually. I shook my head again and strode away. Scanning the dragon-eyed people around us, I began to feel nervous. This was bad. Very, very bad. There was no way for me to spot a real dragon before it was too late. And with Raego picking the dress code, odds were that he wouldn't be alone, and that he had probably sent some dragons here ahead of time. Why else the disguises?

We grabbed drinks, asking the bartender if he had seen anyone that might fit my client's description. He shook his head, and offered us a free dance with anyone we chose as soon as he realized who I was. I declined, although Tory looked disappointed at my choice, arguing that we might fit in better if we looked like we were having a good time.

"So good a time that we won't see a real dragon come up behind us and snap our necks?" I retorted, quietly but severely. She sighed, nodding agreement, and we continued searching the roof for my client. I began to feel stupid that I had never pressed him harder for a name. I mean, he was paying me a lot of money, and I had procured a book for him; a very, very dangerous book, apparently. But I had let him get away with not answering the question.

In the future, I would have to remedy that. It would have made things easier if we could have passed out a name to the over-eager waitresses who never seemed to be too far away to suggest luxuries we might enjoy while we wait. Some of those luxuries promised to be quite strenuous. "Would you care to take your pick of two dancers to one of the private rooms?" One asked. I shook my head, the pain from not getting release from Indie's affections earlier threatening to cripple me like a fist in the gut. "How about three, Master Temple?" Again, I somehow managed to say no, and we found a seat on one of the couches.

We chatted idly, eyes searching the crowd. It was unsettling to see so many dragon eyes around me. Even when I glanced at Gunnar and Tory I would flinch instinctively. After a while, we finally began to relax, and that was when Aphrodite and her sisters came to play with the mortals.

CHAPTER 34

T HE FIVE GODDESSES SWAYED OVER TO US, EYES FOR
no one else. Two sat beside Gunnar after scooting him over to a
separate chair wide enough for three. One sat on either side of me,
and the last sat directly in Tory's lap. It happened so fast that none of us
could even protest. They were experts, and only prior knowledge let me realize that they weren't *actual* goddesses, but just extremely talented dancers.
They wore just enough to tease, and little enough to lock your eyes in search
of straps or buttons that magically seemed to hold the sparse fabric in place.

Tory's eyes were wide as the dancer leaned down and licked the hollow
of her throat, but that was all I had time to notice before my own strippers
dove upon me without abandon. One leaned in, her rose-scented hair cloying
my nostrils as she licked my earlobe. Her lacy top brushed my cold drink and
she moaned at the contact, the sound muddling my brain.

"Mmmm… *Archangel* is here to take care of us. Whatever shall we do?"
She asked the other, wrapping her arms around my neck as she settled herself
firmly in my lap. She used one hand to place my own upon her smooth rear
end, able to cup the entire naked cheek in one palm.

That was it. The wizard was officially useless.

The blue dragon-eyes of the woman straddling me made it all the more alluring as she arched her back, leaning backwards to the second woman, who
promptly reached out and gently grabbed a pleasant handful of breast. Her
green dragon-eyes met mine as she did so – sexual hunger filling her gaze.
They parted, staring into each other's eyes hungrily. "I say that we should do
whatever the *Master* wishes of us." They turned to face me, as the one on my
lap slowly continued to lean back until her spine rested on my knees, gravity
pulling her breasts slightly to the side as her hands gripped my ankles and
she ground her panties into my abdomen.

We had attracted quite a crowd. I managed to notice the dancers with
Gunnar in various Chinese acrobatic positions across his body, and I saw one

dancer fiddling with a fuzzy handcuff type bracelet in her hands as the other smothered his face with her chest, throwing her head back with a laugh. Gunnar was surprisingly enjoying himself, which was totally out of character for him. The thought scattered to nothing as my own duo regained my attention with well-placed bite-marks on my thigh.

One of the green-eyed dancer's hands found the book in my back pocket. "Hmm… a librarian. I have always wanted to play with a librarian. Do you like games, librarian? We know a game involving handcuffs…" Her eyes sparkled down at me as she withdrew a pair of handcuffs from out of nowhere. "I think this book is getting in the way. Perhaps we should remove it to reach what is underneath… Which one of us would you choose?" The green-eyed dancer moaned, her horizontal pupils dilating to a solid bar across her eyes. My haze evaporated in a blink, but I didn't show it.

"I'll have to flip a coin to decide…" I pulled the coin Asterion had given me from my pocket, hoping for the best, and flipped it up into the air. The coin instantly turned into a shield, slamming into the green-eyed dragon's – because that is what she truly was – jaw. I felt blood spray across my face, and one of her teeth landed on my shirt as she flew across the dance floor. I drew my power, embracing it to its fullest, and felt the telltale signs of mind control that had been clouding us. I grabbed the blue-eyed dragon by the throat, carefully plucking the book from her fingers. Then I shoved with all my strength, fueled by a riptide of magic, and launched her into a wall. She struck the wall with a solid smack, immediately silencing the music in an explosive shower of sparks, and fell to the ground in a crumpled heap, spine broken.

Dead was good.

I heard the snap of metal and turned to see the dragons with Gunnar smiling as their handcuff clasped around his wrist. His eyes immediately changed – even behind the contacts – glazing over. He was no longer home. Tory was oblivious, making out with her red-haired dancer. I grabbed the bitch by the hair, yanked, and threw her a dozen feet behind me with an added boost of air. Her bare skin screeched in a horrendous wood burn as she skidded across the dance floor. Tory's eyes widened as she saw me looming over her, her shirt tugged down over her stomach so that she was naked from the waist up. I saw the handcuff on her wrist, but thankfully it was unclasped. Feeling something on my own wrist, I glanced down and saw a similar handcuff dangling, unclasped. I shivered, flinging it off into the night out over the railing of the roof.

Tory bound to her feet, pulling her top back up into a semblance of decency. My own fly was unzipped. Damn. Aphrodite had *nothing* on them. I hadn't even noticed their power. The dragons stood from various positions around the floor where I had thrown them, but the two with Gunnar continued smiling up at me, one holding a thin chain attached to the bracelet in their fingers. "Good, wolfie..." The blue-eyed, red haired dragon cooed in his ear. Gunnar's shoulders relaxed at the praise.

"Gunnar, get away from them. Now." I demanded.

"Don't want to." He said, struggling with the words. "I'm happy here. So happy. They love me..." I slammed my power into him, but it struck an invisible dome emanating from the handcuff, bouncing harmlessly away. Shit. One down. I had to kill these bitches now, or I had no idea what would happen to Gunnar.

The Regulars around the dance floor watched drunkenly, several shooting angry glares my way as they had just seen me hurt three strippers. Good men, but they had no idea of the truth. I wouldn't have time to differentiate between Regulars and dragons if it came to a fight, and if a couple of these drunken men thought they were protecting an innocent woman, they might wake up in a hospital tomorrow morning. *Shit, shit, shit.*

A cop appeared out of nowhere, brandishing his pistol, and aiming it in my general direction, yelling at me to stop hurting the women, his eyes wide as his overweight frame sloshed back and forth at any sign of movement. The green-eyed dragon dancer strode up to him, blood dripping from her mouth, eyes innocent and afraid. "He hurt me. Do something, officer. Please! Help me!" She was holding his arm in mock fear. His eyes turned on me, rage blinding him.

"Don't!" I yelled, as he began to raise his gun.

Her hand moved quicker than I had ever seen, tearing his throat completely from his neck to reveal a purplish white spine beneath the gore. Blood spurted into the air, painting the green-eyed dragon's face. Then she shifted into her true form, her legs kicking out a couch that had been too close. She wasn't as big as Misha or the silver dragon I had killed, but she was easily twice as long as a man from rump to snout, and green like a forest in summer.

216

Then mass chaos erupted. People ran, eyes wide, not even realizing where they were running, abandoning all ties with either their loved ones, dates, strippers, or friends. Screaming tore at my ears, making it hard to notice anything else, but I kept my eyes on the dragons, ready for the fight of my life. Four versus two. A sudden blast of fire ignited a nearby couch, and four more dragons emerged from the flames.

Okay. Now we were really screwed.

I realized I had the book in my pocket and groaned. The book they had been tearing up my city to find. If they turned Gunnar against us we were in serious trouble, because I couldn't see myself hurting my best friend. He wouldn't know what he was doing, but he was one of the most dangerous things I had ever seen when in werewolf form. It would also ruin his career if they made him shift.

Tory tugged at my arm, letting me know she was ready for battle. I waved a hand at the cop, but she shook her head, lifting up hands stained with blood. "He's gone." Crap, a dead cop. Kosage was going to be furious, and once again, I was present at the crime. What would that make him think? But I didn't have time to worry about that now. The fire spread to the beams that held up the glass ceiling, thick dark smoke cloyed the air.

"Well then. I think it's time for you to earn your own nickname." I murmured, unleashing the same whips of fire and ice I had used at Alaric's hotel room earlier. Another couch burst into flame as my whip licked it with the faintest brush. "Come on down, bitches. Let me show you what I did to your big sisters." I grinned, flashing teeth, and then I began to cackle.

I think the non-masculine sound had to do with the suddenly power-drunk status of my body trying to figure out what to make of the new reservoir of magic I had been given earlier in the day. Regardless, it made the dragons hesitate.

Then they began to move, freaky fast, like, well… snakes.

I slung the liquid ice whip around the green dragon's throat, and her eyes went wide enough that I was curious they would pop out. Then, as I tugged back, her neck simply shattered into fragments of frozen dragon-meat cubes. Her body crashed to the dance floor, twitching. I slung the fiery whip over Tory's head as she darted low, and managed to latch onto the back legs of another dragon mid-shift. It knocked her completely off her feet, and sent her tearing through the protective railing bordering the roof, cloaked in flames, screaming as she fell.

"Stop!" A voice bellowed over the crowd, somehow penetrating the din of screams. I smelled that odd smell of cold rocks and snakes again, and froze. No, not snakes. Reptiles. How had I not recognized it earlier?

I realized that all the Regulars were gone, except for the now terrified, wide-eyed bartender holding a broken bottle in one hand, looking like a very scary person – the kind of person whose actions are completely unpredictable; a potential spark for the powder keg around us. Everyone froze, except Tory. She sequentially broke a dragon's forearm, her reptilian kneecap, and then a heel-kick sent her adversary screaming off into the black night, snapping out her wings as she fell off the side of the building, luckier than her sister who had fallen in a wash of flames. I turned, along with the remaining five dragons and Tory, to the new voice that emanated near a particularly dark part of the roof beside a dead fire pit.

A familiar figure stepped out of the shadows, and I blinked. My client.

"What are you doing here, *Rogue*?" The blue-eyed, red-haired dragon hissed, still clutching Gunnar's makeshift leash in a possessive dragon claw.

"The name is Raego, despite its definition. You would be wise to remember it, Tatiana." My client growled back, shadows shifting and eddying about him menacingly.

"The book is ours, *Raego*." Tatiana spat. "You have no claim in this city. You forsook your titles long ago."

He nodded, taking a step closer, and I swear the shadows moved with him. "I seek no claim, only the safety of the humans. I will not allow him to do this." They obviously knew who *him* was, but not me.

I raised my hand.

Raego turned to me, and blinked at my upraised hand. Then, not knowing what else to do, he nodded. "Thanks," I said. "But who is this elusive *him*?"

"Close thy lips, wizard. This is none of your concern, and neither is the book. Hand it over, and we will give you back your wolf. If not, you and everyone you care about dies."

Raego was silent, watching me. "Can I kill her without offending you?" I asked.

He laughed, a deep, calming sound. "It wouldn't offend me, but it might not be wise to attempt it. We're kind of outnumbered, if you hadn't noticed."

I wanted to ask so many questions, but there were too many people present, and I knew that knowledge was strength. If anyone thought I had no clue what was going on, I was screwed. So I put on my mask. "Later then. I guess I'll just have to kill her later then."

She took a step towards me, but Raego's voice boomed again. "Do not even think it, Tatiana. You may already have a master, but you don't want to tempt me into breaking you here and now. I can do it without breaking a sweat, and you know it. It's why I was banished. Competition doesn't work well in our family." Tatiana took another step forward, and then Raego shifted. One moment he was the tall unobtrusive kid I had seen in the alley, and the next he was a black dragon, easily over nine feet long. He was heavily muscled, and he slammed a claw down onto the ground, making everyone freeze.

"I dare you..." The voice was lower now, throatier, and full of a raw power I had never heard from him before. The fire continued to spread, and I could hear sirens in the distance.

Tatiana immediately turned to the roof entrance, eyes angry as she sniffed the air. Then she leapt off the roof, her ocean-blue wings unfurling with a loud snap. Her heavily muscled reptilian forearms cradled Gunnar like a toy as the remaining dragons followed suit. I caught myself absently humming the song from *Monty Python* about Brave Sir Robin bravely running away, so stopped. Tory chuckled lightly.

Raego was still in dragon form, staring off into the night. "They have gone back to roost." He looked at me then, his huge black eyes showing no horizontal bar since they were so dark. "We'll get your friend back. But first, I assume you brought the book with you?" I nodded. "Good. Hold onto it. Everything depends on keeping it out of their hands."

My patience snapped. "You know what?" I began to yell, stalking towards him near the edge of the roof. "God Damnit. I am sick, and fucking tired of this book."

"You do know that God's last name is not *Damnit*, right?" I flipped him off.

"I risked my life to get it, not even knowing it was the same one those bitches were razing my city for, and now you want me to just *hold onto it*? I could have left it with—" I wisely kept myself from uttering the Minotaur's name. "With the person that I obtained it from if you just wanted it kept safe." Raego took a step away from me, holding up his massive claws as if he didn't want to get one step closer to either the book or me. "I don't know what is so fucking important about this book, or why so many people want it, but the one person who has it wants nothing to fucking do with it. Me. I am not holding onto this thing one second longe—"

Something suddenly punched into my kidneys, knocking my breath away as my entire back clenched up in unbelievable pain. I tripped, stumbling over the railing as I heard a familiar man's voice yell behind me. "Not him, you idiot!" The book flew out of my fingers as I fell. I saw an orange blur leap off the building opposite us, snatching the book in her talons before the dragon sped off into the night, her rusty wings pummeling the air as she increased her speed.

As I neared the beautiful street below, I felt something suddenly latch around my stomach, painfully halting my descent, and then I was flying. I glanced up to see Raego holding me tightly against his warm scaly, stomach, his wings beating in wide thumps like helicopter blades starting up. Flames were flicking all over the roof of the club now, and I saw a group of people staring at us as we escaped. One was Tory. I hoped she would be okay. The pain from the initial blow made me curl up in his grip. I wondered if I had broken my back as I struggled for breath.

I knew I would have the always-pleasant experience of pissing blood in the morning, if I was still alive that is.

CHAPTER 35

AS IT TURNS OUT, I DIDN'T EVEN HAVE TO WAIT UNTIL morning to piss blood.

I barely had time to make it to Raego's bathroom after we touched down from our flight. Instant gratification. It's the little things that make the world a joyous place, folks.

After painfully relieving myself, I had the honor of seeing the infamous black dragon's digs. Raego's pad was questionably hygienic. By this, I mean that insects chose their food carefully when rummaging through his fridge, counter, sink, or even couch. I decided that sitting down was not conducive to a longer life, so remained standing. He had flown me here, declaring my shop unsafe. "No one knows where I live. That's a bonus right now."

I carefully adjusted the bag of frozen peas pressed against my genitals – since the pain kept migrating back and forth from my kidneys to my goods – groaning at the Chinese water torture that would eventually, possibly, hopefully, relieve some of my pain from the kidney blow at *Artemis' Garter*, which had apparently not been a fist, or even a well-aimed liquor bottle thrown by that crazy bartender. No, it had been a fucking crossbow bolt shot by my well-intentioned friends the dragon hunters. Luckily, it had only been a blunt-tipped bolt, meant to stun so that they could catch Raego alive.

They hadn't wanted to risk bringing in live ammunition with so many civilians around. I was impressed that they had managed to get in at all, but I was sure that the bouncers had had their hands full, what with all the stampeding customers rapidly evacuating their club, raving stories about some crazy Archangel lighting dragons afire on their roof, or so I assumed.

"You should probably get that checked out." Raego muttered from his stained couch, reclining as if it was a throne. The smell of cold stone and snakes struck me again, but now I thought I knew why. It had to do with his flavor of dragon.

"Nah, I've been hit in the kidneys this hard before. I would know if it was anything life threatening. It feels the same as the other time. It was gone after a few hours, but I'll have a spectacular bruise." I scowled at him. "You owe me. I inadvertently saved your life."

He gave me a disgusted look. "You think something like that would have even made me blink in dragon form? It would have just pissed me off."

"Which is when, I'm assuming, they would have hit you with their true weapon. These guys aren't amateurs. They pack some heavy firepower. It was *supposed* to be a distraction, you dolt."

He shrugged. "Whatever. I can't believe you lost the book. Do you have any idea how much shit we are in now?"

I tried to scowl back, but groaned in agony as I pressed the peas too hard into my groin. When I got my breath back, I resumed my scowl. "As a matter of fact, I *don't* know how much shit we are in, because I have no idea why the book is so important to everyone." I leveled an angry wizard finger at him. "*You* didn't even tell me what it was called. If you had, I would have been able to prevent at least *some* of this from happening."

Raego sighed. "Can you at least sit down? You're making me uncomfortable."

I swept my gaze around the litter-strewn room. "I'll take my chances on my feet. I am fairly certain that a biologist would pay top dollar to quarantine this place and study the unique strains of bacteria found here."

Raego's eyes swept the room. "Yeah, but it's the only place I could find on such short notice, and I've been running around a lot, trying to keep tabs on my family without them finding out I'm in town."

"See, that's another tiny detail. Your *family*? Maybe you could explain that. Did I just kill some of your sisters? Your mother? Aunt?" My voice grew softer at a new thought. "Daughter?"

He smiled, shaking his head. "They exiled me, so I couldn't care less who they used to be, but no, none of them were daughters. I'm still young and spry. I just practice procreating at the moment."

I laughed at that, shaking my head. "You and me both. You and me both…"

I chose the cleanest spot I could find, and sat carefully on the armrest of the couch. Raego turned on the TV as if needing it on so that he wouldn't fidget. I watched him. He was a curious man, always playing with something, or looking over my shoulder, or out a window, cocking his head as he

222

listened to things I could only imagine. A few minutes ago, I had watched as he tensed, darted to the side of the couch, waited motionless, and then after an excruciatingly long period of silence, slammed his foot down on a cockroach as it exited the underside of the couch. He had laughed madly, and then promptly snagged a piece of pizza from the counter. Flies dominated the apartment, but he paid them no heed, eating his pizza as if they didn't exist.

More than once, I wondered if he had lost his mind at some point in his life. Either that, or he had severe Attention Deficit Disorder. Or maybe living a life on the run for so long had cracked part of his psyche. They seemed the same to me.

"So, the book," I began, but he anxiously turned up the volume, leaning forward suddenly. I almost decided right then to take my chances without him, but then I heard my name on the TV.

"Nathin Temple, billionaire playboy, and minor felon?" A petite TV anchor chimed with a smile. *"Should we call him God's child, or Satan's Angel? In one day, he has purchased two six-figure cars, harassed a judge at the courthouse, has been connected to several crime scenes, been involved in a high-speed car chase on the Eads Bridge where he allegedly battled a 'demon', and was seen tonight at a premier nightclub in St. Louis, fraternizing with two alleged call girls. We have video footage here."* They played a clip of the two dancers on my lap, much of the image blurred except for my face. I groaned.

"Eyewitnesses state that the party got 'crazy' shortly after he arrived, and then the entire club suddenly evacuated as the party upstairs became too intense for them, meaning the roof caught fire. Upon investigation, the local police found the charred body of one of their own officers, brutally murdered before being burned up in the fire. Further details have yet to be released to the press.

Information states that the FBI was supposedly involved; with one Agent Gunnar Randulf even reported cavorting at the scene of the crime with his long-time friend, Master Temple. No word from Mr. Randulf or Master Temple at this time. The owner of the club has refused to comment on the matter. Is this who we want running the largest company in St. Louis? With the solar eclipse tomorrow afternoon, who is to say what drunken debauchery he will resort to as his next method of celebration?"

The news continued, but Raego tapped the mute button and turned to look at me. "I'm not that guy. They distracted me." I said softly.

Raego smiled sadly. "They are quite good at it."

I glared back. I realized now why I had never noticed his horizontal pupils before. The black of his irises blended so perfectly with his pupils that it was simply impossible to notice. "You mean that *you* are quite good at it. *You* are one of them too! And you didn't tell me!"

Raego frowned. "Along that logic, I could state that you are no different than Jeffrey Dahmer, as you are both human and share almost identical strands of DNA. But it doesn't make you the same, does it? Ever changing, ever evolving. That's what you preach. That each of you has a soul that separates you from the beasts, but you are no different than us. You can be just as evil when you want to." It wasn't accusatory, and that more than anything made me finally nod back in agreement.

"Touché." I muttered. "The dragon hunters warned me about black dragons." I added carefully.

He shrugged back. "I'm rare. My father no doubt put a price on my head after he exiled me years ago. They've been hounding me on and off for years."

"Why did he exile you?"

"Because I wouldn't submit, and when male sons don't submit, we're exiled or killed. Competition of the women, and all that." He gestured emphatically. "But black dragons are unique. I've never met another, but we do tend to keep a pretty low profile." He jumped to his feet without warning. "I need a beer."

I blinked. No sudden movement around crazies. It's safer. "I'll take one too."

He grunted over his shoulder, plucking two from the fridge. He handed me one and sat back down on the couch, popping the top off onto one of the cleaner sections of the floor. He took a long pull, and then looked at me expectantly. "Oh, did you want me to open it for you or something?" He asked, looking at my face.

I gestured at my bag of peas. "It would be very courteous of you."

He obliged, sloshing a good portion of the beer into the couch before handing it over. I guzzled it greedily, savoring the alcohol, but not daring to look at the Born-On date, afraid that I would simply see a skull-and-crossbones etched into the label. "So, what's your stake in all this?" I asked.

He ticked off a finger. "No more deaths. Which means we have to get that book back before tomorrow afternoon. We can't let him use it." I frowned a question. "There's a lot of dragons in the city right now, from all corners of the world. Up until now, we've remained silent, hiding in the shadows since we used to inspire such avid hunters. For the last few hundred years we haven't been unified. The book which you found for me, and then lost, gives details on how to tap into the power of the eclipse, uniting all the dragons under a single leader, an all-powerful dragon: The Son of the Dying Sun, as in The Son of the Eclipse.

"The solar eclipse resembles a black egg on fire – the legendary dragon egg." I didn't even want to ask if they actually hatched from eggs. Gross. "Once the eclipse passes – if the ritual has been performed – that power is absorbed by the most powerful dragon in the room, the one who performs the blood sacrifice. My father will attempt to gain that great power, and unite the dragons under his call." His eyes met mine for a tense moment, and I saw fear in those black orbs. "Which won't be good. He could reveal our existence to the world, bringing back the fear of the dark ages, making all the mythical stories about dragons become actual fact for the very first time in history. Could you imagine the panic that would create? If Regulars knew we were real?"

I sighed, shoulders slumping. "I know exactly what you mean. All Freaks teeter on that line at the moment. I know I did my fair part of revealing today when I killed the silver dragon on the bridge. Then tonight at the strip club. Sooner or later people will begin to put it all together, and there will be no more hiding from the truth." We each pondered that for a time, sipping our beer. Then another question came to mind, but I murmured it practically to myself between sips. "What I want to know is why my friend, Peter, was searching for the same book as you."

Raego perked up, smiling. "I'll be right back." I waved a hand, no longer concerned with his peculiarities as I pondered my question. Raego stepped into the other room, leaving me in silence. Tomorrow morning, I would need to head back to the expo. Doubly so now that they had Gunnar, and that he was persona non-grata in St. Louis after the news had so expertly smeared his name.

Without Gunnar at my back, I felt vulnerable. One friend had betrayed me for power, and the other was powerless at the hands of a mad man. And I had no bargaining chip to get him out. Just Alaric's warped son as a sidekick. But that wasn't true. I had Tory, if I wanted to risk taking her, and Jeffries, although I doubted that he would be much help in a fight. He was also standing in for Gunnar as spokesperson for the team since Gunnar was on hiatus. Then I remembered Misha. Perhaps she could help.

I saw Raego's silhouette enter the living room again so looked up. But it wasn't him. I jumped back in alarm, dropping the bag of frozen peas and my beer as I prepared a web of offensive magic for protection. "Aye, Aye, Cap'n!" The strange man said in a familiar voice. I blinked, my kidneys throbbing painfully at my sudden movement.

"I don't understand." I finally said, studying the strange man before me.

"It's a disguise!" Raego's voice laughed triumphantly. "A black dragon thing. I've been working for you for weeks now. Jessie at your service, Master Temple." My mind reeled at the thought. Was it possible? The employee Indie had hired stood before me: long blonde hair, a heavily muscled frame, and a cinder-block jaw. As I studied Raego's disguise with my eyes acutely attuned to the magical forces of the world, black tendrils of smoke suddenly swarmed around him like a tornado.

After a few seconds the smoke dissipated to reveal my dark-haired, lanky client again. I shook my head in wonder. Tomas' accusation of shape shifting into entirely different people was true. I had been too wrapped up in my grief to have much to do with the store in the last week. Jessie and Raego… the same guy. It all clicked in my head.

"You switched the title of the book Peter asked for!" I practically yelled.

Raego gave a formal bow. "I must have written the wrong title down when he asked me to leave you a message. Jessie isn't too bright. An honest mistake, really. Although Indie didn't see it that way." He paused, studying me carefully. "She's head over heels for you, Nate. The real deal. She'd take a bullet for you if she had to." His voice grew softer. "You can't ask for more than that." I nodded, suddenly emotional.

"She's just a Regular, Raego. You know how dangerous our lives are. She'd be helpless." He nodded agreement but also shrugged, as if asking why that mattered. I changed the subject. Girl-talk later. Guy-talk now. "Thanks for the help, Raego, but it would've been easier if you'd simply told me about Peter. I could have dealt with him directly. As it turns out, he attacked me for the book just before we went to the club. It fell out of my bag and he saw it."

Raego slapped his forehead, groaning. "That must be how they knew you had it on you tonight. They followed you. Peter must have called them. He's been working for Alaric." I stared, random events slowly joining into one bigger picture in my mind, mentally erasing questions from my list as the answers became apparent. Peter's rich investor was Alaric. I began to shake my head, arguing that Peter would have been unconscious, but then I remembered the power the bracelet had given him. Maybe the dragons had been waiting for him when he got home, and woken him up to get the information.

Or maybe my spell hadn't been enough to fight his newfound power. Either way, what Raego said made a lot of sense. It was really the only logical deduction. The dragons had found me at the club, and knew I had the book. Peter could have told them anything. That I was meeting up with a client for the exchange, for example.

"You're right." I grumbled. "By the way, you're a terrible employee from what I hear. Indie deserved a heavy-handed approach. I can't believe that all this time you were working for me."

"I had to see if you were trustworthy before I asked you to find the book."

"You're fired. Officially. Immediately."

"Can I keep the gun? It's pretty sweet." He said with a smile.

"Did you pass your firing accuracy tests?" He nodded, crossing his fingers in hopes of my affirmative answer. "Then sure." He clapped his hands together in delight. "How long has Peter worked for Alaric?"

"Weeks. Where do you think he got his sudden power? Some of the older dragons can bestow gifts upon their servants, but there's always a price. Finding a book in exchange for becoming a wizard? Of course, he would agree. Which is why I stepped in. As soon as I figured out he was your friend, I knew he'd ask you for it. So, I asked instead, and then switched the title he asked for. It seemed wise at the time. Sorry it didn't work out." He said, genuinely guilty as he averted his gaze.

After a minute, he looked back at me, eyes wary. "How did you hurt them with that coin? As soon as I saw it I knew it was old."

I reached into my pocket and dug out the coin. I had no idea how it had ended up back in my pocket after smashing into the dragon's face – or how it had turned into a lethal projectile – but it had been there as soon as I checked.

"A gift from the Minotaur. He said he got it from Hermes. AKA: the messenger god; guide of the lavish Underworld; god of thieves, commerce, sports, and—"

"I get it." Raego shivered, motioning for me to put it away. "Scary guy. Did you know that he enslaved two of the eldest dragons back in his day, cloaking his Caduceus with their carcasses?" He stopped then, eyes glittering. "Say *that* five times fast!" He chuckled. I shook my head. Who would have connected the two snakes on the immortal healing staff to dragons? Not me. Raego continued. "He knew a thing or two about dragons. How did you get his help?" Raego glanced out the window, as if expecting to see the god hovering outside, ready to drape Raego on his staff as a third adornment.

"We all have our secrets, kid. We need to get some rest before we confront your dad tomorrow at the expo. He's expecting me, and after tonight I would say that he's expecting you, too." Raego nodded, face growing harder. "Are you the youngest of your siblings, Raego?"

Raego grew stiff. "What, you think because I'm the youngest that I can't hold my own? I'll have you know that—" I waved a hand, calming him down.

"No, it's not that. I'm just thinking of something." I winked at him, suddenly a shade happier as a plan began to unfold in my head. "Let's get some shut eye. I'll need to make a few calls in the morning so that we're ready for the family reunion. Until then, I bid you good night." Raego studied me curiously for a few moments before nodding, and clearing out a space in a guest bedroom that was remarkably clean, and even had a small bed to sleep in. Surprise, surprise. I was asleep as soon as my head hit the pillow.

CHAPTER 36

I IGNORED THE THREE MISSED CALLS FROM CAPTAIN Kosage on my screen and dialed a different number. Jeffries picked up on the second ring, despite the early hour. "Agent Jeffries."

"It's me, Civilian Temple." I answered drily, feeling *Master Temple* would be rather vain, but it irked me that others could answer with a title without sounding pompous. I heard the phone shift in apparent excitement.

"Let me call you on a different line. Be available." Then he hung up. I sighed, waiting. Jeffries didn't want to speak on a public line, which meant that the shit storm was bad.

My phone chirped in my hand, an unknown number displaying on the screen. "Hello?" I answered, just in case it was someone else.

"No names. This is White Lie. You're Merlin. What happened to the wolf?"

I recognized the voice, and smiled. "This is cool. It's like a movie or something."

"It's called Covering Your Ass. How bad is it?"

I pondered that simple question, but knew I couldn't reveal too much. "Bad." I answered finally. "But I've got backup. We're moving in this afternoon to extract the wolf, but I'll need you to stay behind to hold up the fort."

"What do you think I've been doing? What the hell happened last night? The news was pretty clear. A cop dead, and the wolf missing. It doesn't look good. He might lose his silver pin for this." His words were heavy with emphasis, and I knew we were talking about Gunnar's badge.

"Fuck. That's his life. It's more than his life."

"I know. There's a BOLO on his new Land Rover, because it wasn't found at the club last night. I just wanted to make sure you knew the stakes. Shit rolls downhill, and he's at the bottom right now. He'll take all the blame for this, despite the truth." I suddenly felt guilty. Was this my fault? Had I dragged him into something that he couldn't get out of? But no, they had been looking into the murders themselves. I had merely provided a link, a lead they could follow. Then I remembered that my name had been slandered too, and that Gunnar was a close friend of mine, and that I had purchased two cars for him in the last few days. It looked terrible. Bribery wouldn't make this look any prettier.

"Alright, White Lie. I'll get him back."

"You're telling the truth, Merlin. At least what you believe to be the truth. Keep in touch." I clicked off after that.

I stared at my phone for a long while, debating on whether I should call Tory or not. I had already almost cost Gunnar his badge, what sense was there in risking Tory's career as well? I already had Raego for backup. Did I really need Tory? I decided that I did, and that she would want in on this, if for nothing else than to save Gunnar. Plus, she probably had no idea where I was, or even if I was alive.

"Nate!" She answered on the first ring, voice shaken. "Where the hell are you? I thought you were dead, but the police didn't find your body."

She sounded as if she had been crying. "I'm alive. Raego took me to his place."

"Good. I'm ready for you to pick me up. We're ending this. Today. No one fucks with you two if I can help it. You're untouchable." I smiled at that. My very own pocket-sized bodyguard.

"You sure you want in on this? It's—" she cut me off.

"Of course I want in on this! The news is all but stating that Gunnar is guilty of everything, and only you and I can prevent that. I'm already on leave for my injuries at the bridge and my… proximity to you. I'm under review. Not sure how long that axe will hang before it drops, but probably not too long. I might have to become a Wal-Mart greeter next week." She sounded sad, but quickly regained her composure. "But it's the right thing to do. So, I'm doing it."

"I'll pick you up soon then. Be armed for bear, but wear something classy since we'll be going back to the Expo. We can't be standing out in the crowd."

She agreed and we hung up. Raego saw that I was finished so opened his front door for us to leave, locking up behind us. "I'll meet you there. I can't go to the Expo with you, but I'll see you at the ritual."

I stared back, curious. "How do you know where we will be?"

"I'll be watching you, but I already have a good idea where it will happen. I called a cab to pick you up and take you back to Plato's Cave. You'll need your car, I assume." I nodded. "Until then." And he left, long black trench coat billowing out behind him as he strode down the sidewalk. I saw the cab on the corner, and pulled out my phone. As I dialed a few last-minute people, I anxiously fiddled with Hermes' coin in my pocket. Here's to hoping it worked a second time.

CHAPTER 37

WE STEPPED OUT OF THE CAR MALLORY HAD PICKED us up in – a vintage Rolls Royce Silver Wraith – and into a sunrise of flashes and noise from both cameras and questions. I smiled my best billionaire playboy smile, twirling the suit coat Mallory had brought me, and strode down the red carpet into the *Eclipse Expo!* Tory on one arm and Misha on the other. Misha wore her same red cocktail dress, but Tory wore a sleek black dress with an extravagant white fur over her shoulders. My smile grew wider as I relished how this would look; a publicity hound's wet dream. I didn't answer any questions about who the women were, what had happened last night, or what was going to happen with Temple Industries. I merely smiled, moving forward as if it was my destiny. It was definitely doing what Turner Locke had advised me not to do, but I couldn't help myself.

The women on my arm looked ravishing, and several reporters tried to get answers from them, but they merely flashed shy, sultry smiles back, looking up at me with adoring eyes like any good piece of eye-candy. The reporters smiled knowingly, turning back to me. "Why are you at such a public event after last night, Master Temple? Don't you think it might be taken the wrong way? That you're ignoring your responsibilities?" One reporter shouted above the rest.

I paused, turned to him, and smiled for the camera. "I wouldn't miss an eclipse for the world. Last night was only the *pre-game* to this afternoon." Then we were moving again. We entered the building and quickly found our seats for what I assumed to be a speech about astronomy or a detailed description of the upcoming eclipse at noon.

We were some of the last to enter, and soon the auditorium was left in silence as the lights dimmed and a finely dressed gentleman strode up to the podium before the several thousand guests in attendance. Alaric, the Dragon Lord. I grimaced.

"Friends and citizens. My name is Alaric Slate, as many of you already know. I am new to this fine city, but I feel no guilt at already calling it *my home*." I grimaced at his double connotation. "St. Louis is full of a quality of life not found in many other places around the world.

"We are all here to witness the coming eclipse, as such a display is a gift to be shared with those dear to you. This eclipse is special in that it will be almost uninterrupted for a full half-hour. A half hour where darkness will battle the light, and eventually the light will prevail... hopefully." He added with a mischievous grin. The audience chuckled as if on cue. The double-entendre was not lost on me. "We have numerous scholars present ready to dazzle you with their years of expertise on this very subject, but allow me to take a moment to relate it in a very Plebian way for those of us who are not as intelligent as them, myself included." He laughed at himself, and the audience leaned forward, won over by his dripping charisma.

But all I could imagine was his dripping fangs.

"We are about to share an experience that our ancestors feared. The infamous battle between light and dark. In recent months and years, our world has been confronted with stories, legends, and myths that seem to have leapt right out of a storybook. Take our infamous Master Nathin Temple for example." He pointed a finger at me without looking, and I barely hid my surprise. As one, the audience turned to follow his finger until I fought not to squirm in my seat. Tory and Misha beamed at the sudden attention, latching onto me tighter. "Some have taken to calling him Archangel as he battled *a dragon* over the Eads Bridge. But dragons are just a children's story, right?" He grinned hungrily at the audience, many women leaning away from the gleam in his eyes. "As are *wizards*, yet here we are, one battling another the same as others might argue over a prized painting for sale. Whether the stories prove true or not, many are starting to believe them, and in that is power. Light versus dark.

"But power like that cannot be allowed to be one-sided. There are obviously unbelievable abilities in our world, and thanks to the advances in technology, more of those inexplicable things are being caught on film for all to see, immortalized as fact no matter what *some* would have you think." He expertly emphasized the last words, causing a hubbub of whispering throughout the audience. He held up a hand, commanding silence.

"But there are those who want you to *see* the truth rather than *hide* from it. Old, dark, dangerous powers are manifesting the world over. But where there is darkness, there is also light, like the coming eclipse. I urge our fellow citizens to come forth with their secret powers, because we all know that the darker powers will do so in order to take advantage of the weak. We must be unified against them. No more *Freaks* and *Regulars*. We are all one family. One race.

"I ask all of you to take a step forward as Master Temple has, and embrace your ability for all to see. Stand to fight against the darkness with Master Temple and I for the benefit of all, so that our children can have a safer future. Now, I humbly ask that you allow Master Temple and I to step aside to discuss our future plans for this coalition." With that, he smiled, stepped away from the podium, and motioned for me to follow him.

The crowd went wild as I stood. What was the meaning of this? What ulterior motives did Alaric have? Why did he want to seem to all these people as my friend? Was it a simple publicity stunt? Misha and Tory followed close behind me, Misha's face blank. Alaric had just blatantly admitted to all that I was a wizard, and that he knew it, and that I should be a spokesperson for all the Freaks out there since I had been brave enough to step out. Several in the crowd wept as I passed them by, reaching out to touch my arm as if I was an angel sent down from heaven by god himself. Others shied away or shot me dirty looks thanks to my recent media appearances. I kept my face neutral, my mind racing. What was Alaric's game? What did he have to gain from this? Chaos?

Alaric waited for me beside the stage as the next speaker approached the podium, looking displeased that he had drawn the straw to follow the charismatic dragon. He was doomed, especially if it was a scientific speech. "What was that about, Alaric?" I whispered angrily once we were close enough, the next speaker preparing to bore the audience with the general astronomy of eclipses in the background. Alaric reached out to grasp my forearm cordially so that the audience wouldn't think anything amiss. I tensed.

"I just saved your name, Master Temple. Last evening's news didn't paint a very pleasant picture of you and your ... well, my wolf now, I suppose. Everyone was focused on what new catastrophe you would cause this afternoon, and now they see you as the savior of their city. I have congressmen ready to back your demands with legal documents in order to promote your decrees into bills for congress to peruse. Bills that will pass. Wouldn't you like to see the Freaks as equals to Regular citizens? All this I give you, in exchange for your simple servitude, so that we may have a working relationship when I rule. After all, you did find my book. I owed you *something* in exchange."

I winced at his smile, letting go of his hand with more force than necessary. I managed to smile back after a second. "How is our partnership going to last after I kill you this afternoon?" His smile wavered this time. "What is your real reason for doing this? You know what would happen if it became fact that we exist. It would be the Salem Witch Trials all over again. Your kind would be hunted down too."

Alaric held up a finger. "Ah, but not if they saw me as the one trying to promote harmony between the factions. They would see you and I as the lesser of the two evils. Come now, Master Temple. You know that it is only a matter of time before our secret is out. Yours sooner than mine. And what will happen then? We will become Public Enemy number One. I do not wish that."

"I'm sure you don't. But it still doesn't make sense."

"I have opened the gates a day earlier than they would have on their own, and by doing so, have gained us a notoriety of sorts that will allow us to not appear as the enemy. You should thank me."

"I would rather damn you, because it's all a ruse. I've peeked behind the curtain." I said with a menacing smile.

"Well, that is rather uncouth, Master Temple." There was that word being used to describe me again. He pondered for a moment, smiling and nodding at a guest over my shoulder before continuing in almost a whisper. "Some people delight in creating things, building cities, painting masterpieces, and then there are those others... the ones who love to walk up and flick that first domino... the domino that sets off a chain reaction of unstoppable chaos, destroying something that was most beautiful." He paused for emphasis. "That would be me. I would rather set off the chain reaction then be the domino stuck in the chaos." He glanced over as two women approached. I could tell by the way they moved that they were dragons, but they must have been wearing contacts because their eyes were quite normal.

"We must vacate this place for loftier heights," He said softly. "We wouldn't want to leave the wolf locked up all day, would we? He probably needs to be let outside. And there is the promise of the thief you wished to meet." He added with a sad smile.

Tory squeezed my arm. "Shall we?" She asked, eyes flaming.

"Oh, yes, shall we?" Misha purred beside her.

"I wouldn't be much of a gentleman if I didn't succumb to such beauties as the two of you." I said with a smile as an elderly couple walked past us, staring at us as if we were rock stars from their youth. I kind of liked the attention. I just hated its cause.

Alaric leaned closer. "I must insist on my own transportation if you wish to visit my home. We wouldn't want any strange vehicles left on the property if you decided to stay indefinitely." The words dripped with the promise that if I crossed him, my body would never leave the property. I nodded back, having expected it. "Good. I will be along shortly. Make yourself at home, of course." We followed the two female dragons away from the Expo, Alaric speaking briefly with two older gentlemen behind us.

I recognized them as congressmen.

Fuck.

CHAPTER 38

WE PULLED UP TO ALARIC'S MANSION HALF AN HOUR later, granted entrance by a small intercom at the wide iron gates a mile down the driveway. The dragons had tried talking to Misha several times, but her face had remained stony, giving them no false understanding of whose side she was now on. Neat. I guess my mind work on her had been permanent. I felt slightly guilty about that, but didn't have the time to worry about it just yet. I felt odd as I noticed her repeatedly glancing at my chest where her dragon tooth hung around my neck. Could she sense it? But I remained silent.

I hoped Raego showed up, because if there were as many dragons as he feared nearby, then I would never make it out alive. And neither would Tory or Gunnar.

Alaric's Bentley stopped, and we were encouraged to get out by a sultry brown-eyed woman, her eyes so deep a mahogany that I almost didn't notice the horizontal slits. We followed her inside a home that seemed every bit as impressive as Chateau Falco, and I wondered how they had acquired such a nice home on such short notice if they were so new to town. Or had they been here longer than I thought? How long had Peter really been working for them? My gut lurched at thoughts of Peter's betrayal. I was pretty sure he would be here. He might have even convinced Alaric to let him keep his new bracelet.

Then I remembered that I would get to see the thief soon, the shadowy silhouette I had watched sneak into Temple Industries on the video feed, the person who even the high-tech camera hadn't been able to identify. That brought my thoughts back to the odd music box that I had stowed away in my secret vault at Plato's Cave.

Tory stumbled as one of the dragons forcefully encouraged her to move faster. Her resulting scowl was frightening if one knew her, but comical if not. She was just so tiny. The dragon didn't seem to care.

We strode past a wide-open room with a ceiling made completely of glass, construction work still apparent in some corners, and I stopped for a second. The floor and walls were rich sandstone, with massive boulders and slabs placed lovingly around the room like others would place chairs and couches. Then I saw a flicker of movement and realized that three full sized dragons were lounging on the rocks, lazily bathing in the sun. I saw the heating coils that spread throughout the room and blinked at the expense. The rocks were heated. Almost like a huge reptile cage that a child would have for a pet iguana. I shivered, and continued on.

We passed many more rooms, but finally headed into a more private area of the house, less glamorous and more dated; rougher stone walls and less decoration. Torches lit the halls. A heavy set of oak wooden doors stood closed at the end of the hall, an Italian phrase engraved into a monolith above them: *Lasciate ogni speranza, voi ch'entrate!*

Abandon all hope, ye who enter here.

Misha shivered. "Not here. Anywhere but here," she whispered. I placed a comforting hand on her soft skin and my power spiked. She blinked watery eyes in appreciation, not feeling the power surge like I had. Our guards opened the large double doors and ushered us into another cavernous glass-ceilinged room. Several dragons leaned against the wall around the room, but our guides remained close to the door like guards.

My two best friends stood before me.

Peter and Gunnar seemed to sparkle in the rays of sunlight that speared down from the ceiling. Gunnar sat in full werewolf form, but was without his characteristic *Underdog* underwear. He was attached to a leash held loosely in Peter's hand. The moon hovered beside the sun in the sky above us. It was almost time.

Peter smiled at us. "So nice of you to join us, Nate. Your *friends* are already here waiting." He motioned a finger at Gunnar, and then at an altar behind him. Raego was chained up with iron manacles, looking dazed. I blinked away the tinge of red from my vision, trying to maintain my composure. Tory touched my arm, and my power jumped again. I knew that I could incinerate everyone in the room as easily as breathing, but that wouldn't solve anything. I needed to kill Alaric, and I didn't know how many other dragons were present. I also didn't know the particulars of the spell. Had he already started the necessary steps? Would killing everyone somehow ignite it?

I took a deep breath, and Peter frowned. "No witty comment? No clever repertoire? It seems might *is* right after all." If Raego hadn't told me Peter was involved, I might have had a heart attack upon seeing him here, but now it just made me furious at the betrayal. Defcon 1 furious.

"Why is he here?" I pointed at Raego.

"Alaric needs the blood of a traitor to fuel his ritual. His own son was almost too much to pass up once we found him snooping around. I have to admit that I was surprised to later discover that he was none other than your employee, Jessie, but now I see how my book request went sour." He backhanded Raego, spittle flying from the dragon's lips. His wrists were bloody around the manacles, proving he had struggled. He opened his mouth in a curse, looking furious, but there was no sound. A spell.

I took a threatening step closer.

Gunnar's white hackles lifted and he growled a warning at my advance. "Ah, ah, ah. I wouldn't do that if I were you." Peter smiled. "Your reputation has increased over the last few days, killing those dragons, but I must admit that I played a small part in the ruckus as well." I stared back, not comprehending him. "The break-in at Plato's Cave, and the gargoyles for example. Even though they seemed to merely inconvenience you, one had to try after you so wisely told me *exactly where you were.*"

I almost killed him. Right there. With my untapped reservoir of new power, I knew I could, but there were also a handful of dragons in the room watching me, no doubt ready to squish the weak humans before them, and Alaric was still absent. If Peter continued his banter, I didn't know if I would be able to control myself much longer.

"Who would have known that this renegade whelp was your client the whole time? Well, I put a stop to that, didn't I, Raego?" Peter backhanded him again.

I threw a sledgehammer bar of air at him before I even thought about it. The dragons tensed in the room, but Peter merely flicked his wrist at it as if swatting away a child's tantrum. The energy slammed back into me, stinging my arm all the way up to my shoulder. For every action, there is an equal and opposite reaction. I began to massage my shoulder, but stopped at Peter's smirk. "Pitiful, Nate. Just pitiful. But I wouldn't try that again if I were you."

"You weren't too hard to take down last night, Peter. We both know who would win if I really tried to hurt you." I sneered. He snarled back angrily. Something was... off in his eyes. I had seen it at my shop, but it had progressed since then, as if madness were creeping in to uncover an entirely different person than my childhood friend. The bracelet wasn't just giving him power. It was changing him. Polishing those darker parts of his psyche until they obscured the rest of him.

"I could have taught you all this, and without the chains!" I yelled.

"Who is wearing chains now, Nate?" He glanced pointedly at Raego. "I made new friends – friends who share my same opinions on justice. Might *is* right. As you shall soon see. This bracelet has granted me what I have wanted my entire life. *Power*." A psychotic gleam twinkled in his eyes. "The only price was servitude. And after seeing what will happen when Alaric arrives, you will understand why that wasn't such a thing to give up. The justice of the strong will prevail. Thrasymachus was correct after all, damn Plato and Socrates."

"Peter, do not do this. I beg you. It is a line you cannot re-cross."

"Oh, I know the lines, Nate. Perhaps it's you who don't. I have lived on the other side of your precious line, and it wasn't favorable. Now I'm on the side of power, but I do not whine and cower like you. I embrace the gift, and will put it to good use under Alaric. I would be a god under a Titan." His eyes danced with hungry greed.

"I am with *him*." He whispered, pointing a finger towards the door. As if it were a cue, the heavy doors creaked open and Alaric strode into the room, three more dragons trailing him.

"Ah, our guests have arrived. Let the festivities commence!" Alaric's voice boomed into the cavernous room.

CHAPTER 39

I RECOGNIZED TATIANA – FULLY NUDE IN HUMAN FORM – with her fiery red hair and glacial blue eyes, but the other two were smaller red dragons in full dragon form, perhaps the size of two Great Dane's mashed together. Misha tensed beside me, her hand rising as if to caress them. They shot her icy, hateful stares but remained beside Alaric.

I heard the faintest of whispers from Misha, raw with grief. "My babies..."

My heart broke. "You die first, Tatiana. I promised, and I meant it."

She smirked back, eyes daring me.

Peter was staring at Alaric like a loyal dog. There was nothing left of the man I had grown up with. Power had corrupted him entirely. I risked a glance at Gunnar, and saw a hopeless fight in his eyes. He was still inside there, but had no way to overcome the leash Peter was holding. It was up to me. To us.

Tory was breathing heavily as she glared at Alaric. Another nude woman stepped closer to her master, and I smiled in recognition. Aria. Tory had broken her arm yesterday in Alaric's suite at the Expo. Then my smile wavered. She lifted up a perfectly healed arm to inspect in the sunlight, twisting it back and forth with a grin. "I can do a better job of it today, if you're unsatisfied." Tory offered, smiling.

Aria hissed back, but Alaric raised a commanding hand, amusement on his face. "Oh, I really like her."

"Do you *like* me, like me?" She teased seductively, taking an aggressive step forward. I managed to hold her back, but it was like grabbing onto a moving car.

Alaric laughed at that. "What spunk!" He turned to me. "Do you like the reference?" He motioned at the epitaph above the entrance to the room.

"*Through me you pass into the city of woe: Through me you pass into eternal pain... Abandon all hope ye who enter here.*" I quoted easily. "But I doubt Dante would think this room worthy of comparison to the nine circles of hell." I said, disinterested.

Alaric blinked back. "That is quite a memory."

I waggled a hand. "Eidetic. Kinda' neat, I know."

"Did you know that Dante encountered Wyvern's – an arcane term for dragons – while traipsing with Virgil through hell?" I rolled my eyes, nodding. "So I would argue that the inscription is indeed *worthy of comparison*."

"Tomatoes, toe-mah-toes." I murmured.

He frowned. "I hope that you now see how beneficial our situation could be together, Master Temple. One mustn't be foolish or make hasty decisions. Our coalition will benefit all." Peter's eyes tightened at the prospect of me joining them.

"But I just can't *stand* the idea of my city being overrun by a reptile dysfunction. It's just not right." There was a long silence, and then Tory bent over laughing, but she was the only one, as the rest of the guests were all dragons, and had no taste for my wit.

Alaric shook his head in disapproval and turned to Peter, appraising him thoughtfully. "I hear congratulations are in order…" Raego struggled hopelessly against the sharp manacles, still oddly silent as his mouth opened wide in a yell of soundless pain.

Peter beamed. "I captured the traitor, Master."

"Only with our aid, human. Don't overstep yourself." Tatiana warned.

Peter shrugged. "Neither of us could have done it on our own, true, but it *is* done, thanks to my aid."

She began to argue, but Alaric interrupted her. "Pride *can* be agreeable… at times." Peter smiled wider. "Come to me," Peter obliged. "Your pet will be fine where he is for now." He dropped the leash obediently.

"You gave him a pet? He can barely take care of himself, and you give him responsibility over another person?" I blurted, laughing.

Peter scowled, but Alaric spoke. "The werewolf is quite securely under my command. Peter as his guardian is not as risky as you might think." Gunnar's eyes had lost their hopeful spark. I wondered what the leash had done to him. Was it permanent, like my control over Misha?

Alaric began talking to Peter in a low voice, and I leaned over to Tory and Misha.

"Be ready." I whispered, feeding my words through the link with them so that no one else could hear what was said.

Tory gave a barely discernable shake of her head. "I hope you two can be extra scary today, or we are all fucked." She breathed.

"Scary is my forte..." I breathed back hungrily. Misha smiled faintly, still glancing with concern at her dragon children. I turned back to Alaric, ready to lay my cards on the table. Part of me died at what I was about to do, a lifetime of memories flashing through my mind as I remembered all my childhood experiences with my two best friends: Peter and Gunnar. But that was all it was now. Memories. Peter was lost. He had chosen the wrong side. Still, I didn't know if I would ever be able to sleep again after this. It would haunt me forever.

But it was right.

"It seems Peter has found a new home with you here." Alaric glanced over. "That's good. From what you say, loyalty is fairly important to your harem." He watched me more intently now, and I saw Peter's face turn stony, apprehensive. "I just find it interesting, curious really, that you're buddy, buddy with a man who happened to kill one of your..." I frowned dramatically. "I honestly don't know what to call her. Your daughter? Lover?" I waved a hand in dismissal. "But I digress. The yellow one. Oily fire dragon?" Alaric's face went blank in recognition. "Yep. Her. She sure didn't like a glacier bullet to the chest from your newest minion. But who would, right?" I laughed lightly, but the tension in the room spiked. Dragons hissed, and Peter opened his mouth to argue.

Alaric reached out and placed a suddenly clawed hand on Peter's shoulder, the claws piercing the flesh hard enough for Peter to cry out. "It seems my congratulations are unnecessary, and punishment is in order. She was one of my favorites... You told me that Master Temple was responsible for her untimely death."

Peter began to answer, but Alaric squeezed his shoulder tighter. Without a word spoken by Alaric, Tatiana grabbed Peter's arm and led him over beside Raego, chaining him up. "For this information alone I would have given you anything you wished, but as this is something I already promised it seems I will be in your debt." Alaric sighed to me.

I blinked, not understanding. Tatiana stepped away from Peter's bound body with a satisfied smile, but not before licking his neck hungrily. "I give you your thief, Master Temple. This is the man who stole the curious music box from Temple Industries…Your best friend." I stared, having momentarily forgotten about the odd box. I was dumbfounded, but suddenly even less concerned about what I was committing Peter to. Not only had he betrayed me, but he had also betrayed my parents.

Un-fucking-forgivable.

My vision pulsed with the blood behind my eyes as I stared into his soul, and I knew that even with his newfound power, part of him stilled in unbridled fear – a delicious fuel for my revenge.

It was a start.

"I see." I managed to say as the room steadily darkened. I glanced up to see that the moon was slowly merging with the sun, blocking out a quarter of the natural light.

"So, it seems we each have a traitor in our mist. Yours, a dear friend from childhood who would betray anything for power… even biting the hand that feeds him." Alaric added the last with a growl. "And mine, my own son who chose to abandon his familial duties." He turned away from the two traitors, and looked me in the eye. "So, who dies first?" He grinned; anxious at the pain the choice would cause me.

No one could ask for a better opening.

"Thought you would never ask." I drew the pistol at the back of my waist, and shot Tatiana directly in the forehead, the explosive sound was deafening in the cavernous room. Remembering Raego's warning about blood and the ritual, I quickly lashed out with a blinding bar of white-hot fire, decapitating her at the shoulders and burning her head to ashes in a single second. My fire even incinerated the gore from the blowback of the bullet wound before it had a chance to touch the ground, and then it scored a charred streak in the rock wall on the other side of the room before I released my power. Alaric leapt back at the first sight of the gun. Tatiana's wound was instantly cauterized, so no blood stained the floor. Her body struck the ground a moment later, breasts wiggling on impact. The room was silent as a tomb as I casually re-holstered my weapon. Alaric finally turned to me, face utterly blank. "I already told you. *She* dies first." I said with a cool smirk.

Tory looked sick to her stomach. "Scary is *definitely* your forte." She whispered.

CHAPTER 40

ALARIC'S FURY WAS PALPABLE. "PERHAPS OUR coalition will not work after all. You will pay for that, *Archangel*. She was my... most precious." His eyes glinted with rage and sadness as he avoided glancing at Tatiana's corpse. "I shall have fun with you later." His gaze almost made me shiver. "But back to business..." He pointed at the two bound men, the room slowly growing darker as the moon enveloped the sun by degrees. One of the dragon guards began lighting several torches around the room.

"Both shall be punished, of that I can assure you, but I only need one to fuel the ritual. Only one's blood must flow to make me the Obsidian Son the dragons have needed for so long." He brandished the book from a pocket, tossing back his robe so that he stood nude from the waist up, baggy pants covering his lower half with a wide silk sash. "Thanks for this, by the way." He caressed the book. "I've had the morning to study her secrets, relishing in our long history of power. The passage you will experience is rather short, but quite... impacting. Now, decide who dies. I'll even let you kill your dear friend yourself, if you wish."

I stared at Peter, my rage even more powerful than when I had first heard of my parents' murder. As agreeable as it sounded, I couldn't do it. It would forever break me. Tory didn't seem to know me well enough, anxiously shaking her head at me not to do it. My power began coursing down my skin almost as if preparing to form Stoneskin for protection, but it was slightly different. I couldn't stop it from happening. Alaric pointed a finger at me, commanding me to stop, but I couldn't.

The power washed out of me like a retreating tide, spilling over everyone in the room. Each of Alaric's minions instantaneously exploded into dragon form as it hit them. I tried to hold it in, knowing that it had only made matters worse for us. With extreme effort, I managed to regain control of it, fearing what would happen if I didn't. I was sure I'd just made matters worse for the home team since the dragons were stronger in their true monstrous form. Shit. Misha purred beside me as the huge red dragon I had met above the courthouse, her tail swishing back and forth. I appreciated how large the room was now. With this many dragons inside, there was still plenty of room to run laps around the perimeter for a workout. Alaric had only shifted his arms, but he didn't look pleased at even that lack of self-control.

I spoke before he could. "Why must I decide? You, who resorted to a level of violence I have never before seen in my city for a book that I obtained so easily, are not even man enough to condemn your own son? Do you value life so low that you would murder before all else? Yet now you cannot take even one life?" I laughed into the cavernous room, my voice full of scorn as it echoed off the walls. "You're a crock."

Alaric stared. "I am merely extending a courtesy to a guest. If your stomach cannot handle that, then I will make the decision. But I would never pay a thief to give back what is mine by right." He hissed.

"Then you could have gone to duel Asterion yourself!" I yelled back.

His face slackened in shock. "You slew the Minotaur?" He asked, suddenly wary. I remained silent, letting him assume what he would. "I must hand it to you, Master Temple. You are quite a formidable adversary. To slay the Minotaur – the bane of every dragon's existence – is no easy feat. A battle between him and a dragon would be muscle against muscle, as he is immune to our powers. And I would not wager on my best ten dragons succeeding... myself included." He added the last in a reverential whisper. "We shall discuss your conquest afterwards, but I must admit that I sincerely am in your debt now. It will be a shame to kill you once the city is mine."

I took a deep breath as Alaric stepped closer to Raego, who was rattling his chains in fury now. The chains must have kept him from shifting when my power leaked out, but I could see the fear in his eyes – not the fear of death – but the fear of what would happen to everyone else if his father succeeded. "I am no one's hound. I wear no leash." I took a step closer. Misha crouched low, spitting a warning stream of fire towards the row of dragons at the side of the room. They hesitated. She was at least twice as big as any of them.

"That's humorous. I recall your werewolf saying the same thing. But he seems to rather enjoy his captivity now, don't you, Gunnar?" The werewolf hunched lower, tail wagging as he licked his massive canines.

246

I tried to stall Alaric as his long, black claws reached out to Raego. The room suddenly grew darker as the moon eclipsed the sun. I was now on borrowed time. I had to do something. Quick. "What did my parents have to do with all of this? Why did they have to die?"

He looked over his shoulder, and I saw the faintest hesitation. But he didn't answer the question. That didn't make any sense. He looked like he genuinely didn't know the answer. "Gunnar, be a good boy and keep Master Temple entertained."

Gunnar growled, and slowly padded towards me, drooling. Then Alaric began to read from the book. Misha abruptly darted into the ring of dragons, bowling some of them over, but a ring of energy surrounded Alaric so that she couldn't cross. The room grew darker, and I had a second to glance up at my timeline. The moon was almost completely covering the sun now. Crap. I dodged a sailing body of a smaller dragon as Misha launched her back. Tory leapt after her, shattering the dragon's snout with one blow. I crouched, unsure of what the hell I could do to keep Gunnar away from me without hurting him too badly. He launched himself at me, and I swung a club of air at him, knocking him clear to the side of the room with a satisfying yelp. But he didn't stay down.

I listened to Alaric's speech as I kept my eyes on Gunnar struggling back to his feet. The recital was surprisingly short, only a page, really. His words mingled with the carnage just as I was sure Dante's *Divine Comedy* must have sounded as two poets sauntered through the depths of hell, conversing amicably. Ironically appropriate, hence the title, *The Divine Comedy*.

Tory switched places with me, keeping Gunnar busy so that I could do what I do best. Destroy shit. I was ankle deep in a war: dragons, a werewolf, and the She-Hulk fighting for all they were worth. Spouts of fire, smoke, ice, stone, and other properties peppered the room as the *Skittle's* bag of dragons used whatever weapons were theirs to control. Part of me wanted to catalog all the different types and colors of the species, but the larger part of me just wanted to survive the next five minutes intact. I heard Tory groan as Gunnar bit her arm hard enough for bone to snap, but her fist to his snout crunched enough for him to jump away, shaking his head. They circled each other warily. "Do something scary any time now," she complained, face tight with pain.

Alaric's voice boomed a conclusion. "I prepare the path for the dragons to thrive. I am the first, the father, and the Son of the Dying Sun!" His words tore through the room, a whirlwind of air swirling around him like a vortex of power fueled by the screams of the dying. A promise of what was to come. His clawed hand reached out towards Raego, inching closer to his son's vulnerable throat. Gunnar leapt at Tory again, and she screamed in pain. I reacted without thinking, instantly making a choice between two terrible options.

Tory or Raego.

I pulled Asterion's coin from my pocket and threw it like a baseball. I'm sure it looked pathetic at first, but then it transformed into an icy spear in midair, slicing Alaric's claw off at mid-forearm, and slamming into the lock holding Raego's chains. Alaric's scream tore through the room, momentarily halting the fighting. Raego's voice finally came out in a roar of such intensity that the hair on my neck stood on end as he freed himself from bondage with an explosion of iron fragments that pelted Alaric like a shotgun blast.

Then Alaric let his control go, and he was suddenly a pure gold dragon, scales gleaming like a pile of moving treasure. He was huge, bigger than any dragon I had seen yet, but he still had plenty of room to maneuver as he lunged at Raego. Ridges and scales covered his golden form like heavenly armor. "I will drink your blood like a fine bouquet of wine, my son." He promised with a toothy grin. Even with an arm missing, he still moved with an unmatched fluid grace. He swiped his good claw at Raego, who managed to duck underneath while shifting into his own impressive ebony dragon form, not quite as big, but big enough to battle his father. He speared Alaric in the chest, tackling him towards me in a rolling tumble of claws and scales and fire. Raego jumped away at the last minute, as did I.

I reached deep inside my power, and called my ace. I whispered the name with every ounce of my will, and he answered the call.

Black lightning struck the edge of the room, incinerating one of the dragon guards posted there, and the thunderous explosion of hell's gates opening up filled the room as the doors to the room kicked in, slamming two more unsuspecting dragons into the stone with a sickening *splat*. Thick, black smoke billowed into the room like fog, but pinpoint silver hooves emerged from the blackness, as well as a set of blazing, fiery eyes. Silver blue fire traced the *clip-clop* of horse hooves as he slowly entered the room, and he snorted a neigh that sounded both feral and hungry, freezing the marrow in my bones. His pearlescent horn seemed to glow in anticipation of the blood he sought. Everyone stopped to look, confused and frightened.

My little pony knew how to make an entrance.

Grimm launched out of the shadows like one of the Four Horsemen of the Apocalypse, ripping the throat out of a dragon with his gleaming horn. He neighed again, a chilling, crawling, bestial noise cast into the room, and all the dragons watched in surprise, and then pure fear. So they were acquainted. It would save me the triviality of introductions. I had asked Raego if he was the youngest of his siblings for a reason.

It made him immune to Grimm's wrath. I hoped.

The unicorn's feathers snapped out in a rattling mane of black and red, and the dragons hesitated as he pawed a fiery hoof at the stone. "Good pony!" I bellowed, but as I turned away, I saw Alaric storming towards me. I quickly launched two balls of liquid fire at his chest, where they splattered over his torso in a wash of oily flame against his scales. He opened his jaws wide and roared, his own stream of fire singing my suit as I dove to safety. I rolled on the ground, trying to extinguish any flames on my clothes before I lurched back to my feet. Dry cleaning could only fix so much, after all.

I instantly threw out a net of icy steel, tripping up Alaric as he reared up for a second attack. He collapsed, his momentum sending him sliding into the pile of dragons. Then Gunnar slammed into me, knocking me from my feet, and I crumpled to the ground, barely dodging his snapping teeth as my best friend tried to eat my face. His eyes looked crazed, as if he were watching a nightmare of his own making, unable to stop it from happening. My head rang as it struck the cold ground, and stars exploded across my vision as I managed to wrestle his jaws from my face by grabbing hold of his ears. Tory grabbed him by the scruff of his neck, tossing him back into a candle-holder on the opposite side of the room. He let out a sad, puppy-like squeal on impact. Misha was down, bleeding from numerous wounds, but so were many of her sisters. I saw her eyes darting about wildly, no doubt searching for her babies in the chaos. Grimm tore through the dragons like a scythe, ending lives as surely as the tool cut wheat at harvest in days of old. Gunnar took a few seconds to get up, and I had time to glance at Raego.

He was standing near Peter, but staring at me with his huge dragon eyes. And in those eyes, was the ultimate question. Raego had heard the conversation while he was bound, and heard that I had condemned Peter to death, but

249

here he was, asking my permission. His words somehow whispered into my ear, one of his abilities perhaps? *It's the only way. One must die to stop this, or we will all burn before his power. There isn't much time before the eclipse is over.* I stared back for an eternity, staring into Peter's pleading eyes.

And I nodded, my soul burning away forever.

CHAPTER 41

RAEGO DIDN'T EVEN HESITATE. HE GRIPPED PETERS hair and drew a talon across his pale throat. Blood spurted across the ground instantly, sizzling as it struck the ground. Then Raego breathed onto his face. My childhood friend instantly turned into an obsidian statue, mouth and eyes wide open in surprise. The power in the room coalesced as he died, spiraling into Raego as the moon overshadowed the sun for a few seconds longer. Everything was silent for a breath, and then a concussive ring of shadows exploded out of him. The ceiling shattered into a downpour of raining glass shards, some much bigger than others. One of the latter slammed straight into my side, piercing me like a sword. I screamed in pain, feeling the hot fire of blood instantly escaping my body, and the sound of my voice was eerily alone as I stared transfixed at the explosion, one hand gripping my gun and the other clutching my cell phone.

Every dragon in the room instantly turned into an obsidian statue except Misha, Raego, and Alaric, who lay panting on the ground, struggling to climb to his feet. The other dragons were frozen in the pain and rage of battle, filling the room like lawn ornaments from a nightmare. I finally spotted Misha's babies, curled up in the corner as far from the fighting as they could get, eyes wide with fear as they held each other, forever frozen in their obsidian embrace. I felt a lump form in my throat at that. Seeing Alaric still alive and unaffected by Raego's blast of power, I hit *send* on the pre-typed text message on my phone, and then sighed, exhaustion and blood loss threatening to consume my dwindling strength. Grimm eyed Raego cautiously, but made no move against him, instead neighing anxiously in my direction as he swished his tail. His wings flared out protectively over Misha as she smiled up at him, ignoring the crimson drops that dripped from Grimm's wings and snout. Fresh blood. On a horse.

Gross.

"Nooo!" Alaric's voice boomed. "This cannot be! I will tear the flesh from your bones, wizard!" Then he was running at me, claws tearing into the stone. I raised the gun, fighting my dizziness, and unloaded the rest of the clip at his face. I'm a good shot, but he was just so big and strong, and his scaly, golden skin really was like armor. Several teeth shattered as my aim hit true, and blood exploded from his skull as first his eye was torn out, and then another bullet went straight up his nostril. Flaps of skin hung from his face, blood pouring over his long, glittering shattered teeth as he continued at me, unperturbed. The gun clicked empty and I groaned, unable to get to my feet with the spear of glass still embedded in my body.

Then three sizzling spears of light slammed into his ribs from the side of the room, and I heard shouting as another swarm of projectiles peppered him, nets tripping up his feet, and more electric spears hammering his frame. He finally went down, sliding just past me as his claws reached out to catch me as he did. His claw scratched my cheek in a blaze of agony, but not enough to decapitate me before he was safely out of reach. I looked up to see Mallory and the dragon hunters' leap onto his body, stabbing him over and over again. Several screamed as they were consumed by his fiery breath or were disemboweled by a stray claw in his last throes of self-defense. So many dead. It all happened so fast that none of my other friends had even moved, if they would have even been able to, that is. Finally, the Dragon Lord was still.

Between one moment and the next, Gunnar collapsed to the ground, shifting back to his very naked human form. Wounds crossed his body, his nose a broken ruin, and several hideous bruises painted his ribs. He breathed, but didn't move. Tory fell to her knees, cradling her broken arm and weeping. Gunnar lifted his head to look at me, smiled, and then closed them again. "Thanks." He wheezed. "Couldn't disobey…"

Misha ran over to Tory, her nude body curling around the little sobbing cop affectionately, smoothing her hair with a bloody hand. Tory smiled up at her new friend with a nod that she would be fine. I hissed as I glanced down at my own wounds, glad to realize that they weren't fatal. One was serious, but as long as I got medical attention soon, I would survive. Tory and Misha finally crawled over to my side, eyes widening as they saw the wound. One-armed, Tory helped prop me up and take off my coat as I struggled not to scream again. With a sharp breath, I withdrew the shard, slicing my fingers in my haste. Tory and I quickly tied my coat around my waist with a sharp pull, making me grunt. I panted, leaning back. "That should hold for now, but I think you should be fired as the groups *fashionista*. No respectable man would ever tie a coat around his waist like that." Tory smiled. I chuckled and she leaned in close, squeezing my upper body with her one good arm. "Thank you, Nate," she whispered into my ear.

We helped each other up. I felt dizzy, but mobile. Blood instantly seeped through the coat, but it didn't spread too fast, which was good. I closed off my perception of the pain like my parents had taught me so long ago. Mallory and the dragon hunters watched, maintaining a safe distance as their lips grimaced at Raego and Misha with distaste. Tory looked at my side, concerned.

"It's alright, but we need to get you checked out too." I said, to her as she continued to watch me. She nodded, cradling her useless arm, her face tight.

Raego was back in human form, glancing at the statues and the hunters, looking impressed and cautious.

"How did they know where to find us?" He waggled a hand at the men.

I shot him a weak grin. "I texted Mallory. He was waiting with Tomas and the Dragon Hunters for my call." Raego shook his head.

"You definitely come prepared for the worst."

"I was a good Boy Scout." I said tiredly, looking around the room at the frightening dragon statues. "What are you going to do with them now?" I asked.

He pondered that for a minute. "Lawn ornaments?" He offered, face questioning.

Tory began to laugh between sobs of pain, struggling to catch her breath. I couldn't help it. I joined in, and soon we were all laughing between pants of pain. Grimm nuzzled Misha affectionately with his bloodstained muzzle and then clopped over to me to do the same. Just a friendly, horned, blood covered, red and black peacock-feathered, death-unicorn. Cuddling. No big deal. Misha glanced at her babies in the corner, faces contorted in pain, and I heard her sob lightly. Raego touched her shoulder and whispered a few words to her that seemed to cheer her up, her eyes widening with hope. I didn't want to ask. I just wanted to get the hell out of here.

Raego plucked the book from the ground, looking over at me. "Mind if I peruse this before returning it? It really is a family tome. I would like to study it before returning it to your guardianship. I don't want any surprises cropping up when I meet up with my brethren... subjects," he corrected. "Of the Dragon Nation."

I nodded. "As long as Tomas doesn't diminish your flock in the mean-time." Raego nodded seriously, glancing at the dragon hunters pointedly. "But I still expect the payment you promised." He laughed, but agreed.

Mallory approached, checking me quickly to assess the damage. Satisfied, he shook his head, grinning. "Ye were right, Laddie. You do know how to have a good time. Want me to start the car?" I nodded, too tired to speak. "I'll take Tomas and the rest with me. Dinna' want any more trouble with your other friend there. Old habits die hard." With a flick of his head, he indicated the dragon hunters and Raego eyeing each other warily. I nodded again. After a few words between the two men, Tomas met my eyes, promising a long talk later, and then rounded up his men to leave, grimly lugging away the bodies of his fallen comrades. I felt sick.

Once they were all gone, Gunnar climbed to his feet, looking drunk, but remained silent, eyes downcast. He had probably found a way to blame himself for everything. He usually did. Drama queen. But there was nothing to do about that now. I felt dizzy from both how much power I had used in the fight, and my wound. I was stunned that we were all alive. Well, all of us except for Peter. Oddly, I didn't even feel bad about that as I looked at his frozen fear-stricken obsidian face. "And how exactly did you come to command the unicorn?" Raego asked softly as he helped Misha – now in her impressively nude human form – into her dress.

"A favor." I answered simply. Grimm neighed one more time, and then flew into a shadow and disappeared. No one spoke as they watched me. At that moment, the room brightened significantly as the moon finally lost its control over the eclipse.

"I owe you, Nate. You could have used that coin to protect your friend, Tory, but you used it to save me instead. I'll never be able to thank you enough."

"It was a gamble, kid. Sometimes gambles work, and sometimes you go belly up. I was just lucky." I looked around the room. "We were all lucky."

"Son of the Dying Sun, or Obsidian Son, but not kid. Not ever again," Raego said softly.

"Maybe, but that's a mouthful. I'll stick with *kid*."

Raego shook his head, smiling. He motioned for us to leave the room, supporting Misha as we left. The rest of us supported each other. The house was mostly empty, few of the dragons from earlier visible. I wondered why, but Raego shook his head as I opened my mouth. "They can feel my power. Any loyal to my father were turned to stone, but the others have fled to no doubt spread word." As if verifying that claim, we did see several more dragons frozen into statues as we left. Creepy. "I will receive dignitaries soon, especially since all the big names are already in town. Everyone is covering their ass right now, no doubt preparing gifts appropriate for their new Lord."

We were quiet for a few hallways as we all recovered, regaining our strength. Gunnar finally piped up as he and Tory carried each other. "I am not fit to lead a team if I can't even protect myself from two dragon's seductive wiles," he said guiltily. "She took me too easily at the night club. I was useless."

I waited a moment and then smiled at him. "But they did have huge racks, Gunnar. I mean, they were beyond glorious. Many men have fallen for less."

Tory grinned darkly. "Hell, I would have done anything to see those up close. I could rule the world with a pair like that blonde's." We each looked at her, surprised. She blushed, and began to laugh, but was cut short by a jolt of pain in her arm. Misha was there in an instant, supporting her weight. Tory nuzzled her head into Misha's neck.

"So, what happened after I was captured?" Gunnar asked carefully, face hard.

Tory and I told him the story, the full story about the media and the dead cop. His shoulders sagged further with each word. I even told him what Jeffries had said about the very likely possibility of him losing his job. He was quiet after that. We exited the house, stepping out into the large circular drive before he spoke again. The dragon hunters had apparently all left, but I spotted Mallory at the wheel of Gunnar's Land Rover, patiently waiting for us. He must have had a spare key on him. Gunnar finally spoke. "That was my life. Without it I have nothing. The FBI won't be able to stand up to the Freaks if they continue to crawl out of the woodwork. Even though I was under their control, I heard everything. I saw him talking to congressmen. He was giving them… gifts. Bribes. His dragons were seducing them in a back room. He owned them as much as he owned me. I don't think people are going to stand for his coalition, despite support in political channels. I think a revolt is coming. At least major ripples in the pond anyway. The Regulars don't want to accept us as humans with equal rights, and I don't blame them after the crimes I've seen."

Everyone turned to me as if waiting for the axe to drop. My name had been smeared across the media the most, and my secret was out, completely, stark naked for all to see. I looked them each in the eye. "Well, I've been thinking." Gunnar immediately groaned and Tory smiled. "As I was saying…" I continued, frowning at Gunnar's grin. "I *am* a billionaire who has no chance of spending all the money at my disposal. What do you say to me privatizing our little club here?"

Everyone's eyes widened at that, and I smiled, proud of the shocked reactions. Misha looked anxious, but the others hadn't overcome their shock.

"Like Vigilantes?" Gunnar blurted, face full of disapproval.

"No, no. That's illegal… But kind of." I flashed a guilty grin. Tory watched me curiously. "Perhaps consultants would be a better term?"

Raego remained silent, but was smiling alongside Misha. Tory turned to Gunnar, arching a brow. Finally, Gunnar nodded. "That sounds legal. Kind of." He grew more enthusiastic as he realized that perhaps his life wasn't over. "I like it. Black Ops Mythical Freaks Assemble!" He cheered, smiling like a child.

"Again, kind of a mouthful. How about Black Ops Wizards?"

"But I'm not a wizard." Gunnar argued.

"Neither is the she-hulk or Obsidian Son, but it sounds much catchier, and there is that Kentucky Senator who declared all Freaks were the spawn of wizards anyway." Everyone quickly agreed, nodding enthusiastically.

"We'll need to discuss pay though since we aren't all billionaires." Gunnar began. "For instance, we'll need enough to pay bills, healthcare, and—"

"Six figures work for everyone who wants to do this full time?"

My words cut like a knife. Tory blinked at me. "That…" She cleared her throat. "That is enough to buy me as your sex slave for eternity." She said before catching herself with a fierce blush. I realized I was focusing so much on my stomach pain that my power was leaking out again. I struggled to juggle the two so that she could answer honestly. She scowled at me, glancing at Misha first in apology. Misha grinned hungrily. "What I *meant* to say is that I come from a very poor family, and that is more than I have ever hoped to make in law enforcement."

"The job will be tough, and as you saw today, very dangerous. I will pay

256

accordingly." I glanced at Gunnar. "With full health expenses covered out-side of that, of course." I raised a hand for silence as Gunnar guffawed. "With no deductible."

The silence was thick, and then Tory spoke. "Nate Temple for president?"

Everyone laughed at that. I looked over to Misha. "I assume Raego will be needing you. I release you from my power." She blinked at me.

"It wasn't your power that kept me around. You wear my tooth." I blinked, but she continued. "And you promised sex once this was all fin-ished." It was my turn to be embarrassed, and that is no easy task. Everyone else joined in on razzing me after that. Misha looked from face to face. "I was serious. He promised." They laughed harder.

Gunnar's conscience had a say. "This still sounds shady. I stand by my pledge as a federal agent, and don't want to do anything illegal."

"We will be dancing on the fringes of the law, hence the term Black Ops. But the government will be hiring *us*, so that should appease you. Otherwise we'll freelance into cases of our own choosing."

"They aren't going to like it…" Gunnar said carefully.

"Of that, I'm sure. But that's also the fun of it. No more red tape stran-gling innocents to death. You will have the agility to act swiftly. Think about it. People will cease to care once they realize who allows them to tuck their kids in safely at night." I paused to let that sink in. "Now, who wants to be Robin to my Bruce Wayne?"

Gunnar growled. "No fucking way. You went there."

Tory beamed. "I'm Catwoman!"

Raego rolled his eyes. "You can't be Batman. You don't even have any cool gadgets."

"I can make some." I argued.

We approached the Land Rover as Raego said his goodbyes to everyone. Misha agreed to stay with Raego for a little while, but made me promise her a date first. My mind was already working on a way to substitute Tory for myself, and Misha didn't act like that would be a problem.

We climbed into the car with Mallory at the wheel. He waited for my in-struction. I reached into my pocket and felt a tiny slip of satin. I grinned from ear-to-ear. "Now, I think we all need to visit a doctor. Shall we drop you off at the hospital?" I asked.

"What about you?"

I grinned wickedly. "I have my very own doctor. Don't worry about me. I'll be fine." Tory and Gunnar gave me odd looks, but finally shrugged at my silence. "We can discuss details of our team later."

"So, it's official. I bet we'll even have Paparazzi soon." Gunnar groaned.

"Welcome to the lifestyle of the rich and famous," I smiled, already thinking of my *good doctor*, Indie, as Mallory pulled out of Raego's driveway.

CHAPTER 42

I LEANED BACK IN THE BED OF MY MASTER SUITE AT Chateau Falco, twining a red silken strip of cloth about my fingers, pondering wizardly thoughts as I stared into the fireplace at the edge of the room. The smells from the tray of fresh fruit on the bedside table beckoned to me, but I stoically resisted, content to just relax until my nurse came back to check on my recovery from the battle at Alaric's home. I glanced at the coin Asterion had given me, which sat on my nightstand, and pondered the god's involvement in the dragon mess. It was devoid of its power now, but was still a powerful relic that I had yet to study in depth. Later. So many things to study. I would meet the Minotaur to try and get some answers, both about his history with the dragons and my musings about Hermes.

I had put out a few fires since the eclipse, and was still recovering in – and getting used to – my new home at Chateau Falco. I missed Plato's Cave, but I couldn't complain too much. Here I had a Butler! And Indie had delegated duties to all the employees at Plato's Cave with ruthless efficiency. It was business as usual, just how I liked it.

I had managed to get a grip on my new power after an intense personal assessment. The distortion of chance was gone, which was good, as well as the leakage factor on those around me. Double good. Once I was fully healed I would have to look into it more specifically in an attempt to figure out why and how it had happened. I briefly wondered if my parents had done something to pass on their power to me upon their deaths, even though I thought the idea impossible. But it wasn't important at the moment.

People and newspapers both discussed the topic of Alaric's *coalition* openly and fearfully, but seemed pleased that it seemed to fizzle into nothing at the man's disappearance from St. Louis' social scene. Raego had cleverly issued a statement about Alaric moving back to Europe, complete with travel itineraries and everything. No one questioned it, thankfully. Detective Kosage had been forced to make a public statement renouncing my involvement in the recent crimes after I had put some weight on the mayor about moving my company to a new city. Kosage had been none too pleased, but no love lost there. In fact, I had no intentions of moving the company, but no one else knew that. Even if I had wanted to move the company, I had too many things to do to even entertain the thought at present. I still had to figure out what the Pandora Protocol – my parents' secret project at Temple Industries – was, and what importance the mysterious music box held. Why had the thief stolen it?

My fingers flexed about the satin in a brief surge of anger. The thief... Peter. But had he also been my parents' murderer? The video feed had said *Titan!* at the moment of their deaths, and I had a hard time believing that Peter would have been strong enough to take them out. Even with his new power.

And he was definitely no Titan.

A small part of me missed my old friend. Not the psychopath he had become, but the boy who had been with me since childhood. Gunnar and I didn't talk about it, except to answer a few phone calls about him joining Alaric in Europe. Again, no one seemed to question it. Raego had come by to drop off the book that had started it all, and to discuss the topic of the break-in at my company. He had no real answers – even having met with all the dragons in town for a brief oath of fealty to their new leader – but was confident that Peter had been the thief, but not the murderer. Alaric had had no reason for their deaths, and Peter had been unable to act of his own volition without the charismatic Dragon Lord's approval. Which meant that the murderer was still at large. But there was no one left alive to question now, what with Alaric slain by the dragon hunters.

I sighed, running the material through my fingers again therapeutically. The dragon hunters had met Raego at my home under a white flag, learning that Alaric had used them as pawns the entire time. Tomas had been disgusted at that. Their enemy had tricked them into inadvertently working for him to take out Raego. They had agreed to a truce of sorts, that is, until one of Raego's dragons broke a law or stuck his neck out too high. Raego had smiled, nodding his wholehearted agreement.

Tory and Gunnar had healed without complications, and then promptly been fired. Of course, that wasn't how it was worded, but the result was the same. Jeffries had been the one forced to give Gunnar the news – against his will – as Special Agent in Charge, Roger Reinhardt, leaned on him. Ah, bureaucracy. Kosage didn't mind firing Tory. My friends didn't mind too much, what with the new pay raise from a certain billionaire benefactor, although Gunnar's heart did seem to break a little at the situation. So, I had cleverly arranged a self-esteem boost by asking Ashley Belmont to meet me for a very important business discussion at one of the priciest and most romantic restaurants in town. Somehow, I had forgotten to put anything in my planner, despite the fact that I had double-booked Gunnar to meet me at the same time and place for an altogether different business discussion. Gunnar and Ashley both showed, but I stayed home. I hadn't heard much from either since, other than the brief text message from Gunnar hours after the appointed meeting time. *I owe you one, asshole.*

Raego had informed me that Tory had been spending quite a bit of time with Misha as well. He also told me he'd been able to release her two children from their obsidian prison, and after an oath of fealty to the Obsidian Son, they seemed to be recovering nicely, wrestling all around Raego's inherited house with Tory, of all people.

I smiled at all the happy endings, then hissed softly as I put too much weight on my healing wound. I adjusted myself, leaning back into the pillows more comfortably. Then the bathroom door opened, and a silhouette stood before me, limned by the candle light behind her and the fireplace before her. "Ready for your hourly check-up, Nate?" A sultry voice asked. Indie took a few steps closer, and my testosterone replied hungrily. She stood there in a nurse outfit, smiling darkly.

"Of course, my *good nurse*. Of course…" Flesh, hands, and lips met in a sweaty jumble, which hours later, I couldn't quite remember accurately. But I did feel better, healed. Completely healed… Ready to soon dive back into the fray and discover the truths behind my parents' murder.

The world was a darker place without them, but I wasn't going anywhere, and I hoped my new team would be a benefit to society. Someone had to be there to keep everyone safe. It was our duty. We had the ability to protect the weak, so it was on our shoulders. I sympathized with the Titan, Atlas.

Indie breathed softly, asleep on my chest, her sweaty hair tickling my arms as our warm bodies melded together as one. Someone was going to pay for what they did to my parents. Dearly. But not tonight. No, not tonight.

Sleep soon pulled me under, glorious, peaceful sleep.

And that's when the night terrors started…

Turn the pages to read an excerpt of the next installment in the Nate Temple Supernatural Thriller Series, BLOOD DEBTS…

Quick description for BLOOD DEBTS:

An Angel, a Wizard, and a Horseman of the Apocalypse walk into a bar…

ENJOY THIS BOOK? YOU CAN MAKE A HUGE DIFFERENCE...

Reviews are the most powerful tools in my arsenal when it comes to getting attention for my books. Much as I'd like to, I don't have the financial muscle of a New York publisher. I can't take out full page ads in the newspaper or put posters on the subway.

(Not yet, anyway).

But I do have something much more powerful and effective than that, and it's something that those publishers would kill to get their hands on.

A committed and loyal bunch of readers.

Honest reviews of my books help bring them to the attention of other readers.

If you've enjoyed this book, I would be very grateful if you could spend just five minutes leaving a review (it can be as short as you like) on my book's Amazon page.

Thank you very much in advance.

BLOOD DEBTS

SHAYNE SILVERS

CHAPTER 1

T HE GNARLED OAK DESK QUIVERED AS A SUBSONIC blast shook the entire room. I flinched involuntarily, my drink tinkling lightly between my long fingertips as the lights flickered. I blinked eyelids that seemed to weigh a ton. *What the hell was that?* Had I been asleep? I couldn't remember the last few moments. Perhaps I had been drinking more than I thought. Indie must have already abandoned me for bed by now because she wasn't beside me. And where was Dean? Or Mallory, for that matter? Surely, they had heard the sound. *Felt* the sound. The hair on my arms was sticking straight up in response to my sudden adrenaline spike.

Then I heard the scream. Like someone was being skinned alive.

I bolted from the leather chair in my father's old office – now *my* office – at Chateau Falco. Another distant blast shook the foundation of the house as I darted out the door and onto the landing that overlooked the first floor. Before I could move any further, a fiery comet suddenly screamed through the second-floor stained glass window, barely missing my skull before it crashed through the banister beside me and blazed into an adjacent room. The furniture inside instantly caught fire with a hungry *whoomp*. Dust and debris filled the air as I looked up in time to see the remnants of the window crash to the marble floor, shattering into a billion pieces that looked like a detonation of Fruity Pebbles. The cloying stench of smoke instantly filled my ancestral home as it began to burn. Fast.

More screams and shouts raged through the night amidst a barrage of gunfire and explosions as I crouched, trying to ascertain from where the sounds originated. After all, it was a huge fucking house. Seventeen thousand square feet was a lot of space to search. The single scream I had first heard didn't give me any time to check on Indie, Dean, or Mallory. Someone was dying, right now, his or her scream full of tortured anguish. My home was under assault, by what sounded to be the combined efforts of the Four Horsemen of the Apocalypse.

Unforgiveable.

I briefly entertained what I would do to the prick that dared attack my ancestral home. Then I was running, formulating plans and discarding them just as fast, drawing the magical energy that constantly filled the air around me into a protective cloak. The energy that most people didn't believe existed.

But I was a wizard. Special. A *Freak*, as some called us. I could *see* magical energy. Feel it. Taste it. Hold it. And *use* it… To dish out all sorts of hell when I felt so inclined.

And oh, did I feel so inclined right about now.

As I raced past empty room after empty room, aged paintings seemed to grimace in distaste at my lack of protection… as if I was the ultimate embodiment of failure for a once powerful family. I grunted, shrugging off the pain of those looks. It was my imagination. They weren't *really* disappointed in me. They weren't even *real*. After all, I had instantly reacted to the attack, right? *Or were you dozing through obvious signs of intrusion, awoken only by the sound of their victory in kidnapping one of your friends…*

My Freudian Id is not a pleasant person. I ignored the smug son of a bitch.

I heard the scream again, and determined that it was coming from outside… along with the incessant gunfire. What the hell was going on out there? I sprinted down more hallways, zigzagging back and forth in an effort to get outside faster. Who was screaming? The voice was either in so much pain or so much rage that I couldn't even determine if it was male or female, let alone human.

I finally reached the front entryway, grabbed the massive handle to the front door, and heaved hard enough to tear it from the frame as a surge of magic fueled my strength. I tossed it into the foyer behind me and launched myself into a scene straight from hell. The icy wind struck my face like a finely woven blanket of cold steel, sobering me instantly. I practically shit myself with my eyes wide open.

The night was chaos incarnate.

Dragons the size of utility vans stormed the skies, blasting fireballs at my home from every direction. The ancestral home of the Temples was on fire, and the centuries old construction wasn't faring well. The porte-cochere above me leaned drunkenly, one of the supports abruptly cracking in half. I immediately dove to safety before the roof collapsed, nearly dying before I even had time to fully comprehend the situation. I rolled onto the balls of my feet, scanning the darkness amidst the dust, explosions, shouting, and dying. The fountain in the center of the drive was now a pile of useless rubble, and bodies decorated the once elegantly stained concrete. But now it was stained an altogether different color. The color of fresh blood.

A dozen of my security guards lay in smoking... *pieces* throughout the manicured lawn – bodies still steaming to my magically-enhanced vision. Energy quested hungrily through the air, the waves of power coursing like gossamer threads of colored smoke. Power was *everywhere*... I grinned darkly. I could use that to my advantage. I saw a dragon or two also littering the lawn, betraying the fact that my security hadn't been caught entirely off-guard, even if their Master had been dozing in his office over a glass of whisky. I shook the guilt from my head. Despite the truth of it, I didn't have the time to feel sorrow. My guards knew the risks in defending my home.

Right? Had *I* even expected an attack of this magnitude?

I shivered as the guilt of their deaths threatened to overpower me. I shoved it down harder. Later. Instead, I sprinted towards a small pocket of humans battling each other near the horse stable turned car garage a hundred feet away. I didn't know friend from foe, but I was heartened to discover that at least *some* of my men had survived. Reality seemed to abruptly shift, my vision rippling for a second like I had seen a mirage in the desert. I shook my head, frantically searching for the attacker that was messing with my perception.

But there was no one near me, and the group of humans was too busy fighting each other to bother with little old me, and no dragons were close enough to sneak up on me.

After a few tense seconds, I took off towards the fighting again, dodging a small, jeweled box lying discarded in the grass. Thievery? A horde of dragons seemed like overkill for a robbery. I growled to myself. I would figure out the *reason* for the attack later. Now was time for *action*. I instinctively made a choice, and launched a crested wave of ice at the most unsavory looking group of men. Some collapsed under the onslaught while others remained upright – now frozen solid – but all as dead as a doornail. The remaining faces that turned to me hissed with a sneer of triumph. Shit. Wrong group.

The survivors launched themselves at me with a unified roar of bloodlust, casting battle magic at my face like I had just slapped their grandmother at a holiday dinner party. Dragons *and Wizards?*

I managed to dodge the majority of the numerous elemental attacks, feeling only a single blast of fire sear my forearm, but I ignored that pain. I shattered an arm at the elbow as I came within physical reach, too close for all but the most skilled wizard to use his birthright. It was my only chance against so many foes. I quickly realized I needed backup. A smile tugged at my weathered cheeks.

I bellowed out a single name into the darkness, never ceasing the lethal swings of my arms as they both physically and magically pounded my enemies. A deafening peal of thunder shook the heavens, followed immediately by a crackling bolt of black lightning, which spliced an unlucky dragon neatly in half, causing reptilian blood to rain down upon me. In its wake, a lamenting *neighing* sound filled the air with a very noticeable physical vibration.

Grimm – a seemingly Demonic black-and-red-feathered unicorn the size of a Clydesdale – entered the fray. The single pearlescent, gnarled, and thorny horn protruding from his skull instantly gored one of my attackers through the heart. I might have hesitated for a second as I saw the unicorn catch a quick swipe of blood with a hungry tongue. I might have shuddered with unease, but I was glad the Minotaur had introduced me to him. He had helped me battle dragons once before... to their detriment. I hoped we would do it again tonight. Flaming, orange eyes met mine in a brief, appreciative greeting before we both focused back to our enemies. I called out familiar whips of fire and ice, utilizing them like Indiana Jones on crystal meth to eliminate the crowd of wizards attacking me. I spun in circles of crackling volcanic and arctic fury, lashing a leg here and a face there, feeding off their dying screams as I lost myself in the mayhem. What could have been an hour later, I realized that all were dead. Grimm was staring at me with wide, concerned eyes. I was covered in gore, blood, and ash: And I realized that I was grinning maniacally.

Before I could prove to the unicorn that I hadn't lost my mind, a familiar cry split the night. *"NATE!"* The agonized scream shattered my mind into a million fragments of torment.

My breathing came in ragged grunts as I slowly turned, recognizing the voice.

The dragons had Indie. My girlfriend. The love of my life. My Krypto-

268

nite. My Achilles Heel. I spotted her standing atop the garage, a giant golden dragon gripping her in his talons.

Alaric Slate, the leader of the dragon nation.

My mind went fuzzy for a moment, my vision again rippling like a desert mirage. But... *wasn't he dead?* No. He *couldn't* be dead. He was right in front of me. Holding the woman of my dreams in his razor-sharp golden claws. A swarm of dragons I hadn't noticed until now unfurled just above our heads, simultaneously striking Grimm from behind. The mythical creature was obliterated in a millisecond, shredded into organic matter like he had fallen into a pool of piranhas. I screamed with vengeance at the death of such a magnificent beast – my friend – and cast my power at the earth around me in a fifty-foot radius. The dirt and rock exploded skyward, dropping the dragons into a ten-foot deep hole. A second later, I slammed the earth back over them like a heavy quilt, burying them alive. Tucking the monsters in for bedtime. Permanently.

An amused chuckle filled the night air. I could hear Indie struggling, but I knew it was futile. I turned slowly to face Alaric, my vision throbbing with rage. He stood like a vengeful god – half shifted into his dragon form – a single golden talon pressing into Indie's soft skin like a hot knife resting on a plate of butter. "Hand me the box, Temple," he growled greedily.

I... blinked. I honestly had absolutely no clue what he was talking about. If I did, I would have given it to him. Hell, I would have given him *anything* to save Indie. Even my own life.

Indie screamed. "Don't do it, Nate!"

He silenced her by shoving his talon straight through her gut, causing her to grunt in utter shock, and then agony. I realized that I was suddenly closer, having instinctively raced towards him with murderous intent. He held up a claw in warning and I froze with one foot still in the air. His other talon was still embedded inside my girlfriend's stomach. I was stunned, in shock, unable to think straight, but I slowly lowered my foot to the cold earth. How had it escalated so quickly? He had barely warned me. I glanced down at my feet, trying to control my rapid breathing while frantically assessing the situation for a way – *any* way – to save Indie's life. Her wound was fatal, not superficial. Alaric was a hunter. He knew my plight. He knew my skills. He had effectively demanded my obedience. He knew I would do anything to save Indie. Give up anything.

269

"Please!" I begged. "Take whatever you want, just release her!"

He nodded. "Of course. The box. Bring it here. Now. She doesn't have long without medical attention." Several new dragons were suddenly pumping their vast wings above me, hovering hungrily as an added threat. I followed his gaze and glanced to my side, only to see the same box from earlier sitting in the bloody, frosted grass. *Wait… that can't be right. I saw that near the fountain…*

In a confused daze, I reached down, my fingers numb, discarding the single rational thought.

"Easy, Temple. No surprises. Bring it here." I hesitated, not with any rebellious intent, but with simple confusion about how the box could have appeared beside me when I had seen it a dozen feet away only minutes ago. Alaric shook his head with a sad smile, abruptly twisting his talon inside Indie with a violent, final jerk.

"Nate…" She whispered between tortured gasps.

My senses instantly shut down. I was numb with disbelief and impotent fury. My body began to quiver, rattling the forgotten jeweled box that I apparently still held in my now numb hands. The lid began to pry loose from the box. I looked down curiously. *Yes, do it. Do it now…* a strange voice cooed in my ear. I listened to it, not even caring about its origin, and began to open the box, knowing that Indie was already dead. A part of me was now dead too. Only ashes remained of my heart. The world could burn, and thank me for it. I no longer cared.

"No!" Alaric's voice boomed as he tore his claw entirely through the love of my life, effectively slicing her in half. I felt the mass of dragons dive for me as one cohesive unit, a pack of claw and fang. As if in slow motion, I realized that my death would be a painful one, and I also realized that I was fresh out of fucks to give. I deserved it. I had inadvertently allowed this to happen. Allowed them to kill the woman I loved. So, I opened the box.

A wail of despair from the very pits of hell filled the night before my vision turned an amber-tinted urine color, tunneling out to a single point. Indie.

The dragons' claws tore into me, trying to prevent me from opening the box. But they were too late. The world ended in a climactic symphony of pain and sound as I embraced death.

I *became* death.

Then nothingness.

CHAPTER 2

I JOLTED AWAKE, SHATTERING A GLASS OF LIQUOR THAT was clutched in my fist.

The other patrons of the bar sprang back from their stools with a shout. The man beside me was the only one to remain in his seat, casually raising his drink to his lips. I was panting heavily as if I had just finished a marathon. Adrenaline coursed through my veins, my eyes darting back and forth, trying to make sense of my new surroundings, desperately searching for Indie and the dragons. But I wasn't at Chateau Falco. I was in a seedy bar.

What the hell? Then it hit me. It had been another of the night terrors – now turned *day* terrors – that had plagued me since the aftermath of the dragon invasion a few months ago. They were happening more often now. Escalating in their brutality. But I was getting used to them. Kind of…

I began my usual mental process of rationally stating the facts in order to calm my racing heart. *The dragons are no longer a threat. Indie is safe. I'm not at Chateau Falco…* After a few repetitions and deep breaths, I began to calm down, and reality began to emerge from the depths of my fractured mind. I glanced at my watch and scowled. *I'm in a seedy bar waiting for an unpunctual appointment. The man who called me with information on my parents' murder. I had dozed off. Again.* By sluggish increments, my breathing returned to normal.

I had lost track of the numerous variations of my terrors, but the mysterious box was always center-stage, and the vision only ended when I opened it. But while in the dream, I never at first recognized the box. Not until I opened it. Then nothing but pain.

I waved at the bartender. "I'll sport a round for the bar. Sorry, guys," I muttered. The bartender eyed me warily, no doubt wondering what would happen if he told me to leave. After all, I was the infamous 'wizard' and local billionaire, Master Nate Temple – the *Archangel* – as some now referred to me. Or as I liked to imagine myself, the Notorious N.A.T.

Biggie Smalls had nothing on me.

"I'm fine. Really. Let me make it up to everyone. Get me another one while you're at it," I muttered, plucking a few pieces of glass out of my now bleeding palm. I pressed a napkin in my fist to staunch the blood flow. After a few moments, the bartender finally conceded. Several of the men shook their heads and decided to drink elsewhere. I couldn't blame them. The calm man next to me still hadn't moved.

The bartender placed a new glass of cheap, gasoline-spiked whisky onto the warped, sticky oak counter. I scanned the room with a frown of both anger and disgust. It had been many years since I had been in a *Kill* – a bar where violence was commonplace, even encouraged, and the hygiene equally dangerous – and was eager to pay my tab and get the hell out. After I got the supposed information about my parents' murder from the cryptic caller who had asked me to meet him here. If only that fucking appointment wasn't late I could be home already.

I sighed. No use. I was already here. Might as well wait a bit longer. My notoriety was apparent, judging from the hateful glares cast my way from various patrons of the bar. Which might say something about me. After all, a Kill was where only the most nefarious of supernaturals – or Freaks – hung out. My reputation had really jumped after the Solar Eclipse Expo a few months back, when a harem of weredragons had decided St. Louis was the ideal place to host a ritual spell that would ignite the rebirth of the ultimate god of all dragons, as well as being a convenient locale to announce to the world that magic was in fact very real. I hadn't agreed.

And they hadn't survived.

Now, even the *locals* were apparently terrified of me. And when I say *locals*, I'm of course referring to the *magical* locals. *My* people. Where I arrived, death and destruction was now expected to follow. That dragon event was what led me here tonight to *Achilles Heel* – this supernatural Kill – waiting on my unpunctual appointment.

I swiveled a bit on the squeaky wooden stool, scouting the seedy bar in a way that I hoped seemed nonchalant, doing my best to look inconspicuously lethal...

And my clumsy bleeding fist knocked the drink plum out of the old gentleman's hand beside me. Some of the liquor splashed onto my open wound, causing me to hiss in pain. I instinctively called to my gift, filling myself

272

with magic in order to defend myself from the Octogenarian, doing my best to ignore my stinging palm.

Sure, he might *look* like a frail old man, but you never knew in a Kill. Plus, he hadn't freaked the fuck out when I had my conniption a few minutes ago. He had steel nerves. Which usually resulted from having a severe case of *badass-itis*.

The man smiled amiably at me, waving me off with a forgiving hand motion. "It happens. No worries." His eyes twinkled like arctic ice, seeming to glow. The silence stretched as I waited for him to make his move. His smile grew wider. "You can release your power now. It was just a drink." I let loose the breath I hadn't known I'd been holding, and then, slowly, my magic.

This was when he would attack. I *knew* it. *Wait for it...* I was ready for anything. I would never let my epitaph say '*The dragon slayer that was slain by a nursing home patient.*'

He shook his head as if amused at a child's antics, and turned back to the bar, for all intents and purposes seeming to dismiss my distrust. I swiveled back myself, still tense as a spring. *What the hell? Courtesy?* I slowly began to relax. "Huh. Paint my lips and call me Suzie. You meant it."

The man turned his mercurial gaze my way, and I briefly noticed purple flecks in his icy blue eyes. "Why would I call you Suzie? You are Nathaniel Laurent Temple, of course. Kind of a big deal." He seemed amused at that. "And why would I say something and act otherwise? Is this a riddle? Or one of those New Age things? Are you a... *Hipster*?"

The word sounded unfamiliar on his lips, but I could see that he was proud to have used it, as if it was one less thing pulling him from the grave, a last clutch at his youth. But as I appraised him, I began to wonder if he was really as old as I had originally thought. He had a youthful... *vibrancy* to him. I managed to stammer a response. "No, never mind. I thought... you know... this *is* a *Kill*." I finally grumbled, as if he were the one being strange. He shrugged and began to completely ignore me as he studied the bottles of liquor behind the bar, apparently deciding on his next drink.

Which was extremely odd. See, my reaction was an important stance in a place like this. I compared a Kill to an African watering hole – where one went to do his business, grab a drink of water, and then efficiently retreat to his hidey hole – all the while watching his back for any threats. The place wasn't full, big surprise, with it being cold as balls outside and a weeknight to boot, but enough patrons lingered here and there to justify the sultry guitarist idly strumming cover band music in the corner. And it was vitally important to keep this crowd entertained.

For they were primarily Freaks, as the *Regular* folk called them, or supernaturals.

Even though my new glass was a few inches from my hand, a distinct chime overrode the guitarist in the corner, as if I had tapped my glass with a fork. "Get him a replacement, please." I mumbled to the bartender, and then reached out to down my drink. "Me too. But not this swill. Get me a decent whisky." The grizzled barkeep grunted, and I received a new glass of Johnnie Walker a few moments later.

I lightly sipped the new drink in an effort to fuel my lidded eyes from drooping further. *Mustn't fall asleep again.* I shivered to clear my head, noticing a pair of men down the bar whispering to themselves and glancing pointedly at me. I shrugged to myself. "I have enough friends." I muttered under my breath. I wasn't in the market for new ones.

The older gentleman rapped idly on the gnarled wooden counter with a bony hand as he spoke out of the side of his mouth for my ears only. "You can never have enough friends. *Never*. Also, this doesn't seem like an ideal place for sleeping." No one else had heard, I was sure of it. "I'll take a *Death in the Afternoon*, Barkeep." He requested in a louder voice to the bartender, who seemed to be respectfully waiting for the man's order. *Absinthe and champagne*, I mused, immediately interested, and a little alarmed at what quality of champagne they might have behind the bar. If any at all.

"Nice choice." I spoke, suddenly curious that this might be my contact. He had been here since before I had arrived. Had he been assessing me before deciding to follow through with his information? I was suddenly glad I hadn't stormed out.

The man glanced over at me, his unique frosty blue eyes twinkling in amusement. He was gaunt, skeletal even, but wiry with a resilient strength underneath, and he sported long, straw-colored blonde hair in a man-bun. He was dressed sharply; formal even, and seemed to fairly reek of money, looking like Don Draper from *Mad Men*. I concluded that he definitely wasn't as old as I had originally thought. Just frail. He plucked a cigarette from an ornate silver case, casting me a curious brow as if asking my permission. "Coffin nail?" He offered me one. With a Herculean effort, I managed to decline, waving him to go ahead. He lit up, speaking softly between pulls. "I became infatuated with the drink many years ago. It's the color, I think. Silly reason, but there it is."

I nodded distractedly, trying to catch a whiff of the second-hand smoke. I had recently quit, but still craved a drag. "It's an inspiring drink." I dredged through my exhausted eidetic memory. *"Anything capable of arousing passion in its favor will surely raise as much passion against it."*

The man grunted in recognition. "Hemingway was a great man, even though bull-fighting is slightly antiquated." He appraised me with a sideways glance. "Shouldn't you be attending some high society function or ritzy ball rather than entertaining a barfly in a Kill?" He asked with a refined degree of politeness, as if only making idle conversation.

"The public has always expected me to be a playboy, and a decent chap never lets his public down." I winked, trying to flummox him with a different quote.

"Not many have read Errol Flynn. Learn that at one of your fancy dinner parties?" he drawled, unimpressed.

I leaned back, surprised at his literary knowledge. I nodded. "Sociability is just a big smile, and a big smile is nothing but teeth. I didn't feel like entertaining the crowd again tonight." I decided, for simplicity's sake, to refer to this stranger as *Hemingway*, after his drink of choice.

Before I could ask if he was my contact, I felt a forceful finger jab my shoulder, sending a jolt of power all the way down to my toes. Hemingway chuckled in amusement at the stranger looming behind me. I lifted my gaze to the bartender and realized he was not moving.

At all. Not even to blink. Then I realized that *no one* else in the bar was moving. No one but Hemingway, the stranger, and myself. In the blink of an eye, my sense of alarm reached a crescendo.

The sizzle of power still tingled in my feet from the stranger's touch. This person was juiced up to a level I hadn't seen in a while. And he had apparently gone to the trouble of stopping the flow of time in order to speak with the notorious N.A.T.

Knowing my luck, the night was about to get even more interesting. And I had allowed myself to become distracted by Hemingway.

Who apparently *wasn't* my contact.

CHAPTER 3

I LAZILY SWIVELED ON MY CREAKY STOOL TO FACE THE man. Time seemed to move slowly, whether a result of the stranger's power or my sleep deprivation, I wasn't sure. Delicious tobacco smoke drifted through the air in lazy tendrils. Every surface of the room was wooden, splinter-laden, and filthy – coated with decades of blood, smoke, and various assortments of dried booze – an arsonist's wet dream. When fist-fights and worse were frequent, why spend the money to spruce things up? Especially when the owner was Achilles, the legendary Greek Myrmidon, and sacker of Troy. No one dared challenge his aesthetic vision. Or lack thereof. Unless they liked having pointy things shoved through their jugular.

The man before me stood out like the Queen of England had entered the *Kill.* He was dressed too nicely, and when I say *nicely* I mean nicely as in formal wear a few hundred years or more out of date. He had a pompous air about him, as if about to check his shoes for filth. He sniffed idly, as if smelling something that personally offended him. He scowled at Hemingway's polite grin with equally polite disdain before returning his fiery eyes to mine. His long, black hair was pulled back into wavy order like a Disney Prince. "This is a courtesy call. I apologize for my tardiness; however, your methods of travel are unreliable." His gaze assessed me as I pondered his odd statement. "Stop digging into the murder. Nothing good can come of it. Accept that fact like the rest of them do."

My rage spiked at his tone alone, not even taking the time to get angry at his message. "Them?" I asked in a snarl, surprised that this person was my contact.

"Yes, the humans. Do try to keep up," he answered, sounding annoyed.

I didn't dare risk asking him *what* he was, in an effort to not appear ignorant, but I noticed a faint glow around the man, something that would be visible only to wizards. Odd, because he was definitely *not* a wizard. I just didn't know exactly *what* he was. He was wearing a bulky 1980's era trench coat that clashed with the practically archaic dress clothes underneath, and he was much taller than me. He sported a clean-shaven, baby face, and moved with the grace of a Calvin Klein underwear model. My wizard senses picked up the smell of frost and burning gravel. Odd combination... I had never seen anyone quite like him. And the fact that he didn't know how to dress to fit in with the modern-day humans was unnerving. It meant he didn't belong here. On Earth. No doubt a smart person to avoid.

But the cheap liquor and his unexpected warning had me wanting to vent off some steam.

"Am I to understand that you arranged a meeting with me – to which you arrived abhorrently late – in order to tell me to stop meeting people with information on my parents' murder?" He nodded. "Our phone call would have sufficed. Otherwise, I might be inclined to think that you were *deliberately* wasting my time. And very few people would consider doing that to me." The man shrugged, unperturbed. "What if I keep digging?" I pressed, idly assessing my surroundings for collateral damage, shivering as I remembered that everyone was frozen and unable to escape. That changed things. Hemingway took a sip of his drink, watching the exchange with interest. Why was he not immobilized?

My contact assessed me up and down, not with overt disrespect, but merely as if wondering what form of creature sat before him. "This is a Heavenly affair, not your... jurisdiction. But it's your funeral." Hemingway immediately burst out laughing. I frowned at him. Was he drunk? My appointment was obviously powerful, and Hemingway looked as if a strong wind would blow him away like a kite. Something the man had said drew me back away from the frozen patrons of the bar. The man had casually said *Heavenly*. Was he being literal?

"This is none of your concern." The man hissed at Hemingway, causing my drinking partner's grin to split even wider, revealing dazzlingly white teeth.

Him threatening my brand-new drinking buddy pissed me right the fuck off for some reason. "Are you," I began, giving the stranger a mocking head-to-toe appraisal, "threatening me?" The man... blinked, as if seeing a kitten suddenly sprout horns. It fueled my anger even more. I mean, I wasn't the scariest kid on the block, but I was formidable.

Wasn't I?

"I don't need to threaten a man hunting for death." The stranger shared his glare with Hemingway and gave a faint grunt. "Just a polite warning." He began to turn away, business obviously concluded.

But I wasn't finished. Not at all. He needed a lesson in manners. Since Hemingway seemed content to merely watch, and the other patrons of the bar were immobilized, that left me to teach him.

I pulled the energy that filled the room from all the supernatural presence surrounding us deep into my soul into a cocoon of raw power. Enough that my vision began to twinkle with black flecks, and then I let loose a wallop of pure power straight into the stranger's stomach. It punched him about as hard as a Mack Truck, and he went sailing out the front door, taking half of the frame with him. I grunted, nodding proudly. Hemingway's eyes shot wide open in disbelief and then alarm.

I was instantly surrounded by shiny, pointy things, all resting at my throat. I hadn't even seen anyone move. Wasn't everyone in the bar frozen? I swallowed. Carefully. Apparently, I had misread the situation.

I looked at one of my assailants, my gaze cool despite the uneasiness squirming in my belly. "I don't take kindly to pointless meetings, pointy things at my throat, or threats."

"Don't speak, mortal, or I will carve out your jugular," the pompous ass threatened.

I shrugged slowly, trying to appear unconcerned as I studied the gang of swords. They were professional. Not a single wrist quivered, and eyes of cold, merciless justice met mine. They were pros. And they each wielded Crusade Era swords. The creature I had sucker-punched strode back into the bar a minute later, shaking off dust and debris from his trench coat, his face a thunderhead. For the amount of force I had dished out, he looked perfectly... unaffected. "Did you need some fresh air?" I sneered.

He halted before me and his gang lowered their weapons. "Do you have any inkling of what you just did, and who you did it to?"

"Man, if I had a nickel for every time I heard that line." I muttered.

"Don't be coy, wizard. You just struck an Agent of Heaven. I have every right to carve out your eyes."

"But then that would make *me* the holy one, and I was under the impression that was your shtick."

The man scowled at me with disgust, not amused by my blasphemy. I could take any number of insults, but *disgust*? That was just... confusing. Who had the balls to feel *disgust* to wizards? I mean, we were some pretty heavy hitters on the block of the supernatural community.

He stared me dead in the eye as I somehow managed to formulate a parting threat in retaliation to his disgusted look. "Words have consequences. You should be careful how you speak to one such as me."

He met my gaze, shaking his head with arrogant disdain. "One such as you..." he mimicked in amusement as if at a child. My anger was only growing stronger at the lack of respect he was showing my kind. He didn't acknowledge my threat, but sniffed the air curiously. "You stink like Demons. This whole town does." He leaned closer, taking in a big whiff of all the glory that is my aroma. "Especially you." He added. His mob of thugs inched closer as if to protect him, despite the fact that I had just laid him out with my best punch, and he had merely shrugged it off.

I blinked at the change of topic, uncomfortable with a strange man smelling me so deliberately. "Do dragons count as Demons?" I asked, feeling the weight of the new bracelet against my forearm. The bracelet that held the late Dragon Lord's teeth.

The stranger cocked his head. "It's not your trophy. It's *you*. Have you been consorting with Demons in your search for the murderer?" He accused, somehow seeming to gain a few inches of both height and width. His thugs grew tense, swords slowly rising again, ready to stab on command.

"No." I answered honestly, too surprised to take offense. "Listen, you probably shouldn't hulk out here. Achilles wouldn't like it. He's territorial like that." My mouth wouldn't stay closed.

He grunted, slowly returning back to his normal size. "It would behoove you to wash the smell away, lest it offend your betters. We believe that your parents' murder was directly caused by Demons, which you stink of. We have people on the case, but these people," he smiled proudly, holding out a hand to his gang of backup dancers, "are the kind to stab and exorcise first, saving questions for later. We wouldn't want any damage of the... *collateral* nature now, would we?"

"Okay. If you want me out of it, that's fine. But I demand progress reports."

The man blinked. "Only *One* commands us, and you are not *H—*"

"Daily." I continued as if he hadn't spoken. "Yes. Daily progress reports should suffice."

The man actually let out a stutter of disbelief, then a momentous silence. I managed to control the urge to fidget. Barely. Then he finally spoke. "I would be cautious if I were you, mortal. Everyone has limits. Everyone should know their place in the world."

"Hmm. I'll take that as a *No* on the progress reports then. If that's the case, I will not drop my investigation." I leaned forward. "I *need* answers to this. There is more at stake than my grief. Although that is reason enough." I leaned back into the bar, reaching out for my drink. I took a sip as I considered my next words. *Why not poke the bear a bit more?* the insane Id of mine whispered. I very stupidly listened. "I'm sure you know what it's like to lose a father figure without explanation." I managed to smile before I was suddenly slammed up against the bar. Although the man hadn't moved, he was fairly tingling with blue power, and his shoulders were quivering as if threatening to bust out of his trench coat. Was he sporting a pair of wings under there?

Hemingway sputtered out his drink, but the hulk of a man dropped me immediately, holding up his hands, placating... to Hemingway.

Huh.

"Peace!" The man commanded. Still, his tone was nothing but threatening. "Be careful to whom you blaspheme. My Brothers are not so tolerant. And my sons have no compunctions against violence in *His* name. That is their purpose, after all." His smile was ice. You've been warned. Consider yourself lucky."

I let out a nervous breath. "And you've been given your answer as to my next move, pigeon." I was playing a wild card, assuming by his words that he was an Angel, but the drinks had me feeling courageous. And I was pissed that he had slammed me into the bar without even a reaction on my part. A heavy hitter for sure. I would need to be on my A game if I wanted to tussle against him and his brothers. I was sure that Angels couldn't simply 'off' someone. Which was why he had immediately backed off when Hemingway reacted. Hemingway knew *what* he was, and knew that he had crossed a line. Apparently, there were rules. There were *always* rules. There *had* to be rules...

I *hoped* there were rules...

"Out of respect for what you are going through, I will let this minor annoyance slide, with a warning. If you ever strike a Knight of Heaven again, you won't even have time to apologize. We will smite you out of existence. If our nephews and nieces, the Nephilim here, don't find you first. They have less scrutiny about their daily duties than we Angels." With that, he turned on a proud heel, nodded to his gang of warriors, and they all left the bar. His shoulders fluttered anxiously underneath his coat as if alive. Then he was gone, ducking slightly through the broken door.

I sat down, breathing heavily.

I had sucker-punched an Angel, and I was still kicking.

I noticed that a man down the bar was appraising me thoughtfully. Somehow, he also hadn't been affected by the Angel's manipulation of time. He didn't look impressed at my bravery.

Or maybe stupidity.

Time jolted, and everyone in the bar seemed suddenly surprised at his or her abrupt locomotion, as if wondering whether or not anything odd had happened. Even the Freaks hadn't sensed the Angel's ability to stop time. I heard the bartender begin shouting about the broken door. His eyes quickly flicked towards me but I was still at the bar, obviously nowhere near the damage. His brow furrowed in thought, no doubt wondering how I had done it. Hemingway finally belted out, "*Balls*! You've got a titanic pair of balls. Or you have a *death* wish." He exclaimed between bouts of laughter.

"Shut up and drink, Hemingway."

Hemingway smiled at my nickname, lifted his glass in salute, and downed his drink, shaking his head as he continued to mutter to himself.

What had I gotten myself into?

CHAPTER 4

I CONTINUED TO STARE AT THE BROKEN DOORWAY WITH A frown of concentration, noticing the chill air from outside sucking out a good chunk of the bar's heat. Thanks to me. People began putting on their coats, but remained inside.

I was too tired to connect the dots. I needed to clear my head. So, I stood and strolled outside, hoping to catch a glimpse of the Angel again. I entered the street, but saw no sign of him or his thugs. Just the typical *Mardi Gras* revelers.

Curious.

Apparently, someone sent from *upstairs* wanted me to stay out of my parents' murder investigation. I just wanted justice. Nothing more. But someone was watching me. Did that mean I was close to the answer? Why were freaking *Angels* investigating their murder? And to top it all off, I apparently reeked of Demons. But… *why*?

I had no idea. Shivering, I stormed back inside, ready to pay my tab and leave.

Sauntering over to the bar, the TV caught my attention. Someone had turned up the volume. As the words reached my ears, I groaned inwardly. Hemingway seemed to be listening with rapt attention. It was the now familiar news rehash about me from the last few months. "*Master Temple is still refusing to comment, so the world is full of speculation. As everyone is aware, a few months ago, our beloved benefactor, Nate Temple – recently nicknamed the* Archangel *– and heir of Temple Industries after his parents' murder, was allegedly involved as a person-of-interest in a murder spree the likes of which St. Louis has never seen before. At this time, he is not considered a suspect.*" Her tone said otherwise. "*Alaric Slate – Master Temple's business partner in a so-called coalition of* supernaturals *– is apparently missing, so no interviews with him have been forthcoming.*" The news reporter then went on to declare that the high-speed car chase over the Eads

Bridge involving a *Demon* was no doubt a monstrous hoax. A woman *had* been found at the bottom of the river, but it was determined that she was most likely just an innocent crash victim. They had yet to determine her identity. I scowled. She hadn't been an innocent bystander. She had been a silver-scaled dragon intent on mutilating me. My best friend – werewolf, and now *ex*-FBI agent – Gunnar Randulf had barely helped me out of that one. Literally. Silver and werewolves were not bed-buddies.

I idly fingered the bracelet of misshapen teeth on my wrist. Dragon teeth. Acquired from the late Dragon Lord, Alaric Slate. I had killed Alaric, and used his dental palate to make a fashionable bracelet. It had made me feel marginally better. When Alaric's ritual had backfired, thanks to yours truly, the spell had then transferred the power and designation *Obsidian Son* to his offspring, Raego, making him the new de-facto leader of the dragon nation.

A two-fer if I ever heard one.

Raego, always savvy, chose to break the morbid news to his fellow dragons by making my bracelet an award, like a god-damned Purple Heart, declaring me a friend of dragons everywhere. One phrase stuck in my eidetic memory like a persistent hunk of caramel corn. *"He is the ultimate death for us. Our very own Grim Reaper for those who wish to act terrible to humans... or those who disappoint me."* I fingered the bracelet angrily. "I won't be Raego's fucking hit man." I growled.

I felt Hemingway turn to study me acutely. "What?" I snapped, nervous at the attention the news story might have caused, as well as my last comment.

But he didn't acknowledge my idle comment. "Grandma, what great big balls you have!" He chimed in a falsetto voice, grinning widely.

"You already said that." I muttered. He chuckled. I pondered my recent encounter. "You really think so? He didn't look too tough. Although he walked off my sucker-punch pretty well." I continued, regarding my departed appointment.

"Well, does it take more guts to twice traverse a staircase in a burning building or to make a one-time leap into a volcano? Damned if I know, Kemosabe. All I know is when you're making those kinds of calls, you're up in the high country."

I chuckled. "Never heard that before."

Hemingway nodded. "One of the Greats. S. H. Graynamore. Interesting character." He took a deep pull from his drink. "I hate those amoral asshats."

I choked a bit on my drink, biting back a laugh. "Pardon?"

"That was Eae, the Demon thwarter. But he's nothing compared to the Archangels." He looked me up and down. "The *real* Archangels..." his eyes twinkled, referring to the nickname the media had granted me.

I felt an icy shiver crawl down my spine. "That really *was* an Angel? I thought he might have just been a temp employee. *Eae?* For an Angel, that name's pretty... lame."

Hemingway simply stared at me. Like, *really* stared at me. I began to fidget after what felt like a full minute of silence.

"Okay. It's a badass name. Terrifying. The Demon thwarter... interesting job description." He continued to stare. I decided to change the topic to avoid his gaze. "Why didn't you stop me from pissing him off? He could have *smote* me... *smited* me... no, that's not right either... Anyway, I could have used a warning."

Hemingway's gaze finally broke with an amused grin. "You handled yourself well. Except for launching him into the street. You shouldn't make that a habit. You wouldn't look good as a pillar of salt. Then you called him a *pigeon!* In front of the *Nephilim!*" He roared in laughter. "*Pigeon...*" He muttered again before taking another sip. "He was right, you know." He added, almost as an afterthought.

"About what?" I grumbled, still trying to wrap my head around the fact that I had just sucker-punched a freaking Angel. And *then* mocked him. And in front of his crew no less. I pondered his thugs. Nephilim – the offspring of Angels and humans. Supposedly powerful soldiers of Heaven, although I had never crossed swords with any of them before tonight. I hadn't even believed they were actually real.

Boy, was I damned.

Hemingway scouted the bar carefully. Having already scoped the place out myself several times – keeping track of the people who had entered and exited – I noticed the man who also hadn't been affected by the Angel's time manipulation. He was down the bar, and glaring pure frustration at Hemingway. I turned back to Hemingway and watched him nod amiably at the scarred man. The Irish-looking man continued to scowl back, but finally gave a dismissive nod in return, swiveling to instead watch a pair of particularly cute vampires playing pool. I assumed the man was one of Achilles' generals. Playing bouncer 2,000 years later must suck after such a glorious feat as starring in *The Iliad*. Hemingway didn't seem concerned with the stranger, so I let it go.

Maybe I was reading too much into things. I mean, it's not often that an Angel arrives in a bar to politely tell you to *cut it out*. How many other Angels were in the bar? Or Nephilim? Jesus. I had never considered tussling with an Angel. I hadn't even known they were real, let alone on our plane of existence. Thankfully, no one was close enough to overhear us as Hemingway took a long pull from a fresh cigarette.

My nervous fingers ached to reach out for the cancer stick, but I managed to compose myself. I had successfully remained smoke-free for a few days now, and was proud of my discipline. But I had just survived a smiting. Perhaps I deserved one. Just one. I shook my head defiantly. *No*. "So, what was the Angel right about?" I asked instead.

"You smell like Brimstone. It's a pungent odor, and it could get you murdered quick if some of his more blade-happy brethren caught you unprotected." I sniffed myself, picking up the light sulfuric smell, surprised that I hadn't noticed it earlier.

"I don't know why I smell like that. I haven't summoned any Demons. Lately." Hemingway blinked at me with those eyes that seemed able to weigh my soul and judge my guilt. Was he an Angel too? Eae *had* seemed nervous of him. "Honestly," I said, holding up my hands.

Hemingway shook his head. "I believe you, but regardless. This town reeks of it. And so do you. The rumor mill does hint at Demons being involved in your parents' murder." I blinked, suddenly pissed. This mysterious stranger, among others, seemed to know more information about my parents than I did. Hemingway continued, unaware of my frustration. "Get rid of the odor as soon as possible. It will only attract the wrong kinds of attention, as you just noticed. Angels don't make a habit of appearing to mortals, but when they do..." his voice and gaze grew distant. "Nothing good comes of it." He finally finished in a soft voice.

He studied me for a moment before deciding to continue. "I once heard a story from a down-and-out farmer about Angels and Demons. It might put things into perspective for you, as it did me. Especially since you're not bright enough to leave well enough alone." He winked. "It shook me to my core. But I was a different man then. A virgin to the true ways of the world.

Perhaps wiser. Perhaps less." His eyes grew far away.

He shook his head after a moment. "Anyway, the man was distraught, filled with grief. And despite offering him a ride the following morning, I never heard from him again. He fled in the middle of the night. I've thought of him often as the years have passed me by, curiosity getting the best of me. Perhaps he was telling me *his* story." Hemingway winked again, face mischievous. "Alas, I never discovered his identity..." He took a sip of his drink, gathering his thoughts. I nodded for him to continue and hunkered down, ready to listen. I would stay a little longer to hear this.

His next words enveloped me like a warm blanket. Stories from an experienced raconteur could do that. "I'll tell it to you like it was told to me." I nodded. He cleared his throat again, his voice changing slightly as he began to tell me a tale.

An exhausted local farmer was on his way home from selling his wheat at the market a day's ride away. It was drizzling, but a true rain would fall soon. He knew these kinds of things after farming for so many years. He didn't know how he knew, but he was right more often than not. He was eager to get home and see his family after a long day, eager to share his success, and eager to revel in the more important joys life had to offer... family. He wasn't an established farmer, with vast fields and many clients. No. He worked only for himself and his family.

A prideful, peaceful, god-fearing man.

He trotted beside his horse and cart up the final hill to his home only to discover his son's broken body on the lawn that led to the front porch. The farmer froze, unable to even blink. His boy was not even ten years old. His beautiful, daring, carefree son had been left to suffer, the long smear of blood trailing from the porch and down the freshly painted steps to the lawn a statement of his tenacity to escape. But escape from what? What could so terrify his bold, courageous son in such a way? Especially while mortally wounded? The farmer could not even begin to fathom, let alone truly accept the death before him.

His heart was a hollow shell of ice, liable to shatter at the slightest breeze. The wind began to howl, heralding the approaching storm, but it was a distant, solemn sound in his ears. He carelessly dropped the reins to the horse and crouched over his son's broken body. He brushed the boy's icy-blue eyes closed with shaking fingers, too pained to do more for his fallen, innocent offspring. But what he would see next would make him realize that his son had been the lucky one. The farmer managed to stand, stumbling only slightly in the growling, approaching wind, and entered the small, humble foyer of his home. Like so many times before, his wife greeted him immediately, although those past circumstances were never as abhorrent as this.

His wife had been tied down to face the open doorway. Her dress lay in tatters beside her nude marble-like form. There were many empty wine bottles on the ground, and several piles of ash from a pipe. Enough ash to signify that several men had bided their time in this room while he had been away at market bartering higher prices for his wheat. The house reeked of tobacco. And he wasn't a smoker. He subconsciously knew that his future path would now lead him to darker places than he could ever imagine. His life would be forever changed.

I shivered, feeling the dark story touch a part of me that I had to fight to squash down. I had enough frightening memories to fuel my recent night terrors. I didn't need another. But I knew Hemingway would tell this story only once. Also, this story would be my only knowledge about Angels and Demons outside of the Bible. If Angels were watching my movements, I *needed* the information. I waited for him to continue, signaling the bartender to refill Hemingway's glass. The storyteller nodded in appreciation.

Upon seeing his dearly beloved murdered, the farmer crashed to his knees, the forgotten purse of money that was clutched in his fist dropping to the floor like a sack of wheat. The coins spilled across the gnarled wooden planks, one coin rolling toward the tear-filled, terror-laden gaze of his wife, before briefly brushing her long lashes and settling flat against the floor in a rattle that seemed to echo for eternity. That and the desperate panting of the farmer's breath were the only sounds in the haunted house. But they were enough to fill it completely. He had been anxious to see the look of joy in her eyes at the coins.

The sensation of pride from her meant everything to him. It lent him his own pride. Instead he received this glassy, empty stare that would forever haunt his dreams. The woman who had made his life worth living, the woman who had saved him from his own darkness, the mother of his beautiful son, the woman who had made the endless hours of toil in the fields worth it lay before him, filling his vision like a never-ending scream that tore at the very fabric of reality. Thunder rumbled outside as if an extension of his grief. He would never be able to look at a coin again without remembering this scene. He had been proud to come home. Proud of his success at market. Proud of what the money would mean to his family. The prideful, peaceful, god-fearing farmer felt a scalding tear sear his weathered cheeks.

He distantly realized that he was no longer a prideful man.

A cold, amused voice emanated from the shadows. "Do you seek justice, farmer?"

The farmer jolted, hands shaking with fear... and something else. A feeling he had not experienced in many years. White-hot rage. He stared into the shadows, only able to see a hazy silhouette, wondering if it was one of his wife's rapists mocking him. If it was, so be it.

Everything that mattered in his life lay dead before him. He would welcome the cold, merciless slumber of death in order to escape this haunting grief. Or he would avenge his grief on this wretched soul. It was a long time before the farmer answered, knowing that farming held no interest to him anymore. Nothing *held any interest for him anymore. Well, one thing did...*

Vengeance. The sight of their *blood on his weathered knuckles, the scent of* their *fear filling his nostrils, the feel of* their *dying struggle under his blade. The sound of* their *endless, tortured screams was the only sensation that would appease this once prideful, peaceful, god-fearing man.*

"I do." *The farmer rasped, realizing he was no longer a peaceful man.*

Lightning flashed, the thunderous crack instantaneous, rattling the open windowpanes, and billowing the curtains. With it came the downpour of rain that had been biding its time in the dark skies above. A new voice entered the conversation from another shadow of the room.

"Together, then. We must each give him a gift. To represent both worlds. He must agree to neutrality. To live in a world of grays, as the final arbiter of truth." *This voice was deeper, more authoritative, and obviously hesitant at the situation, judging by his tone. The voice addressed the farmer again.* "After your vengeance is complete, do you agree to forget this past life, and embrace your new vocation? I cannot tell you what it might entail, but you shall never be able to deviate once the choice is made. I can promise that you will not be alone. You will have Brothers to aid you in your cause."

The farmer nodded. "If I can obtain justice first, I agree. I have nothing else left to me."

The first voice grunted his agreement with a puff of stale sulfur that the

288

farmer could taste even from across the foyer. What could only be described as a Demon slowly uncoiled into the light, red eyes blazing with anticipation, his leathery, scaly skin covering an almost human-like frame. The horned, shadowy creature, pulsing with physical shadows of molten fire and ash, handed the farmer a gift, placing it over the man's face, which instantly transformed the approaching darkness into a hazy green, the shadows evaporating under his newfound night-vision. The Demon stepped back, appraising the man before him with satisfaction and uncertainty... even fear, before waving a hand in the direction of the other voice. The farmer turned to assess the second creature, eyes no longer able to show surprise. The man-like being that stood before him crackled with blue power, like lightning given form. An Angel. Wings of smoking ice and burning embers arced out from the creature's back, sparks drifting lazily down to the wooden floor, dying away before contact. The Angel extended a marble hand, offering up a gleaming silver gift. The farmer took it, the item familiar in his hands.

The two creatures spoke as one. "Gifts given. Contract made. He shall be the first. Now, ride forth into your new life. You shall find a new horse befitting your station waiting outside." *Twin peals of thunder, and the once peaceful, prideful, god-fearing farmer was alone again.*

The farmer stood in the empty house, and realized he was no longer a god-fearing man.

Over the coming year, he found every last culprit in the crime that had destroyed his life. Their screams unsuccessfully attempted to fill the empty void in his soul, and he reveled in every sensation he created from their broken bodies. Immensely. But it was never enough. Then he faded from this world, to fulfill his new responsibilities, forever regretful of his decision to accept those cursed gifts.

The story continues. Get your copy of BLOOD DEBTS today:

www.shaynesilvers.com/l/44

GET YOUR FREE BOOK!

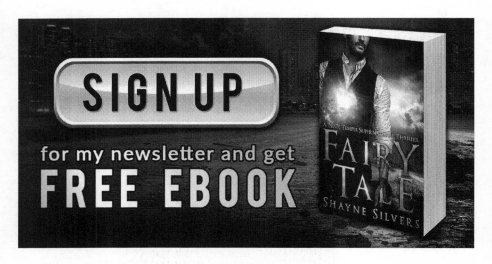

The family classic, Grimm's Fairy Tales, is not the collection of bedtime stories Nate Temple thought it was, but actually the keys to a veritable prison housing the most dangerous bloodthirsty hit men of the supernatural community. This reckless wizard must find a way to lock up the prison for good before his city becomes a buffet table for the Brothers Grimm...

SIDE NOTE: Be sure to read Obsidian Son first, as the Fairy Tale novella assumes you are already familiar with Nate's world and the characters in it.

Discover Nate's origin story, and get a sneak peek into the events that lead up to GRIMM, Book 3 in the Nate Temple Supernatural Thriller Series. To get your digital copy of FAIRY TALE as well as a digital copy of OBSIDIAN SON (*share it with someone who loves to read!*), and lots more exclusive content, all for FREE, you just need to tell me where to send them.

www.shaynesilvers.com/l/134

ABOUT THE AUTHOR

Shayne is a man of mystery and power, whose power is exceeded only by his mystery. In other words, a storyteller.

Shayne currently writes the Nate Temple Supernatural Thriller Series, which features a foul-mouthed young wizard with a chip on his shoulder attempting to protect St. Louis from the various nasties we all know and fear from our childhood bedtime stories. Nate's been known to suckerpunch an Angel, cowtip the Minotaur, and steal Death's horse in order to prove his point. His utter disregard for consequences and self-preservation will have you both laughing and cringing on the edge of your seat.

Shayne holds two high-ranking black belts, and enjoys conversing about anything Marvel, Magical, or Mythological. You might find him writing in a coffee shop near you, cackling madly into his computer screen while pounding shots of espresso. He is currently hard at work on the fifth installment of the Nate Temple Supernatural Thriller Series coming March 2017, and hopes that you enjoyed reading Nate's Story as much as he enjoyed writing it.

CONNECT WITH SHAYNE ONLINE

My Website:
www.shaynesilvers.com

Facebook:
www.facebook.com/shaynesilversfanpage

Twitter:
@shaynesilvers

Pinterest:
www.pinterest.com/shaynesilvers

Instagram:
www.instagram.com/shaynesilversofficial

Goodreads:
www.goodreads.com/author/show/6876556.shayne_silvers

Don't forget! If you've enjoyed what you've read, please leave me a review for OBSIDIAN SON on Amazon.

Thank you in advance.

41827376R00179

Made in the USA
Middletown, DE
24 March 2017